SPIRITS
OF ASH AND
FOAM

ALSO BY GREG WEISMAN

Rain of the Ghosts

SPIRITS OF ASH AND FOAM

A Rain of the Ghosts Novel

GREG WEISMAN

 St. Martin's Griffin ❧ New York

SPIRITS OF ASH AND FOAM.

Copyright © 2014 by Greg Weisman. All rights reserved.
Printed in the United States of America. For information, address
St. Martin's Press, 175 Fifth Avenue, New York, N.Y. 10010.

www.stmartins.com

Designed by Anna Gorovoy

Map by Rhys Davies

Library of Congress Cataloging-in-Publication Data

Weisman, Greg (Gregory David), 1963–
   Spirits of ash and foam : a Rain of the ghosts novel / Greg Weisman. — First edition.
       pages cm
   ISBN 978-1-250-02982-9 (trade paperback)
   ISBN 978-1-250-02981-2 (e-book)
   1. Supernatural—Fiction.   2. Talismans—Fiction.   3. Ghosts—Fiction.
4. Vampires—Fiction.   5. Schools—Fiction.   6. Grandfathers—Fiction.
7. Islands of the Atlantic—Fiction.   I. Title.
   PZ7.W44639Spi 2014
   [Fic]—dc23

                                                          2014008059

St. Martin's Griffin books may be purchased for
educational, business, or promotional use. For information on
bulk purchases, please contact Macmillan Corporate and Premium
Sales Department at 1-800-221-7945, extension 5442, or
write specialmarkets@macmillan.com.

First Edition: July 2014

10   9   8   7   6   5   4   3   2   1

TO SHEILA AND WALLY . . .

A COMPOSE FOR ALL THEIR LOVE AND SUPPORT . . .

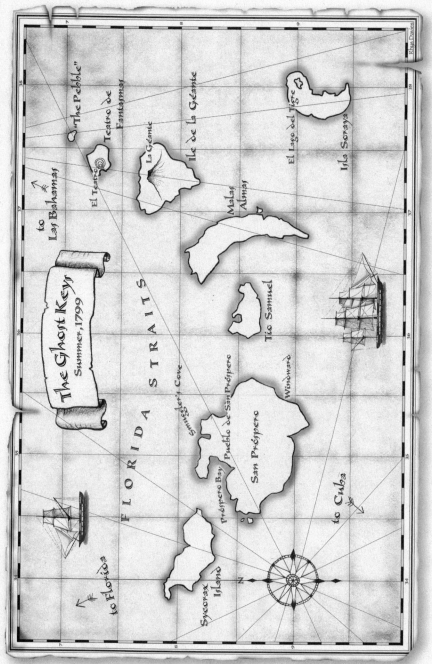

The Ghost Keys
Summer, 1799

FLORIDA STRAITS

to Las Bahamas

"The Pebble"

Teatro de Fantasmas

El Teatro

La Géante

Ile de la Géante

El Lago del Tigre

Isla Soraya

Malas Almas

Tío Samuel

Smuggler's Cove

Pueblo de San Próspero

Próspero Bay

San Próspero

Windward

Sycorax Island

to Florida

to Cuba

N

Rhys Davies

SPIRITS OF ASH AND FOAM

CHAPTER ONE

DETRITUS

MONDAY, SEPTEMBER 8

I must have dozed off. With a start, I woke up beneath a mahogany tree to find the clearing deserted. Only minutes before, or so it seemed, the N.T.Z. had been packed with local teens celebrating the end of summer. Or celebrating *despite* the end of summer, I suppose. But now there wasn't a soul in view. Or a ghost, for that matter.

I got to my feet and stretched, arching my back and craning my neck. What had been a roaring bonfire was now a cold, wet fire pit, but there was no shortage of light. The nearly perfect circle of an almost full moon illuminated the nearly perfect circle of the clearing. I padded over to the sandstone slab at the edge of the cliff and looked out over the Atlantic. A heavy quilt of mist had descended upon San Próspero below. Competing smells—orchids and bananas and ozone from the storm that had passed through earlier—tickled my nose. Mostly, I was hungry.

I scoured the place to see if the kids had left anything behind, but half a corn chip does not a meal make.

So I took off, slipping under banana plants and into the dense jungle that surrounds the N.T.Z. Heading down Macocael Mountain, dodging low-hanging vines and leaping over exposed roots, I passed "The Sign." I glanced back over my shoulder to confirm it hadn't changed. *Because,* as Maq is fond of saying, *in these parts, you never know.* But the incongruous artifact remained a true constant: a stolen PED X-ING sign with two iconic pedestrian-tourists surrounded by a hand-painted red circle with a line through it. Above the figures, the hand-painted, slashing red initials **N.T.Z.** marked the hidden, semisecret clearing above as a haven for local kids only. No Tourists Allowed in the No Tourist Zone.

Near the bottom of Macocael, I passed into the wet blanket of mist and, reaching Camino de Las Casas, paused to violently shake myself and fight off the damp. Then I trotted down the Camino toward Próspero Beach. I knew Maq would be there, and I knew he'd have something for me to eat.

I wasn't wrong. (I rarely am.) Maq had a small driftwood fire going on the sand, which would have been lovely and warm, except he had constructed it ridiculously close to the incoming tide. A baby breaker spilled water into flame, extinguishing about half of the already minute blaze. But Maq didn't seem to mind. He cheerfully fed more driftwood into what remained of his fire and a nice piece of fresh snapper into my mouth.

"It's long after midnight, Opie," he said. "Where've you been?" I was too busy wolfing down my meal to answer. Still, he seemed satisfied with that response and nodded sagely. I swallowed, and he said, "Want some more?"

Well, we are feasting tonight. I barked my approval, and he rubbed his knuckles across the yellow fur between my ears, while dropping another chunk of fish into the sand in front of me. I wagged my tail. *(Okay, yes, I'm canine. Get over it.)* Another wavelet sloshed into his shallow, struggling fire pit, as I snapped up the snapper.

Seconds later, I was bouncing around him like a *batey* ball, hoping for more—before realizing there was none. So I settled in beside my best friend and watched him contemplate the universe from beneath his straw hat. Maq stared down at the fire as the ocean finally put it out for good with an accompanying *hissss* and a cloud of steam, smoke and ash—all instantly carried off by a stiff breeze from the east. The water receded, leaving behind a layer of dirty seafoam amid the soaked coals, the foam quickly absorbed by the sand beneath. Maq, more pensive than I'm used to seeing him, considered this and nodded once again. "So many things are fleeting," he said, in that voice he had appropriated from W. C. Fields, back when the famous Hollywood actor had come to party on the Ghost Keys in 1935. "But even the most fleeting things return."

At first, I didn't have the slightest clue what he was talking about—but I was pretty sure he was talking about something. So I widened my perception beyond the beach, beyond the Pueblo, beyond San Próspero. And there, across the bay, I found what I was looking for on Sycorax Island: Isaac Naborías, bushy gray hair peeking out from under the hat of his official Sycorax Inc. security guard uniform, paused before the silent archaeological excavation at the mouth of the old bat cave.

It was part of Isaac's lonely, 4:00 A.M. rounds: a trip about the Old Manor, past corporate headquarters, between the three factories and the cannery, and then out to the dig and the cave—soon to be the site of a fourth factory. *(Or is it a second cannery? Naborías wondered, none too sure.)* Normally, he'd take a quick peek inside the cave, shining his heavy flashlight into its depths to make sure none of the late-shift employees were in there smoking anything funny. But tonight, just as he took a couple of shuffling steps toward the mouth, a lone bat flew out—right into his face. Naborías, eyes screwed shut, waved the thing away frantically; he *hated* bats! When he opened his eyes it was gone. He thought the exterminators the boss hired had taken care of those pests. Poisoned most of them and driven the rest away. Unfortunately, the cave was clearly still infested. He'd write that up in his nightly report, of course. That was his duty. But there was no way he was going inside there with those flying rats. So Isaac walked away in a huff—thus completely missing the bloodless, pale corpse lying faceup, not five feet away on the dark, sandy floor of the cave.

CHAPTER TWO

MONDAY, SEPTEMBER 8

Rain Cacique's alarm clock woke her at 6:00 A.M. sharp. While Maq slept off the previous night on a bus bench, and I scratched at some sand fleas beneath it, Rain vaulted out of bed, excited to begin what she was convinced would be a brand-new chapter in her life.

Quickly, she skittered into her bathroom, turned on the hot water, stripped out of her pajamas and jumped in the shower. Steel drums played in her head, the morning's mental soundtrack: bright and warm, tangy and full of promise, just like her life since gaining . . . *it*.

As the near-scalding water rained down on her copper skin, she touched the two golden snakes entwined around each other and around her upper left arm. One snake, the Searcher, had tiny chips of turquoise-colored stone for eyes; the other, the Healer, was sightless. Together, this armband of braided snakes—which for years she had seen her grandfather wear casually on his wrist—was the *zemi*. She wasn't exactly sure what a *zemi* was or even what the word *zemi* meant, but she knew the thing had mystic powers. The night before, the Healer snake had emitted a golden glow and mended a nasty scratch on her arm from a harpoon. (*A harpoon!*) Within the same hour, the Searcher snake had emitted a blue glow that helped save herself, her best friend Charlie and a whole bunch of ghosts from, well . . . from an evil, killer hurricane-woman! *Okay, yeah, it sounds crazy,* she thought, *but that's exactly what happened!* And she couldn't be more pleased. She soaped up, rinsed off and was soon toweling dry in front of the mirror.

She stared into it, while brushing first her teeth and then her long black hair. She studied her face, staring into her almond-shaped, almond-colored eyes. She felt sure she should look different now—now that she had . . . superpowers. *I see dead people.* She giggled. Of course, the most important dead person in her life was her grandfather, her Papa Sebastian. But his ghost was somehow asleep inside the *zemi* and wouldn't wake and emerge until sundown. And, oh, she couldn't wait until sundown.

She got dressed: panties, bra, khaki shorts and a royal blue sleeveless tee with absolutely nothing imprinted on it that could label her as part of any circle, faction or clique. She searched for her favorite shoes . . . and then remembered Charlie had been more or less forced to drop them overboard last night while they were trying to escape from that jerk Callahan. The World's Most Dangerous Tourist had stolen the armband, somehow knowing it was important even before Rain had figured things out. But Rain had stolen it back, leaving Callahan none the wiser. And now *she* knew it was the key to unlocking the ancient mystery of the Ghosts, the chain of eight islands on which Rain had spent her entire life—all thirteen years of it.

Was it only a few days ago she had felt so trapped? So completely locked into a tedious existence of school and work, making beds and cutting bait for tourists? An existence that would transition when she graduated only into a tedious *eternity* of making beds and cutting bait for yet more tourists? *Okay, sure, graduation is a long way away.* In fact, today was the first day of the new year, the first day of eighth grade. Well, she could live with that, knowing what she now knew: The *zemi* wasn't the only Searcher/Healer. Rain was also the Searcher and the Healer. She picked out another pair of deck shoes (honestly, she had like a hundred pairs anyway—well, okay, five) and put them on. Then she began braiding her long dark hair into the tight, thick rope she favored.

Relying on muscle memory alone, her fingers deftly and automatically danced the three lengths of hair into the braid, while her mind raced over all she had learned. Her *zemi*—a gift from her grandfather, who had himself received it as a gift from his *abuela* long ago—was only the first of nine *zemis* she had to somehow search out and collect, so that she could heal a "wound." She had not a clue what the wound was, how she could heal it or even where to look for the next *zemi*, but all those questions hardly weighed down her soaring thoughts now. Right now, all that mattered was the soaring. She didn't feel trapped in a small life anymore. She had real purpose, real responsibilities, and ironically, that made her feel free. *The rest I'll figure out,* she thought. *I mean, one down, eight to go. How hard could it be?*

She pulled her backpack out of the closet and her battered notebook off a shelf. It was jammed with notes from her various seventh-grade classes. Without a moment's hesitation, she clicked open the binding and dumped every single sheet of used paper into the trash. Then she refilled it with a fresh, clean stack pulled from the plastic bag of school supplies she had purchased yesterday morning—a lifetime ago.

Also in the shopping bag were a couple of new pencils, a couple new pens, a fluorescent yellow highlighter, a two-pocket folder for handouts and assignments, and a very old framed photograph of ten World War II airmen in front of their B-17 bomber, the *Island Belle*. She studied the photo for a moment or two. They were all dead now, except Old Joe Charone. There he was, decades ago, as an injured young tail gunner. And there was Sebastian Bohique as a dashing young bomber pilot: not the old, warm, gray Papa 'Bastian she had known, worshipped and loved—but a Dark Man with a very dangerous smile. Beside 'Bastian and Joe, their crew: the Eight. All gone now. Released, at last, to their final rest, thanks to 'Bastian, Charlie and herself. She carefully propped the picture up on her dresser and finished packing for school.

She exited her room, carefully locking the door behind her and double-checking to make sure. She didn't want any more unwelcome visitors lifting her stuff as Callahan had done. Then, with backpack slung over one shoulder, she descended the front staircase of the only home she had ever known: the Nitaino Inn.

Her father, Alonso Cacique, was at the front desk, checking out the DeLancys and the Chungs. It was the standard routine: asking how their stay was, suggesting they recommend the Nitaino to their friends, etc. Rain was about to continue on through the dining room to the kitchen to help her mom serve the breakfast portion of the Inn's "Bed & Breakfast" promise, when the front door opened and a crowd of bodies noisily poured in.

She recognized Timo Craw, who led the way, hefting two very large rolling suitcases over the lip of the threshold. Timo was one of San Próspero's half-dozen full-time cabdrivers, and, of course, Rain knew every local on the island. He was followed by an Asian woman in her mid-thirties, who—in addition to Sherpa-ing multiple airplane carry-ons—was trying to shepherd three very sleepy kids, ranging in age from eight to four. This brood was followed by their disheveled father, an Asian man about the same age as his wife. He also had two large rolling bags, which he had carried up the four cobblestone steps in front of the Inn, but which he had put down just short of the door frame. Now he was struggling to roll them over that last small speed bump with little luck or joy.

With a wiry grace, Alonso instantly slid out from behind the desk, dodging his slim but muscular six-foot form around a DeLancy here, a Chung there, until he had reached the side of this newest paterfamilias and effortlessly taken charge of his bags. (*All those years working the charter boat had to be good for something*, Rain thought.) Alonso introduced himself as one of the Nitaino's proprietors, and the exhausted, somewhat befuddled, but certainly grateful dad shook his hand and said, "I'm Fred Kim. This is my wife, Esther Kim. We're the Kims."

Alonso nodded to Rain, who knew the drill. While her dad did the heavy lifting, she crossed behind the desk and turned the register to face their new guests. "Hi, I'm Rain. I can check you in."

Esther Kim eyed the thirteen-year-old. "You work here?"

"Kinda have to. My folks run the place."

Mrs. Kim nodded and started to sign the guest book. Meanwhile, Timo had sized up the situation. The lobby of the Nitaino was generally considered large and warm and welcoming. However, with four guests checking out, five checking in, plus a ton of luggage, two Caciques, a cabdriver and a postcard rack, things had become decidedly cramped. To Timo Craw, that meant opportunity: "You folks need a ride to the airport? I got room fo' four."

John DeLancy and Terry Chung glanced at each other uncomfortably. John stammered, "Uh, w-we're n-not—"

"—Together," Terry finished.

Timo shrugged. "Sharing cab be cheaper, Captains. But it good with Timo either way. I take one couple now. Come back and take the other couple . . . sooooon as I can." Rain smiled at Timo's cheek. A second taxi could be there in five minutes easy— but the gamble paid off.

"Well, if it's cheaper," DeLancy said.

"Don't want to miss our flight," said Chung.

So, despite the dirty looks from Elizabeth Ellis-Chung and Ellen DeLancy, Timo was soon clearing some space in the lobby as he escorted the two couples and their luggage out the door— though not before Ms. Ellis-Chung had slipped an envelope into Rain's hand: her tip for serving breakfast, cleaning bathrooms and making beds. Rain smiled and thanked her and watched her go.

The click of the door shutting behind them seemed to act as some kind of ON switch for the three Kim kids: the whining started instantly.

"I'm so tired . . ."

"What are we gonna do here anyway?"

"Mommy. Mommy. Mommy. Mommy. Mommy."

Mrs. Kim handed Rain her credit card and then turned to crouch before her kids. "I'm right here. I'm right here. I'm right here."

Rain ran the card immediately to secure the Kims' deposit *before* they could be told the inevitable bad news: Check-in time wasn't until 1:00 P.M., and the two connecting rooms the Kims had reserved had only just been vacated by Timo's latest fares and weren't yet ready for occupation. Rain glanced down at the guest register and read the following names upside down:

Rebecca Sawyer, Hannibal, MO
Mr. & Mrs. John DeLancy, San Francisco
Terry Chung and Elizabeth Ellis-Chung, Cambridge, Mass.
Callahan

Judith Vendaval, New York.
Fred, Esther, Wendy, John & Michael Kim, Seattle

Wow, Rain thought, *they came all the way from Seattle! They must have been flying all night.* The inevitable bad news was going to be *really* bad news. She looked at the other names. Mrs. Sawyer and Ms. Vendaval were still staying at the Inn, but Callahan, *thank God,* was long gone.

At her first opportunity, Rain returned the credit card to Mrs. Kim and disappeared into the dining room—just as Alonso was saying, "You're going to have to give us a little time . . ."

Tourists. They were Rain's life—in fact, practically the sum total of her life until this past weekend. She lived with her parents in the Inn, which was almost never completely empty of guests. Among other chores, she served them breakfast, cleaned their rooms on weekends, and, every couple of weeks or so, helped crew her dad's charter boat for them. Now all that had changed. Tourists had become a side venture. Her life now was with the *zemi,* and she wanted to shout it to the world.

Although maybe not to Rebecca Sawyer. The old woman was sitting alone in the dining room, reading a Lew Archer mystery novel and sipping black coffee. A half-eaten fresh-baked scone sat on her bread plate. She glanced up over the top of her paperback and smiled. "Hello, Rain."

"Hi, Rebecca." The first morning after she had checked in, Mrs. Sawyer had insisted Rain call her Rebecca or Becky. Rain had settled on the more formal of the two options. "I'll have your breakfast in just a minute. Mom took your order?"

Mrs. Sawyer confirmed as much, and Rain passed through the swinging doors into the kitchen.

Instantly, she was hit by the wonderful smells of her mother's cooking. Iris Cacique had three skillets going on the burners. In one, she was sautéing onions, mushrooms and tomatoes in salted butter, while flipping a half-cooked omelet in a second and frying a few links of La Géante sausage in the third. There was a large bowl of mixed berries on the big wooden table where the family ate their own meals, alongside carafes of fresh orange and pineapple juice chilling in the ice bucket.

A cheerful Rain hung her backpack on the hook by the back door. "Morning!"

"Morning, baby," her mother said tenderly, glancing briefly at Rain, who could instantly tell Iris had been crying—and *not* because of the onions. For a second or two Rain searched her brain for an explanation, and then it hit her: *'Bastian!* Her mother was still mourning her own father, who had only died three days ago. The funeral and the wake had followed rapidly, a Ghost Keys tradition, as it's not wise to let a body linger on a tropical island. Now life was supposed to go back to normal, *but what was the new normal?* Most days when Rain came down for breakfast, Papa 'Bastian was already sitting at the table, reading the paper and eating his Lucky Charms. Not today, and not ever again. Of course, Rain knew that tonight—at sunset—'Bastian would emerge from the *zemi,* a bit pale, transparent and ethereal but otherwise none the worse for being dead. Iris, however, didn't know that and grieved still. Rain felt an irresistible longing to ease her mother's pain by telling her everything, the whole adventure—even the parts she knew would get her grounded for life. It was all so exciting, and she wanted to share it. *But how can I? She'll only think I'm nuts—or worse, on drugs or something.*

Rain settled for kissing her mom on the cheek and then setting up plates and spooning berries into a bowl, as Iris Cacique finished preparing Mrs. Sawyer's order.

"Anyone else out there?" Iris asked.

"Just Rebecca."

"That's a relief. I thought the Chungs or the DeLancys might want something before hitting the road."

"They might've. But Timo rushed 'em out the door before they could think. Oh, but the Kims checked in early."

Iris growled under her breath. Rain smiled. That growl was very normal.

Two pieces of whole-wheat toast popped into view. A well-oiled machine, the Cacique women were on the job. Rain used two fingers to pluck the hot toast from the Inn's industrial toaster, dropping both pieces on the breadboard. She sliced them in half diagonally and arranged the two sets of triangles on a plate. Iris wheeled about with her saucepans, and soon the toast was joined by an onion-mushroom-tomato-and-jack omelet and sausage links. Rain was quickly through the swinging doors with the meal, serving Rebecca Sawyer with a smile. Seconds later, back in the kitchen, Rain was being asked what she wanted for breakfast.

"Actually, that looked really good."

Her mother's eyebrows raised a good half inch in surprise. Iris Cacique's only child wasn't generally one for a big breakfast. But Rain was still flush with all the changes in her life. *A new day. A new way.* Besides, she had burned a *lot* of calories the night before, you know, fighting for her life and everything.

Iris started cooking again, and Rain poured herself half a glass of orange juice, topping it off with the same amount of pineapple. Iris asked, "You looking forward to eighth grade?"

Rain groaned, not so much because she dreaded school but mostly because it seemed expected. Not that she *was* looking forward to it. Eighth grade would just get in the way of her new quest. After all, she was the Searcher and the Healer. *I should totally be exempt!* Suddenly, she remembered the form. She hopped up from the table and removed it from under the magnet on the fridge. "Mom, you still have to sign this."

Iris glanced back over her shoulder at Rain's Eighth Period Exemption Form. "I'll sign it if you want. But wouldn't you like to take an elective this semester? Photography, maybe?"

"Noooo. We talked about this. Work. Homework. It's enough. I need some free time—at least until volleyball starts."

"Right, because we wouldn't want you all *stressed out* from taking pictures of seashells and breakers, now, would we?"

"Mommmm."

"I said I'll sign it." She did too, after serving Rain's breakfast. Rain ate quickly, despite multiple pleas to slow down.

Iris cleared Rain's dishes while Rain cleared Rebecca's—just as Alonso escorted the five Kims into the dining room. "Why don't you sit here, relax, have some breakfast—on the house—and we'll have your rooms ready by the time you're done eating."

Fred Kim grunted his acquiescence as Esther Kim attempted to pour her seemingly liquid children into three chairs at one of the larger tables.

"I'm not even hungry."

"I want cereal."

"Mommy. Mommy. Mommy. Mommy. Mommy."

With a sigh of relief, Alonso followed Rain into the kitchen, only to be greeted by his wife's glare. "Tell me I did not hear the words 'on the house.'"

Rain watched her father stick his tongue into his cheek and take a deep breath to maintain his cool. "I've just spent twenty-plus minutes arguing with Mr. Kim about his rooms not being ready. Hell, I could've *gotten* 'em ready in that time. I had to do something."

"Offering them breakfast, I understand. But they weren't

supposed to check in until this afternoon. Breakfast is only served until ten."

"I know that."

"So why are they getting it for free? How are we supposed to earn a living if you keep giving away free food? Especially when I'm the one who has to do the cooking."

Scooping up her form, Rain glided back from the tête-à-tête and quietly lifted her backpack off its hook—but not before her father shot a look her way. "Hold it, young lady. I need you to go strip the beds in Rooms Four and Five before you leave."

"Gee, Dad. I'd love to. But you took away my master key."

And with that, she slipped out the back door before her exasperated father could formulate a reply.

CHAPTER THREE

AND LIFE ENDS

MONDAY, SEPTEMBER 8

O f course, the reason Alonso Cacique had taken away his daughter's master key to the Inn was that Rain had used it to ransack Callahan's room in a failed attempt to take back the *zemi* he had stolen. Since her parents didn't believe their guest had stolen anything, Rain had just seemed crazed—or at best, extremely immature and irresponsible. So her key was confiscated. Fortunately, the *zemi* was later recovered aboard Callahan's boat. All things considered, Rain had no complaints about either outcome.

She walked—practically skipped—through Old Town under an ascending sun as the island of San Próspero rapidly warmed past 79° with relatively low humidity, meaning her clothes weren't yet sticking to her skin. (September was a pleasant month, generally. Frankly, most months were pretty darn pleasant, generally.) Rain checked her tip envelope from the Chungs. Ten bucks. *Not bad.* (Not bad at all, I say. Maq and I could feast off that for a couple weeks, easy.) She threw the envelope away in the wrought-iron refuse can as she turned the corner of Goodfellow Lane onto Rue de Lafitte and stuffed the bill in the right front pocket of her shorts.

She made her way inland, away from any tourist draw, toward the island's large ten-year-old combined campus, which housed San Próspero Elementary School (kindergarten through fifth grade), San Próspero Junior High School (sixth grade through eighth) and San Próspero Senior High School (ninth through twelfth), each in its own building with shared facilities (cafeteria, gymnasium, etc.). As she drew closer, the kids began to amass, approaching from every direction: individuals, groups of two or more, entire cliques even. There was the occasional parent escorting his or her youngest, but that was to be expected on the first day of school. Within a month, even the kindergartners would be walking to school with only their older siblings or friends as chaperones. Mainland parenting and mainland paranoia hadn't yet found a toehold among the locals. To most, San Próspero was still an island paradise where everyone knew and watched out for each other. (Dead bodies in caves notwithstanding.)

Rain spotted Charlie Dauphin, who was standing in front of his locker on the west wall of the junior high building. He was wearing shorts and a gray shirt that read LOCAL COLOR in gold letters. She snuck up behind him and put her hands over his eyes. "Guess who?"

Charlie didn't have to guess. He recognized her voice—and he recognized the electric rush that came every time she touched him. He tried desperately not to do *anything* that might reveal these . . . feelings. It was still deeply humiliating to Charlie that he had fallen in love/lust with his best friend. They had been babies together, had grown up side by side, spent practically every waking moment in each other's presence. It was neither right nor fair that he was afflicted—*yes, afflicted*—with these disastrous longings. "Hi, Rain," he squeaked.

"Ah, you guessed." Rain stepped back, removing her hands, which was both a relief and a sudden horrible void to young Mr. Dauphin. Shutting his locker, he turned to face her, struggling to maintain a neutral expression, which Rain read as despair. She wasn't that far off, though she had the cause all wrong. "I know," she said. "School starts."

"And life ends," he said automatically.

"And life ends. Ten more minutes. The horror. The horror." It was their routine.

With a physical effort akin to me shaking off rainwater, Charlie snapped himself out of it. "It's not all bad," he said. "Eighth grade means we're at the top of the food chain. The biggest fish in the middle school pond." They looked around. From where they stood, the high schoolers were all out of view, and everyone around them was their age or younger. That didn't suck.

But Rain had much bigger—and much stranger—fish on her mind. She leaned in to whisper as her right hand wrapped itself around the armband on her left biceps. "We need to talk about finding the next *zemi*."

Charlie scowled. "Maybe first we should find out what a *zemi* is." He had shared the weirdness of their inaugural adventure—and seen some truly mind-boggling stuff along the way—but he wasn't quite as enthusiastic about the project as the Searcher-slash-Healer was. He hadn't yet been granted a fancy title on this quest and was beginning to feel his only role was that of Rain's sidekick. He couldn't deny the accuracy of the term, but it didn't particularly jazz him either.

"Look," she said, "as soon as school's over, let's head back up to the Cache, okay?"

"Why?"

"What do you mean why?"

"What are we going to see there that's new?"

Rain screwed up her face. She had no answer, but he didn't seem to have caught the spirit of the whole venture, which was frustrating. "Okay, fine. Then come over to the Inn right before sunset, and we'll talk it over with 'Bastian."

"You mean *you'll* talk it over with 'Bastian. I can't see or hear him, remember?"

"I'll translate, okay?"

Just then a new voice interposed, "Translate what?"

Charlie and Rain turned to see Miranda Guerrero standing a couple of feet away. Miranda had been born on the Ghost Keys but had spent most of her life in England, France and Spain, before returning to the Ghosts this past summer. It meant she was technically a local, but she was also the new kid. Rain and Charlie were the closest thing Miranda had to friends on the islands, and she wasn't always sure about Rain, who was now eyeing her suspiciously. "Were you eavesdropping on us?"

Miranda took a step back. "Um, no. I mean . . . Was I?"

"How much did you hear?"

"Something about translating something," Miranda fumfered. She had the slightest hint of a Euro-Spanish accent. "That's it, I swear."

As usual, Charlie intervened. He stepped forward and smiled at Miranda, welcoming her with his wide, kind, cocoa-brown face and dark brown eyes. "It's all right," he said. (And Miranda felt a certain rush of her own.) "We were just talking about watching a DVD of this Spanish movie."

Rain relaxed, liking the cover story. "Right. And Charlie doesn't speak Spanish, so I offered to translate."

"What movie?" Miranda asked.

"Some ghost story," Charlie said. "I forget the title."

"Oh, I love ghost stories," Miranda offered—and then immediately regretted it. Her attempt to generate an invitation was way too obvious.

Fortunately, Rain changed the subject eagerly. "So, who do you have for homeroom?"

Relieved, Miranda pulled out her schedule. "Um, I don't know. It doesn't list homeroom."

"Homeroom is the first ten minutes of whatever your first-period class is," Charlie offered.

"Oh, well, then, I have, um, Mrs. Beachum?"

"Yeah, so do we," Rain said, putting a hand on Miranda's shoulder. "Consider yourself adopted."

Rain smiled, and Miranda beamed. Charlie watched them. *They're so different—but they're both kinda hot.* Rain was his height, tall and slim, her build still a *little* tomboyish. Miranda was shorter but definitely curvier. She had light skin, brown eyes and Kewpie doll lips, with maybe just the subtlest hint of lip gloss, eye shadow, and mascara as accents. That makeup and her clothes—a blouse and skirt, tennis shoes with Peds, small gold hoop earrings, and a crystal pendant around her neck—were all modest enough, but Charlie knew they would further mark her as an outsider at their school. It was all just a little too expensive and made her look more like a tourist than a local. Rain, of course, wore no makeup, *ever,* and—like Charlie and nearly everybody else they knew—bought all her clothes at the local Island Mart, often for ninety-nine cents per item. Functional, not fancy. *But, whoa, they both have really great smiles.*

Charlie knew from personal experience that Rain could snap from foreboding to charming in an instant. And back again. So it was nice seeing her let Miranda at least a little of the way in. The truth was Rain liked Miranda well enough and certainly recognized that the poor kid was going to need all the help she could get. Still, Miranda couldn't be allowed to interfere with the Search. That was Priority One.

The bell—the first of the school year—rang. Charlie and Rain instantly turned toward the door, and Miranda scampered to catch up. Rain heard a slapping sound and looked down. Charlie was wearing deck shoes that were clearly three or more sizes too big, and he seemed to be favoring his left foot. "What's with the clown shoes? And the limp?" she smirked.

He narrowed his eyes at her. "Well," he said, "I had to wear Lew's old shoes, because for *some reason* I couldn't find mine. And I'm limping because I dropped an air tank on my foot last night."

Rain gulped, realizing she had just asked a couple of *very* stupid questions. When they escaped from Callahan's boat the night before, Charlie hadn't quite made it out unscathed. "Sorry, sorry," she said and touched his arm gently with her left hand. Suddenly, the Healer snake on her *zemi* glowed with a golden light, which flashed down her arm, crossed over to his, then raced down the length of his body, before disappearing into Lew Dauphin's oversized shoe.

Panicked, she stepped back and looked around. No one else seemed to have seen the light, and she had to consciously remind herself that such perceptions were a part of her new ghost-sight powers—and quite invisible to everybody else.

Charlie's expression did change, though. He looked perplexed as he trod gingerly on his right foot—and then stepped down on it with a sudden, unexpected confidence. Then he smiled, and Rain noticed his limp was gone. She wanted to shout, to tell the world, *Did you see that? I healed him!!* Instead, she sighed and smiled, glad that her friend's pain had ceased—and still a little amused that the *zemi* couldn't do anything about Charlie's older brother's big floppy shoes.

CHAPTER FOUR

THE HORROR

MONDAY, SEPTEMBER 8

Homeroom and first period.

So, along with twenty-one other teens—together comprising exactly half of San Próspero Junior High's eighth-grade class—Rain, Charlie and Miranda found seats in Mrs. Beachum's classroom. Rain sat by the window in the second-to-last row, having learned long ago that the *last* row attracts too much attention from teachers accustomed to its occupation by their worst slackers. Charlie sat at a desk to Rain's left. Miranda hesitated. She was definitely a front-of-the-class type of student, but she didn't have the courage to leave her two friends, particularly now that they had officially "adopted" her. She sat next to Charlie, inadvertently cutting off Renée Jackson, who was about to take that very desk. Renée glared down at the new girl in her fancy clothes before taking the desk behind Miranda, who remained blissfully unaware she had already made a powerful enemy before the second bell had even sounded for homeroom.

Rain, head angled down, glanced through her lashes up at Mrs. Claire Beachum, who was writing her full name on the board at the front of the classroom. The fact that the teacher had her back to her students hardly mattered, since Rain was quite convinced Mrs. B had eyes in the back of her head—probably hiding somewhere in that tight bun of dirty-blond hair. She had been Rain's history *and* English teacher in seventh grade and had not been charmed by Rain or Rain's lack of effort in either subject.

The bell rang. Mrs. Beachum turned to face the class. "Good morning. As most of you know, I'm Mrs. Beachum, and I have all of you for homeroom and history—and most of you for English at the end of the day." She picked up an attendance sheet and scanned the faces of her students. Her eyes lit briefly on Rain and crinkled slightly. (Rain knew—*just knew*—Mrs. B had it in for her.) Finally, the teacher's eyes rested on the only unfamiliar face in the room. "You're Miranda Guerrero?"

"Yes, ma'am."

Claire Beachum winced; she was only twenty-eight and didn't particularly like being ma'amed. " 'Mrs. Beachum' will be fine," she said. "Normally, we'd start our morning with school announcements, but it's the first day, and the office is a tad disorganized. So we'll just move forward and hope for the best. Charlie, Rain, Renée, Carlos. Please distribute these books."

Charlie and Rain exchanged a look and then rolled their eyes in sync before rising and making their way to the front of the room. There the four summoned teens scooped up piles of hardcover history textbooks and paperback copies of Eduardo Galeano's *Memory of Fire*, carrying them along the four columns of desks so every student could take one of each. Some grabbed the books eagerly. Others stared as if the volumes might bite. Since the books were heavy, Rain grew impatient and snapped at Gladys Hernandez, "Just take 'em already."

"Rain," Mrs. B said.

Charlie glanced over at his friend in time to see her first bristle at the reprimand and then tamp down her obvious displeasure. *Rain reins in her reign,* he thought and turned away so she wouldn't catch his grin.

Rain forced a not-so-pleasant smile onto her face. The whole thing was intolerable. *How could the Searcher be reduced to this? If only Mrs. Beachum knew the truth! If only they all knew!*

"Now, these *History of the Americas* textbooks are new, never before used. Same with *Memory of Fire.* You can highlight passages, but do not write or doodle in the margins. Remember, you're just borrowing these books for the school year. You'll give them back in June, undamaged, or you'll pay for a replacement. And they're not cheap."

Considering multiple options, Renée reached Miranda's desk but decided not to show her cards yet. Smiling, she allowed Miranda to take her books and then sat down again behind her. The distribution complete, Carlos, Rain and Charlie sat too.

Just then, Linda Wheeler, a high school junior, entered and handed Mrs. B a photocopied memo. "Today's announcements," Linda said.

Second period.

Miranda followed Rain and Charlie to their next class—but stopped short of entering. She looked down at her schedule. "Um. This isn't the right room."

Charlie checked his own schedule. "Algebra One with Coach Brinque. This is it."

Still focused on her schedule, Miranda shook her head. "I'm

in Geometry Honors with Ms. McKellar." She looked up at her two friends and found them staring at her as if she were some kind of alien. She swallowed hard and shrugged. "I took algebra last year."

"And where exactly were you last year, *Sugar*?" a voice dripped from behind them.

Miranda turned to face Renée Jackson and thus missed the appalled looks on Rain and Charlie's faces. They'd grown up with Renée and knew she only called her worst enemies "Sugar."

"The American School in Madrid," Miranda was saying.

"Well, that's so interesting. I want to hear all about it. I'm Renée. I'm in geometry too. I'll show you the way." Renée linked arms with Miranda and escorted her toward the staircase.

Miranda looked back over her shoulder and waved. "Bye, guys. See you at lunch?"

Rain and Charlie nodded dumbly. They both had an impulse to follow, but the bell rang. So, reluctantly, they entered the classroom.

"Miranda looked so happy," Rain said weakly as she again took a seat by the window in the second-to-last row.

"You don't think Renée'll lock her in a closet or anything?"

"Nah. She's too twisted for something that obvious. Wait for it though."

"*How* did Miranda get on Renée's Sugar List so fast?"

Rain had no idea and no opportunity to formulate a theory before Mr. Brinque called class to order. And asked Rain to help distribute textbooks.

Third period.

Rain caught up with Miranda for P.E. in the girls' locker room of the gym. The Amazonian Renée stalked nearby, an elegant black jaguar ready to pounce. Whatever she was planning clearly hadn't happened yet, as Miranda was still smiling and not curled up in a little ball in the corner. Rain wanted to find a way to warn her, but this wasn't the place or time.

Coach Viki Hernandez (Gladys' twenty-three-year-old sister) assigned gym lockers to all the eighth-grade girls. Then she distributed towels, gym shorts and T-shirts, which were all to be dumped in bins at the end of class in exchange for clean laundry on a one-for-one basis. As the coach related the school's widely ignored requirement that students shower after every physical education class, a horrified Miranda whispered to Rain, "Can't I bring my own gym clothes?"

Rain shook her head, but Renée answered, "I don't see why not."

Rain suppressed a groan.

Fourth period.

Charlie moved slowly forward in the lunch line, glancing back over his shoulder. He saw Rain enter the cafeteria with Miranda . . . and Renée. *Ugh.* Rain grabbed Miranda's hand and pulled her forward. Miranda grabbed Renée's hand and did the same. *Double ugh.* Charlie opened up a space to let the girls in—and instantly felt a large hand on his shoulder.

"No cuts," said Jay Ibara, a six-foot-tall senior. "You want to eat with your little friends, you move to the back of the line, scrub." The four eighth graders stared up at Jay for a second, and even Renée looked slightly cowed. Silently, heads lowered, Charlie, Rain, and Miranda gave way. Renée departed with them, but not before unleashing a sly-voiced "Whatever you say, *Sugar,*" as she went.

Almost instantly their spots were filled by seniors Ramon

Hernandez (Gladys and Viki's brother) and Hank Dauphin (Charlie's brother), laughing and taking cuts with Jay's full approval. Just two days ago, all three had attended 'Bastian's funeral and had at least made an attempt to be civil and sympathetic toward Rain. Ancient history already. Nor would Hank cut his younger brother any slack. *Antislack,* Charlie thought. *That's what he cuts me.*

"So much for the top of the food chain," Rain said.

All three schools shared the cafeteria. The seniors ruled, of course, but there was an unspoken commandment among all the high schoolers to be nice to the grammar school kids. Sure enough, Charlie watched as Hank waved over their youngest brother, Phil Dauphin, and his entire fifth-grade computer chess club clan and gave them cuts.

So, inevitably, the junior high kids dwelled at the very bottom of the food chain, below seniors, sophomores, kindergartners, etc. Last in the chain to get any food—with no chocolate pudding left by the time they got to the front of the line either.

Emerging with their trays, Rain, Charlie, Miranda and Renée searched for a table but found no immediate prospects. Here, Renée seemed slightly conflicted. Rain watched her carefully. Strictly speaking, Renée was more intimidating than popular, but she did run with their grade's popular crowd, which had managed to commandeer one table near the kitchen. *But would she abandon her target?*

"C'mon, Sugar," she said to Miranda. "I think there's room for two over here."

Now Miranda looked conflicted. Renée had been so sweet, but she felt sure her first loyalty should be to Charlie and Rain. "Couldn't we find room for four?"

Rain stepped between Miranda and Renée, saying, "I think we'd rather eat outside. Fresh air, you know?"

Renée's dark eyes hardened. "That sounds great, *Sugar*. You don't mind if I join you?"

She glared at Rain so hard, Charlie could practically see the daggers. *Great. Now Rain's on the Sugar List, too. And if Rain's on it . . .*

Renée turned to Charlie. "C'mon, *Sugar*. Let's go eat outside with the bugs."

Fifth period.

Rain sat in Spanish Two, not really listening to Señor Recino outline the year's syllabus, shaking her head over the conversation that had just taken place in the hall.

Rain had said, "What do you mean you're taking French? Aren't you already fluent in Spanish?"

Miranda had hesitated over what felt like a trick question: "Yeah . . . I'm *already* fluent in Spanish. So I'm taking French. Aren't *you* fluent in Spanish?"

"Yes. Which is why I'm taking it. It's my one easy A."

"Oh."

" 'Oh?' What is 'Oh' supposed to mean?"

"It means, 'Oh, you're a disappointment, *Sugar*,'" Renée volunteered helpfully.

Rain watched Miranda, Charlie and Renée head off to French Two.

Suddenly, a light slap on the back of her head jarred Rain back to the present. She looked over her shoulder, wondering how her large Colombian teacher had managed to get behind her without her noticing.

"*Lluvia*," he said. (Armando Recino called Rain *Lluvia* when he was annoyed with her or feeling particularly clever.) "*Los libros, Lluvia. Distribúyelos, por favor.*"

Sixth period.

Charlie sat on a stool at a lab table with Rain. Both felt bad for Miranda, currently partnered—cheerfully and ignorantly—with Renée at the next table over. Of course, neither had felt quite bad enough to break up their own partnership in order to assure Miranda wouldn't get stuck with San Próspero's one true *demon child*. But I suppose there are limits to human altruism.

Charlie glanced over. Miranda, eyes bright and wide and innocent, listened attentively to Coach Brinque, who was glorying in the wonders of their eighth-grade science curriculum, subtitled *The Natural World*. Charlie had the short, stocky, bald and coal-skinned Brinque for algebra, science and P.E., and the thought was just dawning that this one man controlled nearly half Charlie's G.P.A. *I really should pay closer attention.*

Instead, he glanced over one more time. Renée was looking right at him. She smiled mirthlessly. Mirthlessly or mercilessly. Either way, Charlie shivered involuntarily.

Seventh period.

For Rain, this endless day was ending where it had started, with almost the exact same group of twenty-four eighth graders back in Mrs. Beachum's classroom for English C. For the first time, Rain had not been asked to distribute the books. *Mr. Brinque asked me twice!* But that wasn't Mrs. B's style, so Isabel, Juan, Lacey, Josh, Wilma, Matt, Stephanie and Jason passed out the four volumes that comprised the fall semester's reading list: *To Kill a Mockingbird* by Harper Lee, *Persepolis* by Marjane Satrapi, *The Tempest* by William Shakespeare, and *Their Eyes Were Watching God* by Zora Neale Hurston. Mrs. B explained that they would be studying the Shakespeare play as a prelude to seeing a live production that the P.K.T.B. (the Prospero Keys Tourist

Board) was presenting as part of its annual Shakespeare Festival on Teatro de Fantasmas in November. All her class heard was "Field trip!"

Eighth period.

Rain's locker and her backpack were both now stuffed with books. She transferred *Persepolis*, *Tempest* and *Eyes* to her locker, replacing them with the math and history texts she'd need to do her homework. (*What kind of monster assigns homework on the first day?!*) Miranda approached, carrying some kind of small instrument case. Charlie and Renée flanked her, with Charlie tossing the occasional nervous glance Renée's way.

Somehow, Rain's day—the first in what should have been this new chapter of her life—had been commandeered by Renée Jackson, despite the fact that Renée hadn't actually *done* anything yet. But Rain and Renée had known each other all their lives, and Rain was very aware it was only a matter of time. She glanced up to look into the eyes of the 5'9" beauty. Though only thirteen, Renée already had a knack for standing quite still in poses that emphasized her statuesque height and exaggerated her resemblance to a cast metal sculpture, her bronze skin reflecting the light in myriad interesting ways. On the other hand, her dark eyes and cold smile reflected no light whatsoever.

Over the years, Rain had been on and off Renée's Sugar List easily a half-dozen times for one perceived slight or another. In fact, the only thing Rain could say in Renée's favor was that once Renée finished doling out her "revenge" in the form of some brand of devastating humiliation, she almost always wiped the slate clean. For example, since the time Renée had stolen all of Rain's clothes after a volleyball game on Malas Almas last spring, they hadn't had a single run-in. (And since fifth grade, Rain had known

better than to bother with any attempt at retaliation. It only esca-
lated and extended the conflict and gave Renée more opportuni-
ties to work her dark magic.)

"Do you guys want to come over after school?" Miranda was
asking.

Rain shook her head. "Actually, I'm leaving now."

"What about eighth period?"

Rain pulled out her form. "I have an exemption, because I
work. For my folks. At least until volleyball starts in the spring."

Rain stared a challenge at Renée, who was forced to admit
with her full begrudge on, "Yeah, me, too." She recovered quickly,
sounding cheery once again. "But I'm not working *today*. So we
could meet up after. Where do you live, Sugar?"

Miranda hesitated, knowing what would come. "On . . .
Sycorax."

Renée stared at her. "Nobody lives on Sycorax."

Miranda sighed. "I do. With my dad."

"Does he work for Sycorax?"

"Y-yeah. Kinda."

Wheels began turning in Renée's head. Rain and Charlie's too.

"Wait a minute," Renée said. "You're last name's Guerrero,
right? Are you . . . Pablo Guerrero's daughter?"

Miranda shrugged, trying to pretend it wasn't a big deal that
her father basically owned Sycorax Inc. and the entire island that
came with it.

But this was clearly a mighty revelation to the other three
teens, who all exchanged glances. Charlie and Rain felt particularly dense for not having put this together before, even though
they had known Miranda lived on Sycorax and had gone water-
skiing with her and, what, her chauffer? Her bodyguard?

Renée actually looked shaken. "My mom works for Sycorax."

Miranda felt like she was about to hyperventilate. "It's not a big deal," she said desperately. "I just take the ferry over every morning and back every afternoon. I have a pass, and I can get you on for free. I mean, not that you need that, but—"

Renée pulled herself together. "You know, that sounds fine, Sugar. I'll meet you at the ferry at, what, three fifteen?"

Miranda brightened. "Great! How about you guys?"

Rain hated to leave Miranda to Renée's mercies, but ultimately the Search had to take precedence. Placing her right hand over the *zemi* on her arm, she shot a glance at Charlie, which neither Miranda nor Renée failed to notice.

"Um, how 'bout a rain-check?" Charlie asked guiltily. He *really* thought they needed to protect Miranda from whatever Renée was planning, but he couldn't help himself. Following Rain's lead was practically ingrained in his D.N.A.

"Well, that's all right," Renée said. "We can manage without you. Right, Miranda?"

The bell rang. Charlie jumped at the opportunity. He pointed at Miranda's music case. "Flute, right? I'm percussion. We better get to orchestra. Madame Conduttore hates it when we're late."

Rain and Renée watched Charlie drag Miranda away. Then they turned to face each other. Renée smiled her cold smile at Rain and shrugged. *Game on.*

Rain sighed and shrugged back. Then, backpacks over their shoulders, they took off in opposite directions.

Charlie hesitated outside the door to the orchestra room—another resource shared by all three schools. Miranda watched him look back at the departing Rain. *Dios mío, he's so into her, and she doesn't even—*

Just then, he seemed to notice Miranda's attention and turned an embarrassed smile toward her, before leading the way inside. *Dios mío,* she thought, as she followed him. *That is one great smile.*

CHAPTER FIVE

THE PALE TOURIST

MONDAY, SEPTEMBER 8

Jean-Marc Thibideaux cut a striking figure in his dress white uniform as he strode past tense and curious Sycorax employees toward the cave where they had found the body. Forty-five years old, Thibideaux was a fit and slim 5'll" with coffee-and-cream skin, close-cropped black hair and distinguished graying temples. As the top man at the Prospero Keys Constabulary (known locally as the Ghost Patrol), Constable Thibideaux was on his turf and in his element and dreading the job at hand nonetheless.

Thibideaux was based out of San Próspero, but the P.K.C. had jurisdiction over all but one of the Ghost Keys' eight islands. (Only tourists, the tourist board, various government agencies and official maps referred to these islands as the Prospero Keys. To the native born, like Thibideaux himself, they were the Ghost Keys or simply the Ghosts.) Five other islands—Tío Samuel,

Malas Almas, Ile de la Géante (where Jean-Marc was born), Teatro de Fantasmas and "The Pebble"—curved to the northeast of San Próspero in a gentle arc. Tío Sam's was the one hundred percent domain of the United States Navy, and Teatro and the Pebble were uninhabited rocks (though a single constable was routinely stationed on Teatro during the Shakespeare Festival to discourage rowdiness). The last island in the chain, a storm-tossed jungle known as Isla Soraya, lay some small distance south of the others but was also uninhabited. So most of Constable Thibideaux's (mostly alcohol-related or theft-oriented) business originated on Próspero, Almas or La Géante. Sycorax Island was to the west of San Próspero, just across the bay, but since 1995—the year Sycorax Inc. finally privatized its island—company security had dealt efficiently with virtually every concern, so it *would* take something like a corpse to bring Thibideaux here.

Two deputy constables and three Sycorax security guards—including an embarrassed Isaac Naborías—stood in a semicircle near the cave. They made way for Thibideaux, who checked his watch (2:33 P.M.), then checked the sun to confirm the time. The bright orb stared into the entrance, illuminating what to Jean-Marc looked like the World's Palest Tourist, lying on his back as if asleep in a Hawaiian shirt, Bermuda shorts and Mexican sandals. Dr. Josef Strauss knelt beside the body. The German-born transplant did double duty as an emergency room physician at San Próspero Island Hospital and as the territory's lone coroner. He glanced up at the constable, nodded, and spoke in slightly accented, staccato sentences: "Male. Caucasian. Age thirty-five to forty. No I.D."

"Cause of death?"

"Loss of blood. To put it mildly."

"I don't see any blood, Josef. I don't see any wounds."

"Here," Strauss said, using a steel pencil to indicate the victim's neck.

Thibideaux crouched to get a better look. There were two open sores on the throat of the Pale Tourist. Anyone who had seen a movie in the last eighty years knew what those marks meant. Thibideaux looked Strauss straight in the eye and deadpanned, "So. Vampire?"

Strauss tried not to smile and largely failed.

But for Naborías, smiling was the furthest thing from his mind. He vividly remembered the bat that had flown into his face in the wee hours of the morning—the bat that discouraged him from entering the cave. Still, he quickly brushed all thoughts of vampires and vampire bats aside without voicing them.

Strauss had swallowed his half-smile and was back to business, again using his steel pencil to indicate points of interest on the person of the Tourist. "He's got dirt under his fingernails. Recent scrapes on knees and elbows. And he's also covered head to toe with this rash. I'll know more after the autopsy and labs. But right now I can't rule anything out. Could be accident. Could be foul play. Could be something else entirely. I'll keep you posted."

"Time of death?"

"I'm estimating one A.M."

Naborías winced audibly, saying, "This is my fault."

The constable and the coroner both stared up at the security guard. Thibideaux rose with a questioning expression. "Isaac?"

Naborías sighed and explained. "I was hoping this happened after my shift. But I guess not. Should have checked the cave. Usually do, but I didn't last night—or, uh, this morning. He must have been here when I walked past on my last rounds at around four A.M. I know he wasn't here at eleven P.M. I did check then."

"That fits," Strauss said.

"You don't recognize him?" Thibideaux asked. "He's not an employee?"

"He's not Sycorax," Isaac said, turning toward his fellow guards for confirmation.

Both nodded, and Jimmy Kwan said, "Between the three of us, we know everyone who works for S.I. Dude's a complete stranger."

"Okay," Thibideaux said, "but I'll need to confirm that later."

Naborías nodded. "Of course. Mr. Guerrero was here a few minutes ago and told us to cooperate fully."

"How gracious. Where is your boss?"

"He had a teleconference with Lipton—or, uh, maybe he said Lisbon. But he wants an update from you before you leave."

Making an effort not to bristle at the demand, Thibideaux instead changed the subject. He nodded toward the excavation. "What's going on here?"

"They want to build another factory," Naborías said.

"Another *cannery*," Jimmy corrected.

"I think it's going to be a store for the folks who take the tour," said the third guard, the one Thibideaux didn't know. "They'll sell honey, guava, pineapple. Sycorax T-shirts and hats. Everything."

Naborías glared at his fellows. *Who has seniority here, boys?* Both lowered their gaze and shuffled back a step or two. Isaac turned back to Jean-Marc. "Whatever the end result, they want to start construction. They already had E.I.R. clearance, so . . ."

"So now they needed the archaeologists to check the site and give the go-ahead." This was standard procedure anywhere on the Ghosts, even on Tío Samuel. All proposed construction was preceded by an Environmental Impact Report. Once that was approved, a committee from the University of Florida's Department of Anthropology would initiate a dig to make sure the site wasn't concealing priceless pre-Columbian indigenous treasures.

"They started two weeks ago," Naborías was saying, "but the cave was full of about a thousand bats. One of the professors thought one looked rabid and wouldn't work until the bats were . . . relocated."

Thibideaux looked from Naborías to the Pale Tourist to Strauss. "Could this be rabies?"

Strauss shook his head. "No. Besides, we haven't had a case of rabies on the Ghosts since I moved here in 2004. Sounds more like that professor suffered from chiroptophobia." Thibideaux cocked his head impatiently.

Dr. Strauss clarified. "A fear of bats." Then he pulled a pocket flashlight off his belt, clicked it on and shone it around the cave. "I don't see any here."

Now Naborías clarified. "They hired exterminators. Laid out poison. Only had to kill a couple dozen before the rest moved on. Mostly." Naborías, who had his own issues with chiroptophobia, cautiously reached past the constable and pointed—without actually crossing the threshold—into the cave. Strauss followed the sightline with his flashlight and quickly found a poison trap. Then another and another. There were traps spread throughout the cave.

Again, Thibideaux turned a questioning eye on the Pale Tourist and his last physician. "Poison, maybe?"

Strauss shook his head again, but he looked less confident. "No, I don't think so. But I need to get the body to the morgue."

The constable turned back to Naborías. "Any protests against the proposed construction or the exterminations?"

"Not that I know of." He turned back toward Jimmy and the third guard, who both smiled at again being included in the investigation—but knew better than to push their luck. "No" and "No" was all they said.

"So we're back to vampire," Jean-Marc said with a growl of frustration.

Just then a cell phone rang. Thibideaux reached for his own automatically, faster than his brain could register that the ring-tone was wrong. He heard Strauss clear his throat, and he looked up to find the good doctor holding up a clear plastic evidence bag containing one cheap burner. "It belongs to our friend here," Strauss said, tilting his head toward the Pale Tourist and handing the sealed bag to Thibideaux.

Carefully, the constable pressed the hard black plastic AN-SWER button through the soft clear plastic of the evidence bag and placed the whole package against his ear. "Hello," he said in a neutral tone.

"Where are you, mate?" asked a slightly muffled and clearly miffed Aussie-accented voice. "I told you I want *daily* reports."

A hundred options played out in Jean-Marc's mind, but he settled on "Yeah. Sure. Where do you want to meet?"

There was a pregnant pause. Then the line went dead.

CHAPTER SIX

SOMETHING IN THE AIR

Callahan, scowling as usual, tossed his own burner phone off the deck of the *Bootstrap* and into the water of Pueblo Harbor. He knew a copper when he heard one. *Damn that Cash. If he got pinched, he's on his own. And he'd better not talk!*

Callahan ran his dry tongue over his chapped lower lip and his gorilla paw through his short spiky hair. All the big blond Australian could think about was the fifty thousand dollars Silas A. Setebos had promised him in exchange for the second *zemi*. One would think Callahan would be satisfied with the fifty thousand he'd already received for the first *zemi*. (Especially since he'd received that reward for unknowingly delivering a forgery, a copy of Rain's armband he'd commissioned in order to make an undetectable switch, but which our Rain had managed to switch back, leaving both Callahan and Setebos none the wiser.) No, the first fifty only made him hungrier for the second.

Setebos hadn't provided many clues. Didn't even really describe what the thing would look like this time out, saying only, "It will incorporate the image of a bat." But he had told Callahan he'd find it somewhere in the vicinity of the archaeological dig on Sycorax Island. Fortunately, Setebos had paid off or blackmailed one of the university professors into delaying the dig with some excuse or other in order to give Callahan a few precious weeks to search for it. But with Callahan still occupied securing the first *zemi*, he'd subcontracted the after-hours task of searching for the second prize to Cash—who'd clearly blown the gig. On the plus side, at least Callahan wouldn't have to pay the man now. *Besides, if you want something done right . . .*

With surprising agility for a man his size, Callahan swung himself off the deck of the cabin cruiser, his heavy boots landing hard on the dock. He'd make a supply run now, to make sure he had everything he'd need to last him, oh, at least a week. Then tonight, he'd slip out of the slip under cover of darkness so no one saw his heading. By midnight, he'd be dodging the Sycorax rent-a-cops in the pitch black and searching the dig. With a little luck, he might even put his hands on the *zemi* before morning.

Clomping down the dock, he passed the Sycorax Ferry and Renée Jackson, who stood in one of her frozen poses, running complex theoretical equations in her head. She was trying to calculate exactly what Charlie might have told Miranda after orchestra, exactly what Miranda's reaction would be, and exactly how Renée could find a way to turn it all to her advantage. Miss Jackson was nothing if not calculating.

Exiting the pedestrian gate, Callahan passed under the large WELCOME TO PUEBLO DE SAN PRÓSPERO sign without giving it a glance—or giving any notice to the young girl who lingered beneath it, quite troubled. Charlie had warned Miranda that Renée was "a piece of work"—a true specialist in the art of making everyone miserable. He thought he was helping. Now, though, she didn't know what to do. She liked Charlie. And Rain. But they still weren't really making her a part of their world. They had adopted her. Like a stray cat. But she wasn't their friend. Not really. Not yet, anyway. Maybe not ever. And the only other person she had even connected with was—according to Charlie—a witch. *So now what?*

"So many balls in the air!"

Miranda turned toward the voice and, despite her teenaged torment, couldn't help but smile at Maq and me. Maq was juggling old, split tennis balls he had found in the Dumpster behind the Versailles Hotel. Every thirty seconds or so, I'd pick up another ball off the dock with my teeth and fling it toward him. Without missing a beat, he'd absorb the ball into the routine. Soon I was fresh out, and he was easily juggling some eight or nine tennis balls. It was seriously impressive. I swear I've known the guy forever, and until today, I had *no idea* he could juggle.

Of course, I'd lay odds *he* had no idea he could juggle either. Maq can be rather fuzzy on those sorts of details. His memory is as thin as his old straw hat, which was currently on the ground in front of us, collecting no small amount of change from passing tourists wowed by our antics. Unfortunately, said antics turned suddenly clownish as the balls came tumbling down, bouncing and rolling every which way, some right off the dock and into the water. I scooped one up, but Maq had already forgotten them. There was no thought of collecting the tools of his recent success to repeat the exercise later. Now he was focused only on the money in the hat and the meal it would provide for us within the hour. Maq, you see, is extremely distractible. Then again, tell me, who *could* focus on the present or the past when able to see into the future? Maq knows where our next meal will come from.

He knows where the next *zemi* will be found. And that prescience of his makes up for a lot.

As for me, I can't see the future, and I'm not all that interested in the past. I'm canine. I focus on the now. But I am *very* good at the now. In fact, I'm virtually omniscient when it comes to the now. For example, I knew that right now Miranda—cheered by Maq's foolishness—had resolved to face Renée with a smile, an open mind and only the tiniest bit of caution. In that moment, I knew her mind better than I know my own tail. To be clear, I had no idea how it would all turn out. But at present, I knew Miranda was going to give Renée—and herself—the opportunity to be friends.

I also knew that at present, Rain was in the N.T.Z., standing before the sandstone entrance to the Cache.

CHAPTER SEVEN

STUDY HALL

MONDAY, SEPTEMBER 8

The air was still and smelled too sweetly of vanilla orchids and banana plants, as if the N.T.Z. were a dessert left out to curdle in the thick humidity and afternoon sun. Worse, after the fast-paced journey uphill through the jungle, Rain's T-shirt was sticking uncomfortably to her back and chest and stomach. Dropping her backpack on the ground, she tried tugging the top away from her damp skin, flapping it to create a bit of breeze, but it helped little.

Shadows were just starting to lengthen but as yet provided no real shade.

She took a quick glance around to assure herself she was alone. Then she slipped the *zemi* off her arm and knelt beside the sandstone slab at the edge of the cliff. She pushed aside a couple of stray vines that partially covered the circular indentation in the stone. She placed the snake charm in the indentation, twisted it a half turn and pulled it out, exactly as she would the key to her room at the Inn.

Instantly, the sandstone began to glow with blue light, a blue to match the eyes of the Searcher snake on her *zemi*. The sight—*the Sight*—was one of Rain's gifts: her ability to *see* the magicks that greased the wheels of her quest. Rain jumped back as those mystic wheels caused the block to move. The night before, the first time—perhaps in centuries—that it had opened, this movement was accompanied by a *grinnnndinnng* loud enough to wake the dead. Today, the slab was practically soundless as it glided aside along the frictionless blue glow to reveal the stone steps that led down into the Cache.

Rain descended a few steps and paused to breathe in the cool air washing over her skin. She reached out a hand to slide it across the smooth stone walls . . . and felt a curving groove. The light was dim, so she leaned in close. It was another circular keyhole for her snake charm key. *This is perfect!* She had been worried that while she was down in the Cache, a hundred other local kids could have shown up and found the sandstone slab open to the world. She reached up and yanked in her backpack. Then she placed the *zemi* in its interior slot and twisted. She ducked her head as the block glowed again and slid closed with an echoing *thunk,* leaving her in semidarkness and making her nervous about what would result if someone happened to be in the way of that slab when it thunked. It brought on her icky-face and a shiver and a conscious effort to push the thought away before descending farther.

In her head, Rain heard a bassoon with violin accents as she followed the indirect light down the circular stairway. She passed the extinguished torch on the wall and issued a command: "Light!" Nothing happened. "Torch!" Nothing. She tried to remember the exact words she had used to bring it to flaming life the night before, but she couldn't quite recall, and ultimately it didn't matter. There was enough illumination leaking up from below. *Maybe that's why the torch won't light. It isn't truly needed. Or maybe, like 'Bastian, it doesn't work before the sun goes down . . .*

She emerged into the Cache, a wide terrace cut into the cliffside and open to the elements directly in front of her. Shadowed by its stone ceiling thirty feet above, which provided a floor to the N.T.Z., the air in the Cache was easily twenty degrees cooler. While there had been no breeze atop the cliff, down here a gentle zephyr of salt-scented sea air washed over Rain's skin, causing her to breathe a satisfied sigh of relief. She slid her backpack off her shoulder and gently lowered it to the floor.

To her right, along one side of the rectangular cave, were nine stone thrones, carved out of the wall itself. She ignored these and crossed to her left instead. Here was the long stone shelf, and behind it the wall that still bore the charred message that had *officially* launched her on her quest:

BIENVENIDO, BUSCADORA, A LA CACHÉ.

BIEN HECHO. HAS ENCONTRADO EL PRIMER ZEMI.

COMO TÚ, ES EL BUSCADOR Y EL CURADOR.

COMO TÚ, TAMBIÉN ES EL PRIMERO DE NUEVE.

TENEMOS POCO TIEMPO Y SÓLO UNA OPORTUNIDAD
PARA CURAR LA HERIDA.

ENCUENTRA LOS NUEVE. PARA TI Y PARA ELLOS
SON LAS LLAVES QUE ABRIRÁN EL VERDADERO
ACERTIJO DE LAS FANTASMAS.

Once more, Rain made her best approximate mental translation from the Spanish. "Welcome, Searcher, to the Cache. Well done. You have found the first *zemi*. Like you, it is the Searcher and the Healer. Like you, it is also the first of nine. We have little time and only one chance to heal the wound. Find the nine. For you and they are the keys to unlocking the true mystery of the Ghosts."

Rain found herself smiling. *I'm the Searcher. I'm the Healer. I'm the key to unlocking this mystery!* It was pretty great. She turned toward the nonexistent fourth wall and came very, very close to shouting that to the world. *After all, shouldn't they know?* Shouldn't the whole world know this quest was hers?

Still, a part of her was quite aware she'd never be believed, and what little she could prove could easily be taken away from her. The *zemi*. The Cache. These could be classified as archaeological finds and put in the hands of the very people who would laugh derisively at her ghost story—even with Charlie as a witness. And if they took the *zemi*, they'd be taking 'Bastian away from her too. She could not allow that. So except for an unintelligible grumble, she kept her mouth shut.

She ran her hand along the stone shelf, studying each of the nine indentations carved to house the nine *zemis*—or they would house them, once she'd found the other eight. The first indentation was yet another circular keyhole for her snake charm. The second was a small cylindrical hole. The third was a thick equilateral triangle. The fourth looked something like a cross. The fifth was a shallow cup; the sixth, a circular ring; the seventh, an oval ring. The eighth was a deep widening groove that called to mind a gigantic dagger or maybe the kind of stake one used to stab an oversized vampire. The last—the ninth—was carved into the distinctive shape of a skull.

She backtracked along the shelf in reverse, pausing to look

once again at the second slot, the next slot to fill. She stuck her index finger into the hole and could just barely touch the bottom. She had no idea what the second *zemi* would look like, but it seemed to be more or less the shape of a roll of quarters. Not much to go on. She needed another clue.

Then she had an idea. She was still holding her armband. She placed it in the first slot, hoping for another message of flame to appear on the wall, as it had the night before. No dice. She twisted it like a key. Nothing. *Oh, well. Worth a try.* She sighed again, but she didn't really feel defeated. She felt . . . at home, strangely at home.

It was still a few hours until sunset. She had time to kill, and she didn't really feel like going back to the Nitaino just yet. She glanced down at her backpack and shrugged. *Might as well.* She opened it up, pulled out *To Kill a Mockingbird* and took a seat on the largest and most central of the stone thrones. It wasn't immediately comfortable, but she found that if she leaned against one of the arms and swung her legs over the other, it fit her just fine. She cracked the book and started to read. *"When he was nearly thirteen, my brother Jem got his arm badly broken at the elbow . . ."*

CHAPTER EIGHT

GOOD TALK

MONDAY, SEPTEMBER 8

R ain had lost track of the time. When she returned to the Inn—at a few minutes to seven and less than an hour before sundown—her parents already had dinner on the table. There were three place settings now. Iris and Alonso stared at the empty seat, which only four nights ago had been filled by the warm old man with the kind gray eyes that neither of them would ever see again. Rain saw her mother on the verge of tears again, and even her father was forced to shove his tongue into his cheek and draw a deep breath to keep from choking up. They were still grieving 'Bastian in a way Rain herself was not. She knew that at sunset he'd emerge from the *zemi* and be with her once more. She wanted to reassure them, to *tell* them. *He's not really gone!* Instead, she spontaneously reached out with both hands and touched theirs.

And it happened again! Just as with Charlie's foot, the eyeless snake on her charm flashed gold. The warm light—light only she could see—split in two, running down her left arm and also across her chest to her right, before leaping from Rain's outstretched hands to Alonso and Iris.

Rain's eyes went wide, and she froze.

But immediately, she could see the positive effect. Glancing from mother to father and back again, she saw them both smile. These were bittersweet smiles—brought on by fond memories of Sebastian Bohique—and hardly negated their grief. For a time, however, the sadness was chased away. Iris straightened in her chair, and Alonso said, "Dig in!"

Raising an eyebrow for her own benefit, Rain withdrew her hands and picked up her fork. *Chalk up another win for the Healer,* she smirked. She twirled some pasta and shoved it in her mouth.

It was simple fare, Alonso's bachelor recipe, made with sautéed onions and mushrooms and half a pound of Malas Almas ground beef, which, along with garlic salt, garlic powder, onion powder and a hefty amount of Parmesan cheese, was stirred into mainland tomato sauce (that is, from a can). This concoction was allowed to simmer on low for a *long* time before being poured over and tossed with al dente spaghettini and then doused with still more Parmesan. Plus there was garlic toast. The meal wasn't going to win any prizes, but it was a family favorite.

Alonso, mouth half full, asked about Rain's first day of school. Just to give him a hard time, Rain said, "I'm sorry, what was that? I know there are words coming out of your mouth, but all I see is bits of cheese and sauce."

Alonso shut his mouth, smiled wryly, and swallowed. "Sorry. How was school?"

"Okay, I guess. Mrs. Beachum still hates me."

"She doesn't hate you, Rain," Iris admonished. "She'd just like to see you put more effort into your work."

"You say tomato; I say tomahto."

Alonso squinted at her. "Do you? Do you really say tomahto?"

Rain shrugged. Her parental units spent the next fifteen minutes eking out the tiniest slivers of information about each of her classes.

Then, giving up, Alonso changed the subject. "The Kims have chartered the boat for all day Saturday. They're bringing all three kids, so I'll need you to work."

Rain rolled her eyes, practically an involuntary response.

"We know how you feel about babysitting tourist kids . . ." her mother started.

"But we don't want any arguments," her father finished.

Rain wasn't arguing. She was resigned to it. *For a day, the Searcher would be the Babysitter.* Her cross to bear. Still . . . "Three kids are a lot. I mean, safety-wise. Even if I grab hold of one with each hand, the third could still jump off the boat and tragically drown."

Both Alonso and Iris knew what she was getting at. Iris, the family bookkeeper, was more inclined to hold the line, but Alonso relented quickly. "Fine. Tell Charlie I'll pay the usual."

Rain grinned. "Great. He'll be here any minute. I'll ask him."

Iris shook her head, astonished—though she knew she shouldn't be. "He's coming over tonight? Didn't you spend the whole afternoon with him? You only just got home. And don't you have any homework?"

"I wasn't with Charlie, and I did all my homework already."

Rain's parents stared at her. Talk about astonished. Even Rain was a little surprised. "I know, I know. But I found a quiet place, um, near the N.T.Z. And I just started reading my English assignment. The book's not bad, and it was only the first three chapters, so I finished pretty quick. So then I moved on to my math worksheet and my Spanish worksheet, and then I did the history reading, and then I was done. I mean, it's the first day back; they didn't assign *that* much."

Alonso's jaw hung open, despite a mouthful of spaghettini. Iris was more demure but no less stunned. Rain almost never did her homework voluntarily. Getting her to buckle down often involved *hours* of procrastination, whining and wheedling. Of course, it *was* only the first day. Plenty of time for Rain to revert. Even so, this was a good sign, and the Caciques would take it.

Alonso shut his mouth, swallowed and shook off his disbelief the way I'd shake off a light drizzle. Then he reached into his pocket and slid a key over to Rain. It was her copy of the Nitaino Inn's master key, the one he had taken away from her only the day before as "punishment" for ransacking the contents of Callahan's guest room. He said, "Well, if you've suddenly matured into a responsible individual, I think you can have this back."

"You mean you realized that without it, I can't make the beds or clean the toilets."

"Yeah, well, that too."

"But," her mother said, "this key does represent real responsibility and trust."

Keys are like that, Rain thought, smiling. "Don't worry. I'll be good. No repeats of the other night. I swear."

There was a pause, as Iris seemed to consider her next words: not what she was going to say, but whether or not she was going to say anything at all. Finally, she spoke, more haltingly than Rain was accustomed to hear from her normally decisive mother. "There's one more . . . thing. You mentioned . . . Well, yesterday, you said . . ."

Iris paused again. Rain couldn't imagine what her mom was getting at. *What did I say yesterday?*

Alonso rescued his wife. "Your mom and I talked it over, and if you'd still like to move into 'Bastian's old room, we think it's okay."

Iris more or less found her voice. "It's bigger, and it's not on the guest floor, which is probably a good thing. You'd definitely have more privacy, which is probably a very good thing. So . . . do you still want to change rooms?"

Rain had completely forgotten that on impulse she had asked for 'Bastian's room. The very moment it had come out of her mouth, it had seemed wildly disrespectful to his memory. Of course, that was before she knew Papa 'Bastian would be hanging around as a ghost. She wondered whether or not he'd approve— then decided he'd prefer to have the room go to her than to an unending chain of tourists. Besides, 'Bastian was stuck with the armband, and the armband was sticking with Rain, so this was more or less a way for him to *keep* his room. Tentatively, she said, "I think I do. If it's okay with you."

Iris nodded. Even smiled a little. "It is. I think he'd like that."

I'll double-check at sundown, Rain thought.

Alonso was already moving on to logistics. "We don't want the move to cause a lot of disruption for the guests. Mrs. Sawyer's checking out Wednesday morning, and that'll just leave Ms. Vendaval and the Kims. We've got another couple checking in Thursday afternoon, the Bernstein-Shores. So that really makes Wednesday after school the best time for the move."

"O-okay," Rain said. *This is happening fast.*

"So I want you to have your stuff packed up and ready to move before then."

"Right. Got it." She was beginning to get a little excited about it.

"Hi," Charlie said, entering through the swinging door from the dining room. "It's almost sunset."

While Iris and Alonso thought about the seeming non sequitur, Rain whipped around in her seat to look at Charlie, then whipped back to look out the window at the fading light of the day. Then she shoved another huge forkful of pasta into her mouth—she was, after all, her father's daughter—swallowed hard, and leapt to her feet.

She grabbed Charlie's hand, saying, "Let's go to my room."

Charlie inhaled sharply, feeling that wonderful, horrible electric rush. Though his mouth was pasta-free, he swallowed hard too and glanced, terrified, at Rain's parents.

In fact, Alonso and Iris were not blind to Charlie's crush on their daughter. They gave each other a silent look that spoke volumes. *These kids are getting older. When do the new rules start?*

Rain remained oblivious, asking to be excused without waiting for an answer and tugging Charlie toward the Inn's back stairs.

Iris said, "Rain, wait. Maybe Charlie would like to sit down? Have some pasta? Or dessert?"

Charlie appeared on the verge of accepting the latter invitation. "What do you have—" But Rain caught his eye and nodded toward her armband. "Um, never mind, Mrs. Cacique. I already ate."

With that, the two teens raced upstairs.

CHAPTER NINE

GHOST RULES

MONDAY, SEPTEMBER 8

Rain didn't release Charlie's hand until they were standing in front of her door and she was pulling out her room key. She slipped it into the lock, but what they were about to do seemed clandestine enough that she found herself looking back over her shoulder toward the guest room across the hall— the room Callahan had stayed in, as if the big Aussie might still be there, watching her every move. Of course, no one was staying in Room Six now. She chided herself and opened her bedroom door.

She let Charlie in and then plopped down on her unmade bed. (Rain rarely made her own bed, feeling she made more than her fair share at the Nitaino. Her mother attributed this to laziness, but Rain just called it logic.) She had left enough space for Charlie to sit beside her. He hesitated. Then crossed the room and sat at her desk chair.

They waited in tense silence for the sun to set.

Then Rain said, "Oh!" and slipped the snake charm off her arm, setting it carefully on her nightstand. They both stared at it as it did absolutely nothing. Seconds ticked by.

Charlie suddenly remembered, "Oh, I warned Miranda about Renée."

"Oh, good." Then, "How'd she take it?"

"I think she felt pretty bad."

"Yeah."

More silence. Rain felt like she was in Mrs. Beachum's class at the end of the day, waiting for that last bell to ring, when the minute hand on the clock over the chalkboard moved so slowly, it sometimes felt like it was about to click backward.

Rain said, "I'm moving up to 'Bastian's old room on Wednesday. Um, assuming he doesn't mind."

"That's cool."

"Yeah."

Daylight was fading in the room. Then, just as Rain was about to stand and hit the light switch, she saw it: a soft white glow emanating from the *zemi* on the nightstand. Of course, only she could see it, and an unaware Charlie clicked on her desk lamp.

Like a genie from a very different kind of lamp, the late Sebastian Bohique emerged in all his translucent glory. He wasn't exactly a dead ringer for the grandfather who'd been part of Rain's life for the past thirteen years, an old man of way past eighty with long gray hair and soft gray eyes. No, that octogenarian look just didn't fit 'Bastian's self-image. Instead, this was the ghost Rain had dubbed the Dark Man: twenty-one years old and in his prime, neat as a pin in his World War II Army Air Forces uniform and bomber jacket. His black hair was cut short in back, while in front it swooped up like hawk feathers. His eyes were two orbs of polished onyx. That's how 'Bastian Bohique saw himself, how perhaps he had *always* seen himself. And now, now that he was dead and "living" by his own personal definition, this was 'Bastian Bohique once more.

He spoke. That is, his lips moved. But the words were indistinct, impossible to grasp, fleeing from Rain like smoke or the tide. She couldn't hear him.

Mentally, she kicked herself. She had thought it would be awkward for 'Bastian to emerge while the *zemi* was on her arm, but she had forgotten she needed to be holding or wearing it in order to hear him clearly.

Charlie, watching her carefully, said, "Is he here? What's he saying?"

"I don't know," she said, snatching the snake charm off the nightstand. "I took the armband off."

"Well, why'd you do that?"

She rolled her eyes at him, and he rolled his right back.

'Bastian watched all this with some amusement. It was somewhat reassuring that even after his death, so little had changed in the world he hadn't *quite* left behind. He spoke again. "Can you hear me now?"

Rain beamed. "Yes! Loud and clear. I mean, roger that, Captain Bohique!" She saluted.

He saluted back. "Acknowledged, Lieutenant Raindrop."

Grandfather and granddaughter fought the impulse to hug. Both wanted it badly but knew it to be impossible. 'Bastian had no substance, and their arms would simply pass right through each other. They had quickly learned that the failed attempt was sadder and more frustrating than not trying to hug at all.

Charlie saw his friend's bittersweet smile. Concentrating, even squinting, he tried to perceive 'Bastian in the space in front of her. He could imagine the same sad smile on the old man's face. Rain's smile—all sixteen varieties by Charlie's count—had skipped Iris' generation, but everyone who knew them agreed Rain had inherited hers from her grandfather. Try as he might, though, Charlie just couldn't see the ghost, let alone read his expression. Giving up, he said, "He's here, right?"

"Yep. Right in front of me." Her eyes never left her Papa 'Bastian.

"Okay, great," Charlie said. "So now what?"

That stumped all three of them. The ghost was in the house. *Now what?*

Rain raised a questioning eyebrow at 'Bastian. Dead or alive, he was still the only adult in the room.

He shook his head. "Don't look at me. You're the Searcher, kiddo."

Rain growled under her breath but ultimately nodded. She said, "Fine. Let's review what we know. See if we can figure out how this works and what we should do next."

"Sounds good," Charlie said, simultaneously with 'Bastian's "Makes sense."

"I never saw any ghosts during the day," Rain continued. "You, your bomber crew—none of you ever showed up until after sundown or later, and you always disappeared at sunrise."

"That's right," 'Bastian said. "Honestly, I'm not even sure I *exist* during the day. I have no memory of anything in between sunrise and sunset."

"What's he saying?" Charlie asked.

Rain held him off with a slight wave while speaking to 'Bastian. "I thought you slept in the *zemi* during the day?"

"It's more like I'm stored in there. It doesn't feel like sleep. And if I've had any dreams, I sure don't remember them."

"Maybe ghosts don't dream."

"You got me. There's no owner's manual for being dead. Although I'm not sure why I'm surprised. There's no owner's manual for being alive, either."

"Rain," Charlie grumbled. It had only been two days, and already he was way tired of constantly being left out of her spirit-talk.

"Sorry, sorry. He's been saying he doesn't have any memories of the daytime. Not even dreams. And he doesn't know how being a ghost works."

"So try some stuff," Charlie suggested. "Can he walk through walls?"

Rain looked at 'Bastian, who nodded. "Well, I did some of this yesterday, but I guess a little experimentation couldn't hurt."

He crossed to her door and hesitated. "I feel a little silly." Then, out of habit, he took a deep airless breath and stuck his head through the door.

Rain narrated: "He just stuck his head through the door. Now he's walking all the way through it. I can't see him. Now he's back." She turned to 'Bastian. "How'd that feel? Does it hurt? Is it weird?"

"Doesn't hurt. It's a *little* weird. It's like . . . It's like . . . *humidity*. You know when you walk outside on the stickiest day of the year . . ."

"And you feel like you're walking into a wall of yuck," she said, nodding again.

"Something like that."

"Okay," Charlie said, mostly to prove he was getting the gist of things. "So the wooden door feels like a wall of yuck. What does a wall feel like?"

'Bastian shrugged and crossed to the outer wall of Rain's room, beside the window looking out on Goodfellow Lane. Rain watched him, and Charlie used the movement of her head to follow the action.

'Bastian felt a little like a trained seal, doing tricks on command. *On the other hand, I probably* should *learn my limits.* He stuck his head and upper body through the wall. Hanging out over the second story, he felt a sudden, discomforting rush of vertigo. He was afraid of losing his balance and tumbling forward. He grabbed for the edge of the wall, but his hand passed through; there was no way to anchor himself. He caught a glimpse of the streetlamp clicking on below before yanking himself back inside—mostly through sheer force of will. "Okay, I didn't like that!"

"Walls are harder than doors?" Rain asked.

"No, going through felt the same. But I was hanging off the edge there, and I nearly fell."

Rain turned to Charlie. "He nearly fell."

Charlie frowned and shook his head. "Wait a minute. This is exactly what I've always wondered about in movies. Ghosts can move through walls, so how come they don't drop down through the floor? I mean, is he even standing on the floor?"

Both 'Bastian and Rain instantly looked down. Then Rain abruptly sprung off the bed into a low crouch to study 'Bastian's feet. She let out a tiny gasp. "He's not. He's sort of floating. I mean he's near the floor, but one foot's a bit above it and the other's a little ways . . . *in* it!"

Charlie smiled and even made a fist, as if he had just scored a point. "So the floor. It's really just a habit!"

Rain turned to a stunned 'Bastian. "It's like when you were in the water yesterday. You just stood there. Upright. Like you were on a platform or something that wasn't there at all."

"That's right," 'Bastian remembered. "I could even feel the water moving through me. And when I wanted to sink down or float up, I just . . . did."

"See, he can control it," Charlie said, almost as if he had heard the dead old man's words. "'Bastian, try to sink down through the floor. Just concentrate and see if you can."

Now even 'Bastian had caught the bug of the kids' excitement. He took another breathless breath and tried to focus on DOWN. And . . .

"It's working," Rain called out. "He's sliding right through the floor!"

"I knew it!" Charlie whisper-shouted.

'Bastian allowed himself to pass all the way down and into the currently deserted lobby of the Nitaino. He wondered—if he kept going, would he pass right through the Earth itself to the other side? But just shy of the lobby floor, he was brought up short by a tug he recognized.

Seconds later, Rain turned to Charlie. "He's back."

"I couldn't go very far," 'Bastian told her. "The *zemi*. I'm still tied to it. Can't seem to move more than ten yards or so away from it. In any direction."

"What about up?" Charlie asked.

Rain stared at him. Now it really did seem like Charlie was listening in.

Charlie stared back. "He tried down. See if he can go up. You know, see if he can fly."

"Well," Rain said, "he just came up from the lobby."

Charlie considered this. "Is that the same thing? I mean, I'm asking. I'm not sure."

Rain turned to 'Bastian, who squinted his eyes and thought UP.

This was tougher going. He rose four feet or so off the floor, feeling the whole time like he was swimming through molasses. After considerable mental effort, his head poked through Rain's ceiling, past a layer of insulation, and through the floor of his own old room.

Below, Rain watched his progress. She could still see him

from about the waist down, and it suddenly registered that her Papa's upper half was in his room. His room, which was soon to be *her* room. She'd have to tell him—*ask him*—soon. He sank back down. *Soon, but not right now.*

"Up is harder," he said as he descended to the floor.

She turned to Charlie to bring him up to speed. "Up is harder. And he's still tied to the *zemi.*"

"Well, then put it down," Charlie said. "Maybe it'll follow him if you're not holding it."

She was impressed. "You're just full of good ideas tonight."

Feeling the heat in his cheeks, Charlie looked away and shrugged.

Rain placed the snake charm on the floor, then turned to 'Bastian. "Try to go down the hall. We'll see if it slides across the floor after you."

'Bastian nodded and vanished through Rain's door again. Seconds passed. The kids watched the *zemi*, as it did . . . absolutely nothing.

Soon 'Bastian was back, looking and feeling quite frustrated. "It's no good. I tried walking; I tried concentrating. But it's like being tied to an invisible chain attached to a stake!" Rain shook her head. She couldn't hear him. Increasingly aggravated, he kicked at the charm, remembering in the instant before impact that his foot would simply pass right through it.

Except that it didn't. His foot made contact—contact he could *feel*—and the *zemi* skittered across the floor and under Rain's bed.

Charlie leaped to his feet. "I saw that! What happened?"

Rain was still sitting on her bed, stunned. "He kicked it. He just kicked it, and it moved."

Belatedly, she dropped off her bed to reach beneath it, but 'Bastian held out a hand to stop her. "Wait!" he said. "Let me try."

She heard nothing, but his hand was enough, and she stepped away to watch. 'Bastian allowed himself to sink beneath the floor up to his neck. Then he walked forward—acutely aware at this point that he wasn't actually walking *on* anything. He passed from Rain's sight under the bed. All she could see now was his faint ghostly glow. Then he emerged and rose . . . *zemi* in hand.

"Whoa," Charlie said as he watched the snake charm float and bob through the air. He glanced over at the full-length mirror on the back of Rain's open closet door. It was the same deal in the glass: floating *zemi*, but no 'Bastian.

Rain whispered excitedly, "Try putting it on."

'Bastian slipped it onto his right wrist. It felt comfortable there, as it had for the last sixty-nine years of his life. He waved his arm around. The charm stayed in place.

"Try walking with it now," Charlie said.

'Bastian nodded enthusiastically. Leading with his left foot, he walked toward and *through* the door. But the *zemi* was still solid enough, and he couldn't get his right wrist through.

All Charlie saw was the snake charm bumping up against the door multiple times. He ran over and called out to 'Bastian, "Come back in. I'll open it." Charlie saw the armband move backward from the door. He opened it and peeked both ways down the hall to see if anyone was coming. "No one's there. Try walking with it now." Charlie watched the armband float around the door and down the hallway.

Rain crossed to see, but Charlie held his arm out. "No, wait there. Let's see if it's just the snake thing he's tied to or if it's you too."

It was just the snake thing. 'Bastian walked with the *zemi* on his wrist all the way to the far end of the hall, an easy thirty feet from Rain's door. He came back and reentered—just as the door to Room Three opened and a tall Caucasian woman with long dark hair came out. While locking her door, she glanced over at Charlie and smiled. He panicked and ducked back inside, slamming the door shut behind him.

Both 'Bastian and Rain stared at Charlie. "What?" she asked. "What's wrong?"

"Nothing. We just . . . *He* needs to be more careful."

"*I* need to be more careful. Young man, I was following *your* instructions!"

Neither teen could hear him. Charlie said, "A lady came out of one of the guest rooms and nearly spotted him."

Rain waved off the concern. "She wouldn't have been able to see him."

"Okay, fine. But she nearly spotted the *zemi* floating down the hall. Same difference."

This sank in, and Rain turned to 'Bastian, saying, "We do need to be careful. If someone sees it, they'll take it away. I can't risk losing it *or you.*"

'Bastian started to speak, then realized he'd simply be talking to himself. He took off the band and handed it back to Rain, who was about to put it back on.

Then Charlie said, "Can I try it?"

Rain shook off the idea. "What good would that do?"

"I don't know," Charlie said. "Maybe nothing. I know I'm not the Searcher, but the *zemi*'s like an upgrade. You could see the ghosts without it, but you need it to hear them. So maybe if I put it on, I'll be able to *smell* 'em or something."

Rain chuckled, but she was still somewhat reluctant to hand it over. On the other hand, she couldn't come up with a legitimate reason not to, so she held it out to Charlie.

He took it from her gingerly, as if expecting an electric shock, but the charm was static-free. His father's oversized watch loosely occupied his left wrist, so he slowly placed the *zemi* on his right. He thought about sliding it up to wear on his biceps as Rain did—and in truth, his arm was just skinny enough to make that feasible—but he recalled that 'Bastian always wore the charm on his wrist and left it alone. Then slowly he raised his eyes to look at Rain and 'Bastian.

"Wow," he whispered.

"What?!" Rain and 'Bastian asked in unison.

"Totally nothing. I still can't see him. Can't even smell him. Tell him to say something."

'Bastian said, "Now you want me to bark on command? I *am* a trained seal."

Rain saw his lips moving and sent an inquiring look Charlie's way.

"Nothing," Charlie said. He took off the *zemi* and handed it to Rain.

She could see he was pretty disappointed. "Maybe you've got to be part of the family," she offered.

"Yeah, I suppose . . ." Then, a little excited, "But that would mean your mom . . ."

Rain shook her head. "She's the same as you. She hasn't been able to see him."

"I know, but maybe she could with the *zemi*. And if she can . . ."

Now Rain was getting excited. "If she can, I can tell her. About me being the Searcher. All of it."

Charlie screwed up his face. "Well, maybe not all of it . . ."

Rain thought about that and agreed. "Yeah. Like not the stowing-away-on-Callahan's-boat part . . ."

"Or the riding-on-the-haunted-plane-that-nearly-crashed part."

"Yeah, we'd be grounded till *we* were ghosts."

"But you could tell her the rest," 'Bastian said quietly. "Or I could. I could talk to my daughter."

Rain looked at her Papa and made a decision.

Racing down the back stairs, they found Iris in the laundry room off the kitchen. They stopped in front of her and stood there, rather stupidly. Iris folded towels and waited for Rain or Charlie to speak. When neither did—as the two of them and 'Bastian were all trying to formulate some kind of plan to initiate this latest experiment—Iris finally said, "Yes?"

Rain looked from Charlie to 'Bastian, but both stared hopefully at her. So, with no good ideas or excuses coming to mind, Rain simply took off the armband and said, "Try this on."

She held the charm out to her mother. Iris placed the folded towel in a white plastic laundry basket and shook her head. "No, baby, Dad wanted you to have it."

"I know," Rain said, irritated. "I'm not giving it to you."

"Oh." Iris—to her surprise—felt a little let down.

"I, uh, I just want to see how it looks . . ."

"On a real woman!" Charlie offered, trying to be helpful.

Rain turned on him. "What is *that* supposed to mean? I'm not *real* enough for you?"

"No, I didn't mean *real. Older.* On an *older* woman."

Both Rain and Iris shot the boy a sour face. 'Bastian tilted his head away and scratched one spectral eyebrow with a phantom pinky. *Poor kid's doomed now.*

Charlie corrected again. "Grown-up. A grown-up woman. An . . . uh . . . I'll just be quiet now."

For a second, Rain was annoyed enough to have lost track of why they were there. Charlie pleaded with his eyes and then nodded toward the *zemi.*

Still frowning, Rain turned back to her mother. "Ignore him.

It's just . . . I want to see how it looks against your skin from a distance." Charlie could see Rain was proud of the feeble fib, and he was relieved she had found her smile again.

Iris wasn't exactly convinced, but at this point it seemed easier to comply. She took the snake charm from Rain and placed it on her left wrist. She waved her hand in the air. "How's this?"

Rain glanced at 'Bastian and said, "Let me just step back."

She did, and 'Bastian stepped forward. "Iris? Little Flower? It's me. It's your father. Can you see me? Can you hear me?"

But Iris was unaware of his presence and was considerably more curious about her daughter's strange behavior. She watched Rain stare at her and then away. Charlie was doing something similar. She decided this was some inside joke at her expense. "All right, what's going on here? What do you keep looking at, Rain?"

"Nothing," Rain said wistfully as 'Bastian's head sank sadly. "It's just . . . just the light reflecting off the charm. It makes pretty patterns on the wall."

Iris turned and waved her arm again, discovering that this much at least was true. A mosaic of light, mostly gold but with flecks of blue, glinted in time to her movements on the wall behind the washing machine. Iris also discovered there was something about wearing her father's wristband that made her melancholy—a feeling she had been struggling to fight off since he had passed. Quickly, she removed it and handed it back to Rain.

"Okay, are we done?"

Rain and Charlie both looked disappointed, though Iris could hardly fathom why. She picked up the laundry basket and started up the back stairs.

Just then the front desk bell rang. Iris paused a few steps up. "Rain, please see what that is."

"Sure, Mom," Rain said, and Iris couldn't help but notice the same melancholy in her daughter's voice. She watched Rain and Charlie head into the kitchen toward the lobby. Then she shook her head and ascended the stairs.

The two teens—with 'Bastian almost literally in tow—crossed through the dark dining room and entered the warm light of the lobby to find Ms. Judith Vendaval waiting.

"Can I help you?" Rain asked.

"Yes, I was hoping you could recommend a place to eat here in Old Town."

"Sure," Rain said. "There are a bunch of places." She looked at Charlie for confirmation, but as this was the woman Charlie had slammed the door on upstairs, he was currently doing his best to make himself as invisible as 'Bastian. Rain shook her head and turned back. "Are you in the mood for anything in particular?"

"Not just anything. Everything. The famous don't-miss places and the local haunts that no tourist knows about. See, I write travel books, and my next one's on the Ghosts."

"That's kinda cool," Rain said. She found herself studying Ms. Vendaval intently. The woman was truly striking. So much so that after seeing her only once the night she'd checked in, her image had invaded Rain's dreams. The Tall Woman was over six feet in height and in her mid- to late twenties, with long black hair, very pale skin and dusky red lips. Her eyes were dark brown, but they caught the light and twinkled invitingly. She was wearing a blue strapless dress, cut above the knee, with a red belt and purse—not to mention nail polish—that matched her lipstick perfectly. Throw in the cool job, and now Rain found herself *admiring* Ms. Vendaval intently. Until a couple of days ago—before learning of the *zemi* and the Search—this was exactly the kind of woman Rain had wanted to be.

"It's *very* cool, actually," the woman was saying. "I spend a few months in a place where everyone wants to go. And just when I'm about to get bored, I'm off to the next great *where* out there."

Rain nodded. *Exactly* the kind of woman Rain had wanted to be.

"I'm Judith, by the way."

"Rain. And this is Charlie and—" Rain swallowed hard. "And this is Charlie."

"Hi, Charlie," Judith said.

"Hi," Charlie croaked, a little freaked that Rain had come so close to introducing her dead, transparent grandfather to the nice lady.

"I haven't seen you at breakfast," Rain said, desperate to change the subject.

Judith blushed, a little embarrassed. "Well, I'm not exactly an early riser. My target audience is a bit more interested in the island's nightlife. Speaking of which . . ."

"Oh, yeah, dinner. Um, well, Old Town isn't exactly Nightlife Central. That's more downtown or by the beach. But there's Kelly's Bar and Grill over on Rue de Lafitte, which has the best burger in the Pueblo." Rain looked at Judith again and frowned. "Of course, you're a little overdressed for Kelly's, so , um . . ."

"Barcelona," 'Bastian offered.

"*Barcelona!*" Rain said, way too loud. Judith looked taken aback. Rain tried to recover by pointing and saying, "It's just a shout away! Two blocks down and a right turn on Honest Robin Lane."

"I love the street names here," Judith said with a sparkling laugh.

"Yeah, I guess they're . . . quirky. Anyway, Barcelona serves traditional Spanish food. Old World. The paella's pretty amazing. Totally four stars. The place is packed at lunch, but getting a table for dinner's pretty easy. And it's not pricey."

"Sounds perfect. Hey, do you two want to come along? I'm on an expense account, so the paella's on me."

Rain turned again to look at 'Bastian and Charlie and then down at her armband. She shook her head.

Judith looked embarrassed again. "I'm sorry, that was weird, wasn't it? I'm some stranger inviting two kids to dinner."

"No, it's just . . . we already ate. And we have homework."

"Of course, of course. I'm going to be here for five or six weeks anyway. Maybe some time I could invite you *and* your parents to dinner."

"That sounds nice," Rain said. "You all set or do you want a map or something?"

"Two blocks down and turn right? I think I can handle it."

"Okay, um, well. Enjoy." Rain grabbed Charlie's hand and tugged him up the front stairs. 'Bastian paused to admire the Tall Woman, who was a good six inches taller than he. Captain Bohique brushed a hand through his hair, but she looked right through him, her eyes following the teens up the stairs. Then she sighed heavily and headed out the Inn's front door—just as 'Bastian felt that ol' *zemi*-tug yanking him upward.

Seconds later, all three of them were back in front of Rain's door. Glancing involuntarily at Room Six once more, Rain again dropped Charlie's hand to pull out her key.

"It must be kind of sad," Charlie said as he rubbed the hand Rain had just released.

"What?" Rain asked.

"Eating alone every night. I mean, even if the food's great and it's all paid for, you're still eating alone."

"Yeah," Rain agreed, distracted momentarily by seeing Judith's glamorous life from this new perspective.

Then 'Bastian cleared his throat, and Rain unlocked her door. They all went inside.

Rain shut the door and faced 'Bastian. "Mom couldn't see you."

"And there's no point tormenting her with the knowledge of something she can't experience."

"And probably wouldn't believe."

"So we keep the secret among ourselves."

Rain turned to include Charlie. "Only the three of us can know about this. Do you swear?"

"No one else would believe us anyway."

"That's your vow?" she asked, unimpressed.

He held up a hand. "I swear."

She looked at 'Bastian, waiting. He grinned. "Who am I going to tell? *How* am I going to tell? You're the only one who can hear me." She suddenly looked very cross, and he quickly held up a hand. "I swear."

Charlie glanced over at the mirror on the closet door and watched Rain hold up her hand, saying, "I swear too," to empty air. Then he had a thought.

"Rain, can you see 'Bastian in the mirror? Can he see himself?"

Both Rain and 'Bastian turned toward the closet and were stunned by the *lack* of what they beheld. 'Bastian wasn't reflected in the glass. Rain's head ping-ponged back and forth between 'Bastian and no-'Bastian. *This* was almost freakier than the fact that he existed. The ghost himself took a couple of steps forward, as if getting closer might suddenly make his reflection appear.

"It's like you're a vampire," Rain said in a hushed voice.

"So I take it that means no," Charlie said. "Makes sense when you think about it. The mirror reflects actual light, not mystic glows or whatever."

Disturbed, 'Bastian turned his back on the closet. Rain sank down onto her bed. Charlie felt stranded in the middle of the room and ultimately retreated back to the desk chair. They were silent for a while. Then finally, Rain said, "Why me?"

'Bastian and Charlie looked up at her.

"I mean, I'm glad, honestly. I like that I'm the Searcher. But I don't understand why, and I'm a little afraid . . ."

"Of what, Raindrop?" 'Bastian asked gently.

"That there's been some kind of mistake."

They all thought about this for a long minute. Then 'Bastian spoke. "I don't think there's been any mistake."

Independently Charlie said, "Remember Rubio the Pirate?"

"Exactly." 'Bastian nodded in agreement.

Rain rolled her eyes. (Oh, if Maq and I had a quarter for every time she did that, we'd never go hungry.) "Oh, come on," she scoffed. "My imaginary friend from when I was *four*?"

"You used to swear he was real, Rain," Charlie said firmly.

"You used to point to him and say, *He's right there!*" 'Bastian said in a similar tone.

She crossed her arms. "He was. An imaginary. *Pirate*."

"He taught you Spanish," Charlie said.

"He did not!"

"Maybe he did," 'Bastian said, thinking. "Your folks and I wanted you to be bilingual, but we always forgot to speak Spanish around the house. But somehow you were fluent by the time you were five. For a while we thought you were a bit of a genius."

"But you got over that?" Rain asked crossly. In fact, this whole Rubio tangent was putting her on edge in a way she couldn't quite explain to herself.

"It drove me crazy," Charlie remembered. "You were always speaking Spanish to Rubio and leaving me out of the conversation. Kinda like you two do now! Honestly, when I think about it, it's probably why I took French."

"And it wasn't just Rubio," 'Bastian said thoughtfully. "There were others. You'd wander off sometimes and say Martha wanted to show you something or Stefano had found a penny. I never took it too seriously, but it actually worried your parents. And even at age six, you could see they were worried. So first you stopped telling them about your 'friends,' and then you promised you wouldn't see them anymore. Your ghost-sight, Rain. I think you *willed* it to go away."

Rain was stunned. From somewhere in the dim recess of her memory, she could picture Rubio and Martha and Stefano and Guillermo with more clarity than now made sense for figments of her imagination. And when she pictured them, they were always surrounded by a soft white glow. Still she resisted the obvious conclusion. "So if I willed away my ghost-sight, why's it back now?"

"I think because I died," 'Bastian said, "and you wanted to see me."

Charlie had his own theory. "Maybe the *zemi* healed you. The way it healed your arm after Callahan harpooned you."

Or, Rain thought almost against her will, *the way it healed your foot this morning. Or Mom and Dad's hearts at dinner.* Haltingly, she said, "Let's . . . talk . . . about the *zemi*."

"Well, I don't know much more than I've already told you," 'Bastian said. "I got it from my *abuela* when I was injured in the war. It probably saved my life, though I didn't believe that then. After I recovered, I offered to return it, but she told me it wasn't hers to take back or to keep. It had been given to her by her *tío abuelo*. In fact, she told me it had been handed down within our family, for generation after generation, for four hundred years. She said it was my turn, but that when the time was right, I'd pass it on to my child or grandchild. I remember telling her I didn't think I'd ever have kids. She laughed at me."

Charlie waited as long as he could stand before clearing his throat overdramatically. Rain quickly repeated what 'Bastian had told her.

Then she asked her *abuelo*, "Tell me about your *abuela*."

"She was born and raised on Tío Samuel—until the U.S. Navy took possession of the island and the family moved here to San Próspero. She went to Mass every Sunday at the *Catedral*. But she was infamous for laughing at, well . . . inappropriate moments during the service or the sermon. When I was little, she was already old, and my friends used to tease me and say she was *una bruja*."

"Rain," Charlie said.

"She was a witch," Rain said.

"I didn't say she *was* a witch," 'Bastian protested. "That's what they called her. I think she simply valued the old ways along with the new. And that made her threatening to some people who didn't understand."

"She was a *misunderstood* witch," Rain said.

'Bastian sighed heavily.

Charlie was running some calculations through his head. "So 'Bastian wore the armband for . . ."

"Sixty-nine years," Rain said.

Both Charlie and 'Bastian looked at her wide-eyed while mentally confirming her arithmetic. She didn't want them making a big deal out of it. "What? I did the math. I'm a genius, remember?"

"Who said you were a genius?" Charlie asked, mock-appalled.

"He did. Look. Why does the number matter?"

"Well, I was thinking maybe that's why he's tied to it. Because he wore it for so long. But then I figured that if his *abuela* got it from her great-uncle, she probably wore it for at least a few decades. Soooo . . . is she in there too?"

'Bastian was taken aback. Slowly, he said, "I don't think so."

Rain shook her head.

Charlie raised an eyebrow. "So did he displace her when he died?"

'Bastian scowled. "I don't think so."

Rain shrugged.

Then Charlie pointedly asked her, "And if you keep wearing it, will you get stuck in there when *you* die?"

This notion truly horrified 'Bastian. It was one thing for him to stick around and have more time with his granddaughter, help her to complete her mission. The thought that she'd be trapped for all eternity in the snake charm—with no rest, no heaven—was another matter. He whispered, "Rain. Maybe . . . maybe you should take it off."

But on this point, Rain was firm, solid. "No. I'm the Searcher and the Healer. If I heal the wound like I'm supposed to, we won't have to worry about that. I'm not taking off the *zemi*."

'Bastian still felt a little queasy, but Charlie simply nodded. "Okay," he said. "That just leaves us with one real question: What's a *zemi*?"

CHAPTER TEN

NIGHT MOVES

MONDAY AND TUESDAY, SEPTEMBER 8-9

Nine P.M.

They talked a while longer. Rain told them about her trip to the Cache and the roll-of-quarters shape of the second *zemi*. But they reached no further conclusions about what a *zemi* actually was or how they could, would or should go about finding out, let alone finding the next one. Eventually, Alonso knocked on the door to tell Charlie his mother had called and it was time for him to go home. As he got up to leave, Rain hugged him without warning and whispered, "Thanks. I couldn't do this without you." She started to disengage, but without thinking, he gave her one last squeeze before letting her go. Then, terrified he'd revealed too much, he all but pushed her away. She hadn't noticed—though the same couldn't be said of a smiling 'Bastian or a frowning Alonso.

Charlie said his "See you tomorrow" and departed with Alonso as fast as he could manage.

Leaving Rain alone with 'Bastian. *Now what?* It suddenly occurred to both of them that for all intents and purposes, granddaughter and grandfather were roommates for the foreseeable future. *Awkward.*

Ten P.M.

What am I going to do all night? 'Bastian thought. Or maybe he said it aloud. When you're a ghost and all your dialogue is basically psychic anyway, it can occasionally be problematic telling the difference.

Rain said, "I suppose it'll get pretty boring sitting here, watching me sleep." *Maybe a little creepy, too,* she thought—though she didn't like thinking that way. She had *never* placed her Papa 'Bastian and "creepy" in the same sentence before. The fact that he now appeared to be less than ten years older than Rain wasn't helping. "I guess . . . I guess you could put on the *zemi* and go for a walk or something."

'Bastian instantly brightened at the idea. "I'd like that."

"But you need to be supercareful. You're invisible; the *zemi* isn't. You can't let anyone see it floating down the street."

"I'll be careful."

"And don't forget to be home before sunrise. *Way* before sunrise."

"Curfew. Sunrise. Yes, sir, General Raindrop, sir!" He saluted. But she didn't find it as amusing this time.

She took the armband off and slowly handed it to him. He placed it on his wrist. Then she crossed to her bedroom door, opened it slightly and looked around. "The coast is clear," she said. "I'll go down with you and open the back door."

He nodded.

Suddenly, she froze. She wheeled on him and blurted out, "I'm supposed to pack up my stuff and move upstairs to your old room on Wednesday. Is that okay?"

He looked stunned for a moment and then thoughtful. Then he said a bunch of things she couldn't hear. She shook her head. He smiled. It was a relief that even as the dangerous and dashing young Dark Man, he was still capable of her Papa 'Bastian's patented Old Man Twinkle. Almost as big a relief as knowing he was okay with the move.

Just to be sure, she said, "Nod if it's okay."

He nodded.

She beamed. They headed down the hallway.

At the back door, off the kitchen, Rain pointed down at the doggy-door installed ten years ago when 'Bastian had brought home a mutt named Guillermo that Rain remembered slightly better as an imaginary friend/ghost than as a living animal. Guillermo was hit by a car only a month after arriving at the Inn, but because Rain had claimed he was still around, she never needed, wanted or asked for another pet, which, frankly, was a relief to Iris, who didn't want to risk the potential liability, should a dog bite one of their guests. (I genuinely like Iris, but she does have her blind spots.)

Rain whispered, "You should be able to get the *zemi* back inside through that."

'Bastian nodded. *Clever girl.* She opened the door for him and watched him sneak away.

The wrought iron gate off the Nitaino's back courtyard presented a bit of a challenge. However, with a little care, 'Bastian was able to slip the *zemi* between two iron bars, while he himself phased through like smoke.

Then the late, great 'Bastian Bohique went for a walk.

Eleven P.M.

He walked, and he walked.

As 'Bastian passed under a streetlamp, a car sped by without warning. He tried hiding the *zemi* behind his back—then realized how useless that was. Fortunately, the car drove on, its occupant oblivious to the floating snake charm. 'Bastian exhaled another airless breath. *I do have to be more careful.*

He stuck to the shadows as much as possible, but truthfully, the little lanes were all but deserted anyway. Rain hadn't lied when she told Judith that Old Town wasn't the hub of San Próspero's social scene—particularly on a Monday night. It was too far from the ocean, and parking on its skinny cobblestone streets was a nightmare. During the day, Old Town's quaint shops and authentic cuisine attracted an economy-boosting minihorde of tourists, but they generally scattered by seven or eight o'clock at the latest. Now 'Bastian pretty much had these streets to himself.

At first, with Rain's cautions ringing in his ears, this was a relief. 'Bastian had never been a man uncomfortable in his own company. The full moon directly above his head seemed a charming companion, and his spirits were light. But as he meandered without purpose down Rue de Saint-Germain, the thought occurred that this solitary state—in what promised to be night after night of walks just like this—was no longer a matter of choice or occasion. This was his "life" from now on. A few hours between sunset and bedtime with his granddaughter, and then no one but himself and the moon. (And on some nights, not even the moon.)

Which perhaps explains why he ultimately found himself walking down Old Plantation Road toward the graveyard.

Twelve A.M.

The main gate at San Próspero Cemetery was closed but unlocked. 'Bastian couldn't open it, of course. Nor could it keep him out. As with the courtyard gate at the Inn, it simply required a bit of careful maneuvering to walk through it with the *zemi*.

He was no longer meandering. He knew exactly where he wanted to go. He hadn't been present for his own funeral—after all, it had taken place during the day—but he knew where he was buried. Because that's where his heart was buried too. He beelined—walking right *through* various headstones—to *the* headstone. A single slab of carved granite marking two graves, one old, one brand-new. The inscription was simple: ROSE & SEBASTIAN BOHIQUE. LOVING PARTNERS. LOVING PARENTS.

He tried to touch, to caress the stone, as he had touched, caressed it so many times since Rose's passing. Of course, his hand passed right through. He sat down on the ground and was momentarily distracted by the realization that he wasn't so much sitting on the soft earth as hovering more or less even with it, as Charlie said, out of habit. The concern was fleeting. He spoke out loud to his late wife, asking if she was here, if she was near. If maybe, just maybe, she might be willing to appear. (Had he meant for his appeals to rhyme like that? I'm honestly not sure.)

In any case, Rose Linda Nitaino Bohique remained absent.

He missed her and wondered even now, with absolute proof of life after death, whether he would ever see her again. *Or has she found her peace . . . while I'm condemned to this for eternity?* He felt like crying but was stumped by the question *Can a ghost shed tears?*

I watched him from beneath the bougainvillea-covered arch that separated the graves of men and women from the Pet Cemetery. I felt a canine need to ease his pain with my presence and was about to pad over to him. Maq intervened to stop me.

Or maybe he wasn't even aware of 'Bastian. Who knows with Maq? He waved a split half of guava under my snout and lured me deeper into the animal graveyard. We both sat—appropriately enough on this night—by the little bronze plaque that a soft-hearted Alonso had purchased for Guillermo. I had been quite fond of Guillermo both before and after his death. He wasn't too bright, but his rear had a delightful chocolaty scent. I was sorry to see him move on, but after young Rain had refused, for her parents' sake, to acknowledge his ghostly presence, it was clear it was time for him to go.

Maq placed my half of the guava on the ground in front of me. I smooshed my face into it, chewing and licking up the sweet fruit, seeds and all. Maq raised his half up to his face and smooshed as well. When we were through, we smiled at each other, two gooey, smooshy messes.

Then, out of nowhere, Maq said, "*Hura-hupia* owes me a quarter."

One A.M.

Out in the Florida Straits, on the edge of the Bermuda Triangle, *Hura-hupia* was forming out of wind and spray.

The moon took no notice, but the artificial satellites of men would register what briefly appeared to be the formation of a hurricane. Of course, it wasn't just any hurricane but a vintage hurricane: 1945's Santa Julia, last seen only the night before by Rain, Charlie and 'Bastian when it had tried to destroy them all by bringing down their haunted bomber off the coast of Tío Samuel. Julia had been thwarted then. She did not wish to be thwarted now.

Lightning and thunder overhead spooked a pod of dolphins that dove deep and swam away as Julia moved toward Sycorax Island with forty to fifty mile per hour winds as her harbingers. Then, as multiple urgent calls were being exchanged between the offices of the Weather Prediction Center, the National Hurricane

Center and the National Weather Service, the storm coalesced into a human woman with copper skin and black hair the exact same color as Rain's. With eyes that burned red in the dark, Julia stepped down gently on the shore of Sycorax. To the distant authorities, the sudden nightmare of a storm had vanished as quickly as it had appeared. Meanwhile, the true danger walked toward the excavation and entered the ancient bat cave.

There, *Hura-hupia* encountered the *Hupia*. He was just out of sight of the entrance, sucking the juice from a guava of his own while waiting for a more substantial meal: another Pale Tourist (or some such). Thinking he had found his prey, the *Hupia* moved to attack Julia, but she shook her head with contempt, and in that instant, the *Hupia* recognized his old acquaintance, though she looked nothing at all like the woman he remembered. It was the contempt itself that was so familiar. It radiated off her in unmistakable waves.

She made her way into the dark depths of the cave. Curious, he followed. (Neither creature required light to see.) She paused beside a small saltwater pool, only three feet in diameter but deep enough to reach the ocean. She scanned the surrounding area— the same area that had been searched rather ineffectively by the two deputy constables earlier that day. But *Hura-hupia* soon found the item she had sought: a sealed gourd jar that had fallen to the ground and rolled behind a medium-sized stalagmite. As she picked it up and studied the ring of nine carved bats that decorated its circumference, the *Hupia* retreated a yard or two. Then she dropped the gourd into the pool, where it sank away. This pleased her companion, who drew closer.

Then, in a language I barely recall, Julia told the *Hupia* to guard the second *zemi*. He seemed disinterested at first, until she pointed out how his own survival might depend upon it.

———

Two A.M.

On the other side of the island, the *Bootstrap* was anchored just offshore, and another, equally nefarious conversation was taking place between Callahan and his employer, Mr. Setebos.

Callahan, on yet another burner cell phone, listened to Setebos, who had called to ask if the still unidentified Pale Tourist was connected to Callahan and their enterprise in any way.

The question set Callahan's teeth on edge. This was due in part to Setebos' crisp English accent, which bothered the big Aussie just on general principle. But he also wasn't fond of admitting errors, either in judgment or execution. So very begrudgingly, Callahan admitted, "Yeah, I subcontracted the search. But don't lose any sleep, mate. The man knows not to talk."

"He's not talking. He's dead."

This raised Callahan's spirits a bit. Now he *really* wouldn't have to pay Cash. "No worries, then."

"You're not even curious how he died?"

"Is it relevant?"

"How could it not be relevant?" Setebos sounded a trifle exasperated.

"Fair enough. How'd he die?"

"I don't know yet."

"Right. Let me know when you find out."

"Me? Don't you think finding out is *your* job?"

"You're paying me to find *zemis*. Not to play Sherlock Holmes."

"But he was *your* man."

"There's nothing to connect us. Nothing to lead the cops to me, let alone you." Then a new thought occurred. "I get it. You're worried we have competition. You're thinking that's who took him out."

"Actually, that *hadn't* occurred to me. But if that's true, and if he lost the *zemi*—"

The cold fury in Setebos' voice was evident, and Callahan could almost *see* his next fifty-thousand-dollar payment flying out a porthole. He backpedaled quickly. "Let's not get ahead of ourselves, chief. I'm personally taking over the search tonight. Give me a few days—a week—before we start panicking."

"I'll give you *two* weeks," Setebos said. "After that, I'm going to have to seriously consider other options. And other operatives."

Callahan was about to protest, but Setebos had rung off. It was just as well. *Never sound needy. Nothing makes you lose the money's respect faster than sounding needy.* It was one of his axioms.

Three A.M.

Constable Thibideaux headed into Dr. Strauss' cramped coroner's office beside the morgue in the basement of San Próspero Island Hospital.

Strauss was stirring heavy cream into his coffee with a chicory stick. He offered Thibideaux a cup, but the constable declined. "It's too late for me. I drink that, and I'll never get to sleep."

"So you're sleeping now?" Strauss asked, glancing at the clock over the door.

Jean-Marc shrugged. "I don't need more reasons not to, Josef. Like wondering what caused the death of our Tourist."

Strauss tapped at his keyboard and maneuvered his mouse, bringing up his preliminary report on this year's Jean Doe #2, a.k.a. the Pale Tourist, a.k.a. (to Callahan) Cash. He printed out the document, though he glanced at neither screen nor hard copy, as he spoke: "I don't have much for you yet. They're backed up in Miami, and we won't get final labs until Monday. Next Monday."

"You must be able to tell me something."

"What I told you this morning. No visible wounds, despite massive blood loss, except on his neck. I did test a few samples here." He flipped his thumb toward the double doors to the morgue and the small lab beyond it, which both men knew to be inadequate. "His system was pumped full of anticoagulants, which would explain how and why his blood drained so quickly."

"But not where it went."

"No. Not where it went."

"Please don't tell me we're back to vampires."

"I think clearly we are. Though not in the way you mean." Strauss raised an eyebrow, hoping for a response. Since Thibideaux refused to cooperate, Strauss simply continued. "That much anticoagulant in the bloodstream is not a natural phenomenon. It probably explains the rash all over his body. An allergic reaction."

"So you think someone . . ."

"Someone incapacitated this man, shot him up with anticoagulants and drained his blood."

"The marks on his neck?"

"The microscope confirmed they're not the result of a single clean 'bite.' Too messy. But they could be multiple hypodermic needle punctures. Either to inject the anticoagulant or draw the blood . . ."

"Or both."

"Or both."

"And why do that in the same place over and over again, unless you *want* people thinking Count Dracula?"

Strauss nodded.

"Wonderful." Thibideaux sighed, thinking it was anything but. That was all he needed. Someone *trying* to create a vampire scare on the Ghosts.

Four A.M.

Isaac Naborías also had vampires on the brain. Vampires and vampire bats. Of course, Isaac had lived on the Ghosts for all of his sixty-two years, and he knew there were no vampire bats on the Keys. He also knew there was no such thing as vampires. Yet there was as much trepidation as determination involved when he forced himself to finally enter the cave before twilight. His flashlight soon found the guava husk, lying in the dirt. It appeared to be sucked dry and had definitely not been there this afternoon. Naborías knew bats ate guava. He also knew the old stories of his people. *The dead favor guava too.* He shuddered and backed out of the cave. *I'm too old to be this superstitious*, he thought. But he couldn't help it. In the legends, bats are tricksters. *And the dead are tricksters too.* Without trying, his mind summoned up the voices of his childhood, his uncles and aunties, telling him the Myth of First Bat.

Five A.M.

In her bed, Rain Cacique—who had *never* heard such stories from uncles, aunties or anyone—dreamed the Myth of First Bat in excruciating detail . . .

In the First Days, the First Bat was the most hideous creature in the world. All the other birds, brilliant and beautiful in their feathers, made sport of him.

This so crushed Bat's spirits that he asked First God for feathers to hide his shameful appearance. God saw how the birds had been unkind and ordered each to give Bat one feather.

Every bird complied, some graciously, some not. First Parrot gave a green feather. First Dove gave white. First Flamingo, pink; First Cardinal, red; First Kingfisher, blue. And so on . . .

Bat was made gorgeous by this new coat of feathers. He took to the sky, and First Rainbow was created in echo of his flight.

And all the birds admired him, even arrogant First Toucan, who had been so begrudging when delivering his feather up to Bat.

But Bat was not gracious in his new splendor. Perhaps from

Toucan, he had received more than a feather, for now it was Bat's arrogance that could not be checked. He taunted and scattered all the birds, which seemed doubly wrong as it was their own feathers he used to torment them.

The birds gathered and resolved to send First Hummingbird to report to God.

Tiny Hummingbird buzzed around God's ears. She made no accusations. She simply pleaded with God to observe First Bat.

And this God did. Displeased, he sent Hummingbird to warn Bat against further transgression. With some reluctance, Hummingbird followed God's command. But Bat would not hear her. He lunged at Hummingbird and chased her away, taunting her cruelly as she fled. And First God saw it all.

The next day, when Bat took flight, his feathers fell away like rain. He was left naked again, stripped of every single one of his luxuriant feathers, all their colors, all their softness, all their splendor, beauty and brilliance.

But this did not make Bat sorry. This made Bat bitter. And bitter. And bitter still. In the First Days, without feathers, First Bat had never truly been hideous. Not inside. Now he was blinded by his ugliness, his shame, his arrogance, vanity and anger. Blind as he was, Bat shunned the First Light.

Bat became Light's First Enemy, hiding in caves during the day and emerging only at night, still seeking his revenge on those more beautiful than he . . .

Such was the dream Rain dreamt in the twilight hours. But dreams—even true dreams—do not have to be helpful.

CHAPTER ELEVEN

DAYS GONE BYE

TUESDAY, WEDNESDAY AND THURSDAY, SEPTEMBER 9–11

A digest of the days' more significant events . . .

Rain woke up chilled and found her comforter had largely slipped from her bed. Glancing at her digital alarm clock, she saw she still had a few more minutes before she needed to rise. She tugged the comforter up around her and covered her face to keep the sunshine out of her eyes.

The sunshine! 'Bastian! The sun had risen, and he wasn't back!

In a flash, she was out of bed and throwing open her door. The snake charm was on the floor right in front of it. Fast as she could, she picked it up and put it on. *Okay, we didn't quite think this through. He could get back in the Nitaino with the zemi, but not back in my room! We definitely need a new plan.*

———

Rain and Charlie were at their lockers before first bell. Charlie tapped Rain on the shoulder and gestured with his head. Rain turned to see Miranda approaching with Renée. They were laughing and smiling together. *Like girls.*

Charlie spoke cautiously. "You two have fun yesterday?"

"We did," Miranda said pointedly and with some audible defiance.

"That's . . . great," Charlie said.

Renée smiled. "Isn't it, though . . . *Sugar?*"

Charlie flinched involuntarily; Rain stifled a growl.

During eighth period, Rain returned to the Cache, which still offered no new insights. She did get her homework done.

Late that afternoon, on Naborías' recommendation, the exterminators were summoned back to Sycorax to lay more poison traps for the bats in the cave. Isaac even came to work early to supervise. He wanted to be rid of those nasty pests once and for all.

After dinner, 'Bastian watched Rain toss her stuff haphazardly into three cardboard boxes and a couple of duffel bags in preparation for tomorrow's move upstairs. He was sincerely trying to see if she had some kind of arcane system for what she put where but ultimately concluded there was none. During this endeavor they discussed options for 'Bastian's return from his night wanderings. She gave him the armband, and he practiced levitating with it. For tonight, he would leave and enter via her balcony window. They'd come up with a new plan after the move.

'Bastian walked up the back alley behind the Orleans Theatre and waited for someone to exit through the rear doors. It took a couple tries, but he maneuvered his way inside the dark, half-empty movie palace. He settled into a seat and found he had more success maintaining his, well, *altitude* if he tried not to think about it too much. The film was an old print of *David Copperfield*. He'd never seen it before, yet the Micawber character seemed somehow familiar. 'Bastian would have loved some buttered popcorn, but one can't have everything.

Callahan was careful to avoid the Sycorax guards. Not that he was afraid of them, but if he had to take one out, it would simply add to the mess and make his job all the harder. So he kept out of sight when the old guy made his rounds. Callahan appreciated, at least, that the geezer was punctual.

Isaac shone his flashlight into the cave. He saw no bats and no new guava husks and smiled in self-satisfaction. He headed back toward the cannery, turning the corner.

Instantly, Callahan melted out of the darkness. He returned to the dig site to continue his search for the second *zemi*.

All through the night, the *Hupia* stayed but a short distance from the *zemi*, ready to strike should anyone come too close. No one did, however, and the *Hupia* began to wish someone would. The meal he had made of the Pale Tourist was now a distant memory, and the *Hupia* was again feeling . . . peckish.

At dawn, the dolphin pod ended their search off Key Largo, Florida. Together, in a tight formation, the pod commenced their journey back to the Ghosts with their companion.

Rebecca Sawyer checked out of the Nitaino. Rain was sorry to see the kind old woman go—and even sorrier when she gave Rain a twenty-dollar tip! Rain silently wished Rebecca would stay another week and double the money, but Mrs. Sawyer departed, laughing at Timo Craw's horrible jokes.

Now the only guests left were Judith Vendaval and the Kims. Normally, the Tall Woman slept through Rain's morning shift, but today, she was out of the Inn before dawn to go snorkeling, and Iris asked Rain to make up Ms. Vendaval's room. Rain pretended annoyance out of habit, but truthfully, it beat serving breakfast to the Kim kids, who had already—in only two short days—begun to fray Rain's nerves. The idea that she'd have to spend Saturday on the boat babysitting them gave her waking nightmares.

Rain entered Room Three. Judith's bed was a mess. It seemed Ms. Vendaval tossed and turned quite a bit in her sleep—either that or she hadn't slept alone last night. The room was otherwise fairly neat, and even the bathroom was relatively clean. Rain took her sweet time tidying up. *After all,* she smiled, *Mom always says anything worth doing is worth doing right.*

Nevertheless, she still arrived downstairs in the middle of a dry-cereal food fight between Wendy and John Kim, with little Michael absolutely wailing over being hit in the nose by a flying Cheerio.

During sixth-period science, the topic was echolocation and the diverse animals that made use of it. It seemed to fascinate Mr. Brinque that this unique evolutionary trait was common, for example, to both dolphins and bats.

"This is why," he was saying, "bats avoid rain—"

"Yeah, I avoid Rain, too!" Juan shouted, thinking fast.

Rain rolled her eyes, though nearly everyone else laughed, including Charlie.

Seeing Miranda look concerned for Rain, Renée turned around to glare at Juan for his lack of manners—though she stopped short of calling him "Sugar." (Perhaps she already had enough sugar on her plate.) Even so, Juan withered under Renée's gaze. Miranda noticed the entire silent exchange, more convinced than ever that Charlie had been wrong about Renée.

Mr. Brinque raised his voice just enough to be heard over the laughter. "Bats avoid rain because it interferes with their echolocation."

Lacey said, "I hear bats killed a guy over on Sycorax."

Miranda quickly said, "That's not what happened."

Renée backed her up. "Someone died, but it was allergies or something."

"No, it's true," Wilma Vanetti said. "Some tourist was drained of blood by a vampire bat."

Carlos was like, "Does that mean he'll rise in three nights and kill someone else?"

The classroom laughed again, though perhaps a little more nervously.

Brinque said, "Vampire bats are *not* indigenous to the Ghosts."

"Just vampires," laughed Juan, having regained what amounted to his form.

"Vampires are a myth based on vampire bats," Wilma announced definitively. "That's how vampires got the name."

Brinque shook his head. "Wilma, that's almost exactly wrong. The name 'vampire bat' was inspired by vampire folklore. Not the other way around."

Wilma shook *her* head. "No, I don't think that's right."

Brinque sighed heavily.

Through this entire lively discussion, Rain was focused on one thing: A man had died under mysterious circumstances on Sycorax Island—and this was the first the Searcher was hearing about it.

After dinner, 'Bastian watched Rain remove her stuff haphazardly from the three cardboard boxes and two duffel bags as she
unpacked in his old room. He corrected himself: *in* her *new room*.
Given the chaotic nature of her packing job, he was sincerely
stunned by her lack of hesitation when putting things away. She
seemed to have envisioned exactly where every single item she
possessed would go.

Of course, it helped that there was no lack of space. The lone
room on the Inn's third floor, accessible only via the back stairs,
was nearly four times the size of Rain's previous quarters. She
now had a king-sized bed (with brand-new sheets, pillowcases,
and comforter—all purchased voluntarily by the usually thrifty
Iris), a large dresser, a walk-in closet, and a full bathroom with
shower *and* tub.

Alonso had just gone downstairs after assembling Rain's desk
against the wall beneath the window that looked out on the wid-
ow's walk that surrounded the entire floor.

Over dinner, he had asked his daughter if she wanted him to
remove 'Bastian's old Spanish desk. It was more decorative than
functional, and its dark, masculine wood no longer seemed to fit
the occupant of the room. Without waiting to consult 'Bastian,
Rain had said she wanted to keep it right where it was.

Now she found herself studying the antique map unrolled flat
on the desk's dark wood and held in place by two paperweights:
a steel-cased compass and 'Bastian's homemade astrolabe. The
map was labeled "The Ghost Keys" and dated "Summer, 1799."

"It's a forgery, of course. Something to fool tourists," 'Bastian
said, standing over her shoulder.

"Really? Are you sure?"

"I'm sure. Look at the names of the islands."

Her eyes ran across the eight Ghosts from left to right, that is,
from west to east: Sycorax Island, San Próspero, Tío Samuel,

Malas Almas, Ile de la Géante, Teatro de Fantasmas, "The Pebble" and Isla Soraya. "They look right to me," she said.

"Raindrop, no one in 1799 was calling Sycorax by its *corporate* name. It was called Isla Majagua way into the twentieth century. And Tío Samuel wasn't renamed for Uncle Sam until the Civil War. Even then, I don't think it became official until after Pearl Harbor. Sometime in early 1942. I'm not sure 'The Pebble' was a real name back in the eighteenth century either."

"What was Tío Sam's before it was Tío Sam's?"

"*San* Samuel, I think."

"Where'd you get it?"

"What, the map? I bought it."

"Why?"

"That's a damn good question. There was this curio shop on Camino de las Casas. It's not there anymore. Must have gone out of business decades ago. But I wandered in one day and was browsing around. There was a lot of voodoo stuff and 'authentic pirate doubloons.'" He made air quotes with his hands. "I saw the map, and it just appealed to me. Also, I think the old woman that ran the place fast-talked me into making the purchase. She must have thought I was a tourist, and I guess for that five minutes I was sucker enough to be one."

"Huh."

"You sound disappointed." 'Bastian sounded amused. In fact, Rain *was* disappointed. Way more disappointed than she could explain or justify. He tried to throw her a bone. "It's a good map, though. Accurate. But not two-hundred-plus years old."

Rain stared at the map for another two-plus seconds before turning away to finish unpacking the last box. She pulled out a small, faded white pillow, embroidered with irises. Rain propped it faceup—hiding the brown water stain in back—on 'Bastian's big old armchair.

"Now *that's* a real treasure. Your Grandma Rose made it for your mom."

"I know." Rain smiled, the map forgotten.

She emptied the cardboard box, carefully laying two framed photographs on her bed. One was the picture of the *Island Belle* and its crew. The other was a wedding photo with a gold-embossed caption that read SEBASTIAN & ROSE BOHIQUE.

Rain removed a couple of nails from her father's toolbox and stuck one in her mouth. Then she picked up Alonso's hammer and picked out a spot on the wall beside the Spanish desk. She quickly hammered in the nail and hung the wedding picture. With the second nail still between her teeth, she said, "I want to get a copy of Mom and Dad's wedding picture and hang that too. Oh, and one of Grandpa Miguel and Nana Kate."

"That would be nice," 'Bastian said with a warm smile as Rain hammered in the other nail and hung the *Island Belle* over her nightstand.

Callahan was methodical; in three nights he had conducted his own personal excavation of about a quarter of the dig. It was excruciatingly dull, and his back ached. His skin and clothes and hair were caked with sweat and soil. And he had found nothing. Still, Setebos' promised payoff kept him working until the predawn sky signaled it was time to go. He vanished into the jungle moments before Isaac Naborías appeared from around the corner.

Isaac clicked off his flashlight. Though the sun hadn't quite risen, there was just enough light in the eastern sky to allow him to save his batteries. Not that he paid for those batteries, but he didn't like wasting Mr. Guerrero's money.

He walked around the perimeter of the excavation toward the cave, confident there was no longer anything to fear. A mosquito buzzed past his ear, and he waved it away. Then another buzzed past the other ear, very loud. He waved that away too. Then he felt a little sting on the back of his neck and slapped it. He pulled his hand away to gaze at the results in the dim light. There was a dead mosquito—bloated but smashed—on his palm amid a small red circle of his own stolen blood.

This triggered a memory, distant and vague . . . but the search through the archives of his mind was interrupted by the sight of another mosquito landing on his forearm. He slapped at that one too.

Then another mosquito landed on his other arm. And another landed on his nose. And another. And another. And another.

Isaac Naborías slapped and waved his arms and even seemed to dance as the swarm surrounded him, sucking away his blood, one small bite at a time.

He started to run. He ran away from the cave and right across the excavation. He ran east toward the guard shack. Toward the shore. Fortunately for Isaac, toward the rising sun.

The swarm kept pace, biting and buzzing.

Just shy of the guard shack, Isaac stumbled and fell to his knees. The swarm seemed to pounce. It felt like the insects were eating him alive. And that buzzing, loud in his ears—was it Isaac's imagination or did it sound a little like *laughter*?

Just as the sun peeked out to start the day, Isaac struggled to his feet, desperate to get inside the shack. Finally, weak and faint, he managed to lurch his way in and slam the door shut. He slapped at the ten or twenty mosquitoes that had entered with him. Dead and crushed bugs were all over his skin and clothes and hair. He looked through the window, expecting to see the shack engulfed by the bloodsuckers.

The swarm had dissipated and was gone.

CHAPTER TWELVE

FULL CIRCLE

Morning.

Jean-Marc Thibideaux hit the snooze button on his alarm clock but made no attempt to turn over or go back to sleep—since he hadn't actually been asleep in the first place. He reached for his smartphone, unplugged it from its charger and turned it on. He had an e-mail waiting from the F.B.I., who had identified his Pale Tourist from the dead man's fingerprints. Milo Long, a.k.a. Milo Cash, a.k.a. Matt Cash, a.k.a. Miles Tallman, had been convicted on three counts of felony larceny and served three years in an Arizona prison. *Okay, I know who he is. Now all I need is the lab report to find out what killed him.*

Jimmy Kwan, meanwhile, sent an e-mail to his superiors from the computer in the guard shack, though he could barely believe what he was typing. Isaac Naborías—Mr. Responsibility, Mr. Company Loyalty Himself—had abandoned his post *before* shift change, leaving behind his flashlight as a paperweight to hold down a brief signed note: *I resign. Effective immediately.* Jimmy stared at the keyboard for a second, then picked a dead mosquito out from between the *H* and *U* keys and flicked it away.

Noon.

"Come on," Miranda said, exasperated.

"I'm there," said Renée.

Rain and Charlie exchanged a look he had no trouble interpreting. Miranda had once again invited them to come hang at her place—after school the next day. (She figured twenty-four hours' notice would provide less of an excuse to say no.) However, Rain had made up her mind that Friday afternoon would mark the official launch of their Search for the second *zemi*. She still had no idea what that entailed, but they had to start sometime.

Still, Miranda was determined. "It'll be fun. We can play tennis or use the pool or the sauna or *the hot tub* . . ."

Rain and Charlie exchanged a second glance.

And night.

"So what was it?" Charlie asked. "The tennis courts or the hot tub?"

"The dead body and the possible vampire," Rain said. Then, not bothering to suppress a smile, she added, "Although I am bringing a suit. Do you think we need our own towels?" She, Charlie and 'Bastian were climbing the hill toward the N.T.Z. Rain had been to the Cache every afternoon, but this was the first time her male compatriots had come along since Sunday night, when they had discovered the place.

"Wait a minute. What dead body?" 'Bastian asked seriously.

"Some tourist died on Sycorax," Rain told the ghost. "Near an archaeological dig. Rumor is his body was drained of blood. I thought I might be able to talk to him. His ghost, I mean. He might know where the next *zemi* is."

"What makes you think that?" Charlie asked before 'Bastian could.

"Nothing," she said, looking at 'Bastian before ducking under a tree branch. "Except . . . it sorta worked with you." He appeared unconvinced. She shrugged and continued, "There may be no connection. Miranda heard he had an allergic reaction and died of, uh, anaphylactic shock. But it's mysterious, and we do mysterious now. It just seemed worth checking out."

Charlie glanced up as they passed the Sign. Then he repeated Rain's words as a question. "We do mysterious now? Like generally?"

The moon had waned slightly since Monday night, but it was still nearly full and dappled the jungle with pools of light. The Dark Man passed through one of these pools and shuddered. He said, "I think you're grasping at straws, kiddo."

"I *know* I'm grasping at straws. But like you said, there's no owner's manual."

"Like you *ever* read instructions," Charlie scoffed.

Rain shot him a dirty look that more than anything else made Charlie want to kiss her. He looked away fast, and she felt satisfied her disapproval had shut him up. "Look, that's why I wanted you both to check out the Cache with me tonight. Maybe you'll spot a straw or two I've missed."

Or not . . .

The threesome slid between two banana plants to enter the N.T.Z. and instantly knew there'd be no grasping of straws in the Cache tonight. A small fire blazed in the pit, and beside it, Marina Cortez and Hank Dauphin were making out on a blanket.

His back to Rain and Charlie, Hank was too engrossed in his

current endeavor to notice their arrival. Marina faced them, but her eyes were closed as she kissed her partner with *serious* intensity. Rain, Charlie and even 'Bastian were paralyzed by the awkwardness and/or allure of the moment. 'Bastian finally looked away, feeling a little skeezy. But the two thirteen-year-olds seemed incapable of averting their gaze.

Perhaps sensing she was being watched, Marina opened her big brown eyes. Instantly, they went very wide, and she attempted to disengage from the kiss, which turned out to be surprisingly difficult. There were tongues to disentwine, lips to unlock, and the fingers of Hank's left hand were tangled into Marina's long dark hair. She let out a muffled "Wait!" into his mouth, and he finally—if reluctantly—got the message. The two twelfth graders pulled apart, though Hank stared at her with a questioning expression until she gestured with her eyes to look behind him.

It was only then, as his older brother started to turn, that Charlie realized he should not be looking, should not be there, should probably never have been born. *Too late.*

"Charlie!" Hank said in a harsh and very loud whisper. Shoulders hunched, he made a movement to rise—and maybe to do some thumping—but Marina put a hand on his shoulder.

"Shhh," she said. "Chill."

Hank continued to glower at Charlie, but he sat back down.

Charlie said, "Uh . . ."

'Bastian aimed one finger and poked Rain's armband, which nudged her out of her stupor. She said, "We're sorry. We didn't know anyone else was up here."

Marina smiled slyly. "You two have the same idea?"

Charlie looked horrified. *How did she know?!*

"*No!*" Rain shouted. Charlie turned to stare at her, crushed by the vehemence of her denial. 'Bastian felt bad for the boy.

Hank, on the other hand, was constitutionally incapable of not rubbing his younger brother's face in the burn: "Seriously, who'd *ever* want to hook up with *him*?"

A more sympathetic Marina nudged him gently with her elbow. "Henry, be nice."

Hank turned toward her, and she gave him a look that actually succeeded in making him feel guilty. Quietly, he said, "Sorry," though it was more to her than to his brother. Still Charlie felt like something akin to a miracle had taken place, and he wondered how he could arrange for Marina to become a permanent fixture in "Henry's" life.

"Look, we can go," Charlie said, at long last finding his voice.

Marina stood. "No, come on. It's okay. We have marshmallows." She crossed to Rain. "Let's find you two a couple of sticks."

Hank scowled but ultimately waved Charlie over.

As Rain and Marina searched the circular clearing, and Charlie cautiously crossed to join Hank, 'Bastian felt tremendously at sea. He didn't belong here among these teenagers, but he was powerless to depart without the *zemi*, and there was no way Rain could transfer it to him in front of these witnesses. With a sigh, he sat down, cross-legged, before the fire. Then, to distract himself, he tried waving his ghostly hand through it. He felt no heat and stuck his fist into the heart of it. Nothing. For a second, it was just . . . neat. Then it only served to remind him how divorced he felt from the world.

A few yards away, Marina leaned into Rain and whispered, "I'm kind of embarrassed. You must think I'm like a slut or something."

Charlie, curious enough to risk his brother's wrath, simultaneously whispered to Hank, "Dude, isn't she dating Ramon?"

"No," whispered Rain, "I'd never . . ."

"She told me she dumped him," Hank said, trying not to sound guilty.

"It's just . . ." Marina paused, either to gather her thoughts or to pick up a suitable marshmallow stick. "Ramon was nice enough, and he's cute. But kinda . . ."

"Isn't he like one of your best friends?" Charlie asked.

"Brain-dead," Rain offered.

"Totally," Hank acknowledged. "But, dude, have you *seen* her?"

Marina offered up an embarrassed shrug. "Pretty much."

Charlie glanced over at the two girls, though it was unclear—even in his own mind—which he was referring to when he whispered, "Yeah."

"And Hank's better?" Rain asked. She wasn't exactly Hank's biggest fan due to the way he treated Charlie.

Hank ripped open the bag of marshmallows and poked three each onto the two bent wire hangers he had brought along. "I'll make it up to Ramon," he said under his breath. "He's into Linda Wheeler now, anyway. She's more his speed."

Marina looked at Hank and sighed. "Oh, he's better. And there's the other part. I mean, look at him. He makes me melt."

"You mean, like *fast*?" Charlie asked, not sure if Hank was being clever.

Rain picked up a stick and glanced over at the Brothers Dauphin. She supposed Hank was good-looking, but he wasn't kind—or loyal. Not like Charlie. She couldn't ever imagine melting over Hank. "If you say so."

Hank punched Charlie on the arm. "Dude, shut up."

"Trust me," Marina said. Then she turned from the boys to smile at Rain. "Baby brother's cute, too."

"Ow," Charlie said, rubbing his arm.

Rain was about to explain that Charlie wasn't the baby of the Dauphin family, but Marina was already walking away. So, armed with sticks, the girls rejoined the guys. Hank made Charlie hand a wire hanger to Marina, who handed Charlie the stick she'd found. Hank held up the bag of marshmallows, and Rain and Charlie each took one and poked their sticks through them.

While the marshmallows roasted, and while poor 'Bastian found himself longing for one the way he'd never longed for a marshmallow in his life, Hank put his arm around Marina. She settled in against him but turned toward Rain again. "I meant to ask . . . *How are you doing?*" Marina's voice was loaded with enough sympathy that Rain was briefly baffled by the question.

Then it hit her. *She's asking about 'Bastian.* The last time Rain and Marina had spoken, Rain was still mourning her late grandfather, unaware he was still hanging around as the Dark Man. Marina had actually been pretty great for someone who was more or less a stranger. (She lived two islands over, on Malas Almas.) She truly seemed to understand how Rain was feeling at the time, probably because Marina had lost her own sister recently. Now, of course, Rain was entirely over anything that resembled grief. She looked across at 'Bastian, who was currently focused on levitating himself cross-legged up and down, up and down. She smiled and said, "I'm good," and left it at that.

Marina didn't push it. She changed the subject, more or less. "So are you at least keeping busy?"

Rain chuckled. "You could say that."

Charlie rolled his eyes.

Marina's left eyebrow inched upward. "Meaning?"

Rain looked across the fire at the brown-skinned girl. Their eyes met. In that instant, Rain wanted to tell her everything. *Meaning I'm the Searcher! And the Healer! I have this mystic quest that's so important that every single person on the Ghosts should get on board or get out of the way!*

Both Charlie and 'Bastian leaned forward to stare at Rain. Though the idea seemed ridiculous, both *knew* she was on the verge of spilling. Although the possible repercussions were impossibly vague in his head, Charlie started to panic a little and cleared his throat loudly.

It did the trick. Rain exhaled profoundly, pulled the gooey marshmallow off the stick, and shoved the hot, sticky confection into her mouth, as if only its goopiness could stop her from revealing the crazy truth. "Meaning," she said while chewing the hot mess, "I'm busy eating marshmallows." She looked away, feeling strangely guilty that she had, in effect, lied to Marina. Particularly guilty since the eighteen-year-old had always been so open and honest with her. As a consolation prize, she considered inviting Marina to go with them to Miranda's place tomorrow. But that wouldn't do either. For one thing, it really wasn't her invitation to extend. For another, no matter how sympathetic Marina seemed, she was still a senior. *No way she'd want to hang with four eighth graders. Even with the hot tub option.*

By now, Charlie had relaxed, the crisis having passed. Swallowing his first marshmallow, he reached for the bag in front of his brother. Hank shot him a look. *Dude, enough's enough!* Charlie looked from Hank to Marina, who was now resting her head on his shoulder, and got the message.

He threw his marshmallow stick on the fire and stood up. "Well, we should be going. School night."

Rain looked at him confused. 'Bastian shook his head, wondering just a bit at Rain's obliviousness. He rose to his feet and said with some volume, "Rain, I think Hank and Marina would like to be alone."

Rain looked over at Marina, who pretty much *was* "melting" into Hank, then practically jumped to her feet. "Yeah, of course. I mean. School night. We need to go!"

"You don't have to," Marina said, though she was looking into Hank's eyes when she said it.

"Yeah, stay," Hank said, appreciating Marina's gaze and feeling safe enough to lie.

"No, we'll go," Charlie said.

"Yeah, we'll go," Rain said.

"Then go," 'Bastian said.

So our three heroes fled the N.T.Z., each lost in her or his own private desires.

CHAPTER THIRTEEN

THE OTHER HALF LIVES

Miranda Guerrero, daughter of the C.E.O. of Sycorax Inc., led Renée, Charlie and Rain onto the company-owned, company-operated Sycorax Ferry, needlessly flashing a pass to a ticket taker, who knew exactly whose daughter Miranda was. Rain asked, "Why do you even take the ferry? Don't you have a chauffer?"

Miranda made a face. "I don't want Ariel taking me everywhere. It would be weird. I take the ferry to be normal."

Rain and Charlie rolled their eyes in sync; they couldn't help it. Even Renée, who was—when she chose—more expert at concealing her thoughts, had to look away. There was nothing normal about taking the Sycorax Ferry home *to* Sycorax Island. There was nothing normal about living on Sycorax, about being the daughter of the man who also employed an easy third of the

Keys' adult population. There was nothing normal about being the richest eighth-grade girl in the Caribbean.

That was why Renée had decided to play a *long* game. To find her moment and wait for it. Miranda was not going to be the victim of just another prank. No clothes stolen from her locker. No Stinky Spray substituted for her perfume. Renée had her mother to think of and couldn't do anything that might blow back and cause Linéa Jackson to lose her job as a fruit inspector at the Sycorax cannery.

But it was more than that. Striking Little Miss Guerrero off her Sugar-List would be the summit, the pinnacle, the apotheosis. Miranda's humiliation would have to be perfect. It would have to be *sublime*. Renée could afford to be patient. Of course, maintaining that patience would be a little harder with regard to Rain and Charlie. Neither deserved any special consideration . . . except for this: Miranda liked them both. So for now, Renée would be on her best behavior around all three. At least, there was the small consolation of being able to torture Rain and Charlie by reminding them of the inevitable. Renée smiled at Charlie and said, "Beautiful day. Wouldn't you agree, Sugar?"

Charlie forced a smile. Still, he wasn't sorry Renée and Miranda were around. Their presence removed some of the crushing pressure of being alone with his crush. (Or of being alone with his crush and 'Bastian, which honestly didn't feel much different most of the time.) Even now, as the sea breeze played with a wisp of hair that had escaped Rain's thick braid, Charlie had to fight the impulse to reach out and tuck it behind her ear; he had to fight the impulse to hold her hand. Or worse.

Rain's thoughts were somewhere else entirely. Without explanation, she took off up the stairs.

They all watched her go. To Miranda, Rain was still an

enigma, difficult to read and so essentially self-sufficient that even Charlie often appeared to be little more than an accessory. It made Miranda feel bad for him, as he stared after Rain like a puppy. Miranda tried to offer a distraction. "So, did you bring your suit?"

Charlie nodded. "Yeah, I'm ready for the Jacuzzi." Then he swallowed hard. Hot-tubbing it with Rain, Miranda and Renée was something like a wish fulfilled. *Assuming my head doesn't explode.*

On the upper deck, Rain ran up to the pilot's cabin and— ignoring the DO NOT DISTURB THE PILOT sign—knocked on the door. Old Joe Charone, the ferryman, opened it for her, and she slipped inside.

"How you doin', Sweetie?" he asked. Old Joe had been 'Bastian Bohique's best friend. They had flown together during World War II, and Joe had that same photograph of the *Island Belle* hanging on the bulkhead behind him. But Joe had been injured during their last mission over Germany and had missed their final, fatal flight, which had killed the *Belle*'s eight other crewmen. He had also missed last Sunday's ghost flight, which had finally laid the Eight to rest. So unlike 'Bastian and the others, Joe had no closure. For Old Joe, he was the lone survivor with all the accompanying guilt. He didn't even have the benefit of a ghostly 'Bastian's company, and Rain could tell from those four short words of greeting that he was still grieving, still hurting, still deeply soul-sick.

So she did what she could. "I'm feeling a little better," she said and touched her left hand to his right. She watched the Healer snake on the *zemi* flare with a golden light that raced down her arm and leapt from her hand to his before vanishing under his sleeve. Then she watched as he took a breath, straightened his back and smiled at her warmly. Same as with her mom and dad.

The Healer might not always remove the wound, but it sure helped with the symptoms.

"You know, I'm feeling a little better too," he said and meant it. "Must be seeing your shining face, Sweetie."

Isaac Naborías, who was a few yards away on the upper deck, was also feeling better. Not better enough to change his mind or ask for his job back. But Jimmy Kwan had called to tell Isaac his last paycheck was waiting for him, so Isaac was heading back to Sycorax to pick the check up in person and say a proper good-bye to everyone.

His cheek twitched. He checked his watch. It was three thirty in the afternoon, and sunset wasn't until seven twenty-nine. (He knew. He had checked.) *I just have to be off that island before dark.* Nervously, he scratched and scratched and scratched at his many, many, many mosquito bites.

As they approached the Sycorax dock, Joe shooed Rain out of his cabin, and she descended to rejoin her little tribe. Once the ferry stopped moving, the air became quite still. The dock smelled of diesel fuel, saltwater and fish.

They disembarked. Miranda took the lead again with Renée by her side and Charlie following. Rain hesitated. A brush-played snare drum and a bass guitar provided her current mental soundtrack, sneaky and slinky. She slipped past Charlie to tap Miranda on the shoulder, saying, "Hey, could you show us where the guy died?"

Miranda looked uncomfortable. "Wouldn't you rather go swimming?"

"I just want a look," Rain said. She glanced at Charlie for support.

He got the message. "Yeah, it'd be cool."

Miranda looked at Renée, who shrugged. She was a little curious too.

Five minutes later, they were standing beside the excavation, looking across to the cave entrance opposite. Rain scanned the area, mostly checking for landmarks, not really hoping to find anything *zemi*-ish out in plain sight—and not really *wanting* to find something with Miranda and Renée in tow. She pointed toward the cave. "That's where the body was?"

Miranda nodded. "That's what my dad said."

"Okay, we can go," Rain said.

Charlie gaped at her. "Don't you want to look around?"

Rain scrunched her face impatiently. *"Now? No."*

Ah. Charlie understood. *Now, no. After sunset, definitely.*

Rain shifted gears with genuine enthusiasm. "Let's hit that hot tub!"

A relieved Miranda led them rapidly toward her home. She was pretty sure her father wouldn't approve of their little detour and was glad to be back on track. Minutes later, she and Renée were walking up the front steps. Charlie and Rain paused to stare.

Renée smirked inwardly. She knew exactly how they felt, how *she* had felt on Monday when first laying eyes on the place. She had just been better able to hide it.

Miranda lived in the old manor house, originally built by the slaveholding plantation owners of the *isla*. The clean white structure had been thoroughly renovated and modernized by men working for Miranda's father, but it still possessed a certain antebellum charm and grandeur, if you liked that sort of thing. In its day, it had been constructed to impress and intimidate. The latter effect was certainly still in force for Rain and Charlie. They instantly felt out of place and uncomfortable, even unworthy. It wasn't a pleasant sensation. Charlie started to feel hostile toward Miranda, though he knew that was unfair. Rain fought the impulse to check the soles of her shoes to make sure she didn't track anything inside. Spotting a mat at the front door she could make use of, she grabbed Charlie by the T-shirt to pull him up the stairs. *Strength in numbers, right?*

Eyes focused down on the doormat, Rain saw a pair of men's brown loafers step out of the manor. She looked up.

Miranda said, "Oh, Dad. These are my friends. Renée, Charlie and Rain. Guys, this is my father, Pablo Guerrero."

Charlie and Rain muttered greetings. Renée said hello clearly. Pablo Guerrero's response confused all three of them. "Twenty minutes."

He paused, turning his head enough to reveal a small earpiece in his right ear. He continued, "Ariel's warming up the chopper . . . No, don't do anything . . . I'll be at the hotel helipad in twenty minutes. Or less."

He paused again to listen. Pablo Guerrero was about 5'9" and in good shape. His light-skinned face was unwrinkled, and only a bit of salt in his otherwise jet black hair hinted at his fifty years on this earth. He was dressed in tan slacks, a pink oxford shirt and designer sunglasses. The one out-of-place note in the man's otherwise elegant and expensive design was a thick leather band around his left wrist with the word DADDY burned into the leather by a pyrographic stylus. Rain had done something similar for her own father when she was nine, but he never wore it.

"Right. See you soon. Twenty minutes. Twenty. Bye." His manicured finger tapped the earbud, and then, finally, he seemed to take notice of his daughter and her companions. "Hello," he said, with much more reserve than he had used on the phone.

Miranda wasn't sure if she should introduce her friends again— then decided there wasn't much point. "We're going to use the hot tub."

Her father stared at her with an odd expression. Almost as if he didn't speak the language, or perhaps wasn't clear what a "hot tub" was. Finally, he seemed to give up. He shook his head a bit and said, "Ariel's flying me over to La Géante. I won't be home for dinner."

"We'll manage," Miranda said.

He nodded in response and departed without another word, descending the stairs and walking briskly around the corner and out of sight. Rain and Charlie exchanged another look. Renée camouflaged any reaction. Miranda took it all in stride and entered the house through the open front door.

It was noticeably cooler inside. During the renovation, walls had been removed from the interior of the house to create a single, immense great room out of most of the first floor. French doors along the far wall were open to a large patio, creating a cross-breeze to make the atmosphere notably more pleasant inside than out. It was elegant, airy, and light. There was a large chandelier hanging down from the rafters, a grand piano off to the side and almost nowhere to sit.

Rain and Charlie paused to drink it all in—but Miranda didn't, and they had to play catchup as she and Renée ascended the grand staircase to the second floor. They walked along a balcony, which passed over the full length of the great room before becoming a hallway that disappeared into the manor's South Wing.

Miranda paused in front of another open door to listen to the helicopter flying low overhead. It vibrated the crystal fixtures, which tinkled briefly like wind chimes. Once the noise subsided, she said, "This is my room. Charlie, that's a guest room across the hall. You can change in there. You can leave your stuff there too. It'll all be safe. Oh, and don't worry about towels; we've got plenty of them in the *cabaña.*"

Charlie swallowed and nodded and watched Miranda lead Renée and Rain into her room. Miranda waved good-bye and shut the door. He shook his head and opened the door to the guest room.

It was enormous. You could stuff his and Phil's bedroom, Lew and Hank's bedroom and probably his mom's bedroom into this one and still have a bedroom left over. There was a large and fancy four-poster bed, dressing tables with marble tops, porcelain lamps and crystal vases with cut flowers. The sum total effect: Charlie was afraid to touch anything, practically afraid to lower his backpack to the floor. He stood in the middle of the room to change. Changing, of course, consisted only of taking off his cargo shorts. He was already wearing trunks underneath. At home, he'd have left the shorts on the floor. Here that seemed like sacrilege, so he picked them up, folded them carefully in half and looked around for a place to put them. Ultimately, he stuffed them into his backpack and hid that behind the door—to minimize its presence in the room.

He went out into the hallway, but Miranda's door was still closed. *Now what?* He thought about the fact that the girls were changing clothes on the other side of the door. *Don't! Down that path lies head explosion . . .*

Miranda's bedroom was also quite large, but Rain had a pretty big bedroom now herself, so she was less impressed. Still it struck her as odd. It appeared to be the room of a much younger child. It was wallpapered with a pattern of strawberries. Of course, there were no faux-antique maps or World War II photographs or anything like that, but there were also no posters on the wall and no family pictures anywhere. The furniture, including Miranda's own four-poster, was pink and white and pretty and clean—and impersonal. *Well, she only just moved back from like Spain. Maybe she hasn't had a chance to really* live *here yet.*

Miranda dropped her backpack on her bed, crossed to her dresser and pulled out a tankini. Rain noticed it was the same style as the one she had worn when they had gone water-skiing last Friday, but that one had been peach; this was tangerine. Immediately and without the slightest embarrassment, Miranda pulled off her top and started to take off her bra. Rain glanced at Renée, who was doing the same, having pulled a metallic gray bikini out of her backpack. Rain quietly lowered her own backpack to the floor. Like Charlie, she was already wearing her swimsuit (the *same* royal blue one-piece she had worn water-skiing) under her T-shirt and shorts. For no good reason, she was suddenly embarrassed about being prepared—and yet simultaneously glad, as it was immediately clear she was the least developed of the three girls, and she didn't really want the other two to see her naked. Rain usually didn't think much about her body, even when changing among *twenty* girls in P.E. After all, she had boobs, little ones anyway, and she *usually* wore a bra. She definitely wasn't the flattest girl in the eighth grade. Besides, she didn't really care all that much about what other people thought of her. Here and now, though, she felt incredibly self-conscious, and she couldn't help thinking, *They're both so much prettier than me.* So while Miranda and Renée stripped and changed, Rain quietly slipped out of her shorts and kept her T-shirt on.

Charlie felt like he'd been out in the hall for a long time. He had finally made up his mind to knock when he heard Renée speak and Miranda respond. He couldn't make out the words, and he didn't hear Rain's voice at all. He leaned in closer, and the door opened. He jumped back and only barely managed to restrain himself from saying something stupid, if not pervy.

Miranda and Renée joined him in the hallway. Both were wearing two-piece suits—and nothing else—and looked to Charlie like they could fit in nicely with the cast of any teen sitcom on Disney or Nick. Rain followed them out, wearing her oversized Cacique Charters T-shirt over her suit. She didn't look like a T.V.

star, but he thought she was beautiful. There was something else, too, something in her eyes. Something he didn't see in Rain all that often. Vulnerability. It only made her more beautiful. He smiled into Rain's almond eyes. He couldn't help himself, though he worried his smile gave something away. Then her eyes smiled back, and it was all worth it.

As for Rain, she was relieved Charlie was still wearing his T-shirt over his trunks. *That was how they rolled.* She immediately felt like less of a freak, and when he smiled at her, she guessed he felt the same. Her confidence instantly restored—Rain was nothing if not resilient—she actually led the way down the hall.

Downstairs, Miranda pointed to a door off the great room. "The Jacuzzi's in back. We'll just take a shortcut through my dad's study."

Unsurprisingly, it was a very large study. Lots of dark wood and open space. Facing the door was a huge glass and steel desk with a gunmetal gray laptop on it and not much else. On the wall behind the desk was a floor-to-ceiling portrait of one of the most striking women Rain had ever seen. She had café-au-lait skin and long chestnut hair, big brown eyes, and full red lips. She was wearing white and looked to be about six months pregnant. The artist had given the woman the subtlest of halo effects: a white glowing aura against the dark background. To Rain, the woman looked like a ghost. Suddenly, the thought occurred that Miranda occasionally referred to her father but never to her mother. Looking at the painting now, Rain could definitely see the resemblance to her new friend.

"Was that your mom?" Rain asked, already sure it was and confident the woman was long dead.

Miranda nodded. "Antonia Guerrero. Oh, and that's me in there too, kind of."

"She's very beautiful," Renée said.

"She was," Miranda said. "I don't remember her, though."

Charlie looked down at his father's watch, hanging loosely on his wrist. He turned away.

"How long ago did she die?" Rain asked matter-of-factly.

"Rain," Charlie said.

Rain ignored him, and Miranda seemed unfazed by the question. "Thirteen years ago. On my birthday. On my *birth* day."

"Oh, wow. Sorry. That must be awful."

"Rain," Charlie repeated with a bit more edge.

"It's okay," Miranda said. "Really. I *wish* I had known her. But I never did. So I can't exactly miss her, can I?"

Rain didn't think that sounded right. More like something Miranda had practiced to convince herself. "You know you don't have to—"

"Rain . . ." Charlie interrupted, his voice low but tense.

Rain rolled her eyes—positive she hadn't said anything *too* insensitive—and turned around to face him. Then she saw what he was looking at. The entire wall, on either side of the door, was covered with close to a hundred pre-Columbian artifacts. There were idols and gourds, necklaces, anklets, bracelets and armbands, headbands and masks, musical instruments, tools and weapons. Some were made of stone, some of wood, some of turquoise, some of gold. And every single artifact was decorated with human or animal figures: men, women, bats, snakes, fish, crabs, birds, gods.

Rain felt a tingling on her left arm and looked down in time to see the eyes on the armband's Searcher snake briefly flare with blue light. She turned to Miranda. "What—what is all this?"

Miranda shrugged. "They're *zemis*."

CHAPTER FOURTEEN

SEARCH AND RESEARCH

Zemis . . ." Rain whispered.

"But there are like a hundred of them," Charlie said. He turned to Rain. "I thought there were only supposed to be—"

Her look shut him up.

"What's a *zemi*?" Renée asked, unintentionally helpful.

"Well, it's . . . um. It's like a spirit," Miranda said haltingly. "Or it contains the spirit or something like that. My dad collects them."

Rain moved in for a closer look. There were multiple gourd jars all in a row. One was circled with fish, another with hermit crabs, a third with gulls. There was a clay mask composed of writhing snakes. A whistle or flute, as thick as her wrist, carved from driftwood—bleached nearly white from sun and sand and surf—to look like a bat with folded wings. And another right beside it, but carved to look like an owl instead. There was a belt of beaded black and red seeds that depicted a female figure amid the waves or maybe the wind. Though the image was simple and emblematic, Rain recognized Hurricane Julia immediately. "Who made these?" Rain asked.

"I, uh . . . don't remember." Miranda laughed nervously. "If I had known there was going to be a quiz, I would have paid more attention when my dad droned on about them."

"Can we find out?" Rain asked almost breathlessly as she moved to study the *zemis* on the other side of the door.

Miranda and Renée exchanged a *How weird is this?* glance. Then Miranda turned back to Rain. "But . . . what about the hot tub?"

Rain didn't respond right away. She examined a wooden spear. The inlaid carving of another bat was etched into its stone spearhead, which was secured atop the spear by two sinewy cords that then hung down half the length of the weapon. She moved on to a necklace with a bluestone amulet depicting another owl. Then a small ironwood statue of a man with a wide grin and a bowl atop his head. Beside that was a golden armband, inlaid with the mosaic of a dog formed from tiny gray and white shells. Drawn to that trinket, Rain reached out, and a panicked Miranda all but shouted, "I don't think you should touch that."

Rain withdrew her hand but continued staring.

Seeing she was fully immersed, Charlie came to her aid. "Your, uh, dad's collection. It's pretty cool. And the hot tub'll still be there, right?"

Rain finally spoke up. "I really want to know more."

Miranda was stunned. She could tell Charlie was only making an excuse for Rain, the girl who took Spanish—despite being fluent—so she wouldn't have to work hard in school. Now she wanted to forgo the Jacuzzi to study these stupid *zemis*? Even to

Miranda, who was a studious child by nature, this did not sound like a fun way to start their weekend. On the other hand, she wanted Rain as a friend . . .

"Well, I guess just about everything you'd want to know is in those books," she said, pointing to an entire wall of built-in bookshelves, perpendicular to the artifacts.

Charlie looked at the wall of volumes and then turned around to face the open French doors that led outside and, presumably, to the hot tub. *Well, at least this'll reduce the threat of head explosion.* "Great," he sighed. "Let's see what we can find out."

Miranda turned to Renée. "Do you mind?"

Renée *did* mind. Very much. One of the few advantages of holding off on her revenge was the hedonistic pleasure she could take by using what Miranda's lifestyle had to offer in the meantime. Right now, though, Renée's long-term plan required her to appear cooperative and benign. So she said, "No. It's . . . interesting." She moved toward the laptop on the desk. "We could probably find stuff online, too." Since she was forcing herself to play nice, at least she could try to speed up the process.

Hearing Renée's suggestion, Rain mentally kicked herself for never having thought of taking her Search online. Due to the magical way she had first been introduced to the word *zemi,* she had taken it as a given that it was some kind of arcane term. She thought she'd have to find some ancient scroll or tablet to reveal a definition. *Checking on the computer in Mom's office never crossed my mind!* Now, as Renée fired up Mr. Guerrero's laptop, Rain felt like a complete idiot.

She shook her head and crossed to the shelves, trying to take in the hundreds of books in English and Spanish that resided there. One title immediately caught her eye. "*The Taíno Zemi,*" she read aloud as she pulled it from the shelf.

"Hey," Charlie said, "aren't you Taíno?"

"I think so. Or I think 'Bastian's *abuela* was. My great-great-grandmother. Oh, and maybe my Grandma Rose."

Eager to get this over with, Renée was already online. "Should I Wikipedia Taíno or *zemi*?"

"Both," Rain said.

Miranda was positive her father wouldn't want them on his personal laptop. She wished she could pull out her iPhone instead, but she had left it upstairs in her backpack. (In Madrid, she never went anywhere without it, but few of her San Próspero peers could afford one, so she had quickly learned to keep hers out of sight.) Still, she knew Pablo wouldn't be back until after dinner. Probably *long* after dinner. *There's no way we won't be done by then. Is there?*

They were at it for a while.

Rain was an inexperienced and impatient scholar. She would pull a book off the shelf and flip through it, searching desperately for answers to some very specific questions. But she didn't know where to look or how, and if something didn't catch her eye right away, it would wander to yet another title.

For the opposite reason, Renée wasn't doing any better on the laptop. Not particularly interested in the endeavor, she would bounce from one link to another—never quite staying on any single page long enough to learn all that much. Meanwhile, Miranda continued to stress about the incursion into her father's study, the growing history on his browser and the growing number of books removed from his shelves. Charlie—attempting to balance Rain's needs with Miranda's obvious discomfort—spent as much time putting volumes back in their proper places as he did skimming through them.

At one point, they all paused for a good seven minutes when a Web site played music from a Taíno *areyto* ceremonial dance. (And think, for a moment, just how long seven minutes is.) Listening—in my way—from across Próspero Bay, I recognized the once famil-iar sounds of the *mayohuacan* drum and the *baijo* flute. It made me smile. Charlie, Miranda and even Renée found the music strangely hypnotic. (For once, Renée didn't click away instantly.) In Rain, it touched something very deep, something rooted within herself, reaching back into her ancestry, her D.N.A. Saying it im-mediately became her new mental soundtrack doesn't begin to cover it.

The recording ended; the clumsy research continued. Ulti-mately, here's what our odd little quartet learned . . .

The Taíno people, a subset of the Arawak, were the original inhabitants of the Ghost Keys and most of the Caribbean before the coming of Christopher Columbus. When the Spanish landed, they brought a host of ills: diseases for which the Taíno had no immunity, slavery, slaughter and near-total cultural and literal genocide. No, not a pretty picture.

Rain believed she was descended from the Taíno on her moth-er's side. Both her Grandma Rose (Iris' mother) and her Great-Great-Grandmother Concha ('Bastian's *abuela*) were largely of Taíno descent, or so she vaguely felt she had once been told. Yet there was nothing vague about the feelings that rose up unbidden when she read about the suffering of the Taíno under the gold-grubbing cruelty of the Europeans. *This is "the wound,"* she de-cided. *This is what the Healer must heal. But how do I ever heal something this big, this ancient—even with nine magical* zemis?

Still, the *zemis* were clearly the key to unlocking this mystery, and the four teens managed in their haphazard way to learn the basics about them. In the religion, culture and mythology of the Taíno peoples, a *zemi* was a spirit-god. In fact, that's what the word meant in the Taíno language. A *zemi* was also an icon, a talisman created by the Taíno and infused with the power of the spirit depicted upon it—like the two snakes (Searcher and Healer) on Rain's armband. Many *zemis* were sculptures—idols, if you will—but that wasn't mandatory. A *zemi* could be anything. A piece of jewelry. A tool. A weapon. A jar. A musical instrument. Anything that portrayed and housed the animistic essence of the *zemi* spirit-god became a *zemi* itself. Thus the nine completely different shapes waiting for their *zemis* in the Cache. And that was the problem. Nowhere could Rain find any mention of nine special *zemis* necessary for healing a wound. Nowhere could she find a reference to Healer or Searcher. Though she had learned a great deal, she was still caught on the horns of her original dilemma: She had no idea what she was searching for or where to begin her Search.

Charlie crossed back over to Pablo Guerrero's collection. "I don't see anything that looks like a roll of quarters."

Renée wasn't even listening at this point, but Charlie's comment triggered a new line of thought for Miranda. *Something's going on here.* There were looks Charlie and Rain had exchanged. Things they had said as prompts for Renée's online meanderings. Things they had semi whispered to each other. *"There are like a hundred of them. I thought there were only supposed to be—" "Anything about* zemis *having healing powers?" "It doesn't say anything about an Earch-Say." "How many on that page? Count 'em."* Now, *"I don't see anything that looks like a roll of quarters."*

Miranda said, "Are you guys looking for something . . . specific?"

The book in Rain's hands slammed shut! She put it back on the shelf. (And Charlie moved it back to where it *belonged* on the shelf.) Rain smiled brightly and said, "Now, how about that hot tub?"

Within seconds, and with barely a glance exchanged between them, Rain and Charlie had crossed the length of the study to wait by the French doors. Miranda practically had whiplash from

Rain's abrupt change of direction, but Renée (who managed to suppress a "Finally") was on her feet and already heading outside, leaving Miranda to quickly clear the history on her father's browser and shut down his computer. This flurry of activity successfully flustered her enough to momentarily push any question of Rain and Charlie's secret agenda out of her mind.

For now.

CHAPTER FIFTEEN

DEMON CHILD

FRIDAY, SEPTEMBER 12

Their time in the hot tub was pleasant—but brief.

While Charlie tried very hard not to get caught looking at any particular part of any particular girl, Rain tried even harder to keep an eye on the moving target that was his wrist-watch. By the time the sun had crept below tree level, leaving the Jacuzzi in shadow, Rain knew it was time to go. She wanted to be back at the cave by sunset to give her a shot at conferring with its new-minted ghost.

It didn't quite work out that way.

She had her excuse ready. She and Charlie needed to head home now: They had to be in bed early in order to get up early, because they needed to work her dad's charter first thing the next morning.

Miranda was stunningly disappointed. "But . . . we *just* got in the hot tub. And I thought you were staying for dinner. The

ferry runs until midnight, and we could watch a movie or something . . ." She trailed off.

As usual, Charlie tried to make it better. He put a hand on her
arm and tried to catch her eye. "We'll do this again. And you can
come over to my place too. It's not fancy. But Rain and I have
been meaning to borrow some mopeds from my mom's rental
lot."

Miranda's weak smile still managed to show her gratitude for
his effort—and perhaps something more. Renée caught it. Miranda
was crushing on Charlie, who Renée knew was crushing on Rain,
who was—*big surprise*—also crushing on Rain. Bitterly, Renée
thought, *I can use this.* Otherwise, she was pretty happy with
how things were turning out. Rain and Charlie were proving
lousy friends, which would make Miranda even more dependent
on Renée.

Rain was already out of the tub and drying off when Miranda
abruptly got out too. Rain's eyes went wide. "Wait, you don't
have to. Stay here. You know, with Renée. We can find our own
way out."

But despite protests from Rain, Charlie *and* Renée, Miranda
insisted on walking her departing friends down to the ferry. She
turned to Renée and once again asked, "Do you mind?"

It took every ounce of self-control for her to respond evenly,
"No. I'm getting pruney anyway, *Sugar.*"

So they all got out of the water. They all toweled dry. They all
went inside and upstairs to change. They all headed for the Sycorax dock, where they all stood waiting for the ferry. They all . . .
were miserable.

Rain again tried to tell Miranda she didn't have to wait, but
Miranda insisted. If she didn't stay, Rain and Charlie would have
to pay for the ride back to San Próspero. Rain told her that was
okay. Miranda just shook her head.

Rain was beyond frustrated. She turned to look west. The sun was on the verge of setting, but there was no way she was getting to the cave tonight. *And I need to talk to that ghost!* She was furious with Miranda for interfering with the Search. She wanted to tell her off and turned back toward her with something cutting on the tip of her tongue. What she saw stopped her.

It was Charlie, really. The way he was looking at Miranda. On his open, sensitive face, it was clear he felt really bad for her. With Charlie unintentionally—though not for the first time—acting as Rain's own personal Jiminy Cricket, she managed to step out of her own deck shoes long enough to walk a few steps in Miranda's sandals. The new girl had wanted this "play date" badly, and she had wanted it to go well. Sure, Miranda tried too hard. She didn't actually *need* to show Rain and Charlie a good time for them to like her. Miranda didn't know that, though, and Rain had completely spoiled the afternoon from moment one. Immediately, Rain wanted to take it all back. To say, *You know, maybe we don't have to go to bed* that *early.* But it was too late. It would just be too strange to about-face now. Too suspicious.

So instead, she said, "Hey, you know the charter tomorrow?"

"Yeah," Miranda said gloomily.

"Well, the family has three little kids. And kids can get kinda crazy on a boat. That's why my dad wants me and Charlie there. To make sure they don't fall off the side or whatever."

"I understand."

"No, but, see, there are *three* kids and only two of us. I don't know if this would be fun for you—and, well, I don't think my dad could pay you, but—"

"Yes!" Miranda said, happily enough and loudly enough that she was instantly embarrassed by her own enthusiasm. She tried to tone it down. "I mean, if you think I could help?" She was still smiling broadly.

"Yeah, definitely," Rain said. She looked at Renée and smiled evilly. "You're welcome to come too."

Renée smiled back, holding Rain's gaze, acknowledging that Rain had scored a point. They both were well aware that even Renée's vengeance had its limits. Miranda might think it was fun to get up early and work a charter for no money, but Renée knew better. Besides, she had her own job. One that paid. "Sorry, I have to work, *Sugar*. You three have fun without me."

"We'll try," Rain said, triumphant. Then she glanced at Charlie, who was looking right at her. He was proud of her—and not for putting one over on Renée. Rain found herself smiling again, shyly this time. She'd never admit it, but having Charlie think well of her mattered more than pretty much anything else in her world. So she punched him in the arm.

Just like that, none of them was miserable. Not even Renée, who didn't mind a challenge and still had the rest of the evening to further secure her bond with Miranda. The ferry was still a good twenty minutes off, but they stood there chatting easily now.

A few feet up the gangway, Isaac Naborías was chatting easily with a trio of Sycorax employees waiting to head home. Sure, he had planned to simply pick up his paycheck, say a few good-byes and be back on San Próspero hours ago. But when he got to the guard shack, Jimmy had told him his check was being held at the main office. And when Isaac got *there*, he found twenty or thirty people waiting to throw him a retirement party, complete with champagne and a chocolate cake. It was unexpected and wonderful, and he had welled up a bit. He'd had some cake, and maybe a glass—or four—of the bubbly. There were old stories and lots of laughs and many, many hugs. (You'd think he was moving half a world away, when in fact they'd still see each other on San Próspero often. Maybe more often, now that Isaac wasn't working the graveyard shift.) So he'd lost track of the time. Truth be told, he was feeling warm, fuzzy, nostalgic and tipsy enough that he'd even lost track of *why* keeping track of the time mattered. It was in there, though, struggling to escape. Which may explain why his mind eventually wandered where it did.

Juno Lynn, a Sycorax Honey beekeeper, started the ball rolling by bringing up the Pale Tourist, asking if the Ghost Patrol had told Isaac the cause of death. Naborías shook his head, and Suzanne Vanetti (Wilma's great-aunt) stated definitively that the cause was "death by vampire bat."

Again Naborías shook his head. "It was no bat," he said. "It was the *Hupia*."

Nestor Gonzales, head of Payroll, remembered that word from his childhood. *"Hupia?* Isn't that the Taíno word for vampire?"

Now, Rain had not been eavesdropping, but the mention of the dead man had caught her attention and piqued her interest. And once she heard the words "Taíno" and "vampire," the conversation commanded her full consideration. She nudged Charlie and motioned with her head. Fortunately, there was no need to move any closer, as Isaac's semi-inebriation made him louder than usual.

"A ghost-vampire. A demon." Isaac pointed an unsteady finger at Gonzales, whose hair, what remained of it, was still black only by artificial means. "Nestor, didn't *tus abuelos* ever teach you the story of the *Hupia?"*

Nestor studied the question, trying sincerely to remember. Suzanne crossed herself, saying, "No one likes those old stories, Isaac."

But Juno, the only person in that small clique under the age of fifty, encouraged Naborías. "I like old stories. What's a 'hoopya'?"

That was all the encouragement old Isaac needed.

"In the First Days," he said, beginning the way his old *tío* always had, "the Taíno people found the First Murdered Man. He had been an old man and wise. But now there was a hole in his neck through which all his blood had been stolen. The next morning another body was found: the First Murdered Woman. She had also been old and wise. And now she had a hole in her neck too."

Rain and Charlie were no longer the only ones from outside Isaac's circle of friends listening. Miranda, Renée and nearly everyone else within earshot was also. Then the sun finished setting, and 'Bastian materialized from Rain's *zemi*. "Hello, kiddo," he said, smiling.

"Shhh," she whispered and motioned once more with her head. So even the dead turned toward Naborías and paid heed.

"The third morning there was another victim. This was the First Murdered Child. Bloodless now too, like the others. Panic swept through the tribe. Every man was accused of being First Murderer. Every woman of being First Witch. And every morning, there was another corpse."

Suzanne crossed herself again. She wasn't the only one.

Rain heard a mosquito sing in her ear and waved it away.

"The First Chief of the Taíno consulted with First Shaman, who consulted with First God, who sent First Bat to watch at night for the culprit. And just before the break of day, First Bat reported back to First God, who sent a dream to First Shaman, who woke with a start and told the truth of it all to First Chief.

"The murderer was a child, little more than a babe. First Chief found this astonishing. This child had not yet learned to walk. He had yet but one tooth. He could not be First Murderer. So one more night was spent watching, and sure enough, the child crawled on hands and knees from his mother's *bohio* into a *bohio* some distance away. And First Chief and First Shaman peeked inside the *bohio* and watched the child crawl toward one of his little playmates and open his mouth to puncture her throat with his one tooth.

"First Chief grabbed up the boy, preventing the attack. And in the morning, First Shaman denounced the child to the entire tribe as a demon. The boy's mother protested. She did not want to believe. But an old crone confirmed that the young woman was known to be wicked. And it was now believed she had lain with First Demon and given birth to its child. First Chief testified to the boy's crime. And all but his mother agreed that the sentence must be death.

"But the small boy only laughed . . ."

During this telling, all eyes were focused on old Naborías, so no one noticed the cloud of mosquitoes gathering above him. Or no one noticed until the swarm descended en masse. The mosquitoes sang and laughed and danced around Naborías, but mostly they feasted. And feasted. And feasted.

Naborías screamed. And screamed. And screamed. The mosquitoes flew into his open mouth and bit his tongue and his gums, the inside of his cheeks and his throat. They were draining his blood, one tiny sip at a time. Juno and Nestor both tried coming to his aid, swatting at the bugs—and killing many—but there were always more, and they weren't shy about biting every man, woman and thirteen-year-old on the dock.

Only 'Bastian Bohique was completely immune, but he was also completely impotent. He couldn't pull Naborías to safety; he couldn't swat a single mosquito.

So it was Rain Cacique who took a running start and slammed into Naborías with enough force to propel both of them over the railing and into the water below. He struggled to return to the surface, but he was weak from lack of blood, so she was able to hold him still beneath the water until he was calm and understood what she had done and why. Then they both surfaced just long enough to take a deep breath before allowing themselves to sink back down where they were safe from the bugs.

The mosquitoes hovered, waiting for another chance. But the old man Naborías and the young girl Cacique stayed beneath the surface, and eventually the swarm dispersed.

CHAPTER SIXTEEN

SMITTEN

Constable Thibideaux arrived on Sycorax just as the E.M.T. launch was shoving off from the dock to transport Isaac Naborías across the bay to San Próspero Island Hospital. Assuming the old man pulled through—paramedic Joey Fajro said Naborías was in desperate need of a blood transfusion—Thibideaux would have to question the former security guard later.

Instead, he began with the witnesses, methodically talking to each, one by one, pausing only when the Sycorax helicopter passed overhead to land just beyond the trees on the corporate helipad. All eyes watched its progress. The boss was back.

"My father's back," Miranda said. She was still shaken. So was Renée. So was Charlie. Rain wasn't shaken, but she was shivering a little. The temperature had dropped considerably, and though someone had brought her a blanket, she was still soaking wet and far from hot-tub warm at the moment.

"I'm proud of you, Raindrop," 'Bastian said.

Rain nodded. *I think it comes with the job*, she thought. Her mind was racing. *I heard laughing.* It sounded crazy even to Rain. *It was just buzzing, wasn't it? No*, she decided firmly, *when we went over the side—just before we hit the water—I heard the mosquitoes laugh.* The music of the *areyto*, the *mayohuacan* and the *baijo*, was once again loud in her head. *This is all about the Taíno. The zemis are all connected to them. And the story about First Murderer is connected too.*

Trying not to turn her head or be too obvious, she whispered to 'Bastian, "How come you never told me the old Taíno stories?"

'Bastian shrugged. "I don't know them."

"But your *abuela* was Taíno. Didn't she . . ."

"Oh, she tried. But I had no patience. You have to understand, kiddo. In those days, the schools here didn't teach our culture. Heck, they *discouraged* it. Told us we should be Americans. And the mythology of America was George Washington and the cherry tree. But I understand it's different now and they celebrate this stuff." He tilted his head toward her. "So what's your excuse?"

She rolled her eyes at him, which was a relief. It meant she was okay. When everyone else had been paralyzed (either out of fear, confusion or just plain old being an insubstantial ghost), Rain had devised and executed a simple solution to save Isaac's life. Still, it didn't seem right. This was his granddaughter, and she was only thirteen. She shouldn't have to face these dangers. He should be able to protect her.

Charlie moved closer. Rain made her icky-face and urgently whispered, "You're standing in 'Bastian!" Neither of them had noticed, but both now jumped in opposite directions. Miranda and Renée stared at Charlie.

"I, uh, thought I saw a mosquito," Charlie said. The girls nodded and looked around, fairly freaked.

Rain whispered to the boys, "I'd love to sneak away to the cave. See if we could talk to the ghost."

All three looked around at the multiple deputy constables, security guards and civilians inhabiting the well-lit dock. Charlie said, "Yeah, I don't see that happening right now."

Rain brightened. "'Bastian, why don't you go? See if you can talk to him—or bring him back here!"

"I'm not leaving you alone with a killer cloud of mosquitoes on the loose." Even as he spoke, the words rang hollow in his ears. "Anyway, I don't see how you could hand me the *zemi* or how I could walk away with it and not have *somebody* notice."

Constable Thibideaux approached to question Rain. He nodded to Charlie and guided Rain a bit farther down the gangway. 'Bastian followed.

"Why don't you just tell me in your own words what happened?"

Rain considered this question long enough to make Thibideaux wonder at her delay. Once again, Rain was fighting the impulse to spill it all. Eventually, she said, "We were just standing here, waiting for the ferry. And then this cloud of mosquitoes sort of attacked Mr. Naborías. So I pushed him into the water to get him away from them."

Of course, this confirmed for the constable what Nestor and Juno and everyone else had told him. This young girl, Alonso Cacique's daughter, had been the hero of the moment. And though the entire incident was beyond bizarre, it also might fit and even explain what happened to the Pale Tourist, Milo Long. Some weird natural phenomenon . . .

Yet the cop in Jean-Marc *knew* the girl was hiding something. Trouble was, he couldn't immediately think of the questions to ask to find out what. By the time he had settled on a simple *Is there something you're not telling me?* it was too late.

Pablo Guerrero had arrived on the scene, and all attention immediately shifted to him. He seemed to have already been briefed. In fact, it wouldn't surprise Thibideaux if the C.E.O. had been informed of the incident before the P.K.C. had even been called. Guerrero approached his daughter first, to confirm she was all right, but he didn't linger there. He simply took her hand firmly in his and walked her forward to join the constable and Rain.

Guerrero nodded to Thibideaux but was already focused on the Cacique girl. Though they had been introduced earlier that day, it seemed to Rain like this was the first time he had really *seen* her. He thanked her by name for her quick thinking and for saving Isaac's life. A trifle dumbstruck, Rain simply nodded and then thanked him for thanking her.

Then Pablo Guerrero said softly, "I knew your grandfather. He was a good man. I'm very sorry for your loss."

Rain glanced at 'Bastian, who shrugged. "Every once in a while, he'd stop by the Lethe & Styx. If Joe Charone and I were there, we'd all have a few beers."

"Uh, thank you," Rain said. Thibideaux noticed the girl was still hesitant, distracted. *Maybe she's just in shock,* he told himself.

Pablo Guerrero cleared his throat and said, "If there's ever anything I can do for you . . ."

"Well, I guess we could use a lift back to San Próspero. The ferry sort of came and went while we were waiting to talk to the Ghost Pa—to Constable Thibideaux."

She turned toward Charlie and reached out her hand; he gladly stepped forward to take it. Miranda reached back to Renée, who—plan or no plan—was also ready to go.

Rain said, "Or we can wait for the next ferry . . ."

Guerrero waved off the idea. "No, Ariel will take you home." He turned to Thibideaux. "You're done talking with these children." It wasn't a question.

Thibideaux wasn't in the mood to bristle. It *was* getting late. These kids were clearly tired, and he could always catch up with them later. "Of course," he said. "But maybe you and I could speak."

"Certainly. Let me just see them off, and I'll be right with you."

Renée and Miranda ran back up to the manor to get Renée's things. It took them less than five minutes, but by the time they returned, Ariel Jones, Pablo Guerrero's personal pilot and chauffer, was already bringing her boss' sleek thirty-foot twin-engine speedboat around to the dock. How she had known to do this was a bit of a mystery, but even mysteries are merely relative. Given what Rain had just gone through, this one didn't seem worth pursuing.

Pablo helped Rain, Charlie and Renée onto the boat. ('Bastian was on his own.) Miranda said, "Thanks for coming. I know it kind of sucked, but—"

"Sugar, don't you worry about that," Renée said.

"And anyway, it was Rain's fault mostly," Charlie said quickly.

"Well, me and the bugs," Rain said. "You still coming tomorrow?"

"Sure," Miranda said. Then she turned to her father. "I promised I'd help Rain and Charlie work her dad's charter."

She was *way* too excited given the realities of the gig, and her father looked at her as if to say, *And you actually* want *to do that?* But he declined to express the thought out loud.

So Rain said, "Eight A.M. sharp at Harbor Slip Nine. And, seriously, don't be late, because my dad *will not wait* if the clients are ready."

"I'll be there!"

"Great."

They said quick good-byes, at which point Pablo Guerrero nodded to Ariel, who eased the throttle forward.

Rain sat down and turned her face toward the wind. She pulled the blanket tight around her shoulders and cuddled up against Charlie for warmth. Charlie chewed on the inside of his mouth to distract himself.

"Who's that?" 'Bastian whispered.

Rain turned and saw that he was focused on the moonlit form of Ariel. She was in her late twenties with short blond hair. Though the speedboat careened across Próspero Bay, she maintained a preternatural stillness. Even her hand on the wheel hardly seemed to move. Rain glanced over at Renée, who was also staring at Ariel. One of the things that bugged Rain most about Renée was the way she'd strike a pose to accentuate her looks, but that's not what Ariel was doing. No, Ariel was what Renée aspired to be. The blond woman wasn't striking or accentuating anything. Her stillness was harnessed from deep within. To Rain, Ariel was like a single still frame glowing in a movie projector. At any moment, either the film would proceed—or the image would combust.

Rain whispered to 'Bastian, "That's Ariel. She works for the Guerreros."

"She's stunning."

Rain made her icky-face again. "Ewww, Papa, she's way too young for you." She glanced up at the Dark Man, who appeared to be about twenty. "Or too old or something."

'Bastian looked askance at his granddaughter and decided to

have a little fun. "I don't know," he said. "Ariel and Sebastian. It sounds like destiny."

"Ewwwww. She can't even see or hear you."

"All great loves have obstacles to overcome, kiddo."

She covered her ears. "Stop! Just stop!" He laughed. Charlie and Renée stared at Rain, and Ariel turned her head five degrees. Then she adjusted course slightly as the speedboat swept around the recently returned dolphin pod.

Rain scratched at her mosquito bites.

Back on the Sycorax dock, Thibideaux was telling everyone they could go home. He had spoken briefly with both Guerreros, but the man had been on La Géante during the excitement, and the girl simply confirmed what every other witness had reported: Isaac had been telling a story when the mosquito swarm attacked and Rain pushed him into the water.

Miranda and her father walked silently up to the Old Manor, hand in hand. At the door, he said, "So, you're making friends, *mija*?"

"I think so."

"And you're glad I brought you back from Madrid?"

She hugged him. "I was already glad about that."

"Good," he said, hugging her back. They went inside, and he shut the door. Then, without another word to each other, she went upstairs, and he crossed the great room to enter his study.

Hura-hupia wasn't far away. Once again, she approached the *Hupia*, who was back at his post, guarding the second *zemi*.

The Pale Tourist—more pale now than ever—was also in the neighborhood, wandering, at a loss. Nights ago, he had reached the reasonable conclusion he was dead, a ghost. But he had no idea what came next. He'd been looking for a light to walk into or some such, but so far, no luck. He spotted *Hura-hupia* and immediately sensed she was a threat. And, of course, it was the

Hupia who'd killed him in the first place. Never big on confrontation, the Pale Tourist stepped *inside* the trunk of a guava tree to hide.

The *Hupia* expected to be reprimanded for attacking Naborías but was pleasantly surprised when *Hura-hupia* encouraged his appetites. *But next time, if you get the chance,* she told him with a smile, *feast on the girl Cacique.* This was welcome advice to the *Hupia.* He had a taste for Rain now. He was smitten.

CHAPTER SEVENTEEN

SIGHTSEERS

SATURDAY, SEPTEMBER 13

Not wanting to be late, Miranda was at Slip Nine at 7:30 A.M. Neither Rain nor Charlie was there yet, but Rain's father was working on the boat. She recognized him from the day he had told Rain her grandfather had passed, but they had never actually been introduced, and Miranda didn't know if she should approach him until Rain got there. Alonso saw her, smiled and went back about his business. Clearly, he didn't remember her. Miranda decided to wait for Rain under the WELCOME TO PUEBLO DE SAN PRÓSPERO sign.

Forty *long* minutes later, Charlie arrived. He greeted her with a smile and asked how long she'd been waiting.

"Just a few minutes," she said.

"Yeah. I know Rain said eight sharp, but punctuality isn't really one of her strengths."

"Her father's on the boat."

"Yeah, he gets it ready, and Rain'll come with the tourists. That's the system."

"Oh. Okay."

"He didn't want any help?"

"Um. He didn't seem to remember me or expect me or anything me. So I decided to wait up here."

"Well, come on. I'll introduce you guys. And don't worry. Alonso's cool."

"You call him Alonso?"

"Never."

"Right."

Charlie made introductions. It was immediately obvious Rain had neglected to mention Miranda would be joining them. Alonso's face darkened briefly; the thought crossed his mind Rain was trying to turn the charter into a party cruise for herself and her friends.

So Miranda made it abundantly clear she was there to work. "Rain said with three kids you'd need three babysitters—but you don't have to pay me."

"Of course I'll pay you, Miranda." Alonso knew Iris would not be thrilled about the extra expense, but he was a soft touch. "The same as Charlie. It's not much."

"That's fine, Mr. Cacique."

"Call me Alonso."

Miranda glanced at Charlie, who shook his head as subtly as he could manage.

Alonso caught it. "Charlie, I've been trying to get you to call me Alonso since you could talk."

"Yes, sir. You have, sir."

Mr. Cacique tossed up his hands in defeat. "All right, let's put you two to work. Rain should be here any minute with the Kims."

Rain and the Kims were not there any minute. In fact, they

didn't arrive for another two *long* hours. Punctuality might not be one of Rain's strengths, but this one wasn't on her. This one you could blame on Wendy, John and Michael Kim. Or perhaps on a certain lack of momentum, determination or discipline on the parts of their parents, Fred and Esther Kim.

Eight-year-old Wendy had been tired and had refused to get out of bed, even if it meant skipping breakfast. Six-year-old John had thrown a fit in the dining room over getting sausage patties when he wanted links. Four-year-old Michael had refused to put on sunscreen. Then when they were finally ready to go, Wendy declared herself famished. Thirty-six-year-old Esther assured her daughter there would be food on the boat. But when Wendy asked if there would be *waffles* on the boat, her mother gave up and gave in (and an appalled Iris found herself making fresh waffles in a kitchen she had already cleaned for the morning).

En route to the docks in Timo Craw's taxi, Michael remembered he'd forgotten his favorite yellow plastic shovel back at the Inn. Rain pointed out there was nothing to shovel on the boat. But thirty-nine-year-old Fred—in a state of pure exasperation—told Timo to turn the cab around.

So at 10:15 A.M., Rain and the Kims finally came aboard the *Spirit of the Ghosts* to find Alonso, Charlie and Miranda in a virtual stupor from the heat and boredom.

Alonso had to literally shake his head clear, but with a little help from Charlie and Rain, the vessel soon shoved off. Within minutes they were out on Próspero Bay and heading through what locals called the Chapel Ceiling (the gap between Sycorax and San Próspero's closest points, which had once reminded someone of God reaching his finger out to Adam on the ceiling of the Sistine Chapel in Rome).

Miranda, meanwhile, had volunteered to help Mrs. Kim with sunscreen and life vests in the cabin. Normally, Alonso, per his insurance, would never have left the dock unless all minor guests were *already* in their vests, but after sitting in the sun for hours, he got a little fast and loose with the rules. (Don't worry. I'll never bark a word of it.)

The boys loved the vests and couldn't get into them fast enough. But Wendy declared a vest would make her look like a baby and so refused to put it on—until Miranda put hers on first. Then the younger girl cautiously complied, keeping her eyes glued on Miranda to make sure the older girl didn't take hers off.

Michael still protested vehemently against the sunscreen, and Esther finally exploded: "Michael Kim, if you don't put on sunscreen, you'll have to stay below deck for the entire trip!"

This backfired. Michael was happy to stay below deck. He looked out the porthole and said, "I don't like water."

Wendy said, "That means he's *afraid* of the water."

Michael screeched, *"Does not!"*

When John understood that his younger brother was "getting to stay below," he wanted to stay below too. At first, Wendy seemed disgusted by her brothers' choice, but as soon as she stepped outside, she spotted a vestless Rain, let out an anguished cry and fled back below deck.

Miranda explained the situation, and both Rain and Charlie put on vests and entered the cabin to show Wendy. The girl, now in a funk, sat in the corner. She kept her vest on but refused to go back out.

Right about then, Fred Kim was getting seasick over the side of the boat, wasting a little more of Iris Cacique's morning labor by depositing his breakfast into the Florida Straits. Once that was done, the green-looking father descended into the cabin to lie down for a few minutes.

Completely defeated, Esther Kim asked Rain if there were any games or puzzles on board. Now, as bad as all of this may sound, Rain had seen worse. She opened an entire game closet for the Kims. Miranda helped John choose Candy Land and even managed to coax Wendy into playing with her brothers and mother. However, eight people made the cabin feel pretty close, pretty claustrophobic. So Rain nodded to Charlie, and they both went topside.

Shaking his head, Alonso rhetorically asked, "They're *all* down there?"

"Yep," Rain said. "Miranda's got them entertained though."

"She's a good worker."

"Uh-huh."

"Better than you two."

"No argument."

"All right. Chill for now."

So Rain led Charlie to the foredeck and took the opportunity to tell him about the blue glow emitted by the *zemi*'s Searcher snake when they had first entered Pablo Guerrero's study the day before.

"Does that mean one of those things was the *zemi*? I mean, 'the' *zemi*, not just 'a' *zemi*."

"I don't know. I don't think so. It was really quick. And I intentionally leaned the armband toward every one of those artifacts, and it didn't glow again. But I do think it was trying to tell me there was info there we could use."

"Well, that's good. At least we won't walk right past something important without a heads-up."

"Right. So all we have to do is figure out where to walk."

"Where to walk where?" Miranda asked, catching her two friends off guard.

"I'll walk the plank," Rain said, "if I have to spend more time with those Kim kids."

"They're not that bad," Miranda said. "But what's with their names?"

"Yeah," said Charlie.

"What?" asked Rain.

Miranda stared at her. "Wendy, John and Michael? Those are the names of the Darling kids in *Peter Pan*."

"These kids aren't darling," Rain said.

"Yeah, but how does that work?" Charlie wondered.

"I know," Miranda said. "So you have a daughter first and name her Wendy because you like Peter Pan. Are you hoping your next two kids are going to be boys? I mean, what if John or Michael had been a girl? It'd throw off your whole scheme."

Charlie offered, "I guess if John had been a girl, they'd have named her whatever, and no one would know they ever had a scheme."

Rain couldn't believe they were talking about this. "Maybe if John were a girl, they'd have named her Tiger Lily. And Michael could have been Tinker Bell."

Miranda ignored her: "Maybe there was no scheme *at first*. Maybe they just liked the name Wendy. Then they have a son next . . ."

"And they figure why not," Charlie added.

"Then by the time Michael is born, there's no way they're not completing the set."

"Or maybe it's all a big coincidence," Rain said.

Charlie shook his head. "You have no imagination."

"I do too."

He rolled his eyes. "No, you don't. You get to *see* the magic, so you don't think you need one." As soon as he said it, he regretted it. He could see the hurt in her eyes.

"You get to see magic?" Miranda asked, amused.

"Yes," Rain said defiantly. "Ghosts taught me Spanish. And my dead grandfather lives in this armband."

Charlie slapped his hand across his eyes and rubbed it down the length of his face. Miranda didn't know what to make of this. It didn't seem quite funny enough to be a joke, but obviously Rain couldn't have been serious. It must have been some kind of in-joke, and once again Miranda felt excluded.

Rain sighed. "See, I have plenty of imagination." But she wondered if what Charlie had said was true. What if she had no imagination? No ability to make those fanciful leaps? How would she ever find the other *zemis* without the imagination necessary to transcend the visible world with her mind?

Now all three felt crummy. Charlie looked around, trying to find some inspiration to change the subject. It was a gorgeous day. The sun was climbing a cloudless sky, but the spray kept things cool. He glanced from the reflection of the sun in the water to Miranda's light skin and asked, "Do *you* have sunscreen on?"

Miranda assured him she did. She knew his concern had more to do with getting out of an awkward moment than protecting her epidermis, but she was grateful for either impulse. She could help too, or so she thought. "How weird was that, last night? With the mosquitoes."

Charlie shot a nervous look at Rain, who said, "Really weird."

Miranda nudged her. "You were like totally a hero."

Rain smiled and nodded with mock seriousness. "Yes. Yes, I was."

Alonso's voice called out from the helm, "Dolphins on the portside."

Miranda and Charlie both had to stop and think which side he meant. Rain knew her ports from her starboards, though, and immediately crossed to the other side of the boat and pointed. "I see them."

Miranda and Charlie followed in time to see an entire pod of bottlenose dolphins taking turns breaching in the bow wave of the boat, dodging the foam and froth like it was a game. This wasn't exactly an unusual sight to Rain and Charlie, but it was still uncommon enough to be awesome. For Miranda, it was breathtaking.

Alonso called out again, "Tell the Kims."

"They won't come out," Rain yelled back.

"Tell 'em!"

"Fine!"

Begrudgingly, Rain entered the cabin and informed the five Kims. Wendy and John ran out to see the dolphins, which made Michael want to follow. His mother insisted he needed sunscreen first, but he whined that he'd miss the dolphins. So they compromised, and Michael agreed she could put on his sunscreen *while* he looked at the dolphins.

Rain followed Esther and Michael out onto the deck, and a queasy Fred Kim followed her. Wendy and John—with Miranda and Charlie standing directly behind them, gripping their shoulders—were already on the portside, pointing and laughing at the dolphins. Michael, his yellow shovel gripped tightly in his little hand, ran right up to the edge, and Esther made a long motherly reach to grab his arm and pull him back from the brink. He said, "Ow!" loudly and fussed and squirmed while she applied the sunscreen.

The dolphins were truly putting on a show, cavorting and playing and showing off for the *Spirit's* passengers. A few slid right up to the boat. Alonso cut the engine and let her drift.

Charlie led John aft and down the steps to the stern diving deck. Miranda followed with Wendy. Michael struggled to be released, and Mrs. Kim either gave up or felt she had slathered enough goop on the kid to let him go. He rushed off after his siblings, and Rain raced to catch up. The adult Kims followed, and even Alonso joined them.

Still firmly gripping John with his right hand, Charlie reached out with his left to stroke a dolphin that had sidled up close. John was astounded. "He let you touch him!"

"'Course he did," Charlie said. "Because he knows I'm his brother."

"You're not his brother," Wendy said suspiciously.

"I am. My last name's Dauphin, and that means dolphin in French. My people and the dolphins go *way* back."

"Yeah, well, he's still not your brother," Rain said, "because he's a *she*."

They all turned to look at the dolphin again, but it was disappearing beneath the surface.

"How can you tell it's a she?" Charlie asked.

"Maybe I'm using my imagination," Rain snarked back.

"Yeah," said Alonso. "Or maybe she could tell by the size. An adult male is longer and thicker."

"Don't spoil the magic, Dad," Rain said. But she wondered how she *had* known the dolphin was female. Why she was so certain of that fact.

Mr. Kim called out, "There are some on this side now." He and his wife moved to starboard. Alonso followed them.

The kids didn't budge. "I wanna touch one," John said. Wendy and Michael concurred.

Something broke the surface near them, but it wasn't the sleek, smooth, blue-gray skin of a dolphin. It was a wrinkly mottled brown-gray back. Wendy cringed. "Eww, what's that?"

The creature poked its head out of the water. Rain practically gasped. "It's a manatee!" This was a rare sight indeed. The manatee floated alongside the *Spirit*, watching the six children.

John looked from the manatee to Rain and back. "It's looking at you," he told her. The manatee turned to study John, and then Wendy, before lingering to gaze at Michael with small brown eyes partially hidden by layers of fat.

"She seems so intelligent," Miranda said. "So human." Now the manatee was a she too.

"I've *never* been this close to one," Charlie said.

John stretched out his arm. "I can't reach her," he said.

Almost on cue, the manatee moved closer. Wendy and John reached out and touched her. Michael looked up at Rain and asked, "Can't she come on the boat? I don't like the water."

"No, sorry," Rain said, "but I won't let you fall."

"Okay."

Charlie and Miranda moved John and Wendy back to make room for Rain and Michael. Michael reached out and touched the manatee. Rubbed her. Rain said, "Be gentle. Stroke, don't rub."

Pulling his hand away, Michael said, "Her skin's loose."

Very loose. It seemed to be pulling back and off the creature in folds.

"Gross," Wendy whispered, but all six kids were fascinated, and no one else said a word as the process continued and the skin pulled away, revealing black tendrils beneath.

Miranda found her voice. "Is she injured?"

Rain said nothing. *She's shedding her skin. Like a snake.* The black tendrils beneath the manatee's skin moved like snakes, but Rain soon realized they were something else. Hair. Black hair under the water. Long black hair framing a caramel-skinned face and big brown eyes. *It's a woman! A human woman!*

Two dolphins rose up to flank the woman. One carefully took the shed manatee skin in its mouth and swam away with it. The other dolphin nudged the woman, who nodded and lifted her face out of the water. She was young and beautiful, and she smiled at Rain and the other children.

Then she dove down beneath the surface, the water sliding off her smooth bare skin as she went. Then she was gone. Like she had never been there.

Rain looked around. No dolphins either. She rubbed her eyes and said, "You'll never imagine what I just saw."

She turned to look at Charlie and Miranda, their jaws hanging open. Charlie slowly lifted his eyes to meet Rain's. "I saw it too," he said.

Miranda couldn't find her voice, but she nodded frantically.

John snickered. "I saw her butt."

CHAPTER EIGHTEEN

PROOF

SATURDAY, SEPTEMBER 13

T he three adults completely missed the best part of the show. Mr. Kim walked across the deck, saying, "Well, I think the dolphins are gone."

His three children turned slowly to look at him, their faces registering enough awe to make him stop in his tracks. Wendy Kim spoke very slowly. "One of those dolphins was not a dolphin, Dad."

Rain jumped in quickly. "It was a manatee! We saw a manatee over on this side."

John said, "It was a *womanatee*. I saw her butt. Her naked butt."

Wendy swiped at him but missed. "John, that's not appropriate."

"Don't hit me. Use your words."

"I didn't hit you."

"You tried."

Still clutching his yellow plastic shovel, Michael ran to his mother. "She turned into a lady."

Mrs. Kim looked mystified. She looked across at Rain, who offered a ridiculously comical shrug and raised her hands as if she had no clue what those crazy kids were on about. For support, she turned to Charlie and Miranda, who mimicked her precisely.

Alonso said, "Well, you're all up on deck, so why don't we set up lunch?"

A slightly green Mr. Kim suppressed a belch, but Mrs. Kim said, "Yes, that would be lovely."

So Alonso, Rain, Charlie and Miranda brought out tables for the food and clean towels for the deckside picnic. They brought out Iris' gourmet sandwiches, her homemade potato chips and pasta salad. They brought out ice chests with carafes of fresh-squeezed lemonade, bottled water, sodas and a few locally brewed beers. They brought out a key lime pie (made with Grandma Rose's special recipe) and fresh-baked chocolate chip cookies. Plus cloth napkins, plates, and silverware. In short, they materialized a feast.

Throughout all this prep work, Rain's mind was racing. A manatee sighting was rare enough, but a manatee that transformed into a raven-haired, golden-skinned woman was something she absolutely had to check out! She tried to justify the necessity of it by telling herself the Mighty Morphin' Manatee might lead her to the next *zemi*—but she didn't take the idea all that seriously. No, what really fueled her fire was one simple fact: *Charlie and Miranda saw the weirdness!*

A plan was forming. But her father would have to cooperate. At least up to a point.

It took all her willpower, but she kept her mouth shut until the banquet was fully prepared. Meanwhile, Wendy, John and Michael had not stopped talking about the Manatee-Woman, and eventually their parents got the gist of the story. It was too fanciful to be considered a lie and way too fanciful to be considered the truth, so the parents chose to be amused and indulgent, especially since the miraculous event seemed to have distracted their children from repeating their earlier—less pleasant—behavior. Wendy seemed to briefly suspect her mother and father weren't taking them seriously, but when John started detailing scenarios to explain the magical origins of their recent visitor, Wendy dove in with her own theories and forgot to care whether her parents were true believers or not.

Once Esther Kim began preparing plates off the buffet table for her children, Rain made her move. She slid up to Alonso and said, "They'll be eating for at least a half hour, don't you think?"

Alonso said yes automatically—then instantly realized his daughter was winding up her curveball. He tried to stop her before the pitch, but . . .

"Then you won't mind if Charlie, Miranda and I go snorkeling while they eat." There was definitely no question mark at the end of that question.

"Rain . . ."

"Dad, we're roasting. We just want to cool off. A quick dip. We'll be back on board before they get to the pie. You know, Charlie and Miranda have been out here since eight."

She always made it sound so reasonable. Still, he had to at least try to hold the line. "Yeah, well, I've been out here since six."

"You're right. I get it. You three go in the water; I'll do lunch duty."

He lowered his head, soundly defeated already. This was a game they played all the time, and he almost never won. In part, this was because he knew Rain was basically a really good kid. She did her chores—not without complaint but without whining—and this week, she'd even been getting her homework done without him or Iris having to breathe down her neck. So he let her win the little victories. Though just once, he'd love to outmaneuver *her* for a change. Not today, though. "No, you go ahead. But be back before the pie."

She jumped up, kissed his cheek and was gone, grabbing Charlie and Miranda and dragging them below.

As soon as she was in the cabin, she stripped out of the life-vest, sleeveless tee, shoes and shorts she was wearing over her swimsuit. Then she started pulling snorkels, diving masks and fins out of a cabinet. Charlie followed her lead—because he always followed her lead—but Miranda just stood there. Rain looked at her. "C'mon. You are wearing a suit, aren't you?"

"Uh, yes. Are we taking the kids swimming?"

"Um, I don't know. Maybe. After lunch. Right now, we're going snorkeling to look for that . . . that . . . For her."

"Her?"

"Her!"

"Oh, yeah. Um, snorkeling?" Miranda had, of course, been snorkeling before, but not often and not recently. Still, she dutifully took possession of the gear Rain handed to Charlie to hand to her.

Rain removed one more item from the cabinet: her father's new underwater digital camera. His *expensive* new underwater digital camera. She decided against asking for permission. She already knew it was reserved for paying customers, but she figured the Kims weren't the diving type. Besides, Charlie and Miranda had seen *Her* too. If Rain could get some pictures—some tangible *proof* all this weird stuff was really happening—then she could tell her parents the truth. The whole truth. Thus she reasoned she was really doing her folks a favor. *If they knew, they'd want me to take the camera.*

Two minutes later, the three thirteen-year-olds were in the

water. Rain was in her element, scanning the blue for Her (in either form) or for . . . *a dolphin!* It was as if the bottle-nose had been waiting for Rain. It smiled, twirled and swam off leisurely. Rain waved her companions forward and set off in pursuit.

Charlie was right behind her, but Miranda was already having trouble getting the hang of the snorkel. She exhaled hard, successfully clearing it of water. But seconds later the tube flooded again, and she didn't have the breath left to clear it. She surfaced, cleared the snorkel again, caught her breath and realized she had lost track of her friends.

Charlie was swimming even with Rain when—always the gentleman—he glanced back to make sure Miranda was still with them. He spotted her, not far away, but facing the wrong direction and looking about. He tried to mark where Rain was headed and went back for Miranda.

Rain hadn't noticed the absence of her friends. She swam after the dolphin through a forest of kelp. Emerging on the other side, she had to pull up short to avoid swimming right into Her. The woman was floating not far beneath the surface. Tiny bubbles of air were expelled from her small, flat nose. Meanwhile, the cooperative pod was swimming in circles, modestly wrapping long strips of seaweed around her torso like she was a maypole. Rain treaded water, stunned.

Suddenly, she remembered the camera. She held it up for Her to see. The Manatee-Woman tilted her head to regard the object. Cautiously, she reached out a hand to touch the camera with long elegant fingers. This provided no additional information, so she simply offered Rain a questioning look. Rain figured that qualified as permission enough. She started taking pictures. Nonstop pictures. *Gotta love digital! Dad's old camera would already be out of film!* She just held the shutter down and let it click away. The digitally produced sound was artificial, but it carried through the water and made Her smile. Rain was getting some fantastic shots of the woman and of the dolphins around her.

Then suddenly she realized all these pictures really proved nothing at all. A semi-naked woman swimming with dolphins was certainly interesting but hardly qualified as mystic. Rain knew what she needed, looked around and found it. One of the dolphins had the manatee's skin in its mouth. Rain pointed at that dolphin and at the skin. The Manatee-Woman looked back over her shoulder, saw what Rain was indicating and beckoned the dolphin forward until it approached with the skin. Stroking the skin, she offered another questioning glance up at Rain, who was trying to remember not to hold her breath. She sucked in air through the snorkel and nodded.

So the woman carefully took the empty manatee skin and pulled its mouth open wide. She bent her knees up to her chest and slipped both feet into the mouth. Then she pulled the mana-tee skin up over her calves and knees and thighs and hips. Up and up she pulled the skin, and her lithe body somehow filled its potato-shaped bulk, until the mouth was like a bizarre turtleneck around her throat, and all that remained of Her was her hands and her head with its dark halo of swirling hair.

She smiled one last time at Rain—then pulled the top of the manatee head up and over her own. The hands disappeared within the skin. The mouth closed, simultaneously slurping up the last few strands of night black hair. Just like that, she wasn't human anymore. She was the manatee again.

And Rain had video of it all. Nonstop digital footage with time code and no edits whatsoever. The manatee approached Rain, nudging her gently with its bulbous, whiskered snout. Then it somersaulted in the water and swam away, surrounded by the dolphins. Rain didn't even bother following. She clutched the camera to her chest and waited until the pod and the manatee had disappeared into the blue distance. Only then did she look around for Charlie and Miranda. She didn't see them, so she surfaced.

There they were. Charlie said, "There you are. Did you find her?"

Rain spit the snorkel out of her mouth and grinned. "I found her! She transformed back into a manatee right in front of me, and I videotaped the whole thing here!" In triumph, Rain raised the camera high into the air—and a dolphin breached and snagged it right out of her hand!

CHAPTER NINETEEN

MERMAIDS

SATURDAY, SEPTEMBER 13

Now all four of them sat, depressed, at an umbrella-covered outdoor table at the Plaza del Oro Mall on San Próspero just after sundown.

Rain played it all back in her mind. The bottlenose dolphin snatching the camera away. Rain attempting pursuit, swimming with everything she had. The dolphin, holding the camera strap in its beak, taunting Rain by walking backward on its flukes along the water's surface, as if performing a stunt in a theme park show. And Rain having to give up when the dolphin, now an easy fifty yards away, disappeared under the blue water.

They had returned to the *Spirit of the Ghosts*. Her father hadn't noticed she wasn't returning with the camera, because he hadn't known she had taken it in the first place. Soon enough, though, he'd realize it was missing. *At which point*, she thought, *I'm doomed.*

Miranda wasn't feeling any cheerier. When the dolphin had grabbed the camera, Rain swam after. Charlie followed. Miranda couldn't keep up. She flooded her snorkel again and surfaced, choking and coughing. Charlie stopped to make sure she was okay. A second later, Rain surfaced, too, as the dolphin loudly snickered at them and danced away. Miranda knew she had been a liability on the adventure. A dead weight, if not the reason her friends hadn't gotten the camera back. She had tried to make up for it. When they returned to the boat, she had offered to take the kids swimming. But Michael instantly fled below deck with his shovel. John asked if they could swim with the Manatee-Woman. Mr. Kim didn't think that likely, so John went below to find another board game. Miranda volunteered to supervise. Wendy stayed on deck with her parents for a few minutes but ultimately joined her brothers and Miranda in the cabin. Rain and Charlie didn't come down. Rain had barely spoken since, unless you counted her bizarre monologue during the walk to the Plaza, recounting and lamenting everything that had happened from start to finish.

Charlie felt helpless. He knew Rain was in trouble, and he knew Miranda felt responsible. He had tried to reassure the latter and had even nudged Rain into mumbling confirmation, but he knew Miranda wasn't letting herself off the hook. As for Rain? She had lost the proof she had sought *and* her dad's camera. Charlie knew how much Rain hated to disappoint her father.

Finally, there was 'Bastian. He had appeared at sunset to find his granddaughter and her friends walking away from the docks with their heads hanging. Rain had been forced to explain the situation out loud in front of Miranda, who was unsurprisingly perplexed over Rain telling a story the three teens all knew and had experienced. Mostly, this dredged up 'Bastian's feeling of impotence. His Raindrop had been in trouble—again—and he hadn't been there. Couldn't be there. Even now, he felt just as useless.

Miranda's cell phone interrupted their pity party. She recognized her father's ringtone: a snippet of *El Amor Brujo* by the Spanish composer Manuel de Falla. Embarrassed, she pulled the phone out of the pocket of her shorts as she stood and walked away.

"Hi, Daddy."

"Miranda, where are you?"

"At the mall."

"Oh. Well. That's fine. But are you coming home? Ariel's on call to pick you up at the yacht club."

"It's not even eight o'clock yet. Can I just text her when I'm ready?"

Silence on his end.

"Did we have plans or something?"

"No. I have to work."

"Then . . ."

"Yes, I suppose it's all right. But not too late."

"No. Not too late. Bye, Daddy."

"Goodbye, *mija*."

They hung up. Miranda looked toward her friends at the table ten feet away. Then someone tapped her on the shoulder. She turned around.

"Hey, Sugar."

"Oh, hi, Renée."

Renée was dressed for work in the ugly orange and green striped polyester slacks and tunic that comprised the uniform of her fast-food employer, Koko's Caribbean Fries. She smiled coolly. "Did you have fun working the boat?"

"Um, sure." Miranda sounded less than convinced, which basically *made* Renée's evening.

"And the three of you are still hanging out?"

"Yeah . . ."

Renée leaned in. "Okay, but you know Charlie has a thing for Rain, right? You don't want to be a third wheel."

"No, I . . ." Miranda swallowed hard and glanced at the backs of Charlie and Rain, still moping at the table.

"Well, don't worry about it. I'm sure they don't mind you hanging around."

"Do you want to . . . join us?"

Renée looked down at her attire. "Not like this I don't. Besides, after a shift at K.C.F., I'm desperate for a shower. But you three have fun."

"Thanks."

Renée turned and walked away, not bothering to conceal her smile. Miranda watched her go, then turned back toward Rain and Charlie, regarding them with a nauseated expression. It wasn't so much her own small crush on Charlie. That wasn't anything too serious. But she didn't want to be a third wheel . . . Still, it didn't seem like either of them was in a romantic mood at the moment, but she'd have to watch Charlie for signs he wanted to be alone. She sighed and returned to the table.

Rain looked up and asked, "You have to go?"

Miranda was about to sit but froze halfway down. "No. But I can, if—"

Rain shook her head. "Stay. Share the misery."

"Thanks?" She sat.

Rain sighed. "Okay, so here's the deal. I need to replace my dad's camera with an exact duplicate." She pointed at the smartphone, still in Miranda's hand. "Can that thing find out what it costs?"

Thrilled to be of use, Miranda tapped her search engine app and said, "Sure. Do you remember what kind of camera?"

"Action SureFocus Waterproof Digital."

Miranda's thumbs went to work. Soon, she was holding out the screen to show Rain. "Is it one of these?"

"That one. The blue one."

They all leaned in to see. Even 'Bastian walked through the table to get a closer look.

"A hundred eighty-nine dollars?!" Rain moaned in stunned despair. "Okay, okay. I have thirty dollars in tips I haven't spent. And I think I still have some money left over from buying school supplies. But that was only like four and change."

She looked at Charlie, who shrugged. "I have exactly six dollars and twelve cents. But it's all yours."

Then she turned to Miranda, who felt awful but could only shake her head.

Incredulous and a little desperate, Rain said, "I'll pay you back. Eventually."

"It's not that. I just don't have any cash. I've got a credit card, but the bill goes to my dad. If I use it to withdraw that much money or even to buy the camera, he'll know. He'll ask."

Rain looked up at 'Bastian standing in the middle of the table.

"Sorry. You really can't take it with you."

Rain let her head crash into the tabletop, hard enough to make the other three wince. From that position, she muttered, "So we've got like forty dollars. I only need a hundred and fifty more."

"Plus tax and shipping," Miranda said, regretting it immediately when her qualification elicited a painful groan.

Maq couldn't take it anymore. He'd been Dumpster-diving in the vicinity and had scored perfectly edible quantities of Koko's Sweet Potato Fries. Now he strode up to the table and said, "Rain, I have your new magic number, and it's not one hundred eighty-nine."

She raised her head to look up at him—completely baffled. "What?"

"Your new magic number is one." Then Maq turned to Charlie and said, "Yours is six." Then he pointed at Miranda and said, "Three." Finally, he looked right at 'Bastian, but I immediately started barking loudly to cut him off. I didn't think it was time to let on we could see ghosts too. Evidently, he agreed—or else I simply distracted him enough that he forgot what he was about to say. Either way, he smiled and patted me on the head. Then he turned back to the kids. "Okay, the going rate for magic numbers is twenty-five cents per. So that's three of you . . ." He counted the teens just to be sure. "Yes. Three. So that's seventy-five cents."

Rain remained baffled. "What?"

"Seventy-five cents."

Rain looked from Maq to 'Bastian to Miranda to Charlie, looking for some confirmation that it was Maq who was crazy, not her.

But when she looked at Charlie, he sighed and said, "Fine." Then he pulled out his wallet and pulled out a dollar. "I don't have seventy-five cents."

Maq snatched the bill away. "That's all right. I'll owe you the quarter. Actually . . . come to think of it . . . *Hura-hupia* owes *me* a quarter. I officially transfer her debt to you. Good luck collecting." Then he turned on his heel and quickly walked away. He had already spotted his next target. Tourists Bernie and Maude Cohen, in matching Hawaiian shirts of fluorescent green and gold, were exiting K.C.F., each with a large order of Fries-N-Onions. They looked like two heart attacks in the making.

Maude saw Maq coming, grabbed her husband by the elbow and hustled him away. "Come on, Bernie. We have to get back to the hotel and pack." She had met Maq before and no longer found him charming. Maq chased after them, calling out, "It's good luck to share onions with a local! Anyone'll tell you that."

I stayed behind, crawling under a nearby table to watch Rain stare after him. I could tell she wasn't finding Maq so charming either right about now, but something else was nagging at her brain. Something Maq had said that she couldn't quite put her finger on. It fled away, so she turned and punched Charlie in the arm. "We needed that dollar!"

"Ow! Cut it out. I thought you wanted me to pay!"

"Why would you think that?"

"I dunno. You looked at me."

"And that look said pay the man for counting to three?"

"A dollar one way or another's not going to make any difference!"

That shut her up. She knew he was right. After a few beats, she exhaled loudly and said, "Okay, maybe we're going about this wrong. Instead of buying a new camera, let's get the old one back."

They all stared at her. Finally, 'Bastian said, "How?"

"The dolphins were working for Her. For the Manatee-Woman. We need to figure out what she was exactly. Once we know more about Her, we can figure out where she'll go. If she's there, the dolphins will be there. And if the dolphins are there, the camera will be there, too."

"Yeah, no," Charlie said.

"You could pilot Alonso's boat through the holes in that logic," 'Bastian added.

She pounded the table. "If you two have a better idea . . ."

Miranda was already doing another Web search. "No, it can't hurt to try. I'm searching *manatee*." She held up her phone and showed them a picture of a manatee. "Order Sirenia."

Charlie leaned in. "Like the Sirens in *The Odyssey*?" He and

Rain had read Homer's epic poem in seventh grade. (Well, Charlie had read it. Rain had only made it about halfway through—which might explain why he got an A- in English and she got a C+.)

"I don't know. But there's a myths and legends section here."

"What's it say?" 'Bastian asked. Rain repeated the question.

Miranda read silently to herself for a bit, then summarized. "There's a lot, actually. But it fits. In West African folklore, manatees were once thought to be human. Um, oh, wow. Okay, manatees are linked to mermaid folklore. They're thought to be the origin of all mermaid legends. Hold on, there's a mermaid link . . . Whoa, this is a long article."

"Search *mermaids* and *San Próspero*," Rain suggested. Then she caught sight of the Koko's sign out of the corner of her eye. "Or, no, that might be too specific. Search *mermaids* and *Caribbean*."

Miranda complied, skimmed and said, "Both Columbus and Blackbeard the Pirate reported seeing mermaids in the Caribbean."

Charlie looked at Rain and said, "Great. So all you need to do is find their ghosts and ask them *exactly* where those sightings were."

She didn't appreciate his sarcasm. "You make that sound so impossible."

He rolled his eyes at her, and she rolled hers right back. Despite the earlier gloom, they broke out laughing. 'Bastian took it as a good sign.

Miranda glanced up at her friends. *Maybe Renée's right. They are kind of perfect for each other. I should go. Or maybe . . . maybe I can even help.* She started to speak, to say something like *You guys both know you should be a couple, right?* But she chickened out, looked back down at her phone and clicked on another link. "I'm just surfing a bit now. When mermaids die, their bodies turn into seafoam. Chinese mermaids weep pearls for tears. Oh, and *this* is semi-interesting. There's a Scottish mermaid called . . . well, I don't know how it's pronounced, but it's spelled *c-e-a-s-g*. If it's captured, it grants three wishes."

"Wish number one, give me back my camera."

A new voice said, "What's wish number two?" They turned. (I turned too. It was like Grand Central Station around here. Not that I've ever been to Grand Central Station.) It was Marina Cortez, this time without a boy on her arm.

"Hey, Marina," Rain said with decidedly mixed feelings.

Charlie looked around apprehensively. "Are you meeting Hank here?"

"Yeah, but I'm way early."

Charlie relaxed slightly—though he glanced at his watch to make sure he was keeping track of the time. He wasn't sure he'd survive interrupting another of his older brother's dates. He saw Miranda looking uncomfortable and made introductions. "Oh, Miranda Guerrero, this is Marina Cortez. Marina, Miranda. Miranda, Marina."

'Bastian scowled. "That shouldn't get confusing at all."

Marina, uninvited but unashamed, took a seat across from Rain. It had been 'Bastian's seat, but he was still standing in the middle of the table. This made things rather awkward for both him and Rain. She had to look at Marina through 'Bastian's pale, transparent form, and he just felt trapped. Trapped enough to walk *through* Rain—causing her to shudder violently. He turned and stood behind her.

Marina noticed Rain's shudder and said, "Someone walk across your grave?"

"Something like that," Rain said, swallowing hard and shooting 'Bastian a dirty look.

"So what are you guys doing?" Marina asked.

The thirteen-year-olds exchanged glances. Then Miranda volunteered, "We're looking at mermaid legends." The truth seemed the most harmless course of action.

"That's so weird! I totally saw a mermaid once!" Marina said enthusiastically.

They stared at her.

"I know, I know. Everyone in my family thinks I'm crazy. But I was on the commuter ferry from Malas Almas, and I saw a woman swimming in the water, totally keeping up with the boat. And then she dived. And for a second, I saw her bottom half, and she didn't have legs. She had a tail."

"Like a fishtail," Charlie said slowly.

"No." Marina gestured with her hands. "It wasn't vertical like a fish. It was horizontal like a dolphin. But not like a dolphin." She focused past her hands and saw them looking at her with slack jaws. Instantly, she looked embarrassed. "And now you three think I'm crazy too."

While Charlie tried to assure her otherwise—without revealing what they had seen—Rain was trying to work it out. The Manatee-Woman was not a mermaid in the classic sense. She hadn't been human from the waist up and fish from the waist down. But if she had been in the process of putting on or taking off her manatee skin, then it could fit. *A horizontal tail like a dolphin, but not like a dolphin. Maybe like a manatee.* She said, "When was this?"

"Last June."

"And where exactly did you see Her?"

"I told you. On the commuter ferry."

"Yeah, but where was the ferry?"

"Um, let me think. I was heading here. I think we had just passed Tío Sam's. Yeah, I'm pretty sure that's right." She leaned to look over Miranda's shoulder. "What else does it say?"

Miranda was still staring at her, and it took a couple of seconds to focus again and look down at her phone. She read, "Um, it says, 'Mermaids and selkies are perhaps both born of the lost souls of the drowned.'"

"What's a selkie?" Charlie asked.

"I don't know," Miranda said, clicking on the selkie link. "Okay, selkies are mythological creatures in Scottish and Irish legend. They live as seals in the sea but humans on land." She gasped quietly and looked up at Rain. "They shed their seal skins to become human."

"Keep reading," Rain said breathlessly.

"Um . . . 'Selkies are usually depicted as beautiful women. A selkie can only become human for a short time unless another human—usually a man—steals and hides her seal skin. In that case, the selkie falls under the human's sway and often falls in love with her captor. Many fishermen sought out selkies, because they were thought to make true and loyal wives, who gave birth to children with an affinity for the sea. A selkie might remain with her human family for generations, but if a selkie wife found her stolen skin, she would use it to return to the sea, even if it meant abandoning her human children.'"

Miranda paused for a moment. Long enough to make Rain recall the portrait in Pablo Guerrero's study. She glanced at Charlie to see if the same thought had occurred to him, but he was staring at his father's watch. Maybe he was worried Hank was about to show up. Or maybe he was thinking of something—and someone—else.

Miranda cleared her throat and continued. "'There's the story of a selkie that donned her skin to save her human husband when he was lost at sea, even though it meant she could never return to her land family. She would, once a year, appear to her human children as a seal and play with them in the waves. But she'd always have to leave them behind, and she couldn't return at all if her beloved husband was near.'"

"That's kinda tragic," Marina said quietly.

"There's another legend here too," Miranda said. She looked up. "Some selkies lure humans into the water—like Sirens—and neither selkie nor human is ever seen again."

CHAPTER TWENTY

AYCAYIA THE CURSED

The ghost of Cash, a.k.a. the spirit of Milo Long, a.k.a. the phantom of the Pale Tourist (a.k.a. the individual Rain had been longing to talk to), was wandering around the Plaza del Oro Mall, looking for a girl. Or rather, *the* girl he had heard *Hura-hupia* mention as a possible target for the *Hupia*. He wanted to warn this mystery girl, if such a thing were possible. True, he wasn't usually the kind of guy to go out of his way for a fellow human being, but being dead now, he figured he could use the karma points. Besides, that mosquito-swarm-*Hupia*-thing had killed him. *Who knows? Maybe this girl could help even the score.*

But where to find her? Having ridden the Sycorax Ferry across the bay, he thought checking out the mall might be a good bet. That was as far as his thinking had taken him. He had no idea what this girl looked like, and only a single name: Cacique. Still lying under my table, my lower jaw flush with the paved stone floor, I watched Cash wander in and out of shops and stores and Koko's. He had no more luck finding a girl who could commune with ghosts than he previously had finding a spiritual light to walk into.

To be fair, it probably didn't help that Rain was no longer at the mall and had—for the time being—forgotten about him.

She and 'Bastian were walking home. The night had turned sticky, and Rain felt a palpable need for a shower to wash away the saltwater film from her frustrating swim and the sweat accompanying her depressing camera dilemma. All thoughts of proving manatee-Her existed, speaking to recently deceased ghosts, investigating mysterious swarms or finding all-important *zemis* had been pushed from her mind. She needed the camera or the money to buy a new one. Neither seemed within her reach.

Grandfather and granddaughter trod down Goodfellow Lane. Moonrise was still an hour or so away, but the streetlamps illuminated the cobblestones—and lured in mosquitoes. Rain said, "Maybe Miranda could get Ariel to take us past Tío Samuel to look for Her or the dolphins."

'Bastian sighed. "It's a big ocean."

"Yeah." Rain's shoulders sank dramatically. "I don't suppose Mom would give me a year's allowance in advance without asking why?"

"Have you met your mother?"

"Yeah." Her shoulders sank a little more. 'Bastian thought they'd be dragging on the cobblestones any minute. They paused outside the Nitaino, with Rain more than a little reluctant to enter.

Inside, Mr. and Mrs. Kim were at the front desk, telling Iris they were hoping for a little *quality* time tomorrow. That is, a little quality time *alone*. That is, alone *together*. That is, together *without* their kids. They were wondering if Mrs. Cacique could contact that nice Miranda and ask if she'd be willing to babysit.

This put Mrs. Cacique in an awkward position, as no one—not her husband and certainly not her daughter—had mentioned anyone named Miranda. Ever. "I'm . . . not sure Miranda's available tomorrow," she said.

"Well, what about Rain?" Esther Kim asked.

"I'm afraid Rain doesn't—"

"I'm in!" Rain spoke before the door to the Inn had shut. "Happy to do it."

Fred Kim said, "You can handle all three of them? For the whole day?"

"Definitely."

He turned to Rain's mother, looking for some confirmation. Iris tried to suppress her surprise and answered the unspoken question honestly (or honestly enough). "Rain's very responsible."

Fred still seemed dubious, but Esther was quite pleased. "Great. Say, nine A.M. tomorrow?"

Rain looked at her mother, who said, "That should be fine. The Bernstein-Shores will be on an excursion to La Géante, and Ms. Vendaval doesn't usually take breakfast."

Rain said, "Then I'm all yours. Or all theirs, anyway."

Esther said thank you and ushered her husband upstairs before anyone involved could change his or her mind.

Iris eyed her daughter suspiciously. "I thought you swore you'd never babysit tourist kids again."

"I . . . deny . . . ever taking such a vow. Besides, these are great kids. They're so easy."

"We are talking about the Kim kids, right?"

All these white lies were making 'Bastian's eyebrow itch. He scratched at it with his pinky while spending a few seconds contemplating the postcard rack and the question of what would actually make a ghost itch.

Rain, meanwhile, was on a roll. "We had a blast with them today."

"A blast? With the Kims? You, your father, Charlie . . . and *Miranda?*"

"Exactly." Rain kissed Iris on the cheek, said good night and headed toward the kitchen, dragging 'Bastian along behind the armband and leaving her mother exasperated.

In contrast, Rain was feeling worlds better. If she played it smart, she could earn enough money in one day to buy that replacement camera for her dad. Of course, babysitting would be a royal pain, but maybe she wouldn't have to suffer it alone . . .

In the kitchen, she phoned Charlie. Always eager to be her hero, he agreed to help. She hung up to call Miranda, then realized she didn't have Miranda's number. She called Charlie back. He had Miranda's cell phone number. Rain jotted it down on the whiteboard on the fridge. She called Miranda, who was unsurprisingly enthusiastic. Feeling more than a little proud of herself, she went up the back stairs to shower and get ready for bed.

Soon enough, with 'Bastian out on his nightly walk, Rain shut off her lamp and settled into her pillow. It had been a long day, tiring in more ways than one. She was soon asleep . . . and dreaming . . .

In the First Days, the First Chief of the Taíno consulted with First Shaman. "The First Men fight amongst themselves," First Chief said. "What is the cause?"

First Shaman was old and wise and knew the cause. "It is Aycayia," he said.

Aycayia was the most beautiful woman in the cacicazgo. *Every man desired her. And not simply the strong, young warriors. The little boys desired her. Old men desired her. Husbands desired her. Even women desired beautiful Aycayia. First Chief said, "Show me this Aycayia."*

So Shaman brought First Chief to view Aycayia from afar. They approached the bohío where she lived with her six sisters. When the sun rose, First Sister emerged from the bohío. And she was beautiful, and First Chief said, "So this is Aycayia. I see now why the men fight over her."

But First Shaman said, "That is not Aycayia. That is but her eldest sister. Wait."

And Second Sister emerged from the bohío. And First Chief said, "Ah, yes. This is Aycayia. She is even more beautiful than her sister."

But First Shaman shook his head. "That is not Aycayia. That is another sister. Wait."

And so it went, as Third Sister and Fourth Sister and Fifth Sister and Sixth Sister emerged one by one from the bohío. And each was more beautiful than the last. But none was Aycayia.

Finally, Aycayia herself emerged. She pretended not to see First Chief and First Shaman, allowing them to watch her bathe.

The moment he saw Her, First Chief was enthralled. And even old Shaman was not immune to the curve of her hip, the fullness of her breast, to her raven-dark hair and the light in her eyes.

And when she began to sing, her voice was so beautiful that First Chief said, "This Aycayia must be mine. I will kill any man who seeks to take Her from me. And I will make Her my queen!"

And First Shaman turned upon him. "No! I will call on First God, and he will strike you down and give Aycayia to me."

And thus Chief and Shaman, the First Friends of the Taíno, were ready to slay each other over Aycayia.

Thankfully, the old crone Guanayoa appeared. She said, "First Chief, this Aycayia is no woman for you. She is First Witch. She robs you of your will to rule wisely."

And further Guanayoa spoke, "And Shaman, do not call on First God, for Aycayia's magicks are so powerful that no less than

First God would love Her. And using His power, she would bring an end to all the First Days."

Guanayoa's words did not break Aycayia's spell, but the men's heat abated. And Guanayoa was able to lead Chief and Shaman away from Aycayia's bohio. With time and distance from her spell, First Chief and First Shaman regained themselves and were First Friends again.

"What must be done?" First Chief asked. "If she remains here, every man will kill every other man."

"That is Aycayia's desire," Guanayoa said. "She seeks to destroy you all."

"Aycayia must be banished from the cacicazgo," First Shaman said. "Else this First Witch will triumph."

So it was agreed that Guanayoa would take Aycayia far away.

Fourteen Warriors were placed in seven canoes. They were blindfolded, so they could not look upon Aycayia. And their nostrils were plugged with rubber gum, so they could not revel in her scent. Aycayia was led to the First Canoe. She was bound so she could touch no one. And she was gagged so her voice could not enthrall. For Aycayia's magicks were so powerful, all the senses must be thwarted.

Aycayia's Six Sisters sat in the six other canoes. Guanayoa sat beside Aycayia and guided the blind warriors far away to Punta Majagua. There, Aycayia, her Sisters and Guanayoa were abandoned. The Fourteen Warriors were instructed to row toward the heat of the setting sun with their blindfolds in place. Only when night had fallen could they remove them and find their way home.

Guanayoa, Aycayia and her Sisters built a new bohio. And for a time there was peace, as Aycayia was forced to care for old Guanayoa.

But Aycayia would not be thwarted. She worked her magicks, singing to the First Men of the Taíno from afar. And each of the

Fourteen Warriors answered her song. They sat in their canoes and put blindfolds on again. And they remembered their First Journey and crossed through the darkness in the same manner.

The Fourteen Warriors found the bohio of Aycayia on Punta Majagua. They found Aycayia bathing with her Sisters. She smiled at the Fourteen Warriors and sang them a song that taught them that only the strongest might have Her. Thus enthralled, each Warrior did battle against friend and brother. And by nightfall, all Fourteen lay dead on Punta Majagua.

Guanayoa, the old crone, was one of only ten witnesses to the crime. She cursed Aycayia. "There is no land safe from your magicks, First Witch! But I have magicks too! First Magicks! And if no land is safe from you, then you will never be safe on land."

Frightened, Aycayia and her Sisters fled to First Ocean, hoping to escape Guanayoa's wrath. They stumbled through the water, trying to reach the canoes of the Fourteen Warriors. But Guanayoa's curse reached them first. The Six Sisters were transformed into dolphins. And the First Witch Aycayia was transformed into a hideous manatee.

But the magicks of Aycayia the Cursed are still strong. And it is said, she can still become beautiful to lure men into the water with her song, never to be seen again . . .

CHAPTER TWENTY-ONE

ORDER SIRENIA

SUNDAY, SEPTEMBER 14

Primed and ready, Rain staked out the lobby and intercepted the elder Kims, who sent their kids ahead into the dining room. Mrs. Kim, with only the slightest edge of desperation in her voice, said, "Is everything okay? Are we still on?"

"Of course. I just want to make sure we're clear on . . . things."

Taking the hint, Mr. Kim asked the going rate for a day's baby-sitting on the island.

Rain pretended to consider this on the spot—though, in fact, she had thought about little else since arranging the gig the night before. "Hmm. Three kids for about eight hours? I'd say a hundred and forty dollars'll cover it."

He balked. "A hundred and forty?"

"Plus, I'll need expense money to pay for their lunch and dinner."

Mrs. Kim said, "We'll be back in time to take them to dinner tonight."

"Oh, well, then I'll only need twenty for lunch. But I need that in advance."

Mr. Kim stared at his wife. She stared right back, giving him a clearly legible *do not mess this up* look. He agreed to Rain's terms.

Rain smiled, quite pleased with herself and more than a little relieved. The going rate on San Próspero for three tourist kids was twelve dollars an hour. At eight hours, that meant ninety-six dollars, but Rain had correctly estimated the Kims would go for the one-forty. If Rain also cheaped out on lunch, she could toss in most of the extra twenty. Add in the forty she already had, and just like that, the camera was paid for. Or it would be. *All I have to do is get through this one day, and all my problems are solved.*

(Of course, it seemed to me Rain had a host of problems neither money nor a camera could possibly solve. The way humans prioritize has always confounded my sensibilities.)

Just to make conversation—and to move Mr. Kim's mind off the unexpected cost—Rain asked Mrs. Kim how she and her husband were planning to spend their day.

"We're going to a place called Smuggler's Cove," Mrs. Kim said. "It sounds very mysterious and romantic."

"It's very a lot of things," Rain said. She felt a little guilty for not warning them away from the biggest tourist trap on the Ghosts, but she couldn't risk them canceling altogether. *And who knows? They might like it. Someone must. Or else tourists wouldn't go there, right?*

The Kims entered the dining room to join their children at breakfast. Rain followed. Though Wendy, John and Michael had only been alone for a few minutes, their table was already a disaster area. Michael had spilled his milk, and some of it had splashed into Wendy's lap, causing her to throw a fit of the hissy variety. John thought it all quite funny, until Wendy picked up his cereal bowl and turned it over in his lap right in front of their parents and Rain.

This action was, perhaps, extreme, even for a Kim kid, and it was followed by a moment of stunned silence. Even Wendy looked a little shocked over what she had done. Then, inevitably, John erupted. Strangely, his tantrum seemed to be more about the ruination of his Lucky Charms than the dampness of his lower half, but that made him no less voluble. The adult Kims hustled their trio of demon children upstairs to change them into fresh clothes, leaving Rain behind to sponge up the mess and wonder what she had gotten herself into.

Minutes later, Kims and Kimlets were back downstairs. Fred Kim handed Rain a twenty-dollar bill to cover lunch, wished her luck, and got the hell out of Dodge with his wife.

Wendy, John and Michael stared up at Rain. John said, "She's not the one you said."

Wendy crossed her arms huffily. "I know. I like the other one better."

Rain offered, "Miranda and Charlie will meet us at the beach. They're probably there now."

Michael said, "I don't like the beach."

Wendy whispered loudly, "He's afraid of the water."

"I am not!"

"Well," Rain said, "I promise you we'll have a great time." She didn't actually believe this, but it seemed like a worthwhile lie to smooth things over.

John asked, "Will the womanatee be there?"

"Anything's possible on the Ghosts," Rain said, not really be-lieving that either. (Though she should've.)

John shrugged. He was in. Wendy and Michael were also en-
ticed. For the moment, Rain had peace.

Said peace was brief—lasting only until the kids realized they
were *walking* to the beach and at last found a theme they could
unify around: heel dragging.

Charlie, standing in the Próspero Beach parking lot with
Miranda, was stunned to see Rain emerge from the Big Blue Beach
Bus, dragging the three Kims and a large canvas beach bag. "You
took the bus?" he asked incredulously.

"I *paid* to take the bus," she growled. "Four dollars down the
drain. I better get free shipping on that camera."

"What camera?" Wendy asked with a suspicious squint to her
eye.

"Never mind," Rain said quickly.

"I want a camera," John said.

"If John's getting a camera, I want one too!" Michael screeched.

Rain's head dropped. Charlie turned to Miranda and said,
"It's gonna be a loonnng day."

No kidding.

Michael was, indeed, afraid of the water, and as much as he
loved that yellow plastic shovel, he had a real knack for dropping
it, burying it, throwing it, etc. It was practically a full-time job for
Rain just playing fetch, and I don't believe she enjoyed it quite as
much as I would have.

John complained about the sand. He said it was too scratchy.
Plus it tasted bad, got in his eyes, under his shirt, in his hair,
swimming trunks, etc. Charlie was awarded the thankless task of
trying to keep the boy sand-free on a beach.

A couple of college-aged girls were lying on their stomachs,
soaking up the sun and listening to indie pop at a volume loud
enough to bleed from their earphones. Wendy laid out her towel

in emulation. Within minutes, Miranda could see that the girl was frying. "Wendy, didn't you put on sunscreen this morning?"

Wendy didn't answer. (The college girls weren't talking either.) So Miranda slathered sunscreen on Wendy's back and legs. Then the college girls turned over. So Wendy turned over, and Miranda slathered her front. Then the college girls went in the water. Wendy followed with Miranda as her shadow. Then the college girls came out of the water. Wendy came out of the water, and Miranda tried to get her to reapply the gunk. Then the college girls *left the beach*, and that was it. Wendy declared it was time to go, and Miranda was at a loss how to change her mind.

It was Charlie to the rescue again. He spotted Ramon Hernandez and Linda Wheeler playing tetherball at the top of the beach. Linda wasn't in college, but she was a "big girl," and Charlie managed to convince Wendy and John to observe the older teens at play. Rain and Michael joined them, too, and soon all six of them were sitting cross-legged on the sand, watching the white orb swing through the air on its long tether, round and round the pole. Even with Ramon basically ruining any chance he might have with Linda by slaughtering her mercilessly, taunting her lack of skill to boot, there was an elegance to the circular motion that enthralled the Kim children and even their chaperones. When Linda stomped away—with a belatedly sorry Ramon trailing after—it wasn't hard to convince the kids to take up the game. In fact, it looked as if a little tether-tournament might fill the rest of the day.

John certainly enjoyed the planning stages. He used a piece of chalk and the pavement to diagram a bracket displaying who would play against whom and in what order. This required some negotiation, but it remained remarkably civil once everyone conceded Wendy could go first against Charlie (this combination being the closest she could come to copying the Linda-Ramon dynamic). But the planning wound up being the *fun* part, and once they started playing, it was all downhill from there.

Start with Wendy getting rope burn. Move on to John hitting it so high that a crying Michael could never even touch the ball. Mix in Rain attempting to intervene and taking a tetherball right to the nose. End with John stubbing his toe on the metal pole. Sixteen minutes into the tournament, all three Kimlets were either crying or trying very, very hard not to, and it was only 11:00 A.M.

Rain spent six more dollars of Mr. Kim's money buying the children ice cream—just to bring a stop to their tears. Half the twenty gone now, and she hadn't even paid for lunch. So when Michael dropped his ice cream in the sand and demanded another, it was all Rain could do not to cry along with him—especially when buying him a new cone.

John thought he deserved another cone too, and threatened to drop what remained of his in the sand to force the issue—at least until Rain made it perfectly clear that such a course of action would result in *less* vanilla-chocolate swirl, not more. He ate the rest of his confection in brooding silence.

Five minutes later, with the ice cream consumed, Miranda used the sated lull in the hostilities to suggest they all build a sand castle. Charlie upped the ante to "a huge sand fortress!" As this gave Michael an excuse to use his shovel, he agreed to dig in. As did John, who, despite hating the sand, enjoyed planning things. Wendy said she would only participate if Miranda did too. So the six of them went to work.

As locals, Rain and Charlie had chosen a section of Próspero Beach known as the Alcove, because it was semi-hidden from the main strip by an outcropping of rocks. Outside of High Season—when every inch of Ghost sand was packed—the Alcove tended toward the deserted. At this moment, there were only a few people around: a lifeguard in his squat white wooden tower; a couple of twenty-year-old Italian surfers, sitting in their wetsuits in front of their boards; two tenth graders, Connor Kelty and Conner Ellison; and Wendy, John, Michael, Miranda, Charlie and Rain.

The sun was pulling into position directly overhead in a cloudless sky, and the temperature was climbing. Everyone was thirsty. The ice cream truck left the parking lot to find a more profitable location, and John watched it drive away and muttered, "I'm still hungry." On cue, Charlie's stomach growled loudly, which at least made the boys—and even Wendy—laugh.

Rain said miserably, "I better get everyone lunch." She pulled the remaining eight dollars from her pocket, knowing there was no way she could feed six people on that amount of money this close to the ocean. (Prices dropped precipitously as one moved inland, but by the beach, a bag of chips could easily cost $5.95.) *What was I thinking, only asking for twenty?*

Miranda put her hand on Rain's and said, "I can get this." Rain looked up at her. "I can use my credit card to buy food. My dad won't think twice about that, and you won't have to spend your camera money. At least I'll be contributing a little."

Spontaneously, a grateful Rain threw her arms around Miranda. "You think you're not contributing? I could never have managed this without you and Charlie." She pulled back from Miranda but still held onto her arms. "I take him for granted; it's kinda our thing. But I'm *really* grateful you're here."

Rain was emotional due to lost-camera stress, but it was Miranda who pulled an arm away to wipe at her eyes. She said, "Don't get me started. I cry like at everything." Both girls laughed.

Charlie saw all this, smiled and continued to dig the moat per John's instructions.

Miranda took off to buy lunch. Wendy, temporarily engrossed in her own princess tower, didn't immediately notice the departure. Once she did, it was all Rain could do to prevent the eight-year-old from taking off after Miranda, who was by that time out of sight. Wendy stayed, begrudgingly, but clearly resented being stuck there without the older girl. Rain scowled—*I'm a girl too!*—but she was already too exhausted and overheated to maintain her own resentment.

She desperately wanted to go in the water to cool off but knew she couldn't leave Charlie alone with the Kimlets. She stared out at the ocean wistfully.

That's when she saw the dolphin. Right there. Just offshore. Its long head poking up out of the water. Smiling. The Italians noticed it too, pointing and laughing.

Rain stood, fascinated. She'd never seen a dolphin this close to a public beach . . . this close to any beach. *Could it be?* The dolphin dove down out of sight—and then popped back up with the camera strap in its mouth. Rain started running toward the water. (Charlie and their charges were now forgotten.) The dolphin swam backward quickly, rising up on its tail to dance away as before and swinging Alonso's camera around its head like a tetherball. Rain dove into the water and swam.

Charlie stood. He had to fight the impulse to ditch the Kimlets and follow. Then Michael said, "Look." And then . . .

Rain swam furiously, for all she was worth. The dolphin dove down with the camera and waited under the water for Rain to follow beneath the surface and pull close. Very close. Rain was almost within reach of the floating camera. *Almost there . . . Almost . . .* At the last second, the dolphin took off like a shot. Rain followed until the beast was again out of sight. She became aware of a strange sound, something almost musical, singing perhaps, muffled by the seawater. Curious, and, in any case, needing air, she surfaced. And then . . .

Miranda approached with a shopping bag of deli sandwiches, chips and cookies in one hand and a six-pack of bottled water in the other. She turned into the Alcove and stopped short. The Manatee-Woman, torso discreetly wrapped in seaweed, stood on the shoreline, her human feet washed by little waves. Her mouth was open and her head bobbed slightly, but no sound came out—at least no sound Miranda could hear. Yet somehow this soundless cry evoked pain and longing in Miranda. Then this strange and beautiful creature crouched gracefully and beckoned with one hand. Miranda turned: the three Kimlets, smiling goofily, walked slowly toward Her. Charlie stood near the sand fortress, doing nothing, his jaw slack. Miranda looked around for Rain but didn't see her. She did see the two Italian boys, the two local boys and the adult male lifeguard, all staring at Her, all motionless. The Kimlets had nearly reached the Manatee-Woman, her arms opening wide to accept them. Finally, Miranda snapped into action, dropping food and water and racing down the beach. She leaped between the Kimlets and the Siren, wrapping her arms protectively around all three children. They struggled slightly. Anger flared in the Manatee-Woman's eyes. Her mouth snapped shut.

Miranda was terrified, but she squeaked out, "No." Then, shouted, *"NO!"* The Manatee-Woman advanced two steps.

Behind her, Charlie felt like he was coming out of a daze. He shook his head. Rubbed his eyes. Tried to focus. He had a vague memory of the most beautiful song he had ever heard and, more than anything, longed to hear again. Longed to hear Her again.

Rain emerged from the surf, calling out, "Miranda!"

"She's trying to take the kids!"

First Witch! Rain thought. *Aycayia the Cursed!* Rain ran toward them, shouting Aycayia's name. Aycayia's head whipped around; her dark eyes flashed, glaring at Rain. She took one last longing glance at the Kimlets, still gathered together in Miranda's protective arms, and then turned to dive into the water. By the time Rain reached Miranda and the kids, Aycayia had disappeared beneath the waves.

CHAPTER TWENTY-TWO

EXTRA CREDIT

S muggler's Cove was a nightmare. Like spending an entire day trapped on the Pirates of the Caribbean ride—*without* any of the drama, humor or animatronics."

Rain nodded as she poured more tomato juice into Mr. Kim's glass.

Concerned her husband might have insulted a piece of Rain's cultural heritage, Ms. Kim said, "It wasn't that bad. Just not what we were hoping for."

"And what a rip-off! I spent all my cash buying tickets and lunch. I know I owe you for yesterday, but I need to hit an A.T.M."

"You mentioned that last night," Rain said with surprisingly little attitude. On the one hand, she still needed that money for the camera. On the other, she couldn't shake the nagging feeling she was personally responsible for exposing the Kimlets to

Aycayia the Cursed, the murderous First Witch of the Taíno. It made money-grubbing now seem particularly distasteful.

Rain glanced at Wendy, John and Michael. All three glared at her, still angry she had chased away the beautiful Manatee-Woman. They had barely touched their breakfasts. Even John's bowl of Lucky Charms had gone unmolested. Rain held up the orange juice pitcher in her other hand. "O.J., anybody?" As one, the Kimlets—in full huff—turned their backs on her.

Esther Kim observed this and shook her head. "I'm sorry they're being this way. It sounds like you did a great job yesterday."

"Did—did they tell you why they're mad at me?"

"Yes." Esther didn't even try to suppress a smile. "You and Miranda wouldn't let them swim away with the mermaid."

"Womanatee!" John called out over his shoulder, unwilling to face either Rain or his parents.

"What did happen?" Esther asked.

"Nothing really," Rain said. "There was this woman on the beach. I guess she was singing, and she was about to go into the water. And the kids tried to follow her. And we stopped them—because Miranda had just brought our lunch."

Wendy turned back around, looking betrayed. She tried to form words, to articulate how Rain was *lying with the truth,* but it was a practice beyond Wendy's previous experience—and she couldn't work out how to explain it. So she snapped her mouth shut and glared.

Rain swallowed hard and looked away. *Another thing to feel guilty about. I'm shattering their innocence.* She didn't want to overdramatize the situation, but still there was a fog of unease left over from the day before. She tried to sound casual as she said, "So . . . what do you guys have planned for today?"

"Nothing too ambitious. I think we're just going to the mall," Mrs. Kim said.

"To spend *more* money," Fred Kim groused before stuffing a good third of a cheese omelet into his mouth.

Rain was relieved. *As long as they're staying away from the ocean.* She wished them luck, poured orange juice unbidden into all the Kimlets' glasses and returned to the kitchen.

Iris was taking inventory. "We're low on bacon and sausage. Oh, and Lucky Charms. That kid eats a lot of Lucky Charms."

Not today, Rain thought as she put down the two half-empty pitchers of juice.

"I'll phone in the order to Rusty," her mother said. "On your way home from school, stop by and pick it up, okay?"

"Sure, Mom."

Mrs. Cacique's eyebrows rose slightly. She wasn't used to her daughter acquiescing to additional chores without complaint. "Thank you," she said.

Rain smiled at her mother, then grabbed her backpack off its hook. She took a step toward the back door but paused and gave Iris a kiss on the cheek first.

A speechless Iris Cacique watched her daughter depart for school.

Mrs. Beachum was lecturing about something, but all Rain could think about was the Taíno. This ancient people—*her people,* at least in part—were connected to everything: the *zemi,* the mosquitoes, the dolphins, Aycayia—probably even a corpse. She didn't know what the connections were, but it was clear the key to unlocking the truth was with these original inhabitants of the Ghosts. She started doodling on a blank sheet of paper in her notebook. Crude drawings of dolphins, manatees and bugs. Crude drawings of the *zemis* in Pablo Guerrero's office. She started writing down questions. Finally, in big block letters, she wrote WHAT DID THE TAÍNO WANT? across the bottom half of the page.

She glanced at Charlie, who was focused forward. She ripped the question out of the notebook, and the sound of the tearing paper got Charlie's attention. He watched her fold it up small and reach across to hand it to him.

Mrs. Beachum said, "Passing notes in class? Seriously, Rain, this isn't third grade."

Charlie and Rain had that deer-in-the-headlights stare. They said nothing.

"All right, Charlie, bring it up here," Mrs. Beachum commanded.

Charlie looked to Rain. He didn't know what she had written, how incriminating or how insane it might read. For a second, he seriously considered swallowing the wad of paper to save his friend. Then Rain surrendered with a shrug. Charlie nodded, stood and shuffled to the front of the room.

Mrs. Beachum took the paper and began unfolding it. "I assume this was important enough that the entire class should hear it."

Rain actually smirked. Mrs. B wanted to embarrass her, but . . .

With mild but growing surprise in her voice, the teacher read the note aloud. "What did the Taíno want?" Then she paused. It was taking her a moment to compute this. She looked up at Rain. "You read ahead in the textbook?"

Now Rain was surprised. *We're studying the Taíno in class?!* She said cautiously, "I'm . . . interested . . . in local history."

Mrs. B said, "I . . . I've never seen you take an interest in history before." She had to stop herself from saying, *I've never seen you take an interest in* anything *before.*

Rain shrugged again.

Mrs. Beachum considered her next move for a moment or two. Then she picked up a marker from the chalk tray. "All right, here's your punishment. I'm giving you an extra credit assignment due Friday morning. An oral report."

Rain's eyes went wide. "Can't I just have detention or something?"

"No. Now, I want you to source this. Don't just search the Internet. Anyone can put anything up there. Doesn't mean it's true." She pulled the cap off the marker and waited.

Finally, Rain said, "What am I searching for?"

"I want you to define for the class the Taíno word *cacique*." She wrote *CACIQUE* up on the whiteboard, but she pronounced it *kah-see-KAY*, Spanish fashion, with three syllables. (Rain and her family always pronounced it in the French style, as the two-syllable *kah-SEEK*.)

Rain was stunned. Mrs. Beachum, turning back from the whiteboard to face her, smiled a Cheshire grin. "So you didn't know your name meant something in the language of the Taíno?"

Rain shook her head.

"Quite a coincidence, then." It was Claire Beachum's turn to shrug. "Small island."

CHAPTER TWENTY-THREE

BAD TASTE

Distracted as she was, Rain had every intention of picking up the bacon, sausage and Lucky Charms for her mother. During eighth period, while Charlie and Miranda were rehearsing with Madame Conduttore, Rain was walking up to the automatic sliding doors of Rusty's Wholesale Market when *he* exited. They stood there, glaring with equal measures of undisguised contempt and barely contained fury: Rain Cacique and Callahan.

His first impulse was simply to wring her neck. But the parking lot was half full, and though his massive form practically filled the doorway, impatient shoppers exited and entered the store by slithering to either side of him. No, Rusty's was too open and too public for him to murder a meddling kid in broad daylight. Instead, he smirked down at the little twerp and, shopping bag tucked under his thick arm, stepped around her and walked away, going about his business and at least taking some satisfaction in knowing there was absolutely nothing she could do to stop him.

Rain watched him stride away, clomping off in his heavy boots. Perhaps the most frustrating thing about Callahan was not the fact that he had stolen her *zemi* or even that he had tried to kill her—since he had ultimately failed at both crimes. What bothered her the most was that somehow this big jerk had known the significance of her *zemi* before either she or 'Bastian had figured it out. *And I'll bet he still knows more than I do!*

So she followed him to find out what else he might know. It was easy. He took an obvious route back to the harbor, and, being as familiar with the geography as she was, she knew exactly where and when to move and where and when to hide. She maintained a more than discreet distance but was never in danger of losing him; his height and his spiky, blond head made it easy to keep track of him from afar.

Of course, Callahan wouldn't be worth his exorbitant rates if he couldn't spot a tail in broad daylight, let alone a thirteen-year-old's tail. He knew she was there the whole time, and he didn't care. In fact, he reveled in her wasted effort. He climbed aboard the *Bootstrap*, sporting a big old grin, and rapidly prepared to launch.

When he was ready, he turned to face her. He knew she had ducked down behind the RULES OF THE HARBOR sign, and he waited patiently, or patiently enough. When her head popped up, she found him looking straight at her. "I'm hunting *zemis*," he said. "Wanna come along?" He thought she would run and was unpleasantly surprised when she hesitated, as if actually considering his offer.

Finally, she shook her head. "No thanks," she said. "I'll find them myself first."

His face crushed inward on itself into a dark, murky scowl. His upper lip twitched. He shouldn't have mentioned the *zemis*. *What is it about this tiny sheila?* She got under his skin so easy; he was constantly slipping up around her. Again he thought of snuffing out her life, fantasized about dumping her body out at sea, permanently removing the bad taste she left in his mouth. Unfortunately, there was an old bum in a straw hat going through a garbage bin not ten meters away. He thought of killing the bum too, but the bum had a dog, and the dog might cause a ruckus. Plus, Callahan didn't like killing dogs if he didn't have to. (Oh, yes, I was *so* touched by the sentiment.)

Callahan growled and turned his back on Rain. He brought in the lines and turned on the engine. Rain watched the *Bootstrap* leave the harbor, taking note of its general heading toward Chapel Ceiling. This surprised her. For some reason, she'd thought he'd be heading directly across the harbor to Sycorax and the bat cave. Unconsciously, she scratched at her few remaining mosquito bites.

"Mosquito Boy's had a taste of you now."

Rain turned to look at Maq, who had folded his entire upper body into the garbage bin. His voice echoed from within the metal container. "No one can eat just one."

"Excuse me?" Rain asked.

"No one can eat just one." Maq sprang up, holding a half-eaten bag of Lay's Classic Potato Chips. He reached into the bag, pulled out a chip, blew a fly off it, and popped it into his mouth.

I was jealous, but Rain made her icky-face. "Hi, Maq," she said, and then, "Gotta go." She took off at a fast pace up the dock.

I wondered if it was really just her nausea that distracted her from questioning my companion or if he was somehow *casting* to prevent her from focusing on his obvious connection to her quest. Either way, Maq only seemed interested in warning her *uncon-*

scious mind. And unconscious or not, I felt he might have done some good dropping a helpful hint about Aycayia as well. Clearly he didn't agree, and hints—helpful or otherwise—aren't my department.

We watched her go. "I wonder where she's off to," he said through a mouthful of chips. But I bet he knew. Her determination was as loud as any hound baying at the moon. She was headed to Island Hospital to visit Isaac Naborías.

CHAPTER TWENTY-FOUR

THE EVIL LEGEND
OF MOSQUITO BOY

MONDAY, SEPTEMBER 15

R ain glanced out the first-floor window. A hummingbird flitted from flower to flower outside. Rain watched it for a few moments and then turned back to Isaac Naborías propped up in his hospital bed. Just looking at him made her itch. Thanks to her *zemi*, most of her mosquito bites had already healed. But Isaac's skin was still covered with tiny welts. He had lost a lot of blood during the attack, but he crossed himself and whispered painfully through swollen lips and an inflamed windpipe that his prognosis was good, though his hands were wrapped to keep him from scratching.

She stepped up to the side of the bed and took his hand. The *zemi*'s Healer snake glowed its golden light, which sped down her arm to her hand—only to be thwarted from crossing over to him by his bandages. Rain realized she needed skin-on-skin contact.

Okay, this is going to be awkward. He was already looking at her a bit strangely.

She reached out again, this time gently touching his forehead. The glow made the leap, but it seemed weaker, spreading thinly around his face before disappearing beneath his bedclothes and bandages. Weak or not, Isaac seemed to receive some relief. He straightened up in his bed and smiled for the first time since Rain had entered his hospital room.

The smile quickly vanished when Rain asked, "You know a lot about the Taíno and their stories, don't you?"

He shook his head. "Nothing. Very little." Still, the *zemi* had done its job; his voice was clearer, less ragged.

"Do you know any of the old words?"

He repeated, "Very little."

"Do you know what Cacique means? I mean, kah-see-KAY?"

Now he couldn't help grinning. He even chuckled a bit. "Do you mean to tell me, Rain Cacique, that you don't know the meaning of your own name?"

She shrugged and tried to look appropriately embarrassed.

"*Cacique* means chief," he told her.

"Like First Chief?" she asked, stunned.

"Exactly. And do you know the Taíno word for First Shaman?"

She shook her head quickly.

"*Bohique,*" he said. "Like your grandfather 'Bastian. You are descended from First Chief and First Shaman. The ones we call Great Searcher of Truth and Great Healer of Ills."

Rain's mouth had gone dry.

Isaac said, "You are true *nitaino.*" He watched her eyes widen further. "Yes, that's the name of your parents' inn and the maiden name of your Grandma Rose, I know. But it is also the Taíno word for nobility. And you are descended from true Taíno nobility.

Not like me. I'm mere *naborii*. A commoner. A peasant. But still, going back, we are all cousins. All family." It warmed the lonely old man to think of Rain as his family.

Rain always knew she had Indian blood, but this was something else, something new and something very, very old as well. This was a heritage. A legacy. Better still, this was an *explanation. This is why I was chosen. Why the Searcher couldn't be Dad or Mom or even Papa 'Bastian. I'm the only one that unites the bloodlines of the Caciques and the Bohiques. The only one who could be both Searcher and Healer.* Tears of gratitude welled up in her eyes, and she wiped an arm across them. *Get a grip,* she thought. *This is great, but you're not done.* She gripped Isaac's hand again and squeezed it tight. The old man squeezed hers back.

"Mr. Naborías," she said, "Cousin Isaac. I need you to finish telling the story of the *Hupia.*"

Instantly, "Cousin Isaac" lost his grin and pulled his hand away. "I can't remember it," he said.

"It's important."

"Best to leave those stories alone."

"No, it's not best," she said. "A man died. You nearly died. And that thing is still out there."

"The constables. The scientists. Leave it to them."

"We both know they're not equipped."

"And you are?"

She stared at him. *Why can't I tell him at least? He'd have to understand.* But she sensed that less was more. "I have to be," she said. "He's got a taste for me now."

Isaac swallowed hard. He didn't want anything to happen to this girl. This girl who saved him. This *Cacique-Bohique.* His new Cousin Rain. Still, he was afraid. "Just stay away from Sycorax," he said.

"I have a friend who lives on Sycorax. Miranda Guerrero. What if she's next?"

"Tell her to leave."

"Mr. Guerrero's daughter? How would that work?"

He looked away, knowing it wouldn't, couldn't.

She pleaded, "At least tell me what a *hupia* is . . ."

He mumbled something.

"What?"

He glanced at her angrily and glanced away. When he spoke, his voice was still quite low but very clear. "It is the Taíno word for ghost . . . or for vampire."

"And that's what we're up against?"

He shook his head. "No. We can't fight it. All we can do is stay away."

"You don't have to go back there," Rain said, urging him on, "but I need to know the full story. How can I protect myself—or help anyone else—without knowing the full story?"

Isaac still wouldn't look at her. But after a few seconds he nodded curtly. Then he cleared his throat. Despite his reluctance, he easily fell back into the old rhythms, the old ways of telling . . .

"In the First Days, the First Murderer was discovered to be a child. First Shaman denounced the child to the entire tribe as a demon. And all but his mother agreed the sentence must be death.

"But the small boy only laughed. He said, 'There is only one way to kill a demon. And you do not have the courage for it.'

"But First Shaman knew the method for killing demons. And First Chief had the courage. Together, they dragged First Murderer to the First Fire, eternally burning in its great pit. Again, the boy laughed, saying, 'You have not the courage . . .'

"And so First Chief and First Shaman consigned the child to the pit, to the fire, to a true demon's death. But First Murderer had fooled them both. For although the flames consumed him, his ashes rose into the air and became the First Mosquitoes.

"And the plague of death continued worse than before."

Isaac looked up at Rain, as if to say, *Do you see now? Do you see the* Hupia *cannot be stopped?*

Rain frowned, answering his unspoken questions. "But somehow the Taíno must have found a way."

Naborías' head wobbled back and forth, up and down, not quite nodding yes and not quite shaking no. "But the stories don't say how. And there are other whispers too."

"What whispers?"

"It is said that in 1566, the Spanish conquistadors released the demon again. And it all but destroyed them."

Another voice spoke from the doorway. "It wasn't your demon that devastated the Spanish. It was malaria."

Rain and Isaac turned. Dr. Strauss stood in the doorway. He looked cranky. He hadn't meant to be caught eavesdropping, but he couldn't stop himself from asserting science over Cousin Isaac's myths. Now, as he entered and made a show of checking Naborías' chart, he wasn't sure if it was the old man's superstition or his own inability to let it slide that was making him cross. He decided it was the latter and surrendered to it. "There was a malaria epidemic in 1566 that devastated the Spanish community on the Ghosts. That's how the French were able to come in and rout them in 1567."

"But what if it wasn't malaria?" the girl asked.

Strauss grimaced. *This is why superstition is so dangerous. It's more contagious than any disease. And the old pass it on to the young.* "The symptoms of malaria include fever and headache, shivering, vomiting and joint pain. And, yes, some people blamed vampires. But staking a scapegoat isn't going to provide a cure."

Maybe it was that German accent, but Rain didn't like the

condescension she perceived in Dr. Strauss's voice. She pointed at Cousin Isaac. "Does *he* have malaria?"

Josef Strauss looked up from the chart and found himself taken aback by the intensity of the young girl's stare. Her almond eyes pinned him in place and forced him to croak out "No."

Rain and Isaac exchanged vindicated glances and firm nods. Strauss could believe what he chose. They *knew*.

Rain absently scratched at her arm.

CHAPTER TWENTY-FIVE

DIAPAUSE

Josef Strauss, more disconcerted than he'd care to admit, returned to his basement office to find his friend Jean-Marc Thibideaux waiting. At that moment I was still with Maq down at the harbor, but I could clearly see (with my eyes closed) the nods they exchanged as Strauss crossed behind his desk. With all due respect to our Rain—the Searcher-Healer, the *Cacique-Bohique*—when I imagined First Chief and First Shaman, it was constable and coroner that seemed to play the parts.

Josef knew why Jean-Marc was there and checked his e-mail straightaway. The lab report from Miami was finally in. He skimmed it and frowned. Then he studied it, and the lines of his frown burrowed deeper into his face. He didn't like what he was reading—and in particular, he didn't like how it dovetailed with the myths he had just dismissed.

Thibideaux waited patiently. Finally, Dr. Strauss nodded and said, "Mosquitoes."

"Milo Long was killed by mosquitoes?"

"The anticoagulant I found in his system was mosquito saliva, which is a natural anticoagulant that also negatively affects the immune system and causes inflammation. Plus, it spreads diseases . . ." He cringed internally. "Like malaria."

"So the rash . . ."

"Mosquito bites. Although not like any I've seen before."

"And we're thinking the same swarm that killed Long attacked Naborías? Ah, the Tourist Board's going to love this."

"Well, mosquitoes can detect and are drawn to octenol and nonanal in their blood targets. Those are both basically alcohol."

"Naborías had been drinking at his retirement party. He may not have been legally drunk, but I've got witnesses who described him as tipsy."

"Also, he was attacked at dusk. And most mosquitoes feed at dusk or dawn. So all that fits, at least."

"What doesn't?"

"The swarm itself. Only male mosquitoes swarm. But only females feed. A swarm that feeds doesn't make sense."

"Could it be a new strain of mosquito?"

Strauss considered this for some time. He was still troubled that the lab report seemed to be confirming Naborías and the girl's superstitions, but he began to see a way to reconcile science with myth. "Or maybe just the opposite," he said.

Thibideaux again waited in patient silence while his friend checked his facts on the Net.

"Diapause," Strauss breathed.

And still Thibideaux waited.

Finally, Strauss' lips curled up into a smile. "I've learned there are legends about these types of attacks. Legends of a mosquito demon child, or some nonsense like that. But if legend has a basis in fact, perhaps we're dealing with an *older* strain of mosquito."

"Josef, I was born on these islands. I've never heard of this kind of mosquito attack before. How could this be an old strain?"

"If it's *very* old. Take the vampire."

Now Thibideaux was getting impatient, and it showed.

Strauss held up his hands. "Hear me out. Take Count Dracula. You put a stake through his heart to kill him. But you also have to cut off his head. If you don't, and if the stake is later removed from his heart . . ."

"He rises again."

"And that's diapause. Or a fictional version of it. It's life on hold. A kind of hibernation. And it's been scientifically proven to exist in some species."

"Including mosquitoes?"

"Especially mosquitoes. Under the right circumstances, it's theoretically possible for an entire strain to enter diapause for decades—maybe centuries—until some environmental trigger brings them back to life."

"So what do we do?"

"Miami's already alerted Vector Control on the mainland. I doubt they've seen anything exactly like this, but they've dealt with Africanized killer bees. They should be able to handle mosquitoes."

"When do they get here?"

Strauss looked at his monitor screen again. Then he shrugged. "It doesn't say. Or rather it only says . . ." He made air quotes with his hands. " 'Soonest.' Tomorrow? Maybe Wednesday?"

"And if another call comes in before then?" On cue, Constable Thibideaux's cell phone chimed. The two friends caught each other's eyes. You could almost see the ashes rising from First Fire between them. Thibideaux exhaled loudly and answered his phone.

At exactly that moment, another phone was ringing. Iris Cacique held off answering it just long enough to give her daughter one last look of disapproval, saying, "Bacon, sausage, Lucky Charms. Was that really so hard to remember?"

"Mom, I'm sorry. I went to Rusty's, but I got . . . distracted."

Iris was hardly satisfied by that explanation, but the phone demanded answering. "Nitaino Inn."

Iris listened with an expression of growing concern. "No. No, I'm sorry, I haven't seen them. Yes, of course. Hold on." She turned back to Rain. "Rain, go check the Kims' rooms. See if the kids are up there."

"What? Why?"

"Their parents can't find them. Wendy, John and Michael are missing."

CHAPTER TWENTY-SIX

COLD HARD FACTS

issing children. This was the kind of call Thibideaux hated the most. He caught a ride on a Coast Guard helicopter across San Próspero from the Pueblo to Windward.

Then came the interviews. With the parents. With witnesses. Then the canvassing for more witnesses. And through it all, the search. The lifeguard who had been on duty had remained at his post, but he'd called in every one of his peers, and they were already checking adjoining beaches and scanning the water as the sun went down. The U.S. Coast Guard used their helicopter and three cruisers, aided and abetted by two U.S. Navy cruisers volunteered by Commander Joshua Stevens (a father of three himself) from the base on Tío Samuel. Of course, the Ghost Patrol was out in full force, calling in deputy constables from Malas Almas and La Géante.

Back to the interviews. Starting with Esther Kim and Fred Kim, mother and father of the three missing children: Wendy Kim, age eight, John Kim, age six, and Michael Kim, age four. (Jean-Marc was struck by the names of the children but couldn't decide if they represented a good omen—or a bad cosmic joke. He caught himself looking up toward the stars, only just appearing, and counting out the second to the right. *And straight on till morning.*) Mr. Kim looked punch-drunk and stunned. Mrs. Kim wavered between fury and terror, between hope and despair. Tears seemed to be perpetually welling up in her eyes—but none fell. At least, not yet.

The facts were these: The Kims had planned to go to the mall that day, but their youngest had begged to be taken to the beach instead, and the older two concurred. Pleased that Michael finally seemed more comfortable near the water—and not wanting either a fight or more whining—Mr. and Mrs. Kim had acquiesced.

So, forgoing the mall, they decided to make an adventure of it. They boarded the Cross-Island Railroad, which cut through the interior jungle of San Próspero with a final stop in the small town of Windward on the opposite side of the island. Leaving the train station, they asked a passerby for directions to the nearest beach.

"But the beach closest to the station is Windward Bar. This is Windward *Strand,*" said the constable.

"I know," Fred Kim said. "That's what the lady recommended. She said Windward Strand would be less crowded and that it was only half a mile farther away."

Jean-Marc frowned. The statement was technically accurate, and perhaps during High Season, or even the summer, useful. But this time of year, *none* of the Windward beaches would be particularly crowded. Any local that knew enough to recommend the Strand would know that too.

Esther Kim read his frown—and read too much into it. "Do

you think she was setting us up? Getting us on an isolated beach so she could grab our kids?"

It didn't seem likely. Especially not with two adults present.

Esther gasped, putting two and two together and getting eight. "Rain said there was this woman who tried to lure the kids into the water yesterday!"

This time Thibideaux was careful his face revealed nothing. "Rain? Rain Cacique?"

"Yes. She babysat them yesterday."

Fred Kim shook his head. "The kids said that woman was young and beautiful. And singing."

"The kids also said she turned into a mermaid!"

"But they were with us when the lady at the station recommended the Strand. They didn't recognize her, didn't say anything to her or about her or—"

"Maybe she signaled them not to."

"Besides, Rain didn't say the woman tried to lure them into the water. She said the kids tried to go swimming with her."

"You don't know what happened. You weren't there. Not *yesterday.*"

The last sentence was clearly accusatory. Thibideaux intervened before the dialogue between the spouses got too heated to be useful. "Why don't you describe this woman to me. The one from the train station."

Fred said, "She was older. About sixty."

"More like seventy," Esther corrected.

"White, black, brown?"

"Black," they said in unison. Esther clarified, "Light-skinned African American with white hair. She had an accent. Maybe Jamaican. I'm not sure." Fred nodded in agreement.

"Anything else? What was she wearing?"

Esther glanced at Fred, who shrugged. She turned back to

Constable Thibideaux. "She was wearing a white peasant blouse and a skirt with vertical stripes." She closed her eyes to picture it. "Green, white, pink, red, blue. Oh, and flip-flops."

"Okay, that's good. That'll help. And I'll have a deputy talk to Rain later and get her to describe the woman she saw the kids with yesterday. But first, just tell me what happened next."

The Kims said nothing. Fred glanced at Esther, but she wouldn't look at him.

"You came to Windward Strand . . ." Thibideaux prompted.

"Right," said Fred. "We came here. Set up shop. The kids played in the sand and in the water."

"We were with them *then*," Esther said, again with the same indictment against her husband, which he made no effort to deny. "We were watching them," she continued. "Watching and playing with them."

The tears welled again but didn't fall. "It was getting late. And we hadn't had lunch."

"Do you remember what time it was exactly?"

Mrs. Kim shook her head and bit her lip, as if not knowing was a great failing. Mr. Kim said, "Two thirty." On that, at least, he could sound definitive. He pointed at his watch, assuming the mere fact it was on his wrist would back his story beyond dispute.

"So I went to the food truck to buy us lunch," she said bitterly, turning to glare at Fred Kim with a fury that threatened to boil over any second. He seemed to wither before her, to shrink into himself.

Thibideaux wished he'd had the foresight to interview them separately. It was too late now, but he took Mrs. Kim's arm and turned her to face him, holding her eyes with his own. "Mrs. Kim," he said, "we're going to do everything we can to find your children. But right now we don't know what's important and what's not, so every detail we get from you matters. Now, stay with me here. Stay with me and tell me everything you remember, no matter how obscure."

Her head bobbed slightly, and she pressed her lips together to stifle sobs. But no sobs came. She gathered her thoughts and then spoke.

Her story seemed ridiculous. One of San Próspero's ubiquitous gourmet food trucks had materialized in the parking lot, and Esther Kim had left the kids with her husband to buy them all lunch. There was no line, but she waited about ten minutes while five different sandwich wraps were prepared. The truck itself blocked her view of her family. When the meal was finished and bagged, she started to head for the beach, but her path was blocked . . . by *crabs*. Twenty, thirty, maybe forty crabs. It was like a march, she said. The crabs walked sideways and drummed their pincers on the ground and against each other's shells.

Then there were the seagulls. When she was about to hop over the crabs, seagulls descended, flapping their wings and cawing, startling her back a few steps. The seagulls landed on the other side of the crabs and, like them, marched in a line with a strange side-to-side gait.

Thibideaux tried to point out that gulls eat crabs, but Esther Kim simply shook her head and said, "Not today."

Esther hadn't known what to make of it all, but it frightened her. She suddenly felt desperate to get back to her kids. Up until this point, she hadn't noticed the shift in the weather. It had been sunny and hot all morning, but fog had rolled in while she was absorbed with the strange dance of crustacean and bird. She could barely see the crabs as she stepped over them. The gulls took flight again, emerging in flashes amid the haze, flapping their wings in her face as they departed. She kept going.

The fog got thicker and thicker. She felt cold and wet and as if she would lose her way—though she knew it was only about thirty feet from the parking lot down to the sand. Something echoed in the mist.

"What something?" Thibideaux asked.

She couldn't articulate what she had heard. Only what it felt like. "Despair. Despair and desire. And the same desperation I was feeling." She found herself running through the miasma. She called out and received no answer.

Finally, she emerged from the fog and found her husband, sitting in the sand at her feet. "He was staring out to sea with the stupidest smile on his face."

The kids were gone.

Thibideaux turned to Fred Kim. He couldn't confirm the crabs or the seagulls. He wasn't even sure about the fog. He did remember being distracted by a song he heard on the wind. He had been watching his children playing in the sand one second. The next second, they were gone.

When Esther heard this, she balled her fists. Finally, the tears came pouring down. Fred reached for her, but she turned her back on him. If these kids weren't found—and perhaps even if they were—she would never forgive him. He would never forgive himself.

Bailey Hall, the eighteen-year-old lifeguard, had a story similar to Fred's. He had seen the Kims arrive on the beach. He had seen the kids playing in the sand near their parents. He had even seen Mrs. Kim leave her family, heading for the Rusty's Gourmet Sandwiches truck. Then he too was briefly distracted by a beautiful song—though he couldn't identify the source of the music. Seconds later, he heard Mrs. Kim shouting for the kids, who were nowhere in sight. Crabs? Gulls? Fog? He didn't know what the constable was talking about.

Cassie Barrett—Rusty's twenty-year-old redheaded daughter—clearly remembered making the wraps for Mrs. Kim. From her vantage in the sandwich truck, she hadn't seen any crabs or gulls, but she certainly remembered the absolutely "freaky fog" and the feeling of sadness it seemed to conjure. She had heard no song, and she never once saw the kids, not before or after the fog. She only came out of the truck when she heard Mrs. Kim screaming. Then she called the Ghost Patrol.

Thibideaux consulted with Deputy Constables Perez and Stabler. He confirmed that everything possible was being done to find the children. He gave them a description of the old woman at the train station and told Perez to call Deputy Constable Mariah Viento—one of the few in the Pueblo not currently deployed in Windward to aid in the search—and have her question Rain Cacique at the Nitaino Inn about the woman she and the Kim kids interacted with the day before. Then Jean-Marc took a breath.

Stabler, a veteran deputy, recognizing the sad inevitability in his boss' exhale, leaned in and whispered, "Doesn't look promising, does it?"

Thibideaux glanced around to make sure no one was in earshot. Then, "We've seen it before. A parent gets distracted. Even a lifeguard gets distracted. And a kid wades out too deep."

"But three kids?" Perez asked, trying to find any excuse to *not* believe the Occam's Razor obviousness of what Thibideaux was suggesting.

"One kid gets in trouble. Another swims out to help," Stabler said. "Boss is right. We've seen it before."

Jean-Marc was already sorry he had hypothesized anything. "Let's not get ahead of ourselves. It's only been a few hours. Keep up the search."

But the cold, hard fact—birds and beasts, fog and song aside—was that Jean-Marc didn't see much hope.

CHAPTER TWENTY-SEVEN

WARM SOFT TAILS

MONDAY, SEPTEMBER 15

A t the Nitaino Inn, Deputy Constable Mariah Viento questioned the minor Rain Cacique in front of her parents, Alonso Cacique and Iris Cacique . . . and in front of her dead and invisible glowing grandfather, Sebastian Bohique, who stood behind Rain, resisting the urge to place a noncorporeal hand on her shoulder.

In her notes, Viento would record that Rain seemed truly torn up about the disappearance of the three Kim children. When asked to describe what happened the day before, Rain seemed horrified—and yet not particularly surprised to learn the two incidents might be connected. She looked guilty enough that Mariah briefly wondered if Rain might not know more than she was saying. (But the young deputy decided this was merely Rain feeling responsible for having been with the children when they met their possible abductor. So Viento's report did *not* mention Rain's guilt-ridden glances over her shoulder.)

Choosing her words carefully, Rain said, "I took the kids to Próspero Beach, to the Alcove. We played in the sand. We played tetherball. It was all pretty normal."

Viento consulted her notes and said, "The parents mentioned something about a woman that wanted the kids to swim with her?"

"I don't *know* if that's what she wanted. I mean, she went in the water. And the kids tried to follow Her. But my friend Miranda had brought us lunch, so we made them wait to swim."

"Miranda?"

"Miranda Guerrero. She's the daughter of Pablo Guerrero."

"*The* Pablo Guerrero?"

"Yeah."

"Who else was there?"

"My friend Charlie."

"That's Charlie Dauphin," Alonso said, trying to help.

Viento wrote the name down. "Anyone else?"

"Not with us."

"Anyone else on the beach you recognized?"

"Ramon Hernandez and Linda Wheeler were there for a while. Oh, and Connor Kelty and Conner Ellison. And the lifeguard, Pedro Serrano."

"Is that it?"

"There were a few tourists there, but I didn't know them."

"Can you describe them?"

"Um, there were a couple white girls. Both blond. Or one was blond and one strawberry blond, I guess. They looked like they were about nineteen or twenty. And there were a couple of guys about that age too. Surfers. They both had curly black hair; they might have been brothers. It sounded like they were speaking Italian to each other. But I'm not sure."

"And that's it?"

"That's it. It wasn't very crowded. No one else was around."

"Except the woman."

"Uh, right."

"Can you describe her?"

Rain swallowed hard. "She was very beautiful. Long black hair, big brown eyes. Skin the color of caramel, like when it's poured over an apple at Carnivale."

Mariah raised an eyebrow at the indulgent description.

Rain looked at her feet and said, "Brown skin."

"How old?"

"I'm not sure. She *looked* like she was in her late teens. Early twenties, maybe. But I suppose she might have been . . . older."

"What was she wearing?"

Up to this point, Rain had attempted to tell the truth, more or less. Now she knew she'd have to fudge a bit more. "Well, she was swimming. So she was wearing . . . a seaweed green suit." That specific phrasing made her feel a little better, but even that smidgen of honesty wouldn't last.

"Had you seen her before?"

"No."

"Do you have any idea why the kids were so interested in her? Did she talk to them?"

"I don't think so. Wendy—that's the Kims' daughter—she kinda liked to pretend she was grown-up and do grown-up things. If she saw grown-up girls, she'd try to do what they were doing. John and Michael sorta followed her lead."

"Mr. Kim said the woman was singing."

"He did? Um, I guess so."

"You don't remember her singing?"

"Vaguely," Rain answered honestly. "I couldn't tell you which song, though."

"Anything else?"

There was a lot else, but Rain shook her head.

Deputy Constable Viento closed her notebook. She turned to address Iris and Alonso, informing them she would question Charlie, Conner, Connor, Pedro, Ramon and Linda and try to track down the four tourists and the woman. Rain noticed she hadn't mentioned Miranda and wondered if Viento had left her out by accident—or if the deputy was intimidated by the Guerrero name and hesitant to question the Sycorax C.E.O.'s daughter.

Rain couldn't have felt worse. Once again, a part of her wanted to scream out the truth. All of it. And if she really thought it might help the Kimlets, she probably would have. But no one would believe her without the pictures on that camera. So the truth would only freak people out about *Rain*. Put *her* under suspicion. She wouldn't be free to conduct her own search. And ultimately, she felt certain she was still the best chance Wendy, John and Michael had. Even if it *was* her fault they had been taken in the first place.

This all played out on her face, and Mariah saw it. She hesitated and then put a reassuring hand on Rain's shoulder, saying, "Rain, this isn't your fault. You gave us a lot of helpful details, and in any case this might have nothing to do with the kids going missing. You didn't do anything wrong."

Rain was not so sure.

Minutes later, up in her room, it took all of 'Bastian's persuasive power to convince Rain not to sneak out to look for the kids that night. To help assuage her, he put the armband on his wrist and ventured out to find them—though he had no clue where to look, short of walking across the open ocean.

Rain went back downstairs and phoned first Charlie and then Miranda to inform them about the Kimlets and warn them about Viento and the version of the truth Rain had related to the deputy. Charlie was quiet for a long time. Finally, he asked the obvious. "It was the mermaid?"

"I don't know. But yeah. Probably."

"Right. Okay. Now what?"

"I don't know," she said again. "But we have to find them."

"Yeah, assuming . . ." He trailed off, but she knew what he hadn't said. *Assuming Aycayia didn't drown them.*

He said, "We'll figure it out tomorrow. Get to school early, okay?"

"I will."

Miranda didn't take it nearly as calmly. When Rain finished her benumbed explanation, she thought Miranda might cry. Then Rain could hear Miranda gasping for breath. *She's not crying. She's sobbing!* Instantly, Rain felt like sobbing, too.

Miranda choked out, "This is . . . our . . . fault . . ."

"I know."

"We've . . . gotta . . . fix it . . ."

"I know," Rain said again. "Get to school early. We'll meet up with Charlie. We'll figure this out." She didn't mention or even allude to drowning.

Miranda said, "Okay," and hung up the phone without another word. Rain stood in the kitchen, holding the receiver for another few seconds. Then she replaced it on its cradle and slowly walked up the back stairs.

Reluctantly, Rain went to bed. She tossed and turned, unable—and then unwilling—to sleep. She listened for the phone or for the front door, praying that a call would come with an update or that the Kims—all the Kims—would simply return. But there was nothing. In fact, it seemed unnaturally quiet. Rain then decided to wait up for 'Bastian. She knew he'd be back just before dawn, but as the night stretched out, having determined to stay awake, sleep overtook her . . .

Rain walked along Windward Bar as the coast curved around onto Windward Strand. A dense fog drifted in from the water, but Rain could see Mrs. Kim cut off from the sand by a strange line of dancing crabs and gulls. Suddenly, Rain felt a sense of urgency. She ran into the fog and immediately lost her bearings. She heard music—no, not music: singing. And the song was beautiful. The song was entrancing. She slowed down again to listen, to attempt to make out the words . . .

But the words hardly seemed to matter. She wandered through the fog, searching for the source of the beautiful song . . .

It was a single voice, a woman's voice . . . and Rain knew this woman, this singer, this Siren, would be beautiful.

Yes. The fog was lifting and there she was. The beautiful Aycayia. Kneeling beside three children. And even from behind, the children looked familiar. Yes, Rain knew these children. Of course she knew them. They were the Kimlets: Wendy, John and Michael. The Lost Girl. The Lost Boys. They were smiling at Aycayia the Beautiful. They were following Her into the water. Mr. Kim and the lifeguard were smiling as they watched them go.

Rain watched the three kids vanish into the surf in pursuit of Aycayia the Beautiful . . .

In pursuit of Aycayia the Cursed!

Rain remembered her urgency. An urgency rapidly descending into panic! She ran; she ran and dove into the water. The water was clear, but she couldn't find Aycayia or the Kimlets.

Then she spotted a dolphin. No, not one dolphin. Six. They swam in a circle, and Rain tried to get past them, but they blocked her path, thwarted her efforts. However, they didn't try to stop her from seeing what took place within the circle. Aycayia the Cursed was climbing back into her manatee skin. Hiding her beauty within a wrinkled, blubbery mass. The three children treaded water beside Her, rapt. How were they breathing? Were they breathing?

Soon the question was moot. The manatee. Aycayia. Her. She tapped each child gently with her tail. One by one, they were transformed. Wendy became a dolphin. John became a dolphin. Michael became a dolphin. These new dolphins were smaller than Aycayia's Sisters. They were young pups. They swam around Her and barked happily.

On the far side of the circle, the Sisters gave way. The manatee raced off, and the dolphin pups followed. Again Rain tried to pursue, but the Sisters barred her. Rain had to surface, to breathe. She came up for air to find Mr. and Mrs. Kim, the lifeguard, Mariah Viento, her own parents, Isaac, Callahan, Pablo Guerrero, Miranda, Charlie, Ramon, Linda, Hank, Marina and Renée standing on the shore, staring at her, pointing at her. "This is your fault," they said in chorus. "You knew she wanted them. You knew . . ."

Rain felt herself sinking down under the weight of their recriminations. She sank away, drowning in her guilt and the warm, soft water . . .

She woke with a start, twisted up unmercifully in her warm, soft covers . . .

CHAPTER TWENTY-EIGHT

GUILTED CAGE

TUESDAY, SEPTEMBER 16

In the morning, the *zemi* was back on the old Spanish desk. 'Bastian had returned before dawn but had chosen not to wake Rain, who had somehow managed to fall back asleep. She wondered if he'd have news for her at sunset—but she knew it was unlikely, and in any case, she couldn't afford to wait.

As she descended the back stairs, she heard her parents talking. Alonso was saying, "Is it horrible to feel relieved those kids didn't go missing on Rain's watch?"

"A little horrible," her mother said. "But I know what you mean."

But it's all my watch! The ponderous guilt weighing her down like lead, she entered the kitchen with shoulders slumped, asking, "Any news?"

Her mother and father shook their heads. Alonso said, "I'm going to take the *Spirit* over to Windward to help with the search."

"Can I go?" Rain asked.

Alonso said, "No," turning to Iris for confirmation.

Iris concurred. "No, Rain. Everything that can be done is being done. You go to school."

"Please," Rain said, "I want to help. I need to help."

Her mother just repeated, "Everything's being done. You need to go to school."

Rain ran a hand through her long hair, pushing it out of her eyes and tucking it behind her ears. She hadn't braided it this morning. She had started to, but she couldn't get her fingers to function properly. They wouldn't work on automatic, and she was overthinking it. Finally, she just gave up. She knew she'd be pushing it out of her face all day, but what choice did she have? She was trapped.

She made a move toward the dining room, but her mother said, "No one's come down yet. Anyway, I've got it covered." So Rain picked up her backpack and headed for the back door. Iris said, "Rain, have some breakfast."

Rain didn't stop. "I'm not hungry." She closed the door behind her.

Rain, Charlie and Miranda conferred outside school, before the bell. Last night, Deputy Constable Viento had stopped by Charlie's place and questioned him in front of his mom. (He'd basically repeated Rain's story.) But as far as Miranda knew, no constables had stopped by the Old Manor.

Rain told them about her dream.

Miranda said, "Is that supposed to be symbolic or something?"

Rain pushed her hair out of her eyes. "I don't think so. At least, I almost hope not."

"You hope not?" Miranda asked, incredulous. She turned to Charlie.

He was chewing nervously on the inside of his left cheek. Then he shrugged and said, "What's the alternative? That the manatee took the kids out and . . ." He didn't want to finish, but Miranda still looked confused. "And drowned them," he said.

Miranda bit her lip and looked away. Tears welled up in her eyes and then tracked down her cheeks.

"Sugar, what's wrong?"

Renée materialized among the trio and, with a real show of concern, used her thumbs to gently wipe away Miranda's tears.

Miranda was too stricken to respond. Rain didn't even want to be on the same planet with Renée right now, let alone explain the Kimlets' kidnapping to her, but some clarification seemed unavoidable. "There are these kids that have gone missing . . ."

"I heard about that," Renée said, still a little mystified. "*Tourist* kids, right?" As in, *Are we really that upset about tourists?*

"They were staying at the Nitaino. And the three of us babysat them Sunday."

"They were so sweet," Miranda said. Charlie's eyebrows went up at that generous description of the troublesome Kimlets, but Miranda misinterpreted. "*Are* so sweet! They are still sweet!"

The bell rang. None of them moved. Rain stared at Renée. "We need a couple minutes. Could you explain to Mrs. B?"

Renée bristled. She didn't like running errands—or doing favors—for anyone. As Rain had guessed, though, it would be tough to say no and still maintain the illusion that Renée . . . cared. She turned to Miranda. "I can stay if you want."

Miranda glanced at Charlie and Rain before turning back to Renée. "No. I . . . That's okay. We'll be in soon. Thanks, Renée." Miranda took it for granted that Renée would fulfill Rain's request. As Renée's mouth twitched slightly, Rain had to suppress a dark laugh.

Renée gave Miranda's arm a squeeze. "Okay, Sugar. See you

inside." Renée did a quick about-face and walked deliberately toward the school building.

As soon as Renée was inside, Miranda turned to Rain. "How is this happening? How is any of this happening?" She was initiating what Rain felt sure was a well-deserved freakout.

Since the full truth wouldn't exactly calm her down, Rain put a hand on her shoulder and said, "Look, it's happening. Does the how matter? We need to focus if we're going to help Wendy, John and Michael. Do you have your phone?"

Miranda nodded and fetched it out of her backpack.

Rain pushed her troublesome hair out of her eyes and said, "In the dream, she turned them into dolphin pups. And she's surrounded by a pod of six more dolphins. So search *dolphins*. And not the science. The legends. The myth. That's how we'll solve this." She sounded way more certain than she felt.

Miranda's thumbs went to work. She searched and skimmed and finally said, "Sailors believed dolphins bring luck."

Charlie chimed in, "For the sailors or for the dolphins?"

Taking his question seriously, Miranda said, "They rescue people. So I guess for the sailors. Hmm . . . the Greek god Dionysus transformed pirates into dolphins."

"Okay, that's starting to sound familiar," Rain said, allowing herself a bit of hope. "How did the pirates get transformed back?"

"They didn't. They were evil pirates. I don't think anyone wanted them back."

So much for hope. "Are you sure? Try another Web site."

Miranda surfed some more. At one point, she nodded to herself and said, "Dolphins can be shape-shifters. They can become human. But it doesn't say how."

Charlie wondered, "The first dolphins, the pod of six, could those be other children the manatee has stolen?"

"No. They're Aycayia's Six Sisters."

"Eye-ka-what now?"

"Aycayia. The Manatee-Woman. That's her name."

He stared at her. "You know her name?"

"From a different dream. Aycayia the Cursed was First Witch. She was punished by being transformed into a manatee. Her Six Sisters were transformed into dolphins."

Miranda stared at her for a few long seconds, then slowly said, "Wow. That, um, fits. This site says dolphin calves are raised by their mother with the help of 'Aunties.'"

Rain tucked her hair behind her ears. "So Aycayia's Sisters are helping Her take care of the Kim kids. That's good, I think."

So it went past the second bell and beyond. Finally, it became clear that if searching the Internet was somehow sufficient for solving mystic mysteries, everyone would be doing it. So Miranda used her phone for something else. She called Ariel and arranged for her to meet them after school with Pablo Guerrero's speedboat. They'd search for the Kimlets themselves.

CHAPTER TWENTY-NINE

OFF PUNTA

The nameless Guerrero speedboat swept out of Próspero Bay with Ariel at the helm and Rain, Charlie and Miranda all scanning the water with borrowed binoculars, looking for . . . *what?* The same exact thought echoed in the heads of all three teens: *What exactly do we expect to see out here?* If Ariel—who had been told only that they were joining the search for the missing tourist children—thought something similar, she kept her own counsel and maintained her standard unknowable poker face. But once Rain pushed the hair out of her eyes, she could see the question clear as day on Charlie and Miranda's worried expressions and knew her own countenance looked no different. *What am I hoping for? That Aycayia and her Six Sisters and her three stolen Kimlets will just swim up to the side of the boat? Well, maybe. They've taunted me before.* But it was a big ocean, and Rain desperately wished she had something more to go on.

Ariel steered the boat southwest, to circle round San Próspero toward Windward, where the navy, the Coast Guard, the constabulary, the lifeguards, the Kims, Alonso Cacique and other volunteers were all focusing their search. But the Searcher lowered her binoculars to desperately surf her own mental Internet for a better clue to guide them. Sure, Aycayia had *taken* the kids at Windward, but there was no reason for Her to stay there with them. In fact, with all the activity on the east side of the island, she'd likely avoid the entire area. *So where would she bring them now? I need to focus on what I know about Her.* There was only one location specifically named in Rain's dreams of Aycayia: Punta Majagua, where Guanayoa took First Witch and her Sisters. But Rain didn't know of any Punta Anything on the Ghosts. *So why does the name sound familiar?*

Rain tucked her hair behind her ears and turned to look at the afternoon sun, sinking slowly toward its nightly resting place beneath the western sea. She wished the fiery ball would simply drop down with a splash and bring on the night, so that 'Bastian would appear. *He* knew these islands better than anyone. *And he knows all the old names . . .*

Then she remembered: it wasn't "Punta" that sounded familiar; it was "Majagua." 'Bastian had told her last week that the pre-corporate name for Sycorax Island had been Isla Majagua. So if there was a Punta Majagua, then Sycorax was where it would be.

Almost embarrassed for not knowing the privatized Sycorax as well as she knew San Próspero, Malas Almas or Ile de la Géante, she turned to Miranda and said, "Do you know where Punta Majagua is?"

Miranda lowered her binoculars and nodded. "Sure. So do you. It's Witch's Finger."

Witch's Finger! Of course! Aycayia was First Witch! And every local knew the little peninsula on the northwest end of Sycorax

Island looked like the crooked finger of a witch pointing toward the setting sun. "That's where we need to go!" she shouted. "That's where they'll be!"

Ariel's head turned a few degrees—not enough to look back at Rain, but enough to acknowledge her words. Then the pilot turned toward Miranda, and a single eyebrow was raised a centimeter in question. Miranda looked from Rain to Charlie and back to Rain. Then Miranda swallowed hard, bit her lip and nodded to Ariel, who immediately put them on a northwest heading, accelerating with the wind at their backs.

Now Rain's untamed black mane was blowing across her face and over the binoculars. She'd tuck it behind her ears, and it would be back in her eyes before she could raise the binoculars. She was about ready to scream when Miranda appeared at her shoulder, saying, "Do you want me to braid that?"

"Oh, yes! Please!"

Miranda immediately set to work, her fingers nimbly intertwining three long strands of Rain's hair almost as quickly as Rain could—on a normal day—do it herself. "It's so thick!" Miranda said.

"I know. It's such a pain."

"No, I mean it's gorgeous, Rain. I wish I had hair like this."

By the time the speedboat was hugging the southern coast of Sycorax and about to come around behind it, Miranda had tied off the end of the braid with the rubber band Rain had worn on her wrist since failing to make her hair behave that morning. It wasn't quite the tight black rope she usually created for herself, but it was a big improvement over the Medusa thing she had been dealing with all day. Rain breathed a sigh of relief and said, "Thanks, Miranda, you're a lifesaver."

Miranda beamed, and Rain shot a look at Charlie, as if to say, *Why don't you ever braid my hair?*

Fortunately, that's when Charlie demonstrated alternate talents. "There!" he shouted, lowering his binoculars and pointing. Dolphins breached the surface in front of them, one after another, as if leading them on procession. Not just any dolphins, either. Rain was sure this was the manatee's pod—Aycayia's Sisters, the Kimlets' Aunties—even before she spotted one of them with Alonso's camera strap between its teeth.

Two of the Aunties teased Rain, tossing the camera back and forth between them. Rain only smiled. She felt certain that— intentionally or otherwise—they were leading the speedboat toward their pups. Toward Michael, John and Wendy. She stepped up behind Ariel and said, "Follow those dolphins!"

This time, and despite the apparent downright silliness of the request, Ariel didn't acknowledge Rain at all but instead maintained a steely eye on the marine mammals, pursuing them around the lower lip of Sycorax's Back Bay, bringing Punta Majagua—the Witch's Finger—into view.

Rain instantly saw Back Bay wasn't empty. A lone but familiar cabin cruiser was anchored just offshore. Stunned—but feeling less surprised than furious—Rain took a few steps back until she was even with Charlie. She whispered in his ear, "It's the *Bootstrap*." They both turned their binoculars toward the deck of the cruiser and saw Callahan using his own binoculars to look straight back at them. *That's why he was heading north out of the harbor,* Rain thought, *to come here!* She still didn't understand all the connections. *Did Callahan have something to do with the Kimlets' disappearance? With Aycayia? Is all this linked to the zemi somehow?* She had no answers, and she didn't like that Mr. Attack-of-the-Killer-Tourist himself was in the vicinity generating questions.

Callahan wasn't happy either. *Those two bloody kids are everywhere! And this time they've brought witnesses.* He especially didn't like the looks of the blonde at the wheel of the approaching speedboat. He was still enough of a soldier to recognize the quality of a warrior in someone else—even at this distance. He'd rather not mess with her, with them, even in the dim light of the setting sun. If they stayed clear of him, fine. He'd let them go about their business. If they interfered—with him, his boat, or his search for the second *zemi*—he'd wait for dark and end them once and for all. He mentally settled in to see what happened next.

On her own initiative, Ariel reduced speed and cut the engine. The dolphins began circling the speedboat. Still there was no sign of the pups or the manatee. Rain caught Miranda's eye. "Is there diving equipment aboard?"

Miranda shook her head. "No, but we have enough back home for all of us. I guess we could head back around the island and bring it here." The idea of another dive did not excite her.

Rain wasn't thrilled either, though for different reasons. She didn't want to leave and come back. She couldn't be sure the dolphins would still be here. Instead, she was taking off her sneakers, getting ready to hit the water without equipment, when the sun finally set and in the low light of dusk 'Bastian materialized from out of the *zemi*.

The instant he saw her, he said, "Rain, I've got news."

"Did you find the Kimlets?"

Charlie groaned audibly as he watched his friend converse with her invisible grandfather, and as he watched Miranda and even Ariel stare at Rain addressing empty space.

"No, no," 'Bastian said, "but I ran into the ghost of the man who died on Sycorax. He calls himself Cash. He followed me back to the Nitaino, but it was dawn before . . ." He paused, looking around. "Say, where are we? Is that Witch's Finger?"

Rain pointed toward the dolphins, circling the boat like

would-be sharks. "We're on the trail of the Kim kids. That's the manatee's pod. Her Sisters."

"The ones who took Alonso's camera?"

"Yeah, that, too. We were hoping they'd lead us to Wendy, John and Michael . . ." She quickly brought him up to speed.

Miranda inched closer to Charlie and asked, "Is she okay?"

"She's just thinking aloud. I do it all the time. Like right now. I'm thinking how *weird this looks!*"

But it wasn't Charlie's outburst that interrupted Rain and 'Bastian's conversation. It was the sudden downpour. All eyes looked toward heaven. Right up until sundown, the sky had been cloudless and clear. *Where had this rain come from?*

And not just rain. The wind was rising, blowing heavy drops into their faces. The temperature was falling rapidly, and all three teens—and even 'Bastian—struggled to suppress chills. Thunder rumbled in the distance. A storm was coming in and coming in fast.

'Bastian scanned the skies, but Rain saw her first. It was Hurricane Julia herself, forming out of the wind and rain: her hair, a mantle of dark clouds; her eyes, the flashing lightning; her voice, the rumbling thunder. "There," Rain whispered.

'Bastian nodded. He saw her. The creature that had killed his B-17 crew nearly seventy years previous. The Dark Man's eyes narrowed.

Even Charlie grokked that Julia had returned. He couldn't see her spirit, but he recognized the locus of storm that he had helped Rain shoot out of the sky just over a week ago.

Aycayia, Callahan, Julia. It was as if all their nightmares were having a party.

The seas were high now, and the boat was rocking badly. Water washed onto the deck from wind-driven waves, and the rain came down at them like pellets. Miranda was again starting to freak a little. "I've never seen a storm come up so fast," she said, screaming slightly to be heard over the wind and not-so-distant thunder.

Charlie growled, "It's getting to be a habit around here." That only confused Miranda more.

Ariel didn't seem to be listening. She was making calculations. In the end, the equation was simple. There wasn't much chance of finding the three lost kids behind Sycorax anyway—and certainly not in this storm. So there was little benefit in putting the boss' daughter and her friends at risk. She fired up the engine and turned the boat around, heading for home and away from the storm.

Rain instantly protested, "Wait! We can't go!"

Ariel ignored her.

Miranda felt the need to make excuses for Ariel; she pled the obvious to little effect.

"But the kids," Rain said, "I know they're close."

"You can't save them if you drown at sea, Raindrop," 'Bastian said sternly; he was starting to admire this Ariel more and more.

Aboard the anchored *Bootstrap,* Callahan was battening down the hatches. He ran a big hand through his soaked blond hair. *Another bloody monsoon! 'Struth, it's like those damn kids bring the bad weather! As if I needed another excuse to put 'em out of my misery!*

Rain was feeling desperate. She was aft, watching the dolphins, who remained behind, within view of Punta Majagua. There might never be another chance. She seemed literally on the verge of jumping off the back of the boat when Charlie grabbed her right arm and 'Bastian grabbed her left by wrapping his ghostly hand around her armband.

"No!" they both declared in another moment of bizarre masculine unison, which was becoming all too common for Rain's tastes.

"Well, we've got to do something!" she shouted. A frantic epiphany found her sliding the *zemi* down her wet, slippery arm and holding it out to 'Bastian. Charlie glanced behind them to make sure his own body was blocking Miranda's view. "Take it!" Rain hissed. "Take it and search Witch's Finger. On it. Around it. I'm not sure. But I know Aycayia and the Kimlets are here somewhere."

'Bastian hesitated. "Even if I find them, what do you expect me to do? Rescuing them may be beyond me. They can't see or hear me, and I can't touch them. And, you know, they're *dolphins!*"

"Then just find them and report back. I'll figure the rest out . . . somehow."

"You know, we're a long way from the Inn. I might not make it back before sunrise."

"Do what you have to do, Papa. But we have to get those kids back to their parents. We just have to."

A few long seconds passed. Finally, the Dark Man nodded and took the armband from Rain's hand, slipping it onto his wrist. Then, with a little concentration, he allowed the boat to continue on without him.

Rain watched as his receding, glowing white form floated above the churning seas . . . and then sank down beneath the waves. She said a silent prayer and leaned her head against Charlie's shoulder. In the pouring rain, it was hard to tell whether or not she was crying.

CHAPTER THIRTY

DEAD AS A DOORMAN

TUESDAY, SEPTEMBER 16

Where the hell do I go? At sunset, the Pale Tourist had materialized in the lobby of the Nitaino Inn. This was where the other ghost, that Bohique kid, had left him before heading upstairs to get the girl, the girl who could supposedly talk to the dead. *The dead like me.* He had been waiting only a couple minutes and had glanced up at the clock on the wall. Then it felt like he had blinked, and everything changed. The clock had jumped fifteen minutes, from 7:10ish to 7:25. It wasn't just the clock, though: the quality of the light had changed too, and suddenly, there was a woman standing behind the front desk. Cash knew she hadn't been there before. He'd have noticed this one: short dark hair, copper skin, nice curves. He couldn't decide how old she was. Anywhere from her late twenties to early forties. She looked a bit like Bohique. Maybe she was the dead kid's older sister. Or maybe all these locals looked alike to him. He stared at her awhile, then waved and said, "Hello, beautiful." He didn't really expect a response and received none.

Cash turned away from Iris Cacique; she was a distraction, and he needed to focus. Belatedly, he realized he hadn't lost fifteen minutes; he had lost *twelve hours* and fifteen minutes. The sun had risen and then set again. During that interval—that is, the entire day—he had simply ceased to exist. *Where the hell do I go?* Not to hell—or heaven, for that matter—unless oblivion qualified as either. There was no sense of the passage of time. Just here, gone, and back again.

He thought about it and figured the same thing had happened to Bohique. He'd probably come downstairs any second. They might have to wait for the girl, though. She'd be in bed at dawn—who wouldn't?—but there was no telling where the kid'd be at dusk. *When I was that age, I pretty much never came home.* Hopefully, this girl—Bohique had called her Rain—was a bit better behaved.

Still, girl or no girl, he wished Bohique would get his translucent butt downstairs again. It had been a relief having someone to talk to finally. Or someone to talk to, who could hear him and would talk back.

Cash had given up looking for the girl at the mall and had been wandering around the beach—though he had no real hope of finding her there either, certainly not at that predawn hour. There had been this dog following him around. Or at least it seemed like the yellow mutt was following him. *Could dogs see ghosts?* Or was it all just a coincidence?

(Okay, yes, that was me. Maq was sleeping off half a beer he'd found in a bottle abandoned on a bus bench, and I was bored and curious.)

Then Cash had seen him. This twenty-year-old kid with the dark eyes and the swooped-back hair. He was in the air force or something, and he was glowing softly white. They had spotted each other more or less simultaneously, and both stood there, kinda stunned. Then the kid had run up to him.

"You're dead!" he had said, demonstrating a tremendous grasp of the obvious.

"You too?" Cash had asked, demonstrating an equally tremendous talent for asking stupid questions.

"My name's Bohique. Sebastian Bohique. Are you the guy who died on Sycorax last week?"

"Yeah, yeah. Call me Cash."

They both motioned, as if to shake hands—then hesitated. For 'Bastian, nothing but the *zemi* had been corporeal to his ghostly form. For Cash, nothing period.

'Bastian shrugged and extended his hand. "It's worth a try."

Cash reached for him, but their hands passed right through each other. For both, it had become a common enough experience. But still disappointing.

The Pale Tourist stepped back. He looked around. "How come you're the only other ghost I've met? Shouldn't these islands be full of spooks walking around? You and I can't be the only two guys who ever died here."

"I think most of them move on. That's what happened with my crew. I think you only stay a ghost if you've got unfinished business."

"Huh." Cash was distracted. This other ghost was wearing jewelry. Some kind of gold band around his left wrist. It looked . . . solid. Real, not spectral. Cash had a sudden urge to touch it, to take it.

"And do you have unfinished business?" Bohique had asked.

Cash refocused on the Dark Man's eyes. He was giving Cash a look that said, *Hands off, bub.* Cash got the message. "I guess I do," he said. "See, I was killed by this . . . Well, I guess it was

kind of a vampire. But totally without the sexy. Anyway, it's looking to kill some girl. So I've been looking for her. To warn her."

"Rain."

Bohique had told Cash a bit about Rain, the girl who spoke to
spooks. He knew where to find her and led Cash to the lobby of
this hotel or B&B or whatever it was. Then Bohique got a little
squeamish and didn't want to take Cash up to the girl's room. He
promised to bring her down.

The sunrise had gotten in the way. Now Cash waited in the
lobby for Bohique or the girl or both, but neither came down. A
couple hours passed. Cash thought about leaving, but where else
did he have to go? He followed Iris around for a while. (Mostly
out of boredom and a little because he liked her looks.) He noticed
she kept checking her watch and staring at the phone. She cooked
a meal that no one ate—not even her. Cash himself lingered over
the food. He wasn't hungry exactly, but he so wanted a little taste.
It smelled so good. Or at least it looked like it did. He wasn't sure
if he could actually smell anything or if he just felt like he could.
It was strange.

Iris wandered back into the lobby, clearly at loose ends, and
Cash followed. Another woman came down the stairs. Another
looker, but totally different from Iris; this one was very tall and
very pale, and not tourist pale like Cash. Judith Vendaval's skin
was creamy and white, and Milo Cash felt an immediate and intense desire to drink her in. Of course, she took no notice of him.

Iris looked up. "Judith."

"Any word on those kids?"

"No. I'm afraid not."

They stood there with nothing else to say.

The front door opened, swinging right through Milo. It wasn't
a new sensation, but as yet, it hadn't lost its disturbing and un-
pleasant qualities. Two men entered: guests of the Inn, Cash fig-

ured. They closed umbrellas and shook off the rain. They seemed oblivious to whatever was upsetting the two women. Both said brief pleasantries to Iris and headed upstairs, passing Judith with a three-way exchange of nods.

Cash moved away from the closing door—and just in time. Before it had clicked home, a girl entered alone, looking every bit the drowned rat. Even so, Cash noticed a resemblance to Iris. The girl had the same copper skin and dark hair—and the same nose.

Immediately, Iris began the interrogation. "Where have you been?" Now Cash knew she was the girl's mother. That tone was unmistakable. His own mother—God rest her soul—had spoken those exact words in that exact tone more times than he could count.

The girl didn't answer right away; she was too busy staring wide-eyed at Cash, who actually checked behind him to make sure he was indeed the subject of her gaze. *Bohique was right. The girl can see ghosts.* He was tempted to approach. To talk to her. She gave him a quick shake of her head. *She's right. Gotta wait till she's alone.* He nodded to her and kept his distance for now.

"Rain."

Rain turned back toward her mother. "Sorry, what?"

"Where have you been?"

"I . . . Well . . . Miranda, Charlie and I went out on Miranda's father's boat to help look for the Kim kids."

"Rain, I told you—"

"Mom, please. I feel bad enough."

"But look at you. You're soaked."

"The storm came out of nowhere. And Ariel took us back as soon as it started."

"Ariel?"

"She's like the Guerrero boat-chauffer or whatever."

Judith moved between them and put a hand each on Iris and Rain's shoulders. "It doesn't seem like any harm was done."

Iris softened, really looking at her daughter for the first time. Rain was on the verge of tears—and had been on and off for a good two hours. Iris wrapped her arms around Rain.

"Any news?" Rain asked desperately.

"No. But I'm sure your dad will call soon."

Then, on cue, what could only be the dad came in the front door. Like his daughter, he was soaked to the bone. Lightning flashed behind him, and the thunder crack followed. He held the door open.

"Anything?" Iris asked.

Alonso shook his head. "Storm drove me back. It's breaking up now, but for a while there . . ." He glanced over his shoulder and moved aside. "Thibideaux's called off the search until morning."

An Asian woman entered, leaning against a uniformed female cop. Cash caught himself looking for an exit—a Pavlovian reaction to the appearance of any badge—and almost had to laugh. For the first time in memory, he was well out of reach of the long arm of the law.

Both Iris and Judith moved to Esther Kim's side. She looked cold and wet, and also numb—though for reasons that had nothing to do with being cold and wet. She said, "Fred's staying in Windward. But he and Constable Thibideaux thought I should come back here, in case the kids called."

Iris and Judith exchanged a glance. Iris said, "Let's get you upstairs. You can catch a few hours' sleep."

"I don't think I could sleep."

"We'll stay with you either way. Do you want anything?"

"No, I . . ." She trailed off.

"Some tea, maybe." Iris glanced again at Judith, who nodded. Iris said, "I'll bring it right up."

Judith wrapped an arm around Esther. The Tall Woman slowly escorted the petite Mrs. Kim up the stairs, under the watchful eyes of Rain, Iris, Alonso, Deputy Constable Viento and Cash.

Iris turned to Alonso. They both looked at Mariah Viento. She shook her head. "It's been over twenty-four hours. Even if we find them, the news isn't likely to be good."

Iris looked away to hide her face. Then she said, "I'll go get the tea."

Cash turned toward Rain, expecting to see her weeping. Then he took a step back. The look of fury on the young girl's face was enough to frighten the dead.

CHAPTER THIRTY-ONE

TEARS

TUESDAY, SEPTEMBER 16

With the storm raging above, 'Bastian remained beneath the surface of the water, propelling himself on *what?* *Ghost power?* Though there was no solid ground beneath his feet, he was, perhaps from sheer force of habit, putting one foot in front of the other, though somehow he doubted his forward momentum had anything to do with his stride.

It was very dark, his own soft white glow providing the only light. When he had left Rain and the boat, he had had a clear view of the dolphins. No longer. He had spent hours traversing Back Bay, from one end to the other, and hadn't seen a single fluke. He surfaced to pouring rain and a view of the rocking *Bootstrap* not too far away, but he couldn't see the Aunties anywhere. He thought perhaps they had sounded, so he allowed—or willed—himself to sink down, too.

He searched deep. *Do dead eyes adjust to the dark?* Because, gradually, the world far below the surface was filled with a strange light. The light of *living* creatures. A jellyfish passed close to his face, seemed to startle, and briefly glowed whiter than the dead, before undulating away. A midwater squid shone like moonlight above him. Below him, various mollusks and sponges shrugged off subtly different shades of pale blue radiance.

Eventually, this bioluminescence seemed to swirl around him, bathing him in cold blue light and illuminating a sextet of dolphins swimming close to shore. With some difficulty, owing to their incessant frolicking, he counted them again, just to be sure. Six large dolphins. No trio of pups. And no manatee in sight. Still, he headed toward the movement amid the glow.

His progress was slow. By the time he reached the silty seabed just off of Punta Majagua, he'd lost sight of the dolphins again. He surfaced. There was no rain on the island. He could still see the nightmare storm—no longer a hurricane but not insignificant— just offshore. But on the beach, the air was calm and sultry, and the precipitation had ceased. He glanced around at the blue flame of dinoflagellate plankton illuminating the water. He tried to read the fire for the silhouettes of the Aunties but saw nothing.

He heard something, though. The slicing of oars through water. He turned in time to see Callahan achieve the shore in a dinghy, which he dragged high up onto the sand. The big man, oblivious to the beauty of the sparkling sapphire sea, donned a pack and marched straight into the dark jungle of the Witch's Finger.

'Bastian hesitated, unsure how to proceed. Like Rain, he couldn't believe Callahan's presence was a coincidence, but like Rain, he couldn't yet connect the dots. The priority right now was finding those lost and transformed kids. They should be in the water with Aycayia and her Sisters, but he couldn't search an entire ocean, and the dolphins appeared and vanished at will. His gut told him to follow the brute, so he followed both gut and Callahan.

Catching up was easy enough. The big man made rapid, determined and steady progress, but 'Bastian could walk in a straight line *through* the drenched flora. Soon he was marching parallel to Callahan, matching the man's pace, step for step—while careful to always keep a tree or fern between the big Aussie and the disembodied floating snake charm on his wrist.

Then Callahan stopped and sniffed the air. 'Bastian couldn't smell anything until both men turned and spotted the rising smoke and heard the distant crackle of a campfire. Then the smell of burning copperwood and copal, ceiba and cedar rushed back to the Dark Man like a memory—which perhaps was all it was.

Instinctively, Callahan's hand slid down toward the knife in his boot, but he stopped himself. He didn't need to go looking for trouble. Avoiding whoever might be out there was not a problem, whereas *dealing* with them—harshly or not—would eat up precious *zemi*-hunting time. He straightened and continued on his nearly silent way.

'Bastian didn't follow. His gut had told him to follow Callahan, but now it was speaking a new language. He could feel it. Something old was calling out to him from afar. He answered that call.

The Dark Man stepped through a ring of mahogany trees and banana plants, not unlike those that encircled the N.T.Z., and found a clearing. In the center was a small, rather pathetic campfire being tended by a crouching woman wrapped in seaweed. Instantly—before he had even seen her face—'Bastian knew this was the enchantress Aycayia. He circled her slowly. From every angle, she was the most beautiful creature he had ever laid eyes upon. A woman he might even have left his beloved Rose for, if the truth be told. She was making some kind of soup, adding herbs and roots to a charred wooden pot and stirring the contents with a stick. Even this simple act seemed to accentuate her loveliness.

So fascinated was the ghost, he didn't notice the clearing's other occupants until one of them spoke. "What's that?"

'Bastian looked around. Michael, John and Wendy—all three quite human and naked as the day they were born—gingerly stepped forward from the edge of the clearing to observe the floating golden snake charm that had attracted Michael's attention as it slowly circled the fire.

Aycayia looked up and tilted her head to observe the *zemi*. Her expression was neither curious nor disturbed. If anything, she seemed . . . numb.

The Kimlets approached the armband. Michael reached up and poked it. John stepped right through 'Bastian's side to get a closer look.

'Bastian said, "Kids, can you hear me?" though he wasn't surprised they didn't respond.

Aycayia tapped the wooden pot with her stirring stick to get the children's attention. They turned and smiled at her, the *zemi* immediately forgotten. They crossed to her on bare feet. From somewhere, she produced three plain wooden cups and carefully poured soup into each. 'Bastian thought it smelled like the *ajiaco* his *abuela* used to make.

The Manatee-Woman mimicked blowing on the broth, and the Kimlets understood, blowing vigorously into their cups before taking their first sips. Whatever the concoction contained, it clearly pleased the little ones, warmed them. 'Bastian could almost see the emotional infrared shining from within.

Aycayia took no soup for herself, taking sustenance from watching Wendy, John and Michael eat. She knelt beside them and stroked the hair of each one in turn while they sipped and slurped. When Michael looked up, sporting a brown soup mustache and a broad grin, Aycayia smiled. It was a smile informed by sadness, 'Bastian knew, but it was so painfully beautiful, he almost didn't care.

He found himself waving his arm to get her attention. He desperately wanted her attention. Firelight glimmered off the golden snakes and caught her eye. She turned to look, and though he wasn't sure, she seemed to be looking at him, not the *zemi*. And for a few long seconds, it was enough.

Ultimately, though, he tore his eyes away to observe the three happy Kimlets, sitting in the sandy dirt, drinking soup from their cups and occasionally glancing over at Aycayia with an adoration he understood all too well. *His* adoration had abated enough that it no longer held enough sway to divert him from his task, the spell sufficiently broken for 'Bastian to remember why he was there.

"You have to bring those kids back," he said. "Or at any rate, you have to let them go." He had no idea if a creature such as Her could hear him let alone understand English or the concept of human love, but he had to try. "We know you're working with Santa Julia. The hurricane-woman. We know she's helping you, sending storms to discourage pursuit. But she's dangerous. She kills people. She killed my crew, my friends. And she tried to kill me. Twice. And my granddaughter too. She doesn't care about the lives of children. But I can see you're different. You're feeding these children, taking care of them. You're tender with them. Their names are Wendy Kim, John Kim and Michael Kim. They have parents, who love and miss them. Parents who are going crazy right now. Parents that these kids *will* need one day. No spell you cast could ever erase the love they have for their father, their mother. Let them go."

Aycayia's eyes had lost focus. She was no longer looking at

'Bastian, assuming she had *ever* been looking at 'Bastian. She wasn't even looking at the *zemi* anymore. He thought perhaps she was looking at something long ago and far away.

Her head tilted down and she stared into the little fire. She listened to the pop of drying wood and the sizzle of flame dancing across mossy bark. Her gaze floated upward, following the smoke and the ash.

Perhaps the smoke made her eyes tear. Perhaps it was something else entirely. Either way, she wept. 'Bastian watched the tears emerge as small but perfect pearls, which dropped into the sand by her knees.

CHAPTER THIRTY-TWO

DREAMS LIE

WEDNESDAY, SEPTEMBER 17

Physically, mentally, emotionally, Rain was exhausted. She'd spent nearly an hour repeating her previous statement to the deputy. Another hour explaining herself to her father. She had looked in on Mrs. Kim, who hardly seemed to recognize her. The poor woman just sat on the bed between Judith Vendaval and Iris, *not* sipping her tea.

Then at last, she was alone in her room with the ghost. The second she had closed the door, he had begun speaking at a rapid pace. She could tell as much by looking at him, but without the *zemi*, she couldn't hear a sound.

Nevertheless, it had been difficult to get a word in edgewise. "Listen!" she finally shouted. "Listen to me! You can stop talking, cuz I can't hear you!"

He said something else then, but all she could read from his expression was confusion. Then he used two fingers to point from his eyes to hers.

"I can see you, but I can't hear you."

He made another hand gesture that she couldn't understand at first. He was holding up fingers near the top of his head. Then he stood at attention and saluted. Then he walked to the wall and put his hand through it.

She got it. He was talking about 'Bastian, with his hawk-feather hair, his Army Air Forces uniform and his noncorporeal body. She said, "I know my grandfather probably said I'd be able to hear you, but . . ."

She stopped. He looked even more confused.

"My grandfather. The other ghost. 'Bastian Bohique."

She thought she saw him mouth the words *That guy's your grandfather?* Or something like that.

"Yeah. 'Bastian's my grandfather. I know he looks young, but he's not."

The ghost spoke again, rambling rapidly, but this time Rain couldn't catch a single word.

"Stop, stop. I can't hear you. Normally, I could. But I need the gold armband to hear you, and 'Bastian has it right now."

The ghost seemed to understand now. He started to speak, then shrugged weakly and closed his mouth.

What had 'Bastian called him? Cash? "Is your name Cash?"

Cash nodded.

"'Bastian will come back. He went looking for the missing kids. But he'll come back, and he'll bring the armband, and then I'll be able to hear you. Or, wait—" She stepped forward, and he reflexively stepped back. She shook her head. "Hold still. I won't be able to hear you. Not really. But I'll sort of know what you want. Maybe."

She reached for him, as if to put a hand against his chest. As

Cash's chest was substance-free, her hand passed into his body, as if reaching for his heart, as if she were touching his soul. He clearly didn't appreciate the sensation and jumped back. But in that second or two, she'd heard one whispered word. Well, not heard it exactly, but she'd felt it. It was liquid, washing in and sweeping away, like a wave lapping at her mind. Or maybe it was a whiff of smoke carried past her consciousness on the wind. One wave, one whiff, one word: *DEATH*.

In any case, neither ghost nor girl seemed anxious to repeat the experiment. Rain looked around the room, frustrated and help-less. Finally, she said, "Could you leave? I need to change for bed, and, well . . ."

Again Cash looked briefly confused, and then he seemed to get it. He headed for the closed door.

Rain said, "If 'Bastian gets back before dawn, we'll come find you. Um, down in the lobby. If not, we'll talk after sunset, okay?"

Cash looked back, started to speak, caught himself and nod-ded. Then he walked through the closed door and was gone.

Rain stood there for a good three minutes, staring after him. Composing herself. Then she got ready for bed.

Wearing a long T-shirt, she turned off the lights and slipped under the covers. The room was dark but not pitch. She stared up at the ceiling. She missed her armband, and not just because of Cash. It had begun to feel like a part of her. It seemed to give her strength. She hadn't been the only one to miss it, either. As Rain and Charlie were getting off the Guerreros' boat earlier, Miranda had noticed Rain wasn't wearing it. Charlie looked instantly panic-stricken. Rain's knee-jerk response had been to lie, to tell Miranda she hadn't worn it today.

Miranda had said, "But I'm sure I—"

Rain had cut her off. "I usually wear it, but I left it home."

Miranda shook her head slightly. Then nodded, suddenly doubting her own memory.

Rain hated lying to Miranda, who deserved better. In fact, she hated lying about this, period, because she—Rain—deserved better. *But what other choice do I have?*

Slowly, all that exhaustion crept up on her. She began to drift. Her last conscious, coherent thoughts were of the Kimlets at the mercy of First Witch.

At that moment, as I felt her fears for the children from across town, I began to growl reflexively. It was a low guttural noise born of my own frustration. I was under yet another bus bench on Camino de las Casas, trying to stay out of the rain, out of the storm caused by *Hura-hupia* to interfere with the search for the kids, not because she cared what happened to them one way or another, but because their abduction provided a useful and serendipitous distraction for Rain that interfered with the Searcher's search for the next *zemi*.

A hand reached down and rubbed my neck, roughly scrunching up the fur and skin, and gently rubbing it back down with the grain, the way I liked it. It stopped me from growling. Maq was above me, lying across the bench with his straw hat over his face. Up to this point, he had seemed oblivious to the rain and indifferent to the fate of the Lost Girl and Boys. But the words he spoke belied that impression. "You know I can't break the rules, Opie. You know that."

I gruffled some sound or other, acknowledging as much.

"Can't break 'em. But no one said anything about *bending* 'em a mite. If *Hura-hupia* can send Rain a dream or three to set our girl thinking down the wrong path, then I can certainly spin one of my own for a minor mental course correction. Heck, I wouldn't even be sending a new dream exactly. If anyone asks, it's really just a do-over of one of *Hura-hupia*'s reveries, spun a bit closer to how *I* remember the story . . ."

I quickly barked my approval. I couldn't really see how a dream would help anyone at this stage, but at least we were doing *something*. So I lowered my chin onto my paws and watched the show playing out behind Rain Cacique's eyelids.

This was the dream Maq sent:

In the First Days, Aycayia the Cursed was in mourning for the death of her child. Aycayia had not eaten, had barely slept and would not leave the bohio, *where once she had cared for the baby and held him close.*

Her six older sisters, who had raised and cared for Aycayia since she herself was a babe, were in fear for their youngest sister's life. They urged her to leave the bohio, *to bathe under the cool light of the moon. But Aycayia would not move. She stared into the fire at the center of the hut and watched the smoke and ashes float away.*

When the sun rose, First Sister tried again. She left the bohio *herself and bathed in the clear, fresh water outside. She called for her sisters to join her, but Aycayia did not budge.*

So Second Sister left the bohio *to bathe with First Sister. And both called to the others to join them. But Aycayia said not a word and did not budge.*

And so it went, as Third Sister and Fourth Sister and Fifth Sister emerged one by one from the bohio. And each began to bathe and each called back. But only when Sixth Sister joined them and all were calling Aycayia did she stir from the flames and smoke and ash.

Finally, Aycayia emerged. She joined her Sisters, who washed the soot from her body. But the ash washed from Aycayia's face was replaced by streaks of tears for her Lost Child. And the song she sang was beautiful but heartbreaking. Yet even in her grief, Aycayia was the most beautiful woman who had ever lived. And that was her curse. Men looked at her and saw the curve of her hip, the full-

ness of her breast, her raven-dark hair and the light in her eyes. But few saw the love that she had borne for her child or the anguish in her heart now that he was lost to her.

When the bath was done, the Six Sisters made a large pot of ajiaco and coaxed Aycayia to eat. The soup was warm and flavorful and brought forth memories of her childhood—not so long ago—in the days before the horror of her wedding night. The smallest of smiles bloomed on Aycayia's lovely face. But this smile would not last.

The old crone Guanayoa appeared. She said, "First Chief and First Shaman have banished you from the cacicazgo."

The Six Sisters protested. They knew Guanayoa had always hated Aycayia and suspected she had poisoned First Chief and First Shaman against Her.

But Aycayia was resigned to her fate. And with her child gone, there was nothing to keep her in the cacicazgo. "I will leave," she said.

Guanayoa was not pleased that Aycayia was not angry. And Guanayoa was even less pleased when the Six Sisters insisted on joining Aycayia in her exile. "We will go with Aycayia from the cacicazgo," First Sister said. "Else Guanayoa will triumph."

The crone argued against it, but the Sisters would not budge, and their loyalty brought a small smile to Aycayia's face. So it was decided that Guanayoa would take Aycayia and her Six Sisters far away.

Fourteen Warriors were placed in seven canoes. They were blindfolded, so they could not look upon Aycayia. And their nostrils were plugged with rubber gum, so they could not revel in her scent. Aycayia was led to the First Canoe. She was bound so she could touch no one. And she was gagged so her voice could make no appeal. For Aycayia's beauty was so potent, all the senses must be thwarted, lest someone take pity upon her.

Aycayia's Six Sisters sat in the six other canoes. Guanayoa sat *beside Aycayia and guided the blind warriors far away to Punta Majagua. There, Aycayia, her Sisters and Guanayoa were abandoned. The Fourteen Warriors were instructed to row toward the heat of the setting sun with their blindfolds in place. Only when night had fallen could they remove them and find their way home.*

But there was no peace for Aycayia. She and her Sisters were forced to build a new bohio for Guanayoa. And they served the old crone as her slaves.

And Guanayoa was cruel to Aycayia in many small ways. But Aycayia would not be brought to anger. It seemed nothing Guanayoa did could harm Aycayia more than her own grief.

But Aycayia's Six Sisters, Aunties to her dead child, could not bear to see Her treated in such a way. And so the Sisters summoned First Hummingbird to take a message back to the cacicazgo, pleading for help. Hummingbird flitted to each of the Fourteen Warriors, and each and every one answered the Six Sisters' call. They sat in their canoes and put blindfolds on again. And they remembered their First Journey and crossed through the darkness in the same manner.

The Fourteen Warriors found the bohio of Guanayoa on Punta Majagua. They found Aycayia bathing Guanayoa with her Sisters. But Guanayoa saw the Warriors first, and Guanayoa was First Witch. She cast a spell upon the Fourteen and told them only the strongest might have Aycayia. Thus enthralled, each Warrior did battle against friend and brother. And by nightfall, all Fourteen lay dead on Punta Majagua.

Aycayia was one of only ten witnesses to the crime. She threatened to tell First Chief and First Shaman of First Witch's evil. But Guanayoa warned, "There is no land safe from my magicks, Aycayia! And if no land is safe from me, then you will never be safe on land."

Frightened, Aycayia and her Sisters fled to First Ocean, hoping to escape Guanayoa's wrath. They stumbled through the water, try-

ing to reach the canoes of the Fourteen Warriors. But Guanayoa's curse reached them first. The Six Sisters were transformed into dolphins. And the First Witch transformed Aycayia into a hideous manatee.

But the beauty of Aycayia the Cursed is still strong, and so too her grief and her loneliness. And it is said, she can still become beautiful to lure children into the water with her song, never to be seen again . . .

Lost in the dream, Rain felt something scrape along her arm. Then her Papa 'Bastian's voice summoned her from sleep. "Rain! Rain, wake up!" Still groggy, she stirred. He poked the armband he had slipped upon her arm, nudging it and her. "Rain. Listen. I saw the kids. Rain!"

Instantly, her eyes popped open, and she all but bolted out of bed—right through her ghostly grandfather, who now stood up behind her. Cash was there, too. She was still confused, half-asleep, but she was dragging herself awake, using her desperation like a rope to pull herself out of slumber's grip. She stepped back so she could see them both. "Did you say you saw the Kim kids? Where are they? What time is it?" She glanced at the clock. It was 5:26 A.M. "Where are they?" she repeated.

"They're on Witch's Finger with Aycayia. I tried to talk to them, to her. But I was pretty useless. The kids couldn't hear me. Maybe she couldn't either—"

"How'd you get back here so quickly?"

He couldn't believe that mattered to her at this moment, but he said, "I ran across the island and hopped the first ferry back. Joe was at the helm. He looked so old . . ."

She couldn't believe that mattered to him at this moment, and she asked, "How were they? How did they look?"

"Fine, actually. Happy. I mean I guess they're under a spell, but they—"

"Were they dolphins?"

"No, human. At least at first. So was Aycayia. She was wrapped in seaweed, which was probably good for my sanity. But the kids were naked—"

"Were they cold?"

"No, listen. Aycayia had built a fire and made them soup. She was *taking care* of them. I don't think she's evil, Rain. I just think she's—"

"Lonely."

"Yes. And sad."

"The dream. I was dreaming that when you woke me."

"Dreaming me finding her?"

"No, dreaming her story. But it was different this time than the last time. I mean it was the same story, but it wasn't. That first dream . . . I think that first dream . . . lied."

Cash suddenly spoke up. "Kid, dreams can totally lie."

This was an odd epiphany for Rain. "Yeah. I guess so. But these dreams, the ones I've been having since all the weirdness started. They're different. They feel so real. And this one tonight seemed . . . true. Or *truer* than the old version of the story, anyway."

The Pale Tourist shook his head. "I don't ever trust my dreams. That's fluff. Spinning off and evaporating like cotton candy for the mind, my friend. You want something to trust, try money. Coin. Lucre. That's the stuff you can bank on. Cold, hard cash."

"Isn't your name Cash?" the Dark Man asked.

"It is now. And that's why."

Rain and 'Bastian exchanged confused looks. Rain said, "Didn't you have something to tell me?"

"Oh, yeah. See, this mosquito swarm vampire thing killed me. And now it's looking to kill you. It's taking orders from this woman, who formed right out of the air."

"Julia," Rain and 'Bastian said in unison.

"If you say so. I didn't catch her name. Anyway, I figured I should warn you. Figured if I did, maybe I could move on." He looked around, but nothing had changed. There was nowhere in particular for him to move. He scrunched his face into a frown. "'Course, I might have gotten that wrong."

Rain visibly shook off Cash's musings and turned back to 'Bastian. "Do you think they're still there, where you left them?"

"No. I stayed with them *until* they left. Then I followed. They went back to the water, and Aycayia had her manatee skin wrapped like a bundle under her arm. I kept up as long as I could. I saw her dress herself and transform back. Then I saw her transform the kids back into dolphin pups with her tail. The other six dolphins joined them, and they swam off faster than I could follow. So I went back to shore and crossed the island. Oh, and Callahan was there too!"

"You know Callahan?" This from Cash.

"*You* know Callahan?" This from Rain.

"He hired me! Sent me to that cave. Sent me to my death, come to think of it."

"Why? Why did he hire you? What's in the cave?"

"Some kind of ancient artifact is supposed to be there. He called it a—"

"*Zemi,*" Rain said.

"Yeah. You know about this?"

Rain pointed to her snake charm. "This is a *zemi*. It's how I can hear you. There are eight more of them, and I'm supposed to collect them. Callahan's in my way."

Cash looked scared, more afraid of Callahan than of Mosquito Boy. "Uh, look. I'd tread carefully. He'll figure you're in *his* way. And he's not the kind of guy to let anyone get between him and his paycheck."

Again Rain and 'Bastian exchanged a look. 'Bastian said, "Paycheck? Who's he working for?"

"No idea. But I can guarantee you he wasn't shelling out my cut on his own dime. Callahan's nothing if not tight with a buck."

"Did he pay you?" Rain asked.

"Dying kinda got in the way of that."

Rain smiled slyly. "So he got you killed and, uh . . ."

"Stiffed you," 'Bastian added.

"Well, that's one way to—"

"So if it came down to it," Rain said, "you don't owe him anything."

"I guess not . . ."

"So you're on my team now."

"There are teams?"

"There are teams." She said to 'Bastian, "Do you think they'll go back? Aycayia and the Kimlets?"

He nodded. "At night, when it's safe."

"Then we need to go back at night."

"It won't be safe. Not for you. Not on Sycorax."

"Whoa, whoa, whoa," Cash said, holding out his arms. "You're talking about Sycorax? That's where the swarm is! You can't go there."

"I have to," Rain said.

"*Why?!*"

"Because now I know dreams can lie."

CHAPTER THIRTY-THREE

WON'T GROW UP

WEDNESDAY, SEPTEMBER 17

T his makes no sense," Renée said.

Rain couldn't agree more—though they clearly had different topics in mind. There were five of them on the Guerrero speedboat now: Rain, Charlie, Miranda, Ariel *and Renée*. From Rain's point of view, the presence of her least favorite schoolmate—at this most crucial place and time—made no sense whatsoever.

Morning had broken on Wednesday, leaving Rain alone. 'Bastian's spirit had returned to the *zemi*, and Cash had simply vanished. Not just Cash, either. The storm that had raged all night over every one of the Ghosts—except Sycorax—had dissipated almost instantaneously with the dawn. Looking out her bedroom window at the clear morning sky, with the rising sun rapidly evaporating the rainwater from the drenched street and sidewalks, Rain had a moment of clarity regarding Hurricane Julia: *She's dead.*

Powerful as she was, Julia could no more stick around in daylight than 'Bastian or Cash. *Or why would she let up now?* No, Rain was convinced Julia was some kind of ghost. That meant Rain would be free of her, safe from her, for a little over twelve hours. If she could get to Aycayia and the Kimlets *before* sunset, then Julia would return too late to intervene.

Not that getting to Aycayia was going to be easy either way. Though Rain was fairly certain the Manatee-Woman would return after dark to Punta Majagua with her Sisters and the Lost Kims, there was no telling where they'd be before then. It definitely raised a question: Why was Aycayia able to operate in daylight when every other mystic creature Rain had encountered could not? *Why didn't* she *vanish with the sun?* Only one answer seemed to make any sense: Aycayia *wasn't* dead. In both dreams, in both versions of the legend, Aycayia and the Six Sisters had been transformed by Guanayoa into sea creatures, but they had not died. On the contrary, they had—perhaps inadvertently—been made immortal.

No wonder Aycayia was so lonely. On the surface, living forever sounded pretty sweet, but beneath the waves, what would it be like for this young girl—this young mother who had lost her child—to live on endlessly in the body of a manatee? The manatee-monotony, even with your Sisters there to maintain your spirits and despite the ability to occasionally transform back into a human, would deaden the soul. Did she have—*could* she have—manatee calves? Would she want them? Or had there been, over the centuries, an endless succession of human children, stolen away and transformed? If so, then clearly Aycayia's power to morph herself a brood didn't include the ability to grant them their own immortality. Otherwise, there'd be hundreds of dolphins and pups by now, not just the original Six Aunties and the three Kimlets.

If these previous Lost Children all aged and died before Aycayia's big brown eyes, the pain of losing her own child would return over and over and over again. The loneliness—even in the midst of caring for each latest "litter"—would be unbearable. And the desperate need to find replacements would continue throughout eternity.

Aycayia the Cursed. Talk about understatement.

Armed with this new understanding, Rain felt maybe she stood a chance of breaking the cycle, if only she could find them before nightfall.

Rain raced to get ready. (Today, she had no problem braiding her hair.) She gathered her things and snuck out of the Inn without seeing her parents or doing any of her morning chores. Ignoring the trouble she'd be in later, she merely left them a brief note claiming she had to get to school early.

Fifteen minutes later, with drums beating in her head, she was outside Charlie's door and filling him in on all she had learned and intuited. They conceived a plan and set about executing it immediately.

There was no point in skipping school. Given that three children had already gone missing on the island, it would only raise significant red flags if they ditched—and besides, they couldn't expect to find Her or the Kimlets until sunset approached. Plus they needed Miranda's help.

So they were both there, waiting for young Miss Guerrero, when Ariel dropped Miranda off at the Columbia Yacht Club. In Ariel's presence, Rain asked Miranda if they could once again go out after school to look for the Kimlets. Miranda turned to look at Ariel, who made a slight glance at the cloudless sky and nodded. Then Charlie asked if they could bring scuba gear. Miranda bit her lip and looked away, but she nodded, this time without bothering to get confirmation from the ever-silent Ms. Jones. Charlie and Rain exchanged shrugs; it seemed it was just understood that Ariel would pick them up after school with diving gear already aboard. They followed Miranda off the slip, and on the way to school, Rain filled Miranda in on the latest relevant weirdness—though not, of course, on anything 'Bastian- or *zemi*-related. By the time they reached campus, Miranda was up to speed on the plan—dreading it, but up to speed—and prepared to do her best.

But they were ambushed entering the junior high. Rain had gone in first with Charlie behind her, but when Miranda followed, Renée had practically pounced. "Hey, Sugar. Miss me?"

"Renée! Hi. I mean . . . yes. I mean, I saw you yesterday."

"I know. But it's been like forever since we last hung out. What are you doing after school? I'm off today."

Renée's work schedule at Koko's Caribbean Fries had kept her at bay—and out of Rain's braided hair—during the current Kimlet crisis. But Renée didn't work Wednesdays, and Miranda was not an adept liar. So before Rain or Charlie could stop her, Miranda said, "Um, well, you see, we're going out on my father's boat to help search for Wendy, John and Michael Kim."

Renée's eyes squinted in confusion, then widened briefly. Truthfully, she had put the missing tourist children out of her mind, and it took her a second to figure out what Miranda was talking about and then another second to get her head around the notion that any of them cared. During second three, she began to see this as an opportunity. She grabbed hold of Miranda's arms. "Oh, I'll come along. Anything I can do to help." Renée glanced over Miranda's shoulder, taking pleasure in Charlie's helpless horror and Rain's grim frustration.

Miranda turned back in time to catch Rain and Charlie's looks—while missing Renée's resulting smirk. It didn't take much effort to read Rain's mind. *It was going to be hard enough hunting for dolphinized children with Ariel around. But at least she'd be tied to the boat. How are we supposed to do what needs doing without revealing the truth to Renée?*

Miranda's own pleading expression spoke a few volumes of its own. *Maybe . . . maybe we don't need to hide the truth from Renée. One more set of eyes, one more diver, might help . . .* but even Miranda, who liked Renée, wasn't truly buying that. If they told her everything, it wouldn't change one inescapable fact: Renée hadn't seen the manatee transform. Without that one supernatural sight to anchor all the rest, there was no way she'd believe. Frankly, Miranda wouldn't have believed it either. So right then and there, Miranda steeled her mind to do what needed doing. She'd try to be as kind as possible, but one way or another she'd exclude Renée from their endeavor; she'd *ditch* her if necessary.

She turned back to face Miss Jackson.

So, approximately seven hours later, Renée was on the boat with the others, loudly mystified by their course and heading. "Those kids were lost near Windward. Why are we looking here?"

Rain's biggest concern was that Renée's appeal to logic might trigger some degree of, well, common sense in Ariel, who, as the sole adult, had the power to turn the boat around, but Ariel didn't give the slightest indication she had even heard Renée. Relieved, Rain said, "The Ghost Patrol and everyone are already searching near Windward. We're helping out by searching less likely spots."

"Less likely?" Renée asked as the speedboat curved around the lower side of Sycorax en route to Back Bay. "Try impossible. How would three little kids have gotten from the east side of San Próspero to the *west* side of Sycorax?"

Charlie shrugged. "Current?"

Renée stared at him. She opened her mouth to speak but was too exasperated to form any words.

Suddenly, Miranda grabbed Rain's left arm, squeezing her biceps just below the armband. In fact, Miranda's thumb grazed the snake charm. It drew Miranda's eyes to it, and Rain watched her friend confirm the *zemi*'s presence. If Rain had to give it up to 'Bastian again tonight, there'd be no convincing Miranda it had been left at home. Rain mentally shrugged. *Worry about that if and when . . .*

Miranda tore her eyes away from the charm and looked over the bow of the boat. Rain turned and followed Miranda's gaze. The Aunties were heralding the boat's arrival, leaping and cavorting along. One even had Alonso's camera.

This time, Miranda said, "Follow those dolphins!" It was a needless statement, as Ariel was already headed that way.

Renée blanched again. "What?!" She started to say more but held her tongue to keep on Miranda's good side.

Charlie offered, "Dolphins are known to rescue people lost at sea?"

Now Renée couldn't help herself. "Seriously? That's the story you're going with?"

By this time, the boat was curving around the southwest lip of Sycorax, heading into Back Bay. Rain could see Punta Majagua—Witch's Finger—to the north. What she couldn't see was the *Bootstrap*. Callahan's boat was gone. It pleased her at first—and then made her nervous. *Rather know where he is than risk him jumping out at us.* Truthfully, though, it didn't change anything. "Okay, suit up."

"Suit what?" Renée asked as Rain and Charlie began stripping down to the bathing suits they were wearing beneath their clothes.

This had been Plan B. When Miranda had failed to dissuade Renée from joining them and had wimped out on just saying no, Rain had the brainstorm to *not* warn their classmate about the dive. She managed to pull Miranda aside en route from the gym to the cafeteria and suggest that when the time came, Renée would be without a swimsuit and wouldn't be able to join them. A grateful Miranda had seized on the opportunity to suggest she stay aboard the boat with Ariel and Renée to keep them occupied and distracted. Rain could pretty much tell this was because Miranda was even less comfortable scubaing than snorkeling, but it made sense. Their new friend would only hold Rain and Charlie back, and the less Ariel and Renée saw the better.

"We're going swimming?" Renée asked incredulously.

"Diving," Rain said as she opened the benches that held and hid the scuba equipment.

"Why?"

Charlie offered, "Part of the search?"

"What are you searching for *down there*? Kids or corpses?" Everyone went silent, and even Renée seemed to feel she had crossed a line. She looked around the boat, exhaled loudly, and said, "Fine," pulling her blouse right over the top of her head.

As she unbuttoned and took off her shorts, Charlie stammered, "W-what are you doing?"

"Well, no one warned me to bring a suit, so I guess I'm diving in bra and panties." She seemed pleased by the lone boy's discomfort.

"That doesn't seem appropriate," Rain said stiffly.

"Oh, grow up," Renée responded as she chose a pair of flippers. "How's this any different from a bikini? Besides, we're doing this for the children. Right, Sugar?"

Rain's face turned copper red. Charlie stood there, slack-jawed, desperately trying not to look Renée's way. Ariel piloted the boat, seemingly unaware of the conversation entirely. And Miranda looked stricken. She had gotten it into her head that she wouldn't have to dive, that her job would be to stay behind on the boat with Renée and Ariel. *So now what do I do?* She hadn't asked Ariel to bring her a bathing suit, and she definitely didn't feel comfortable swimming in her underwear, especially not with Charlie around.

On cue, Ariel reached over and opened another small compartment in the dash. Miranda stared, at first not realizing what the colorful bits of fabric were. Then she took a step closer and knew: Inside the glove box was a collection of rolled-up tankinis and one-piece suits from Miranda's dresser drawer at home.

Miranda sighed a thank you, though even she wasn't sure if the sigh signified gratitude for the swimwear or despair over losing her last excuse not to dive. She offered Renée a choice of suits and grabbed a black one-piece for herself. Renée chose a shiny green tankini, as there were no bikinis available to prove her earlier point.

Charlie was assiduously staring at his flippers until Renée suggested he turn around and not peek. Very, very flustered, Charlie flipper-slapped to the front of the boat to watch the Aunties frolic, mumbling, "I wasn't peeking," while Miranda and Renée changed rapidly. To be honest, it took *all* his willpower not to sneak a look.

Rain also looked away.

Ariel killed the engine. By this time, they were just a couple of football fields away from Witch's Finger. The dolphins stopped too, halfway between the speedboat and the shore. Ariel checked everyone's gear, pausing only briefly to give Miranda a questioning look. They both knew Miranda was trained to dive—and they both knew she had never really taken to it.

"I'll be fine," Miranda whispered with more confidence than she felt.

Rain had a last-minute idea and—while Ariel occupied Renée's attention, checking her tank—leaned toward Miranda and whispered, "Plan hasn't changed. Soon as we get close to *anything*, pretend you're having trouble. Keep Renée busy." Rain could see Miranda's relief through her diving mask. Pretending she wasn't great at diving was something she could definitely manage.

She said to Renée, "Could you stick close to me down there? I'm not really very good at this."

Renée stared at her, still at a complete loss as to what they hoped to accomplish with this dive—and half convinced they were planning some kind of humiliation for her in advance of what she didn't yet have planned for them. Nevertheless, she said, "Of course, Sugar. Whatever you need."

Then Rain and Charlie sat on the edge of the boat and allowed themselves to fall backward into the water. Renée and Miranda took their places and did the same.

It had been a hot and humid day, and the water in Back Bay was swimming-pool warm and refreshing. Rain swam down, swam up and checked her breathing. All seemed well. Charlie moved into position beside her. She looked around to get her bearings. Miranda and Renée were right behind them. The dolphin pod was presumably in front, but even in the clear Caribbean blue, they were too far ahead to be visible. She and Charlie exchanged a look and a nod and swam forward toward the Aunties' last known position. She knew that in the time it took the four teens to get to where the dolphins had last been sighted, the pod could easily vanish, but Rain took the fact that they still taunted her with her father's camera as a promising sign. They knew she was there; they knew she couldn't catch them; they wouldn't run. *They want to play.*

Minutes later, Rain spotted her first dolphin and pointed it out to the others. They kicked their flippers harder to catch up. There they all were: six Aunties, three pups, a manatee and one stolen camera, which was juggled between one dolphin or another—even the Kimlets participated in the game of keep away.

In fact, the smallest dolphin—Michael Kim Dolphin—let it fall from his mouth. It floated there, just barely out of Rain's reach. She probably could have gotten to it before Michael but made the split-second decision not to lose track of why she was there. Rain needed kids, dolphins and manatee to trust her. Taking their stuff—even if it was really Rain's stuff (or in any case, Rain's father's stuff)—was not going to help. She let it float. Michael swam back for it but was beaten to the camera by the biggest of the pups, presumably Wendy Kim Dolphin, who tossed it to John Kim Dolphin as Michael followed along behind.

One of the Aunties took the camera from John, freeing the Kimlets to play without concern. They swam close to each of the teens, lingering particularly around their favorite, Miranda, who gently stroked each in turn. Even Renée, forgetting why they had theoretically come—let alone why she had chosen to tag along— was enchanted. She also reached out to stroke the pups. Michael shied away from her, but Wendy and John clearly enjoyed Renée's attentions.

And all three pups clearly enjoyed teasing Rain. They'd glide in close to her and then quickly back away, snickering. (Obviously, they still hadn't forgiven her for interfering with their first chance to join Aycayia's family.) As with the camera, Rain resisted the urge to reach out and wrap her arms around a Lost Kim and hold on tight. She knew she'd never be able to maintain her grip on one, let alone all three, and she certainly couldn't transform them back—though she did wonder what her healing snake might accomplish and made an effort to rub the *zemi* against one pup or another every chance she got. But neither the charm nor the Kimlets responded to the contact in any way.

Aycayia, meanwhile, was gradually leading the Lost Boys and

Girl toward the Punta shore. Rain and Charlie, and to a lesser extent Miranda and Renée, were following. Then three of the Aunties slid into place between Rain and the Kimlets, creating a sea-mammal screen to run interference for Her. There were bubbles everywhere, coming from the teens' regulators and from the movement of the dolphins, and Rain's vision became obscured. But she didn't need a clear view to know where she needed to be. She had a plan and stuck to it: She'd follow Aycayia and the Kims to land—hopefully before sunset—and make her appeal to all four of them. The dolphins crowded around her, bumping her occasionally, pushing her back. Charlie set his own screens when he could, though, and Rain was able to make slow but steady progress.

The Aunties tried another tack. One of them grabbed the camera and glided within reach of Rain, hoping to lure her off. Rain didn't take the bait and continued forward with deliberate determination.

Now the smiles of the Six Sisters seemed to turn sinister. They became more aggressive, slapping at Rain and Charlie with their tails, bumping them harder. Not for a moment, however, did she think these six loving Aunties would truly risk hurting four thirteen-year-olds. When they pushed, she pushed gently back, calling their bluff. So the Sisters tried something more desperate.

One of the dolphins—First Sister, Rain was sure—swam right up to her. As Rain moved to swim around the creature, the Auntie slid her beak behind Rain's air tube and abruptly yanked to the right. The regulator popped right out of Rain's mouth. The Auntie swam away, but Rain kept her cool and calmly returned the regulator to her lips. A noise caused her to glance back over her shoulder.

Three other Sisters had perpetrated the same trick on Charlie, Renée and Miranda. The latter was panicking. At first Rain thought—or at least hoped—it was merely an act: Miranda's attempt to feign distress to distract Renée. It soon became clear Miranda wasn't faking anything. She thrashed about, unable to breathe, unable to either grab her regulator or even surface. Renée was doing better and had returned her regulator to her mouth, but she was also a bit freaked and too distracted to notice Miranda's distraction.

Leave it to Charlie to save the day. Having recovered his own regulator, he swam up to Miranda and grasped her shoulders. She struggled, but he slid his hands down to her arms and held tight, until she steadied. He grabbed up her regulator and slowly placed it back in her mouth. Then, with a glance back at Rain—who nodded—he swam up to the surface, still holding Miranda's arm. Renée followed them.

Rain continued on alone.

CHAPTER THIRTY-FOUR

THREE PEARLS

The drums were back, building in her head as she swam toward shore in pursuit of Aycayia and the Kimlets. The Sisters approached—perhaps to shut Rain out again—but before they could, she shot them a *don't mess with me now* look borrowed from her mother, and they peeled off and out of her way.

Or maybe the dolphins simply knew this confrontation was inevitable.

The water became shallow. Rain surfaced, pulling out her regulator and pulling off her mask, in time to see Aycayia very close to the beach, working her beautiful form free of her manatee skin, of her animal identity. The three pups played nearby, swirling in circles. Rain turned around. The Aunties were behind her, spread out in a half circle, as if cordoning off the area. First Sister had Alonso's camera. Beyond them, Rain could make out Ariel helping Charlie, Miranda and Renée back onto the boat. Charlie glanced Rain's way—then pointed in the opposite direction. The boat sped off, leaving Rain alone. The stage, so to speak, was set.

Rain faced forward again, in time to see Aycayia stand, half in and half out of the water. The manatee skin was folded neatly in her arms, and her arms were folded across her breasts, but otherwise she was nude—at least from the waist up. Rain was flushed and embarrassed but could no longer risk looking away. *I might not get another chance.* The light was low; the shadows, long. She pulled off her flippers, found her own footing in the soft silt beneath the short waves and began walking toward Her.

Aycayia watched Rain approach, allowed Rain to approach— then seemed to regret it, realizing Rain now stood *between* her and the swirling, chattering Wendy, John and Michael. Rain saw anger flare in the Manatee-Woman's eyes. Aycayia took a step toward the pups, but Rain stopped her with a word.

"Sorry."

Aycayia pulled up short and studied Rain, as if suspecting a trick.

Rain went on, "I'm sorry for what they did to you. Not just Guanayoa, but First Chief and First Shaman too. They didn't understand, but that's no excuse. My name is Rain Cacique. My father is Alonso Cacique, and my mother is Iris Bohique." She pointed at the *zemi* on her arm. "I am heir to First Chief and First Shaman. I am the Searcher and the Healer, and I ask you, Aycayia . . . for your forgiveness."

Aycayia the Cursed stared, and Rain wondered if the Manatee-Woman understood. Rain thought about repeating the apology in Spanish, but Aycayia was from a time before any European had arrived on these shores, and Rain didn't know the true language of the Taíno. All she could do was hope that *somehow* her meaning—if not her words—would bridge the distance.

"I'm sorry for the child you lost," Rain said. "I can't imagine that pain. I hope . . . I hope it's something I never truly know. Once, not that long ago, I had a taste of it. I lost my grandfather for just a little while, and it was almost unbearable. So what you've been through . . . well, I . . . I don't have the words. But I can see the pain in you . . . and in Mrs. Kim—the mother of these three children."

Rain glanced back at the pups. They were no longer swimming in circles. Their little bottlenosed heads poked out of the water, *listening* to Rain—*but watching Her.* Rain wanted to do something to attract their attention, something to create eye contact, but she could *feel* Aycayia's gaze upon her and intuitively knew any movement along those lines would be regarded as a threat. So Rain held still, save for turning her head toward Aycayia again.

"I want to help you," Rain said. "I want to ease your pain and prove that my . . ." She searched for the right word. "That my *remorse* is, um, sincere." Slowly, tentatively, she reached out with her left hand. Even so, Aycayia flinched as if expecting Rain to strike her—or perhaps to make a grab for her manatee skin. Rain paused, and Aycayia settled. Rain reached out again and with just two fingers grazed the perfect copper skin of Aycayia's right arm.

Simultaneously, the eyeless snake on Rain's charm began to glow. The golden light raced down Rain's arm to her hand to those two fingers, making the jump to Aycayia's arm and vanishing inside her. Aycayia didn't smile or sigh, but for a few short seconds, she closed her eyes and felt the *zemi*'s healing power. For what it was worth. Rain knew Aycayia's wounds could never truly be healed by an armband. Still, maybe it could dull the pain enough—just long enough—to open her up to Rain's plea . . .

"I know it's not enough," Rain said. "Nothing could ever be

enough to ease your pain. Not even these three kids. They can help—for a while. They can distract you. But really they're only reminders of what was yours and is gone. Forever. They can't take your pain away anymore than I can. And in the meantime, you are hurting their mother and father. Hurting them the way you were hurt. But this time *you* have the power to heal. You can heal an entire family by giving those kids back."

Aycayia opened her eyes. She looked at Rain with an overwhelming sadness that made Rain want to wrap her arms around Her, to stay with Her forever. But the spell was quickly broken as the beautiful woman shifted her gaze toward the Kimlets. She smiled sadly and then slowly turned her head back to meet Rain's eyes.

Neither moved nor spoke. Rain was out of words. Frankly, I was amazed she had been as eloquent as she was. Then she spoiled the moment.

"Um, if it helps, you can keep the camera."

Aycayia smiled. She opened her mouth and a sound emerged that was something like the bark of a seal. (Certainly not a bark any self-respecting canine would utter.) Rain briefly feared the Manatee-Woman would try to speak in Sea Mammalese and grow angry when Rain didn't understand.

But Aycayia was merely clearing a throat that hadn't uttered a human syllable in centuries. When she spoke again, her voice was halting yet melodious. It was the voice of a Siren, for there was nothing about Aycayia the Cursed that wasn't beautiful, enchanting. She said, "You seek a prize that isn't mine to offer, Searcher."

Rain couldn't help herself. "You speak English!"

"I have listened to the people on the boats. And to the children who have joined me along the way. I know many of their words."

"Then you understood me. You understand their parents—"

"It is not for me to return them to their parents. In my life—in my natural life—I was given few choices. I cannot—I will not—steal away that gift from my young ones."

"They aren't *your* young ones."

"That is for them to decide." She turned to her pups. "Stay with me," she said. "The sea is ours. There will be no sorrow, no rules. Only play and mischief and devotion to one another. You will never know life without love. For you are precious to me, children. More precious than gold. More precious than the most precious of pearls. More precious than mine own life. I love you all."

The pups snickered and called out their approval. Then they turned toward Rain.

Rain stared at them stupidly, not sure what came next. She glanced from them to Her and suddenly realized she was now supposed to make her case to the Kimlets. She wasn't prepared for that. She had spent the entire day going over and over what she would say to Aycayia, but she had no clue how to compete with Her for the kids. How *could* she compete with Her? Immediately, she wished Miranda were there instead. The Kimlets *liked* Miranda. Or Charlie. Rain knew Charlie would have found the words. Even Renée seemed a better candidate. She could probably *intimidate* them into coming back. Rain felt entirely unequal to the task, but the sun continued to sink in the afternoon sky, and she knew she was running out of time. *Now or never.*

She cleared her own throat with her own nervous little bark. She looked at the Kimlets and decided to keep it simple. "Guys. Your mom, your dad, they miss you. They're so scared for you. They're heartbroken. I know—*I know*—you love them as much as they love you. You just can't swim away and leave them alone. They would never, *ever* recover from that. I know Aycayia cares for you, and she's magical and beautiful and everything. But your mom and your dad, well, they're your mom and dad! Wendy, John, Michael, please, please come back to them."

The littlest pup hid his face beneath the water. Wendy nudged him back to the surface. Do dolphins cry? Saltwater ran down both their snouts—but whether it was the sea or their tears, Rain could not be sure. John swam forward toward Aycayia and nudged her. She lifted his bottlenose chin with one hand and stroked it gently, looking into his eyes.

Then she turned to Rain and smiled sadly, saying, "They have chosen to follow you home, Healer."

Before Rain could even register her victory, Aycayia the Cursed leaned over and kissed John's snout. Immediately, he began to transform. Before Rain's eyes, his snout shrank, his skin changed color. Flippers grew into arms; flukes split into legs. Hair sprouted from his head. He actually had a neck again. He became John Kim, floundering a bit before finding his footing in the shallow water.

Afraid to jinx it, Rain didn't move as Aycayia kissed Wendy and then Michael, morphing both into human children once more. The Kimlets clung to Her. Still holding her skin in one hand, Aycayia wrapped both arms around them and said, "I will miss you."

The Not-So-Lost Kims all spoke over each other. They would miss her too. They would never forget her. They loved her. They just loved their parents too. She reassured them she was not angry. She understood. But for each child, she shed one tear: one perfect pearl, her final gifts to her pups.

The four hugged each other as if they'd *never* let go. Until they did. Aycayia the Cursed relinquished her hold on them and stepped away. She nodded toward Rain, who stepped forward. Michael filled the void in his arms by hugging Rain's leg. Even

Wendy took Rain's hand. Only John stood alone as the four of them watched Aycayia unfold her skin and climb back into it. The mouth of the manatee swallowed Her up, and Aycayia disappeared into her animal self. They watched the Manatee-Woman dive and surface and wave one last time with her tail. Then she was gone. The Six Sisters—Aunties no longer—followed, disappearing with Aycayia under the sea.

Rain and the Kimlets stood there for many long seconds, just breathing.

At first, Rain's thoughts were filled only with unadulterated relief. Soon enough, other concerns crowded their way into her head. She said, "Okay, this is good. This is good. Just one last problem."

"We're naked," Michael said.

"Well, there's that, yeah. But I was thinking more about how we're ever gonna explain this to the adults . . ."

CHAPTER THIRTY-FIVE

DUELING REALITIES

Physically, mentally and emotionally exhausted, Rain entered the Nitaino Inn with 'Bastian, Charlie, Miranda and—unfortunately and unavoidably—Renée. The lobby was packed. Iris, Alonso, Judith, Cash and Constables Thibideaux and Viento stood in a semicircle (like Aunties) cordoning off the entire Kim family. Esther Kim was on her knees, holding her boys, John and Michael. Fred Kim stood right behind them with both arms wrapped around his Wendy.

Rain feigned surprise. "You found them!"

Wendy called out, "They found us!" She grinned.

The parents, eyes literally glistening, hugged their kids tighter, then traded kids and hugged again.

Charlie chewed on the inside of his mouth. 'Bastian scratched an eyebrow with a pinky—his standard method of avoiding eye contact, now rather unnecessary, as no one but Rain and Cash could see him. Miranda teared up legitimately. Renée too, appeared touched by the reunion—even as she leaned over and whispered in Rain's ear, "Sugar . . . I own you."

Rain kept a smile plastered on her face and nodded . . .

It had all gone as well as could be expected.

The dolphin pod had done them three last favors, given them three last gifts, easily as precious as their youngest sister's pearls.

Favor One: First Sister, still carrying Alonso's camera, had swum to the far side of Back Bay and gibbered at Charlie—dolphin to Dauphin—summoning him back to Rain. Ariel, expressing no surprise at seeing Rain with three clothes-challenged, Formerly Lost Kims, piloted the boat as close to shore as possible. Miranda and Charlie jumped ship into the shallows with towels to wrap around the Kimlets. Renée stayed aboard with her mouth hanging open. Stunned, she said nothing.

Favor Two: As Charlie lifted Michael into Ariel's arms, Miranda pointed and said, "What's that?" "That" was Wendy's swimsuit floating to the surface of the water, followed by John's and Michael's. Second Sister, Third Sister, and Fourth Sister had preserved them—like manatee skin—for reasons perhaps obscure. The suits were, of course, soaking wet, but not even Michael complained as the three Kimlets put them back on. Renée stared, shook her head but said nothing.

Favor Three: Per Rain's instructions—and Miranda's confirmation—Ariel was gunning the speedboat toward Windward. The danger at this stage was that the authorities—and even volunteers like Rain's father—were out in force, searching for Wendy, John and Michael, and it really wouldn't do to find them with our stalwart teens (and Renée). To this end, the Kimlets lay flat on the deck of the boat, hidden under their towels. They couldn't stop giggling. It was all part of their Awfully Big Adventure, and it was contagious. Despite the ongoing seriousness of the situation—or maybe because they were by this time desperate for a cathartic release—Miranda, then Charlie, then Rain started giggling too. Renée laughed once, a sharp and triumphant bark of her own, but still she said nothing. Ariel did not so much as smile but kept her eye out for other boats and deftly steered clear of any and all. By this time, the sun was within minutes of hitting the water, and Rain feared they wouldn't find a safe landing before Santa Julia reared her stormy head. That's when Fifth Sister and Sixth Sister appeared, leading them to a deserted beach just south of Windward. (By now, the phrase "Follow those dolphins!" no longer required verbalization.) Rain, Charlie and Miranda took the Kimlets to shore. Michael wanted to build a sand castle, but just then the Rusty's Gourmet Sandwiches food truck pulled into the parking lot, sporting a flat. Cassie Barrett got out of the cab, saw the nail in her tire, and began swearing like a sailor—which started John giggling all over again. Cassie heard the boy, turned and spotted the three kids. "Oh, my God!" she said, pulling out her cell phone and dialing 911. She did not see Rain, Charlie and Miranda swimming underwater to the speedboat, which was ensconced out of view, just around a bend in the coastline. A smiling Renée helped them aboard, and still . . . . she said nothing.

Now you couldn't shut her up.

Over and over, she urged the Kimlets to tell their story. She knelt down to their level, fascinated. As previously arranged, Michael took the lead—telling the absolute truth (minus the involvement of Rain et al.)—from their introduction to the Womanatee to their transformation into dolphin pups to their nights as naked wild children eating soup by a jungle campfire, and so on. Of course, the truth played like fiction, and Fred Kim wanted to get to the bottom of it all. As did the constables. Wendy and John took over, telling another version of the story. In this version, the kids were swimming off Windward Strand when they got caught in a tide or current they couldn't fight. It took them down the coast before they could fight their way out of the water to the shore. They walked off, looking for help, but it got dark. They were found by Aycayia and her sisters, and Aycayia took them camping in the jungle and offered them soup.

"And this was on San Próspero? Near Windward?" Renée asked, rather gleefully.

"Yes," Wendy said slowly, her eyes narrowing.

"Did she keep you there against your will?"

"No," Wendy said, showing enough caution toward Renée to raise the younger girl in Rain's esteem by a considerable number of notches.

"Then why didn't she bring you back?" Renée wondered, oh-so-ingenuously.

"She *did*," Wendy emphasized. "Tonight."

"She gave us these," John said, holding up his pearl. Wendy and Michael held up their pearls too.

Everyone, even Renée, marveled. She said, "Those can't be real."

"They're real!" John insisted.

"She cried them," Michael said with a single nod of his head designed to put the matter at rest.

Fred took a few steps back, not at all sure what to make of these recitations. Rain saw him give Constable Thibideaux a questioning look. Thibideaux leaned in and said, "They seem to be all right. It doesn't look or sound like they were abused."

"Abused? I—I didn't even think of that . . ."

"And you shouldn't. But you should have them checked. Just in case."

"You think this woman—"

"We'll find this Aycayia," Thibideaux said—though Rain had her doubts. "Get an explanation. But if I had to guess, I'd say your kids were helped by a kindly drug smuggler."

"*What?!*" This last was said too loudly, and Fred Kim actually hushed *himself* when all eyes turned his way and the room got quiet.

Jean-Marc kept his voice low. "This isn't a serious issue on the Ghost Keys, but we do have the occasional group of amateurs running pot—marijuana—to and from the islands. It's not big business here, but it happens. It's usually mainlanders in their early twenties looking for a little extra cash. And sometimes they're not paid in cash but in things they can hock. I've never seen a payment in pearls before, but it fits."

Cash snorted derisively. Rain wondered if it really did fit—or if the constable was simply trying to create a logic that conformed to his worldview more easily than either Michael or Wendy's tales. Once more, she felt a desire to chuck all the pretense and shout out *her* truths, but she knew better.

Thibideaux went on, "If these young women, this Aycayia and her sisters, were waiting to make a connection, it would explain why they couldn't risk bringing the kids back until the deal was over. Fortunately, it sounds like they took fairly good care of them. Even kept them entertained."

Now it was Michael's turn to stare. John shook his head, and Wendy did everything in her power not to laugh. Michael turned to his mother and said, "Is he making all this up?"

Renée said, "Sure he is. Adults have fairy tales too, you know. Even teenagers tell stories." She glanced pointedly at Rain, who rolled her eyes, despite the danger she knew she was in. Renée was like a bomb waiting to go off, but for whatever reason, she had given herself a long fuse, and Rain made a conscious decision to enjoy the respite—for as long as it happened to last.

Esther hugged Michael again, saying, "She's right. We all have bedtime stories."

"Bedtime?" Michael asked, yawning on cue.

"Yes. Baths first. Then bedtime. Then bright and early tomorrow, we're all heading home." She glanced up—not at Thibideaux but at his female deputy, Mariah, who found herself nodding confirmation *before* checking to see if her boss would concur.

That was all the permission Esther Kim needed. She ushered her children up the stairs—right through Cash, by the way, which served to remind Rain that although one crisis had passed, another had barely been addressed. Briefly, she wondered why there had been no storm tonight. Not even after the sun had set and 'Bastian had materialized on the speedboat en route home from Windward. Perhaps Julia, like Renée, was hoarding her destructive capacity for a more opportune time.

At the top of the stairs, Michael said, "I'm not afraid of the water anymore, Mommy."

"That's wonderful, Michael."

From the lobby, Fred Kim watched his family ascend, until they vanished from view. Then he started to cry. Without shame. Alonso stepped forward, offering a reassuring smile and a reassuring hand on Mr. Kim's shoulder. Fred smiled back at him and wiped his eyes on his sleeve. He crossed the lobby to follow the other Kims—then stopped. He turned back toward Rain and pulled out his wallet. "I still owe you money," he said.

Rain shook her head. "I'm just glad they're safe."

"Thank you, but one thing really has nothing to do with the . . ."

"I couldn't. Really."

Alonso beamed proudly at his daughter. Iris, who had been on an emotional tightrope for days, now sniffed and dabbed at her own eyes—and resisted the urge to hug her daughter, knowing it would embarrass her in front of her friends.

"Really," Rain repeated. She saw 'Bastian raise an eyebrow.

Both knew she felt too guilty over exposing the Kimlets to Aycayia in the first place to take any money. Camera or no camera.

Fred Kim finally took no for an answer. Or perhaps he just couldn't wait to rejoin his family. He said, "Well, thank you," turned on his heel, and practically bounded up the stairs.

Deputy Constable Viento turned to her boss. "Now what?"

Jean-Marc didn't answer right away. He was looking at the teens and asked, "Where have you four been?"

Rain looked at Renée, who stood there, smiling pleasantly. Then Miranda said, "We were on one of my father's boats trying to help with the search." Charlie nodded. So did Rain. Renée said nothing.

Constable Thibideaux seemed to think about this. Then he nodded, turned to Viento and belatedly answered her question. "We look for these smugglers. I'd lay odds they've already left for the mainland, but we put out a description of this Aycayia—"

"Which description? The woman in the seaweed bikini or the manatee?"

Even Jean-Marc chuckled at that. "Yeah, I don't hold out a lot of hope for success here. And frankly, I'm not going to pull out all the stops to find a woman who ultimately rescued these kids, took care of them and then sent them home. But you and Stabler do your best."

"Not you?" Mariah Viento asked, surprised he was delegating.

"I've got to coordinate with Vector Control. They arrived this afternoon to deal with the mosquito problem on Sycorax. They want to set up early, before dawn tomorrow."

The constables then took their leave, shaking hands with Alonso and Iris, then exiting out the front door.

Tall and awkward, Judith Vendaval stood in the middle of the lobby at loose ends. She said, "Well, I should probably, um . . ." She trailed off.

Iris grasped her hands. "Please, join us for dinner?"

"I don't want to put you out. I know it's not included in—"

"It would be my pleasure. I mean, I haven't started *anything* yet, but if you can wait forty-five minutes, we'll have a feast, I swear."

"Can I help? Or at least watch? Local fare is part of what I write about."

"Sure, I'm happy to put you to work," Iris said.

"Putting people to work is one of her talents," Rain sassed.

Iris gave her daughter a *watch it, kid* look, but it came with another smile. Then she invited Charlie, Miranda and Renée to stay as well—if it was all right with their parents. They all accepted. Even Renée.

"Then I'll put you to work, too."

Rain said, "Told you," as Iris led a procession into the dining room toward the kitchen. Rain held back and grabbed her father by his wrist to stop him.

"I have to tell you something," she said.

'Bastian perked up, wondering just how much his granddaughter was about to spill.

Alonso stopped, turned and waited.

She took a deep breath and said, "I lost your camera. I borrowed it without asking, and I lost it."

"I . . . When was this?"

"When we were out with the Kims, and you let us go diving. I wanted to get some pictures of the manatee. But, well, I . . . got startled . . . by a dolphin. And I dropped it. And I couldn't find it."

"And why didn't you say something?"

"Um, you may not like this answer."

"Probably not."

"I was going to replace it without telling you."

"Hope I didn't notice."

"Yeah."

"What changed your mind?"

"Well, for starters, I don't have enough money. Yet!"

"That's why you were babysitting."

"Yeah. But I couldn't take their money, not after—"

"No, I understand that. I was proud of you for that. Not so proud of you right now, maybe. But I'm glad you finally spoke up."

"I *will* replace it, Dad. I swear."

"No, I'll replace the camera. You'll pay me back."

"Okay. I just don't have—"

"I'll take it out of your allowance, which means *no* allowance for the foreseeable future."

She sighed. "Right."

"Okay." He bent down and kissed the top of her head. "Let's go get in the way in the kitchen."

"I'll be right there." She knew she had gotten off easy.

He smiled and entered the dining room, leaving Rain alone with her ghosts.

Cash sauntered up. "We ready to deal with my thing now?"

Since her dad was still in earshot, Rain merely nodded.

'Bastian said, "We'll meet on Sycorax tomorrow at sunset. Rain'll bring me over in the *zemi*. But you'll want to hop the ferry tonight or before dawn tomorrow morning."

"Wait, wait, wait," Cash said, "I don't wanna go back there. And neither does she. They want to *kill* her."

"I have to go back," Rain whispered. "Can't let anyone else get hurt because I'm not doing my job."

'Bastian said to Cash, "And if *your* job is to protect her, you need to be there too."

"We don't know if that's my job."

"Why else are you still here?"

"*I don't know!*" Cash shouted. Both Rain and 'Bastian flinched, but neither bothered shushing him. They just gave him dirty looks, and he lowered his head, appropriately chastened. "All right, I'll be there," he said. Then, out of nowhere, "So . . . is your mom a good cook?"

Rain shrugged and nodded again.

"Great," Cash said. "Then let's hit the kitchen. I may not be able to eat, but I can smell any food I see."

'Bastian nodded too, but then shook his head. "Yeah, but it's torture sometimes."

"'Course it is," Cash said, "but in this afterlife, you take what you can get."

The three of them went to join the others in the crowded kitchen.

Meantime, Maq and I were hitching back from Windward. It had been a long way to go to drop a nail on East Beach Road. But I think it was worth it.

CHAPTER THIRTY-SIX

NONFRONTATION

THURSDAY, SEPTEMBER 18

When the bell rang at the end of English, and as everyone was racing to leave, Mrs. Beachum raised her voice above the clamor to remind Rain she had an oral report due in history tomorrow morning on the Taíno *cacique*. Rain nodded; she thought about saying something clever about the "research" she had already done but—fearing Mrs. B might ask follow-up questions—kept her mouth shut.

That morning, Rain had come downstairs to find no one in the kitchen. She'd crossed through the dining room to the lobby, which was again crowded with luggage, Caciques, Kims and Timo. The Kims were checking out—three days early. *But who could blame them?* Certainly not Iris or Alonso, despite the loss of income the early departure represented. With a nudge from his wife, Fred Kim offered to pay for the extra days, but Rain's parents wouldn't hear of it.

Rain had knelt down to say good-bye to the Kimlets. She knew that even now she wasn't their favorite, but Wendy, John and Michael still gave her big hugs and bigger hugs for Charlie and the biggest hugs for Miranda. (Rain took some satisfaction in knowing there were no hugs for Renée.) Then Wendy did something very grown-up. She took Rain's head in her small hands, tilted it down and kissed her gently on the forehead. Esther Kim noticed this benediction and was about to comment, until Michael said, "Aycayia taught her that." That served to remind Esther she wanted off the Ghosts as soon as mortally possible, and she began ushering her family and Timo out the door.

She paused long enough for Fred to shake Alonso's hand, and for Esther to embrace Iris, and for both to offer their thanks. Rain had held the door open for them, and Esther kissed Rain on the cheek and whispered, "Thank you, Rain."

A few minutes later they were gone. Rain's parents headed for the kitchen, but Rain stopped, spotting Michael's yellow shovel on the floor of the lobby. She went to the window, sure the Kims would be back for it any second. But they didn't come back. And Rain soon realized they'd probably never come back. And that was okay, because she was also fairly certain that Michael didn't need the shovel anymore. Still, she kept it. During English, she drew a crude picture of a manatee on it. It would be Aycayia's *zemi* now. It didn't belong in the Cache, but she'd keep it on the old Spanish desk in her room.

At the lockers, Rain confirmed with Miranda and Charlie that—after orchestra—they'd head back to Mr. Guerrero's study to do more research. Rain would wait for them in the air-conditioned school library, getting her other homework done. (There wasn't enough time to get to the Cache and back.) Renée, "unfortunately," had her shift at K.C.F. and wouldn't be able to join them.

Rain and Renée watched Miranda and Charlie go—then turned to face each other.

"So, really," Rain said, "what do you want?"

"Sugar—"

"No. No sugar, Renée. I'll take it unsweetened."

Renée smirked out loud and thought about it for a while. *What did she want?* "Well, we could start with the truth. You knew those kids would be on Sycorax—nowhere near Windward—and had us looking there on purpose." She nearly said "on porpoise" but decided it wasn't her style. "I don't know what the dolphins had to do with it. But something was up over there, and you've lied about it to everyone else, including, oh, I don't know . . . the kids' parents, your parents and the Ghost Patrol."

"I just wanted to get them back safely."

"I get that. I do. I saw those kids with their mom and dad. You did a good thing. But first you did a bad thing. And that's the piece I'm missing."

"You wouldn't believe me if I told you," Rain said with confidence, knowing Renée had heard the truth already from Michael the night before and hadn't believed a word of it.

"Well, I wouldn't *trust* you if you told me. Let's put it that way."

"So . . ."

"So, I don't know. Not yet, anyway. I'm not busting you. But I'm not letting this go, either. I'll figure it out eventually. I'll get it from Charlie or from Miranda. Or you'll make a mistake, and I'll get it from you."

"Get what? What do you think we're even talking about?"

Renée frowned. Then she took a step forward and said, "It doesn't matter what. But I'm gonna mess you up over it. You and Charlie and Miranda."

"You know Miranda legitimately likes you. She thinks you guys are friends."

"No thanks to you."

"Exactly. We've tried to warn her off, but she won't be warned off. So why not just be her friend and leave her out of this?"

"You know I can't do that."

"Why? Do you even remember what she did to piss you off?"

"Yes!"

"And it's petty, right?"

"Doesn't matter. Can't let it go."

"Yes, you can."

"No. I can't," Renée said. And Rain saw it. Something hard as flint in Renée that couldn't let go of any perceived slight. Ever.

"Okay, so . . ."

"Yeah." They turned and went their separate ways.

CHAPTER THIRTY-SEVEN

SURFING FOR EPIPHANIES

They took the ferry across this time (Miranda said Ariel was busy flying Mr. Guerrero to Miami), but that was all right. Huddled together, alone at the back, they watched San Próspero recede while reviewing what little they knew. Rain retold Naborías' Mosquito Boy legend, which creeped Miranda out. (Not that it made Charlie or even Rain feel particularly warm or shiny.) But it also served to remind Miranda that the other two were keeping things from her. She had been part of the whole Aycayia thing from the beginning, because she had witnessed Aycayia's first transformation, but this . . .

"What exactly are we trying to achieve here?" she asked.

"What do you mean?" Charlie asked back.

"Well, I take it we're not helping Rain prep her oral report."

"That's part of it," Rain said defensively, then more sheepishly, "A little part."

"A very little part."

Rain exhaled. She looked at Charlie, who shrugged. Then she turned to Miranda and decided—with some relief—to spill at least a few of her beans. "Okay, here's the thing. I'm a *cacique* on my father's side and a *bohique* on my mother's. That means I'm the Searcher."

"What's a Searcher?"

Charlie jumped in. "We're not a hundred percent sure yet. But we know Rain needs to search out a *zemi*."

"And we think this particular *zemi* will have something to do with Mosquito Boy," Rain stated, feeling more and more sure she was correct. "Something that'll stop his attacks."

Miranda swallowed hard. "So now . . . we're going to fight this . . . this swarm thing?"

"We did okay with Aycayia."

"Yeah, Aycayia turned out to be misunderstood and nonviolent. And kind of wonderful, really. Is that what you think Mosquito Boy is? Misunderstood? He murdered one guy and nearly killed another."

"Which is why we have to stop him. I mean, that's why I have to stop him." She looked at her two friends and realized she was actively putting them in danger. She didn't want that. After what nearly happened with the Kimlets, she *definitely* didn't want that. "But you guys don't need to be there when it goes down."

"You trying to ditch me?" Charlie asked.

"I'm trying to keep you safe."

"Oh, like last time. With Callahan and the plane and everything? You really think you can deal with this alone?"

"I won't be alone. You know that."

"Who's Callahan? What plane?"

Rain groaned. She looked from Charlie to Miranda and said, "Let's not get ahead of ourselves. I could use help with the research.

Help figuring out where the *zemi* is and how to use it. No one'll get hurt doing that. The rest . . ."

"We'll burn our bridges as we go," Charlie said. He sounded slightly angry. *Sometimes,* Rain thought, *I just don't understand him. He never wanted to be part of this craziness in the first place!* She shook her head involuntarily.

The ferry docked. The kids disembarked. Constable Thibideaux and Sycorax security guard Jimmy Kwan were watching the Vector Control people set mosquito traps at intervals along the pier. Thibideaux, who'd been supervising this rather dull activity since daybreak, spotted Rain, Charlie and Miranda heading for the Old Manor, and the thought crossed his mind that the three of them had been on the fringe of every odd crisis he'd been called in to investigate over the last couple of weeks. Jean-Marc Thibideaux didn't like coincidences and thought that when he had a few minutes to spare, it might pay to have another talk with those kids. Then one of the mainlanders asked him a question, and he turned to answer.

Soon enough, the kids were back in Mr. Guerrero's study, trying to maximize their time by working three sources at once. Rain was skimming more of Pablo's books, Miranda was on her smartphone, and Charlie was using the laptop on the desk, as each searched among a long list of topics: the Taíno, their legends, their *zemis,* vampires, mosquitoes, even malaria—since Rain figured that like Dr. Strauss, other scientists might have mistaken otherworldly events for malarial symptoms.

Not having much luck, Charlie said, "Could really use Phil's help right about now."

Miranda looked up from her phone. "Phil's your oldest brother?"

"Youngest. He's like the Internet whisperer. No, he's the World Wide Web Whisperer. We call him W-4."

Rain rolled her eyes at him. "We do not."

"We should, though. I may start."

Rain shook her head, laughed and turned another page. She spotted something intriguing and read aloud, " 'The Taíno traced their descent through the female line back to a female ancestress.' " She looked up. "Does that help?"

Miranda shrugged. "It's empowering. Kinda."

Charlie grumbled, "I've got to get some guy friends." Then he perked up. "It says here that if a vampire encounters a pile of rice, he's *compelled* to count every grain. We should get some rice."

"I'm sure we have rice in the kitchen," Miranda said. "But would that work on a Taíno mosquito-vamp or just the regular Transylvania Dracula kind?"

"Don't know," he said, "but, hey, the Taíno aren't the only ones with mosquito-vamps. The West African vampire's also associated with mosquitoes . . . or, um, fireflies. It's called an *adze*."

"You're an *adze*," Rain said from behind her book. She couldn't resist.

"*Adze. A-d-z-e.*"

Miranda said, "I bet a firefly vampire's pretty. Bet it sparkles."

Charlie put in, "Hey, when we get the rice, can we get some garlic too?"

"My dad loves garlic. I'm sure we've got a ton."

"Vamps hate garlic for some reason. If I were a vampire, I still think I'd hate anchovies more than garlic."

"Wait," Miranda said. She studied her phone. Then, "The ancient Egyptians used garlic to protect themselves from malaria, and the pharaohs slept under mosquito nets." She looked up at Rain. "I think you were right. Mosquito-vamps and malaria have walked hand in hand for like centuries."

Rain smiled, feeling quite self-satisfied.

Charlie stood and stretched. It was getting close in the room, and he was getting sleepy. He crossed to the French doors and opened them to let in a late afternoon breeze. Then he sat down behind the computer again.

They were quiet for a time. Surfing, skimming, reading. It had gotten very easy between them. Relaxed. Miranda was studious by nature. Charlie had to work at it more but could take pleasure in the process once he sank his teeth in. The surprise was Rain. She had never been one to enjoy perusing a book—for work or pleasure—but perhaps all she needed was the proper motivation. And a killer swarm of mosquitoes paired with her own destiny as Searcher and Healer seemed to be doing the trick. Silently, she read more about the Taíno, new details mixing in with old, and was fascinated by a culture that resonated for her deeply . . .

The word *taíno* means good or noble.

The *Nitaino* were the nobility of the Taíno, and the *naborii* were the commoners, but slavery was unknown. *Caciques*—who could be either male or female—were tribal chiefs. *Bohiques*—also known as *behiques* or *bohutí* or *buhuithus*—were healers and shamans.

The Taíno lived in large multifamily homes. *Sort of like the Nitaino Inn,* Rain thought. There were two kinds of houses: the rectangular cane variety and the round or oval *bohio,* which had high-pitched conical roofs.

Zemis or cemís were spirit-gods or icons of the same, infused with the spirit-god's power and stored in the home of the *cacique.*

Public plazas were used for the *areyto* ritual dance, for recording astronomical events and for the Taíno ball game, *batey.*

There was competition, even war, between Taíno *cacicazgos*—or chiefdoms—prior to the arrival of the Spanish, after which everything changed . . .

From the other side of the large room, Miranda, who had been wandering back and forth with her phone, perked up. "The Taíno drum was called the *mayohuacan,* and their flute was the *baijo.*"

Charlie looked up from the laptop. "That's what you and I play in orchestra."

"Kinda. Listen. There's a lot here about *baijos*. They were played to declare love or to announce the return of a hunting party or to summon guests for a feast. The *baijo* was said to weep or talk, and the sacred flutes granted power to women or men— they could even summon the stars."

Rain and Miranda looked at each other. Something was tickling simultaneously at their memories. Rain put her book back in its place on the shelf. Miranda slipped her phone into the pocket of her shorts. They both approached the wall of *zemis* on either side of the door to the great room.

There were two thick, carved, bleached driftwood flutes on exhibit against the wall. Once again, Rain felt her left arm tingle. Once again, the eyes of the Searcher snake briefly flared with blue light. But this time when Rain reached for the bat with folded wings, Miranda didn't try to stop her; she was too busy picking up the owl-flute herself. Each girl turned her flute over in her hands. Miranda even tried blowing into the owl and played a few pretty notes. Rain stared at the bat and then at her snakes, hoping for some revelation: for her Searcher snake to glow again or for her mind to suddenly open to the *zemi*'s power. Nothing quite that obvious occurred. Rain and Miranda looked at each other— then traded flutes. Rain held the owl, and still no great epiphany came. Miranda tried blowing into the bat-flute, but this time no sound came out.

"This is odd," she said. "You can't play this flute."

"Maybe there's something stuck inside?"

"No. It's not that. The holes are in the wrong place. None run the length of the flute. They go side to side. And this hole at the top doesn't connect up to the others. I can't figure it out."

Charlie said, "I can't see from here."

The two girls turned and held up the bat and the owl.

Charlie searched *bat* first and started reading off a couple items of mild interest. "Bats are associated with vampires, because vampires can transform into bats."

Miranda frowned. "That's so circular."

Charlie ignored her. "Bats are nocturnal and active in twilight."

"That's when mosquitoes are most active, too," Rain said. "In twilight, I mean. So the two kinds of vampires can team up."

"I dunno. Could be they're more rivals than teammates," Charlie said. "This says little brown bats—the kind we have on the Ghosts—eat up to twelve hundred mosquitoes per night."

"Great," Rain said. "So all we need to do is bring rice, garlic and vampire bats to the hunt."

"Little brown bats," Charlie corrected. "Not vampire bats."

Miranda said, "I think there's another bat *zemi* over here." Still holding the unplayable bat-flute, she crossed to examine the wooden spear. The carved bat-shaped stone spearhead could have been the flute's smaller brother. They were stylistically the same. Miranda slid her hand along the two long leather sinews that hung down from the spearhead. She lifted the ends of the two cords and studied them. She held the flute up to the light. "Hmm," she said.

Rain returned the owl to its home on the wall and said, "What?" But she was already feeling something stir. The music of the *areyto* was back, playing in her head with such strength she had to glance over at Charlie to confirm he wasn't on the Web site.

"These go together," Miranda said.

"Maybe they depict the same spirit-god," Charlie said.

"No. I mean, yeah. They're the same spirit-god, the same *zemi*." And Rain knew before Miranda could say out loud, "They're one zemi." She handed the bat-flute to Rain, who held it up, allowing Miranda to thread the sinew through the "useless" hole at the top.

Charlie came around the desk to join them. Miranda knotted the threaded cord to the other sinew. Rain lifted the spear off the wall. The flute hung soundly by the cords, halfway down the length of the shaft. Rain's Searcher snake glowed again—and this time the glow maintained. *The second zemi. It was here. All the time. But in two pieces and too weak to fully register with the snake. The "roll of quarters" shape we've been looking for is the base of the spear! It'll fit perfectly into the Cache's second slot!*

So there was her epiphany. Shame it arrived a minute too late.

CHAPTER THIRTY-EIGHT

RIGHT PLACE, WRONG TIME

THURSDAY, SEPTEMBER 18

All three teens had lost track of time. The sun had set. Night had fallen. 'Bastian emerged from the armband.

But before the ghost could say boo, the mosquitoes poured in through the open French doors. Miranda began to scream, but her cry was choked off as a portion of the swarm attacked her, many flying right into her open mouth. Charlie faired no better; the insects were all around him, biting and sucking viciously.

But the vast majority of Mosquito Boy's . . . *totality* descended upon Rain. She held the bat-spear-flute-*zemi*, but it provided no protection. Her own Healer snake glowed—but even its power couldn't keep up with the bugs' assault.

All three kids swatted at the insects—and squashed a great many. There was mashed bug and the resulting tiny bloodstains on their skin and their clothes. And more mosquitoes every second.

Miranda did an old-fashioned stop, drop and roll, perhaps hoping she could snuff out the mosquitoes like a flame. But this was a spirit from beyond the fire. He—it—they—were ash, alighting on everything, impossible to escape and everywhere at once.

Charlie tried to run to the French doors to shut them, but a wall of bugs forced him back.

And no one was more ineffectual than 'Bastian. All his feelings of impotence, of powerlessness, of uselessness seemed to culminate in that moment, as he tried to swat at bugs that passed right *through* his hands. He couldn't help these children. All he could do was watch.

As if to emphasize the point, a segment of the swarm seemed to coalesce into the form and shape of a small boy, buzzing with a kind of contemptuous laughter that chilled all four of them down to their souls.

Rain tried to pull her mind together, to think of what they could do. *Water! Water saved me and Isaac!* But they were too far from the ocean. She didn't even think they could make it to the hot tub. *But it's our only chance!*

But before she could move or even articulate the plan, Charlie choked out, "Rain, use the *zemi!*"

She yelled back, "It's not doing anything!" Every word allowed more of the creature into her mouth.

"It's a spear! Throw it!"

She had been holding it straight up and down and suddenly felt horrifically foolish. She pulled it straight back over her head, but the spearhead was facing the wrong way—it pointed back toward the wall—and the mosquitoes were still biting, still draining her lifeblood via hundreds of tiny wounds. She had to change her grip without dropping the spear—more difficult than it sounds, given the nature of the *Hupia*'s attack. She wound up twirling it in her hand, so that the point faced outward. The flute hanging loosely from the cords whipped around, emitting a short high-pitched whistle. She lifted it high over her head, brandishing it, ready to throw. About to throw.

In that instant, the entire swarm seemed to hesitate. To pull back and pull off the three children. Then, en masse, it swarmed back out the French doors, leaving its potential victims behind.

'Bastian put his head in his hands. He wanted to cry, but a phantom has no tears. He wanted to speak but felt he hadn't earned the right.

Rain remained frozen in place, breathing hard, spear still poised to strike, just in case the bugs returned. The *zemi* on her left arm continued to glow, continued to swim upstream to heal the tiny punctures and purge the quantity of mosquito saliva under her skin.

Charlie coughed and spit and doubled over, grabbing hold of his shins as he tried to catch his breath.

Miranda cried quietly on the floor—and then began moving in livid spasms, desperately trying to slap away the dead and dying bugs spread over her hair and skin and clothing. She was getting frantic, hyperventilating, and it snapped Rain out of her own paralysis. She crossed to Miranda and knelt to touch her. The snake's glow—invisible to Miranda—struggled uphill to heal her body, but at least it seemed to calm her soul.

"Breathe," Rain said. "It's over." And more quietly, "I'm so sorry."

Miranda stopped struggling; she lay back and took deep breaths punctuated by heaving sobs. She squeezed Rain's hand, then released it, allowing Rain to stumble over to Charlie. He straightened just as she approached—and nearly impaled himself on the spear. Rain kept it aloft, though the muscles in her arm were beginning to burn. With her free hand, she touched his cheek and watched the glow spread to him.

She whispered, "You saved us."

His head shook minutely back and forth. *It was you,* he wanted to say, but he hadn't quite caught his breath.

Rain grabbed his wrist and dragged him back over to Miranda, who was still lying prone on the floor with only her knees up. They both knelt beside her. Rain glanced at 'Bastian and said, "Keep a lookout." He forced himself to nod. He still couldn't speak, but, yes, he could keep watch. *It's the least I can do. And the most . . .*

Cautiously, Rain put down the spear, close enough so she could grab it at the first hint of buzzing. Then she firmly grasped Charlie and Miranda's hands in hers. The glow was faint, attenuated, as it attempted to spread across the three friends to heal every infinitesimal injury. Slowly, however, it worked its magicks upon them. With every passing second, they felt a little bit better, a little bit calmer, a little bit more whole. Charlie had only the vaguest of notions what was happening, and Miranda actually attributed her improvement to the power of friendship. (And maybe she wasn't half wrong.) They stayed this way, hand in hand in hand, without speaking. Eventually, Charlie and Rain helped Miranda sit up.

Thunder rumbled. Rain knew what she had to do. Gradually, she disengaged her hands from theirs. Miranda felt the loss like a void in her heart and spirit. Her confidence seemed to drain away. She reached for Rain, but her friend had already taken up the spear again and was rising. Failing to achieve contact with Rain, Miranda found Charlie's free hand instead. The tears came, but she managed to struggle out, "What are you doing?"

"I have to finish this," Rain said.

'Bastian and Charlie balked simultaneously: "You can't be serious!" and "Are you crazy?!"

"It'll just keep killing unless I use this to stop it." Thunder rumbled again like another warning. "I need to go now," Rain said, "before I have both of them to deal with."

Charlie stood, hauling Miranda to her feet with him. He looked at Rain, staring right into those almond eyes, puffy from the bites around them but still so clear. His own left eyelid was practically swollen shut, and water squeezed out. He wiped it quickly from his face, lest someone take it for a tear. "Okay," he said. "Let's go."

"No," she said. "I'm not putting you through this again."

He said nothing. He wanted to roll his eyes but figured she wouldn't be able to tell. So he simply maintained eye contact to let her know he was serious.

She tried again. " 'Bastian will have my back."

Charlie said, "No. He can scout ahead—maybe call out a warning—but the one thing he *can't* do is have your back. Anyway, that's my job. Always been my job."

Sebastian Bohique found himself saying, "He's right." 'Bastian wanted to stop them. To hogtie them if necessary, but he knew he couldn't. And selfishly, if his granddaughter was going, he wanted Charlie there by her side. It was a horrible, crushing realization: He'd rather risk another life than send Rain out there with only himself for protection.

"What . . . what are you talking about?" Miranda asked in a voice laced with terror. "Who's 'Bastian?" As soon as she said it, she remembered that 'Bastian was the name of Rain's dead grandfather, but that didn't compute, so she said, "You can't go out there!"

Rain put a hand on Miranda's bug-bitten shoulder. It served to heal her a bit and calm her a bit more, but mostly Rain had done it to help Miranda focus. "Listen to me. I want you to go up to your bathroom. Close all the doors and windows. Run a bath so you can get under the water and hide just in case. A hot bath'll probably make you feel better anyway."

"Rain . . ."

"I have to. I have to. I have to." It was a coin flip as to whom she was trying to convince.

The rain was pouring outside in earnest. A building wind splashed the downpour around. The French doors slammed shut, then swung open again. Lightning struck. Rain blinked, and when her eyes opened again, Cash was standing in the open doors. It made her jump, and she nearly threw the spear.

Cash took one look at them and said, "What happened here?" A second later he knew. He said, "You all alive?"

Rain nodded. She said, "Did you see which way the swarm went?"

"Out!" Miranda practically yelled.

Cash said, "Toward the cave. The bat cave . . . where *it killed me!*" He had already grokked that Rain was planning to pursue the *Hupia,* and though he wasn't quite sure why, he still felt like somehow it was his job to protect her—from herself, if necessary. With that in mind, he stood in the doorway, widened his stance, and crossed his arms defiantly.

Rain turned to Miranda one more time. "Close the doors behind us and go up to your bathroom. It'll be okay."

Then she strode across the room and walked right through Cash.

"Ah, man!" he said. "I hate when people do that!" Then he jumped aside to avoid Charlie, who, of course, had Rain's back.

'Bastian was next. As he passed, the other ghost said, "Dude, she's your granddaughter! Can't you stop her?"

"No."

And so the two spirits raced to catch up to the two teens, leaving Miranda quite alone.

CHAPTER THIRTY-NINE

THE PAVED ROAD

THURSDAY, SEPTEMBER 18

ain, wait!" Maybe it was the terror of being left by herself with a vampire swarm on the loose, or maybe it was loyalty to her new friends and fear for their safety, or perhaps a desperate need to cement her place in their world, or an unrelenting desire to learn all the truths still kept from her, or maybe it was all of these impulses, confused and conflicted, roiling through her traumatized mind—but Miranda had chosen *not* to stay behind.

She raced to join Rain and Charlie (and 'Bastian and Cash), stumbling on the paving stones. Rain steadied Miranda with one hand and called out over the rising wind, "You don't have to come with us. You'll be safer inside, believe me."

The warm, heavy rain pelted Miranda's tired, aching, and already itchy body. She opened her mouth to explain, found she couldn't articulate, well, *anything,* and settled for a helpless shrug.

Rain exhaled loudly—articulating her own confused mix of exasperation and admiration—then nodded and used the bat-spear to wave the whole group forward.

They crossed the grounds behind the Old Manor, heading for the cave. The storm seemed intense enough, but it wasn't close to hurricane strength. Perhaps the kids and ghosts thought—if they thought about it at all—that *Hura-hupia* was still in the process of building to her standard raging fury. In fact, she *wanted* this coming confrontation. She felt good about it. She thought it would end the game. No, this time, the storm wasn't a weapon against Rain—it was a tool to keep the rest of the world out, to prevent anyone from stumbling to the Searcher's aid.

On the dock, Tess Mvua—the lead technician from Vector Control—had to shout over howling winds to Thibideaux and Kwan that they could call it a night. "Mosquitoes won't swarm in this weather. I don't care what species or subspecies." Together, they retreated into the Sycorax cafeteria to get coffee and wait out the storm, thus completely missing the three teens and two ghosts who passed useless mosquito traps en route to their destination and destiny.

About twenty feet from the mouth of the cave, Cash motioned with his head at Rain and said, "What's with the spear?"

"It's the *zemi*. It's what the Taíno used to destroy Mosquito Boy."

"No, no, no," said Cash, stopping. Rain and 'Bastian stopped too, and Charlie and Miranda followed suit.

"What?" Charlie asked. "What did he say?"

Miranda looked around. "What did who say?"

Ignoring Charlie, Rain repeated, "It's the *zemi*."

Cash shook his head. "It may be 'a' *zemi*, but it's not 'the' *zemi*. I found the *zemi* in the cave the night I died. It was a container, like a jar, made from a gourd. It had nine bats carved all around it."

Rain held out the spear to show him the carved bat-spearhead and the carved bat-flute hanging from it. Cash said, "Yeah, that's what the bats looked like. But my thing was a gourd."

"What makes you think 'your thing' was the *zemi*? I mean 'the' *zemi*."

"'Cause he was *inside* it!"

"What?"

"Mosquito Boy! The vampire! The *Hupia*! Whatever you want to call him! Look, Callahan sent me to the excavation to look for this jar. He had some Spanish text from 1566, saying 'they released death from a gourd.' So I dug the damn thing up in the cave, but like an idiot, I opened it, and the swarm flew right out and ate me alive!"

'Bastian asked, "So *that's* how the Taíno stopped the *Hupia*? By sealing him in a jar?"

"Uh-huh." Cash nodded.

"They must have done it twice," 'Bastian said. "Once after First Chief and First Shaman burned the demon to ash. And then again after the Spanish set him free."

"Sure, whatever," Cash said impatiently. "Twice. Three times. Fifty. Who knows how often he's gotten out? I can't be the only dumbass in history." He turned back to Rain. "But that's the solution, kid. They sealed him in the jar. If you're gonna fight him, you need to go in there and find the jar. *That's* your *zemi*!"

Rain was stunned. Rocked. The soundtrack in her head had gone silent. She had been so sure. The Searcher snake had "spoken," and she had taken up the bat-spear *zemi* to use against Mosquito Boy, before placing it in the Cache. But if she was wrong, she was leading them all . . . *Wait! There's no way a gourd jar would fit in that roll-of-quarters slot in the Cache. I'm not wrong.* She said, "But when I threatened to throw the spear, he flew away. The whole swarm flew away. He had us. He could have killed us all, but he was afraid of the spear and ran. Flew. You know what I mean. *This is 'the' zemi!*"

Now Cash was stunned.

'Bastian said slowly, "Maybe you need both. It makes sense. If both *zemis* have bats on 'em, maybe they're designed to be used together. Maybe there's a Taíno bat spirit-god that empowers them both."

Rain nodded, feeling better. "So we use the spear to drive the swarm into the jar."

Cash said, "And seal him back inside it."

"And the jar's still in there?"

"Should be. I dropped it when I died."

Charlie said, "Well?"

Rain said, "There'll be another *zemi* inside the cave. A gourd jar with bats carved on it like the bats on the spear. We need to find it. Then we use the spear to—"

"To drive the swarm back into the jar," Charlie said. "Yeah, I heard."

"I heard too," Miranda said. "But how do you *know* that? Who are you talking to?"

"Explanations'll have to wait. Right now, I just want to finish this. We go in. I'll use the spear to keep the swarm back. You guys find the jar. Then it's all over." She made it sound so simple, and no one—least of all Rain—actually thought it would be quite that easy. Still, it made them feel better to have a plan.

They proceeded to the cave, three thirteen-year-olds and two insubstantial ghosts, armed with one wooden stick.

CHAPTER FORTY

BLOOD RELATIVE

Bastian entered first, followed by Cash. A single ghost light on a metal post, set up that morning by Vector Control, illuminated the surroundings. The two spirits spotted the bugs huddled and buzzing—perhaps even cowering—in the back of the cave. That looked promising, so 'Bastian called out for Rain to enter. She came, spear in hand, and marched straight toward the swarm. Once more, the mosquitoes seemed to merge into the form of a small boy. Now it definitely cowered away from Rain—or at any rate, away from the *zemi*—against the cave wall.

Charlie and Miranda entered, and Rain told them to keep their distance from the swarm while they searched. Her words echoed loudly inside the cavern. Miranda stared at the swarm and froze. Charlie grabbed her hand and gave it a squeeze, which worked surprisingly well. (Perhaps Charlie has a bit of the Healer in him too.) Miranda offered Charlie a nervous smile, and they began looking about, carefully keeping Rain and the spear between themselves and Mosquito Boy. Miranda pulled her phone from her pocket and turned on its flashlight app, shining it into every dark space, including around the circumference of the small saltwater pool. She shone the light *into* the pool but barely scratched the surface of its depths.

Rain never took her eyes off the *Hupia*. "Any luck?" she asked.

Charlie said, "Not yet."

'Bastian asked Cash, "Where did you drop it?"

Cash didn't seem to hear. He stared at Mosquito Boy in much the same way Miranda had. *There it is. The creature that killed me.*

'Bastian repeated the question. "Where did you drop the thing?"

Cash snapped out of it enough to answer defensively. "Don't know. I was kinda busy dying at the time, so I just dropped it."

"Well, where were you standing when you opened it?"

Cash looked around, then pointed at Rain. "Pretty much where the kid is."

Rain glanced down at her feet, heard a slight buzzing, and looked up again. The swarm had moved a few inches from the wall—and was losing its boyish figure. Rain tightened her grip on the spear.

'Bastian said, "So it could have fallen to this side of the cave."

Rain said, "I don't want Charlie or Miranda anywhere near the *Hupia*."

The two teens looked up. Miranda started to speak but quickly realized she and Charlie weren't being addressed.

'Bastian said, "We'll look over here."

Cash shook his head. "I'm not going near that thing."

'Bastian got all military on him. "Mister, it can't hurt you now. Start looking!"

A cowed Cash made a halfhearted effort while 'Bastian searched in earnest. He found the loose dirt where Cash had dug up the jar in the first place. He found a couple of broken spearheads, some small animal bones, and a few massive piles of dried bat guano—but no bat-jar *zemi*.

Charlie was searching around a stalagmite in another corner of the cave. It was dark, so he felt around for the jar and didn't find it. He stood up and called out to Rain, "What if the jar's not here?"

Perhaps, in hindsight, it was the wrong thing to say. Perhaps it wouldn't have mattered. It's unclear if the *Hupia* understood English. Either way, it grew bolder, swarming outward from the wall. Rain stabbed at it with the spear, but how do you strike a stake through the heart of a thousand flying insects? She had a brief thought: *Where's the rice and garlic when you need it?* Then Mosquito Boy, no longer afraid of these ignorant children and ghosts, attacked.

Rain—descendant of shamans and chiefs—was clearly his primary target. The swarm could feed on the others later. The Healer snake strove mightily to keep her whole, but it hadn't completely finished healing her after the first attack. It was falling way behind now.

Rain staggered back under the swarm's onslaught of bloodsuckers. She swung the spear, and the swarm focused on her hand and wrist until she dropped it, screaming.

'Bastian and Cash could do nothing but look on as Rain was eaten alive, a very little bit at a time.

Miranda was frozen against the far wall. Charlie took a few steps forward, and the bugs came after him. But their focus was still on Rain, so he ran and dove and scooped up the spear. He rolled up onto one knee and held the spear aloft, ready to throw it. The flute bounced painfully off his head, but he ignored it.

For a second the swarm seemed to hesitate. Then it released

312 · GREG WEISMAN

Rain—who collapsed onto her hands and knees—and confronted Charlie in the form of that laughing, buzzing First Murderer, Mosquito Boy. Charlie took aim, and Mosquito Boy laughed louder. Charlie heaved the spear right at the heart of the demon child. It was a good throw. The spear soared through the air, right on target—and the bugs separated to let it pass through Mosquito Boy harmlessly. The spear thunked into the soft earth, five feet beyond the swarm, out of reach and useless.

As it flew the bat-flute whistled again briefly, and something clicked for Miranda. The Taíno myth of flutes: the *baijo* that granted power. She shouted (practically screamed), "It's not the spear! It's the flute! The flute has the power!"

Unfortunately, that epiphany came too late. The swarm expanded and attacked Charlie and Rain. Miranda—gaining bravery with knowledge—ran forward but was cut off by another wall of bugs.

Rain gasped out, "Papa, it's a *zemi!*"

Suddenly, 'Bastian shared her epiphany. *If I can touch one* zemi, *maybe I can touch them all!*

Sebastian Bohique—descendant of First Shaman—ran to the spear, grasped it solidly with both hands, and yanked it from the ground. He was almost smiling.

Miranda, backing away from the bugs that still attacked her two friends, saw the spear rise of its own accord and flip upright. She saw the flute rise up and for a second she had hope . . .

But 'Bastian called out to Rain, "I can't play it. I have no breath!"

Rain managed to lift her head. 'Bastian saw his granddaughter as a mass of tiny wounds, her face swollen and distorted and covered with bugs. She was dying. He held the *zemi* in his hand, and still she was dying. He held it, and still he could not save her.

In pain and light-headed from lack of blood, Rain saw her

ghostly grandfather standing there with the spear pointing straight up, the bleached white flute hanging from its leather sinews. Despite the fear she would join 'Bastian soon, other thoughts still managed to claw their way out of her fevered brain. She remembered Miranda trying—and failing—to play the flute. *But the holes are in the wrong place. They go side to side.* And another image, another memory, popped into her head: a pole, a white object on a tether. Through swollen, bloody lips, Rain croaked out one word. "Tetherball . . ."

Fortunately, the whisper carried. Miranda understood immediately. "Tetherball!" she called out, and her words echoed. "The ball, the flute, goes *around* the pole!"

Then even 'Bastian understood. He allowed the flute to drop and placed both hands low on the spear. He began to swing it in a tight, quick rotation. The flute swung around on its tethers, picking up speed. As air flowed through its sideways holes, the *zemi's* music began to play. 'Bastian Bohique swung the flute around faster and faster. It whistled louder and higher. The swarm rose en masse off Rain and Charlie. It fled, trying to hide amid the shadowy crevices in the cave's ceiling.

'Bastian could feel the rush of power from within the *zemi* as it flooded hotly up his arms to energize his entire ghostly form. Answering his command, the flute spun faster, its single swirling tone echoing louder and louder off the walls of the cave. And as its pitch moved beyond the register of human hearing, the panicked swarm fled toward the mouth of the cave, only to pull up short and fly back inside, afraid of what was coming, of what had answered the call of the flute's magicks.

Bats.

Julia's storm, her wind and rain, had wreaked havoc on their echolocation. But the call was more powerful than any hurricane, and the little brown bats came.

They returned to their cave in droves and quickly proceeded to eat the bugs comprising the vampire's self. The swarm fled up, down and all around like some parody of a children's game, but the bats were everywhere, rapidly picking the *Hupia* apart—eating him alive—one mosquito at a time. The diminishing swarm tried to find the exit, but more bats came, answering the *bohique*'s call and cutting off all escape.

Mosquito Boy's buzzing screams echoed off the wall. And as Rain reached out to place her hand on Charlie and share her *zemi*'s healing power with him, Miranda pointed at the saltwater pool and cried out, "Look!"

Aycayia the Cursed rose from the pool in human form. Her torso was wrapped in seaweed, and she carried the gourd-jar with its carved ring of nine bats that *Hura-hupia* had dropped into the ocean. Aycayia stepped out of the pool onto the hard surface of the cave floor. Then, opening the jar, she sang a lullaby in the old tongue:

> *Come, my child,*
> *Come and sleep.*
> *The day is long.*
> *The night is longer,*
> *But here in your mother's arms,*
> *You are safe.*
> *Come, my pretty child,*
> *Come and sleep.*
> *Come my love, my child,*
> *Come and sleep . . .*

And the few mosquitoes that remained of the *Hupia* beelined for the jar, as they had in the time of the Taíno and in the time of the Spanish. When all were safely stowed, Aycayia sealed the gourd. 'Bastian stopped swinging the spear. The flute spun around a few more times, slowing, its own song winding down into an audible register and then into silence.

The satiated bats ascended to take possession of their old roosts, their old perches, hanging upside down from the ceiling of the cave.

Rain—the snake charm already beginning to return her swollen face to some semblance of normalcy—sat back on her knees, one hand still holding tightly to Charlie's wrist. She looked up at Aycayia and understood. Though Rain couldn't speak the language and hadn't comprehended the meaning of the lullaby, she *was* able to translate Aycayia's pain. Meeting Aycayia's gaze, holding that gaze in her own, Rain swallowed painfully and spoke aloud to Her. "Mosquito Boy. The *Hupia.* He's your son."

CHAPTER FORTY-ONE

ASH AND FOAM

THURSDAY, SEPTEMBER 18

When Aycayia sang again, she sang in English—or so it seemed to those assembled. There were moments, though, when Rain and Miranda and 'Bastian thought they heard Spanish. Even moments when Charlie and Miranda thought a few words were in French. To me, treading down a poorly lit dock on a different island, it sounded like a plaintive howl. But I think Aycayia the Cursed sang in the old tongue of the Taíno one last time, for such was the power of her song that *all* could understand its meaning.

The song told a story, and the story was this . . .

In the First Days, the most beautiful woman in the cacicazgo was Guanayoa. Every man desired her. And not simply the strong, young warriors. The little boys desired her. Old men desired her. Husbands desired her. Even women desired beautiful Guanayoa.

None were immune to the curve of her hip, the fullness of her breast, to her raven-dark hair and the light in her eyes.

And Guanayoa relished the power over others that her beauty brought Her. And so she sought more. She bargained with First Demon to gain his magicks, and she became First Witch. But there was a cost. There is always a cost. The very magicks that made her powerful and extended her life for many, many years also ruined her beauty. And as Guanayoa's beauty faded, even the memory of that beauty faded from the cacicazgo.

But Guanayoa remembered. And like First Bat, she hated the beauty of those around her. And the one she hated most of all was Aycayia.

But this First Witch was clever. She convinced Aycayia's Six Sisters that she had found a husband for Aycayia, a mighty warrior, a man of power. The Sisters thought she meant First Chief or perhaps First Shaman, and they agreed to the match.

But Aycayia's husband was neither Chief nor Shaman. Her husband was not a man at all. He was First Demon, who took Aycayia as payment for the magicks he had gifted to Guanayoa.

Aycayia's wedding night was a nightmare, one she barely survived. But her Six Sisters—wracked with guilt for giving her up to the Demon—nursed her back to health, and soon Aycayia found she was with child. The Six Sisters feared what the child of such a father might be, but Aycayia loved her baby from the moment of conception. Before he was even born, she named him after Jurupari, the son of First Sun and First Woman. Jurupari, keeper of the Sacred Flutes, who after First Woman's death, used his mother's body to create the First Stars.

And such a name has power. And such a boy might defy his Demon Father and become a great cacique or bohique. But that was not the wish of Guanayoa. She cursed Jurupari in his mother's womb by feeding Aycayia ajiaco tainted with a single drop of human blood. She gave the First Born of First Demon a taste for blood and knew he would never be sated.

And so when Jurupari was born, he became First Murderer. And First God sent First Bat to uncover Jurupari's crimes. And First Bat was horrified by what he discovered. First Bat forgot his anger and all his bitterness over losing his coat of colored feathers and swore to serve the Taíno as their spirit-god to keep First Murderer in check. And First Bat revealed Jurupari to First God, who sent a dream to First Shaman, who told the dream to First Chief.

And though he was but a child, Jurupari was apprehended by First Chief. And First Shaman denounced the boy to the entire tribe as a demon. And all but his mother, Aycayia, agreed the sentence must be death.

But Jurupari only laughed. He said, "There is only one way to kill a demon. And you do not have the courage for it."

But First Shaman knew the method for killing demons. And First Chief had the courage. Together, they dragged First Murderer to the First Fire, eternally burning in its great pit. Again the boy laughed, saying, "You have not the courage . . ."

And so First Chief and First Shaman consigned the child to the pit, to the fire, to a true demon's death. But First Murderer had fooled them both. For although the flames consumed him, his ashes rose into the air and became the First Mosquitoes.

And the plague of death continued worse than before.

And Guanayoa blamed Aycayia for Jurupari's rampage. Guanayoa lied with truth, saying Aycayia had lain with First Demon to conceive First Murderer. Then Guanayoa lied with a lie, saying Aycayia was First Witch.

And Aycayia the Cursed was so beautiful that this lie was believed by all—for they believed that none but a witch could possess such beauty. And Aycayia was banished to Punta Majagua to serve

Guanayoa. But Aycayia's Six Sisters refused to abandon her. And in her way, Aycayia refused to abandon Jurupari.

Fourteen Warriors were placed in seven canoes. They were blind-folded, so they could not look upon Aycayia. And their nostrils were plugged with rubber gum, so they could not revel in her scent. Aycayia was led to the First Canoe. She was bound so she could touch no one. And she was gagged so her voice could make no appeal. For Aycayia's beauty was so potent, all the senses must be thwarted, lest someone take pity upon her.

Aycayia's Six Sisters sat in the six other canoes. Guanayoa sat beside Aycayia and guided the blind warriors far away to Punta Majagua. There, Aycayia, her Sisters and Guanayoa were abandoned. The Fourteen Warriors were instructed to row toward the heat of the setting sun with their blindfolds in place. Only when night had fallen could they remove them and find their way home.

But there was no peace for Aycayia. She and her Sisters were forced to build a new bohio for Guanayoa. And they served the old crone as her slaves.

And Guanayoa was cruel to Aycayia in many small ways. But Aycayia would not be brought to anger. It seemed nothing Guanayoa did could harm Aycayia more than her own grief.

For First Shaman had called upon First Bat to honor his vow and become a spirit-god for the tribe. First Shaman carved a flute from driftwood in the shape of First Bat and tied it to a spear with a spearhead also carved in Bat's likeness. And First Bat entered this flute and spear, and it became his own zemi. And when the zemi played, all of First Bat's little brown children answered its song, and they fell upon the First Mosquitoes and consumed them.

As Jurupari's swarm shrank under this attack, he fled to his mother at Punta Majagua. Aycayia had created a jar from a gourd and had carved the image of First Bat nine times around it. She sang a lullaby to her son, and Jurupari flew inside the jar to sleep in *his mother's arms once more, safe from the bats, which remained outside the gourd. And the Taíno were now safe from him.*

And so the Six Sisters sent First Hummingbird to tell the cacica-zgo of Aycayia's sacrifice. Hummingbird flitted to each of the Four-teen Warriors, and each and every one answered the Six Sisters' call. They sat in their canoes and put blindfolds on again. And they remembered their First Journey and crossed through the darkness in the same manner.

The Fourteen Warriors found the bohío of Guanayoa on Punta Majagua. They found Aycayia and her Sisters bathing Guanayoa. But Guanayoa saw the Warriors first and knew they had come to bring Aycayia back.

And this infuriated First Witch beyond all measure. She cast a spell upon the Fourteen and told them only the strongest might have Aycayia. Thus enthralled, each Warrior did battle against friend and brother. And by nightfall, all Fourteen lay dead on Punta Majagua.

Aycayia was one of only ten witnesses to the crime. She threat-ened to tell First Chief and First Shaman of First Witch's evil. But Guanayoa warned, "There is no land safe from my magicks, Ay-cayia! And if no land is safe from me, then you will never be safe on land."

Frightened, Aycayia and her Sisters fled to First Ocean, hoping to escape Guanayoa's wrath. They stumbled through the water, try-ing to reach the canoes of the Fourteen Warriors. But Guanayoa's curse reached them first. The Six Sisters were transformed into dol-phins. And the First Witch transformed Aycayia into a hideous manatee.

But here Guanayoa betrayed her own interests. For in her haste and fury, she cursed Aycayia and her sisters with all her magicks— even her own immortality. And so Aycayia the Cursed became im-mortal, and ancient Guanayoa was now fated to die . . .

But even Death himself could never bring an end to the magicks or the dark desires of First Witch. Nor could Guanayoa's curse ever taint the beauty of Aycayia or the beauty of her song . . .

Aycayia fell silent, her song now ended.

Tears streaked Miranda's face, and even Charlie wiped his eyes. 'Bastian held the spear in one hand and felt guilty about it. Cash decided he was in love.

Rain still held Aycayia's gaze. After a long pause to absorb all she had heard, Rain said, "Guanayoa, First Witch . . . she's Julia, isn't she? The Hurricane-Woman?"

Aycayia nodded solemnly.

"And she's dead now?"

Aycayia nodded again.

"But it hasn't stopped her?"

This time Aycayia didn't feel the need to nod.

"And she still hates you. And you . . . still love your son." As it wasn't a question, Aycayia saw no need to respond, so Rain continued. "But you have to see that this can't go on. Every few centuries . . ." Here, Rain glanced back at Cash. "Someone will set Jurupari free. And what if the *zemi* can't be found? How many people will die? Or what if it is found and the gourd's lost?"

Aycayia didn't answer.

"We need a more permanent solution."

Aycayia looked from Rain to Charlie to Miranda, all still marked and marred by her son. She glanced at the spear in 'Bastian's hand, and then, for a moment, she even seemed to stare at Cash, Jurupari's most recent fatality. Then she turned back to Rain and spoke clearly. "Only I can stop this cycle."

For some reason, Rain didn't like the sound of that. "What . . . does that mean?"

"It must be. I am the only one who cares for him. And I cannot leave my child alone in this jar for eternity. Not alone."

Quietly but with determination, Charlie said, "You can't let him out."

Rain understood, though. Not the method, exactly, but the means.

Aycayia said, "I cannot let him out. And I will not leave him alone. I know what he is. I know what he's done. But I am still his mother." Her voice was a testament to sadness and grief, but her eyes shed no pearls. She had no pearls left to shed.

Lightning clashed just outside the cave, but *Hura-hupia*— Guanayoa—was powerless to interfere. Just in case she thought otherwise, Maq and I had "borrowed" an old dinghy and were currently en route to Sycorax. We wouldn't have to row even halfway there. Merely the threat of Maq's approach was enough to keep First Witch at bay. She would play by the rules of the game, as established so very long ago.

Aycayia held the jar to her breast like a baby. She rocked it and sang once more:

The day is long.
The night is longer,
But here in your mother's arms,
You are safe.
Stay, my pretty child,
Stay and sleep.
Stay my love, my child,
Stay and sleep . . .

Then Aycayia stepped forward and with what seemed like great effort, handed the gourd to Rain.

"I don't . . ." Rain began, but there was no need to finish.

Aycayia returned to the pool. She knelt down and reached into the water, removing her manatee skin. She said, "I have already said good-bye to my Sisters." And with her back to all assembled, she rent the garment in two. She dropped the pieces on either side of the pool and stepped into the water—or rather *onto* the water. She almost stood upon it as she turned to face Rain.

She smiled then.

And dissolved.

Miranda gasped audibly, but there was no other sound, except a faint bubbling. Before their eyes, from the bottom up, Aycayia the Cursed dissolved into seafoam. The process seemed painless—or at least it seemed to cause her no more pain than her long life and Guanayoa's fury had already inflicted. Her smile never dimmed as her body sank down and down without actually sinking, until all that remained amid a few strands of seaweed was a thick layer of foam coating the surface of the pool.

Rain approached the pool, gourd in hand. She nodded to 'Bastian, who began to twirl the *zemi*, bringing forth its protective tone. Above, in the shadows, the children of First Bat stirred but did not descend. Rain opened the jar and scooped a handful of foam into it, reuniting Aycayia with her child for eternity.

Then Rain sealed the jar again.

CHAPTER FORTY-TWO

STICK-UP

Rain, Charlie and Miranda emerged from the bat cave to face a fading storm. Julia (a.k.a. Guanayoa, a.k.a. *Hurahupia*) knew she had one chance left to keep the *zemi* out of Rain's clutches, and it wouldn't depend on the weather.

"Right. Hand it over."

Rain looked up. A soaking-wet Callahan, his blond hair plastered down over his forehead, stood before the three teenagers with a gun in his hand, which he used to gesture at the gourd Rain cradled in her arm.

'Bastian and Cash had been a few paces behind the teens but were still just inside the mouth of the cave. Raising up the bat-spear-*zemi*—which was shadowed from Callahan's view—'Bastian was more than ready to use the pointy end against the man threatening his granddaughter. He thought about throwing it but didn't trust his arm. Better to run the Aussie clean through what passed for his heart. There was only one problem. Rain was currently in the way.

Her glance moved from the huge, looming weapon in Callahan's hand to the bat-jar in her right arm and then over to the snake charm on her left. The golden glow of the Healer snake was still at work, helping her recover from the *Hupia*'s attack, but the Searcher snake was dormant. There was no blue glow surrounding either the snake or the jar. The gourd was significant, maybe even a *zemi*—but it was not "the" *zemi*. There was no place for it in the Cache, and she didn't need it. *Still, don't want to make that too obvious.*

"This?" she asked, nodding down at it.

"Of course, *this!*" Callahan said with extreme irritation. He had already searched the cave himself and couldn't understand how the girl had found the dingus when he had not. *But that doesn't matter. It's mine now.*

"And you'll shoot me if I don't give it to you?"

A number of verbal comebacks came to mind, but they all sounded clichéd, so Callahan settled for visual eloquence, raising the gun to aim it between her eyes.

Rain nodded and, as solemnly as she could manage, handed the jar to her opponent.

Charlie said, "I wouldn't open it if I were you."

Callahan flashed him a contemptuous look, which hid a certain amount of uncertainty over the oddness of the boy's warning. He shook it off. *Nothing these kids say matters.* He gripped the gourd in his free hand like a rugger ball and started to back away into the jungle. For a few lovely seconds—lovely in his mind anyway—he fantasized about shooting them all. But that would bring more trouble than it was worth. He'd heard about the manhunt for those tourist kids and knew that three more missing brats—*Where had this third one come from, anyway?*—would probably bring a tidal wave of authorities to the Keys. He didn't need that. *Not with more* zemis *to find.* He settled for leaving them with an implied threat. "Don't follow me."

"Don't worry," Rain responded.

"I'm following him," Cash said.

Rain's eyes went wide, but she didn't dare speak or look back toward the cave.

'Bastian said, "What are you talking about?"

"I'm gonna follow him," Cash repeated. "I'm gonna *haunt* the bastard."

"*Why?*"

"Well, for starters, he's the one that sent me after that *zemi*. He's the one who got me killed. So I owe him a little payback. Besides, *I haven't done anything yet!* I mean, why am I still here? I didn't stop the evil-demon-mosquito-thing. I didn't save the girl or even help save her, really. And I still don't see any light or tunnel to walk into. So maybe I can hang with my old buddy Callahan. Figure out his next move. And report back to you guys."

'Bastian nodded.

Rain did her best not to reveal her smile as a scowling Callahan disappeared into the jungle with Cash right behind him. Just before disappearing from view, Cash flashed a goofy grin and said, "See ya!"

And above, Julia raged over Callahan walking off—with the wrong *zemi! Fool,* roared the thunder! *Idiot,* shrieked the wind! She had half a mind to wait until he boarded the *Bootstrap* and then sink the whole glorified canoe with one massive bolt of lightning But she would resist the murderous urge much as Callahan had. There were still more *zemis* to find, and at least a chance that, eventually, Callahan might get lucky enough to claim one for Guanayoa's team—and perhaps a slightly better chance that, eventually, he might get angry enough to take Rain out of the game permanently.

Rain felt exhausted but tested her patience by counting to three hundred to make sure Callahan wouldn't spot them leaving with the true *zemi*. She took Charlie and Miranda's hands in her own—sharing her healing glow with them, as they shared their steadfastness with her.

Two hundred and ninety-eight, two hundred and ninety-nine, three hundred . . . and the three itchy, wet teens—with their spear-carrying ghostly companion—beat a hasty retreat toward the Old Manor through the still-pouring rain.

CHAPTER FORTY-THREE

ELLIPSIS

First period.

Miranda could tell Rain was a little nervous delivering her report in front of the entire class. Rain knew her material cold, however, and as she spoke about the Taíno, their *caciques*, *bohiques*, *cacicazgos* and *bohios*, Miranda could see her friend gain confidence with every word.

As Rain held up the bat-spear and said, "This is a Taíno artifact called a *zemi*," Miranda's mind wandered back to the night before . . .

After their frightening encounter with the big gun and the bigger man carrying it, Rain had taken Miranda and Charlie's hands and led them toward home. Miranda had felt the warmth from Rain's grip extend up her own arm, flowing through her, as it had before, soothing Miranda's fears and pain and even some of the itchiness of her many, many mosquito bites. She looked down at her arms and watched some of those bites literally heal and disappear before her eyes.

But glancing back over her shoulder, she was still disconcerted to see the spear/flute *zemi* bobbing along behind them in midair. Finally, she grew exasperated enough to ask, "Are you guys ever going to tell me what's really going on?"

The Searcher looked at her with some confusion, as if finding it quite miraculous that Miranda didn't already know. By then, though, they'd reached the French doors to Pablo Guerrero's study—which wasn't empty.

Miranda's father was there with Ariel Jones, Constable Thibideaux, Jimmy Kwan and Tess Mvua, the woman from Vector Control. The place, of course, was a mess, with hundreds of dead, squished mosquitoes littering the floor—not to mention the occasional minute drop of teenaged blood. Pablo Guerrero had looked nearly frantic when he had turned around to see the three teens enter. Instantly, he rushed to Miranda and wrapped his arms around her, asking breathlessly, "*Mija,* are you all right?"

"I'm fine, Daddy," she responded, "I'm fine." She patted him on the back reassuringly.

Then came the lying-with-the-truth, which seemed to spring up naturally, even effortlessly, between the three kids.

They kept it simple. The mosquito swarm had flown in through the open doors and attacked them. (Fortunately, Rain had healed them all just enough to make this seem only a mildly scary bedtime story—not a horror movie.) They had run out into the rain to escape the bugs, but the swarm had followed. Then the bats came, and that was that.

Ms. Mvua was shaking her head—until the part about the bats. That was the only piece of the whole thing that *did* make sense to her. "I was told there had been an earlier attempt to exterminate the indigenous bats?" she asked.

Miranda's father confirmed this. "One of the archaeologists was afraid of rabies."

"Well, that might be what caused the problem. The bats had probably been keeping the mosquitoes in check until the former were driven off."

Jimmy nodded. "Balance of nature."

"More or less."

Pablo Guerrero said, "So we leave the bats alone and this swarming problem goes away?"

"Well, I want to complete our study," Ms. Mvua said, "but I wouldn't be surprised."

"Then that's what we'll do." The boss had spoken.

Within a few minutes, the other adults had left, Ariel to ready the boat to take Rain and Charlie back to San Próspero. That's when Pablo turned to his daughter with thin eyes and said, "There are two *zemis* missing off my wall."

Miranda glanced over toward the French doors. Whatever it was that had been carrying the spear had been smart enough to remain outside with it. She said, "They're up in my room." Her father's eyes got even thinner, and she said, "Rain has an oral report tomorrow on the Taíno, and I said it would be all right if she used them for, like, show-and-tell."

"Oh, *you* said it would be all right? And aren't the three of you a little old for show-and-tell?"

"You know what I mean. Visual aids. And *isn't* it all right?"

"Well, I suppose. If you're all *very* careful. These aren't souvenirs. They're priceless artifacts."

"We get that. We've been studying the Taíno; we're learning about the *zemis*. It's actually pretty fascinating."

"I've been telling you that for years."

"I know. I know." She hesitated and then decided to go for it.

"I was wondering—after Rain's report—if I could hang the spear and flute up on the wall in my room?"

Looking dubious, Pablo started to answer, but his phone chirped. He pulled it from his pocket to glance at a text and was distracted enough by what he read that when Miranda said, "Daddy, I'm finally taking an interest," he nodded, though what exactly he was acknowledging was unclear.

But Miranda knew her father well enough—or rather, knew *how to play* her father well enough—to take that particular yes for an answer. She kissed his cheek and waved for her friends to follow her back through the French doors, saying, "I'll just take them to meet Ariel."

Outside, Miranda saw the spear, apparently leaning against a wall. She walked over to get it—but when she picked it up, she met resistance.

Rain said, "Papa, the storm's clearing. There are people around. We can't let them see the spear float down to the dock."

And just like that, Rain's "Papa" let go, and Miranda nearly tumbled backward with the spear. Charlie steadied her—almost as if he had been ready for it—and Miranda held the *zemi* out to Rain.

To Miranda's surprise, Rain hesitated. She said, "I don't need this for school . . ."

"You might as well bring it in, though," Miranda said, "since you're taking it back to San Próspero anyway."

"Won't your dad expect to find it in your room?"

"He never comes into my room. Never. If he thinks about it at all, he'll just assume it's there. Besides . . ." She put it in Rain's hands. "I think this belongs with the Searcher. Whatever that means."

Rain exchanged a glance with Charlie to one side and with

empty air to the other. There were a number of nods exchanged—some, Miranda figured, that she couldn't even see. As they walked to the boat, it was all agreed. They wouldn't just tell Miranda everything; they would *show* her everything. Tomorrow, after school.

Which meant today. Rain had finished her report by playing a brief section of the *areyto* on Miranda's phone, which she had also borrowed.

All eyes turned to Mrs. Beachum, who was frankly stunned. She had thought Rain would look up the definition of her last name and issue a ten-word bare minimum report. That was the Rain she knew from the previous school year. Instead, the girl had done an entire presentation on the Taíno, *complete with visual aids* and *music*! Claire Beachum had never seen Rain so engaged in the material. In *any* material. So the teacher tried, with little success, to keep the surprise out of her voice. "Rain, I'm truly impressed. That was great work."

Rain said, "Charlie and Miranda helped with the research. And this *zemi* belongs to Miranda's dad. Oh, and Renée helped too."

An entire classroom of stunned students turned toward Renée, who couldn't decide if Rain was trying to be nice, trying to get on her good side or trying to embarrass her.

Rain was already returning to her seat. Mrs. B said, "You still learned it. You *memorized* it. Rain, this could be a good year for you. Educational. Informative."

Claire Beachum saw Rain, Charlie and Miranda smile. Smiles to suppress laughter. Mrs. B definitely didn't get the joke.

Fourth period.

Renée moved slowly forward in the lunch line, glancing back over her shoulder. She saw Jay Ibara enter the cafeteria with Hank

Dauphin and Ramon Hernandez. She'd have to time this perfectly.

Rain, Charlie and Miranda were already through the line with their trays and food, but it hadn't escaped Rain's attention that Renée had allowed multiple people to pass in front of her, so she could hover before the now barren dessert section. Something was up, so she stopped to watch, nudging Charlie with her elbow.

Charlie, in turn, nudged Miranda, who said, "What? What's wrong?"

"Shhh," Rain said. "Watch and learn."

As was their custom, Jay and his friends headed straight for the front of the line, cutting in front of twenty or thirty junior high kids. Jay grabbed a tray and silverware and chose the Caribbean Meatloaf and Smashed Potatoes. That's when Renée said, "Is this the last chocolate pudding?" Her voice carried.

Behind the counter, Mrs. Fajro turned toward Renée, surprised there was any pudding—chocolate or otherwise—left at all. But she said, "Do you see any more?"

Renée said she didn't, which was Jay's cue. He nudged her aside with his hip—not violently but firmly—and took the pudding cup.

"Senior prerogative," he said without even bothering to look at his victim.

Renée said, "Of course, it is . . . *Sugar.*"

Jay's meal ticket was punched, and he left the line, taking a seat among the other seniors at the center table. Renée left her empty tray in line and went to stand beside Miranda.

Miranda said, "Aren't you eating?"

Renée didn't answer, and Charlie said, "She gets sustenance from other sources."

"Well," said a confused Miranda, still standing there with her own tray, "aren't *we* eating?"

The others said nothing, their eyes on Jay Ibara. Of course, it didn't occur to either Rain or Charlie to warn him. Charlie did ask himself whether he would have warned Hank, had his older brother been the victim of this confection, but he didn't dwell on it.

Jay went straight for the chocolate pudding, scooping big spoonfuls into his mouth, consuming it all in about four bites. Then he started in on his meatloaf and spuds. And then, slowly, his expression began to change. He looked uncomfortable. Then, perhaps, a little pained. His stomach growled loudly enough for the entire cafeteria to hear—no mean feat in the noisy hall. His best friends laughed at him, and he tried not to look embarrassed, but soon the only emotion he displayed was panic.

Hank stood up from the table, waving his hand in front of his nose.

Then Ramon practically shouted, "Dude, did you just squirt?"

Then Jay was running—if one could call it running with thighs pressed tightly together—to the little boys' room. Laughter followed.

Renée Jackson smiled with satisfaction and left the building.

Rain turned to Miranda and said, "And all Jay did was *not* let her cut in line."

Eighth period.

Charlie and Miranda had orchestra—and of course 'Bastian wouldn't be available until the sun went down—so Rain had time to kill.

She had carried the spear all the way downtown. It attracted some attention, which made her smile. Nobody stopped her, though—not even Deputy Constable Viento, whom Rain waved to as they passed on the sidewalk. It was hard for Rain not to giggle, but she largely maintained a straight face.

Her first stop was La Catedral de la Magdalena, the oldest church on the Ghosts. Her quarry wasn't there, but Father Lopez—who eyed the spear in Rain's hand with more amusement than confusion—said she had just missed her prey, though he might be across the street. "Our friend likes to cover all his bases," Father Lopez said.

So Rain left the *catedral* and crossed El Camino de Dios to the Old Synagogue, the second-oldest Jewish house of worship in the Caribbean.

Obeying the sign at the door, Rain slipped off her shoes, placing them neatly beside a battered pair of men's sandals. The sign said nothing about spears or flutes, so she carried her pagan *zemi* into the synagogue, feeling the clean, warm white sand of its floor under her toes.

She spotted him immediately, kneeling on a straw mat before the mahogany bimah—and the sight of him gave her momentary chills. But she soon realized he wasn't covered with blood but with *bija,* a local remedy that dyed the skin red and was supposed to protect against mosquitoes. She wondered just how far back the tradition went and felt sure it originated with the Taíno.

"Cousin Isaac," she said.

He turned to her, and his caked red face broke into a smile. Still holding the spear in her right hand, she helped him to his feet with the left. (She had switched hands on purpose, so that the Healer snake could work a bit of its magic upon either his body or spirit or both.) Isaac Naborías sighed contentedly, brushed a bit of sand from his knees and said, "Cousin Rain." He glanced at the spear.

"I did it," she said. "I found the *zemi,* and Mosquito Boy—the *Hupia* . . . he's gone. For good this time. You can get your job back at Sycorax. It's safe."

He beamed at her, quite relieved, but he said, "No, I think I'll stay retired. I've earned that. And I can afford it the way I live. Plus, I'm old. I'm not long for this world."

"Don't talk like that," she said. *Why do old people* insist *on talking about their own deaths?*

He waved the thoughts away. "Was anyone hurt?" he asked, touching her right arm and the few mosquito-bite scabs that her overworked snake charm had not quite gotten around to healing—at least in part because she wouldn't stop scratching.

"We're all fine."

Next, he gingerly touched the flute, dangling from the spearhead, as if he thought the bat carved upon it might actually bite. "And he's really gone?"

"Forever."

Naborías tilted her head down and kissed its crown, much as Wendy had done the previous morning. "Thank you, Cousin Rain. You bring joy to an old man's heart." Then he rubbed the back of his hand roughly across his forehead, streaking the *bija*. He smiled. His teeth looked very white between dark red lips. "You hungry?"

"Starved," she said. "I didn't really have time to finish lunch."

They left the Old Synagogue together and walked to the taco cart outside the *catedral*. Isaac paid. He insisted.

CHAPTER FORTY-FOUR

WHAT REMAINS

S
o I know you can't see him, but this is my grandfather, Sebastian Bohique. He's a ghost."

Miranda stared and then squinted in the direction Rain was looking but, as predicted, saw nothing.

"You don't have to try so hard," Charlie said. "I can't see him either."

Rain said, "He says hello."

"Or hear him," Charlie said.

Miranda said, "Hello, sir," in 'Bastian's general direction.

'Bastian smiled. It was odd being formally introduced to someone he'd already spent so much time with. *Then again, what isn't odd about all this?*

While waiting for the sun to set—and for 'Bastian to emerge—Rain and Charlie had used the time to fill Miranda in on everything that had happened over the previous fifteen days, starting with 'Bastian's gift to Rain of the first *zemi*—right up through a fuller explanation of what Miranda had herself witnessed the night before. They tried very hard to leave nothing out, constantly supplementing each other's points of view. It had, on occasion, been a challenge to get the words out—even to those who had lived through it, the events all sounded so preposterous, so fantastic, when spoken aloud—but Miranda had seen enough over the past week to believe anything. If they had told her Martians were landing, I'm quite certain she'd have bought that too.

Rain looked around the N.T.Z. to confirm they were still alone. It was about 7:30 P.M., and since no other locals had shown up to see the sunset, she figured they had a good hour at least before anyone would journey up to start their weekend. Parties did tend to spontaneously erupt in the N.T.Z., but rarely before nine or ten.

Satisfied, she held the bat-spear out to 'Bastian, who truly liked having it in his ectoplasmic hand. It felt comfortable there. It felt right, and he felt strong holding it. Rain slid the snake charm from her arm and approached the sandstone slab at the cliff's edge. Charlie followed her; Miranda followed him, and 'Bastian followed all three. Miranda glanced back to see the spear and flute float after them. She shook her head involuntarily.

Rain knelt and pushed the vines out of the way of the circular indentation in the rock. On either side of her, Charlie and Miranda crouched for a closer look. 'Bastian stood behind them. Rain placed her armband in the circle, twisted and removed it. She and 'Bastian watched the blue glow envelop the entire slab, and all four of them saw it slide aside. Miranda knew what was coming but nevertheless was caught off guard enough to lose her balance, falling back on her butt. She was wearing a short skirt and immediately wished she had chosen shorts this morning, but she forgot her embarrassment as soon as the slab revealed the stone steps leading below.

Rain turned to Miranda and said, "Welcome to the Cache." Then she nodded to Charlie to lead Miranda and 'Bastian down. Rain came last, pausing just inside the entrance to use her snake charm on the interior "keyhole" and seal the entrance behind them. Miranda, who had turned on her phone's flashlight app, watched this with a sense of dread, unable to shake the feeling they were trapped in Aladdin's cave or whatever. She had thoughts of coming out again and finding a century had passed. Frankly, she had a lot of random dark fantasies in quick succession, but really who could blame her?

It was a tight squeeze, but Rain slid past the others to take the lead. They descended single file, Rain, Charlie, Miranda and 'Bastian. Torches flared to life as Rain silently passed. Miranda gave a short yelp at the first one but composed herself quickly and tried to be nonchalant from that point.

They emerged into the Cache, and more torches lit in succession around the chamber, brightening the stone walls and enriching them with a large population of shadows. Rain turned to Miranda once again and said, "Okay, *now*, welcome to the Cache."

The others patiently watched Miranda walk around. She looked at the nine thrones; she looked up at the high stone ceiling and across the open terrace at the spectacular view. A crescent moon reflected off the ocean while a cool breeze danced through the chamber. Miranda turned to face the stone shelf and the charred Spanish writing on the wall. Rain, who knew it by heart at this point, had already told her what it said, but Miranda silently read and translated the original message for herself.

Finally, she turned back to them and said, "What now?"

Rain shrugged. "Now we hope we got it right." She crossed to the shelf and placed the Searcher/Healer *zemi* in the first slot. Then she turned and held out her hand to 'Bastian.

For some reason, he was reluctant to give her the spear. *But that's ridiculous. She's the Searcher.* He handed it over, and Rain carefully placed it in that second roll-of-quarters slot. The bottom of the spear slid in easily and fit perfectly. Nice and snug. Rain heard the music of the *areyto* again in her head, and she was hardly the only one.

All four watched the two *zemis* glow hotter and hotter. Rain stepped back as if from an oven or blazing fireplace. The glow expanded, washing over the entire shelf and then up the wall behind it. The wall burst into flame. Our quartet flinched and blinked as the light flared, too bright for even 'Bastian's ghostly eyes.

By the time they could see again clearly, what remained was flaming letters that moved as if alive. Rain didn't even try to read the words yet—though she felt them buzzing through her head. Slowly the flames burned out, leaving behind black, charred words and a new message in easily legible Spanish:

BIEN HECHO, BUSCADORA.

HAS ENCONTRADO EL SEGUNDO ZEMI. HAS ENCONTRADO EL
SEGUNDO DE LOS NUEVE. EL PROTECTOR DE LOS TAÍNOS.

AHORA DEBES ENCONTRAR EL TERCER ZEMI. EL CONSEJO LO
HA DEJADO EN ESTA ISLA. POR LO TANTO ES AQUÍ DONDE
DEBES BUSCAR EL TERCERO DE LOS NUEVE.

RECUERDA, LLUVIA, EL TIEMPO ES CORTO.
PERO TENEMOS FE EN TI. HEMOS PUESTO NUESTRO
FE EN TI. Y TODAS NUESTRAS ESPERANZAS DE CURAR Y
SANAR LA HERIDA DE LOS FANTASMAS.

BUENA SUERTE.

Charlie studied the words. He felt pretty certain he under-stood the first few sentences, but he didn't know the words *debes* or *consejo* or *dejado* and soon lost confidence he was getting any of it at all. He waited patiently as the other three read and translated for themselves. Rain was mouthing the words, a trait he found endearing. Then he realized he was staring at her lips and quickly looked away. He waited a little longer and a little longer still. Fi-nally, he groused, "Next mystic quest, I want the messages in French."

This snapped Rain out of her reverie, and she attempted to translate. "It says, 'Well done, Searcher. You have found the sec-ond *zemi*. You have found the second of nine. The Protector of the Taíno.'"

'Bastian tilted his head to admire the spear and flute: "So it's called the Protector *zemi*." He liked that.

Rain went on, "It says, 'Now you must find the third *zemi*. The Council has left it on this island. So here you must find the third of nine.'"

Miranda said, "You didn't mention a *consejo,* a council."

"This is the first we've heard of it," Charlie said—and then, unsure, "Right?"

Rain and 'Bastian answered in unison, "Right."

"Okay, go on," Charlie said.

But Rain hesitated before reading the next bit. She exchanged looks with Miranda and 'Bastian. Then she swallowed hard and said, "'Remember, Rain, time is short.'"

"It doesn't say Rain," Charlie scoffed. *That's a word I'd have recognized.*

Miranda said, "*Lluvia* is the Spanish word for rain."

"Wait," Charlie said, "Wait, wait, wait. This Council . . . they're calling you . . . *by name?*"

Rain nodded.

"Is this like an auto-feature for whoever turns out to be the Searcher, or did they . . . know?"

She shook her head. "I don't know." *Except I do. If this were automatic, the wall would call me Rain. But somehow the Council sensed me without fully understanding the English word. Lluvia was the best—the closest—they could come up with. However many centuries ago, they knew the Searcher would be me.*

For some reason, the ramifications of this freaked them all out as much as anything that had come before. Personally, I would have thought it reassuring—a *we knew what we were doing* kinda thing—but humans love to overcomplicate.

Miranda recovered first and took the liberty of finishing up. " 'Remember, Rain, time is short. But we have faith in you. We have placed our faith in you and all our hopes for curing and healing the wound in the Ghosts. Good luck.' "

CHAPTER FORTY-FIVE

FLAME AND SURF

FRIDAY, SEPTEMBER 19

The same moon Miranda had seen from the Cache was shining down through clear skies on the *Bootstrap*, which maintained position at specific G.P.S. coordinates in the Florida Straits. Thursday night, Callahan had—without knowing it, of course—led the ghost of Milo Cash onto the cruiser, where it was anchored off Punta Majagua. Just before dawn, the Pale Tourist had watched the big Australian weigh anchor and prepare to leave. Cash, knowing he was about to dematerialize for the day, had been afraid he'd return to find himself stranded in the middle of Back Bay with no *Bootstrap* or Callahan in sight. So he had been quite relieved to materialize aboard ship at sunset in this new location. *Good to know. Long as I'm on this dinghy before the sun comes up, Callahan's stuck with me.*

Otherwise, he hadn't really accomplished much yet, haunting-wise. He'd followed Callahan up and down the length of the boat, down into the cabin and back on deck, all multiple times, but Callahan was blissfully unaware of his old business associate's presence. Despite the boredom, Cash was at a loss as to how—or whether he ought—to change the situation. Still, he had nothing but time to figure it out.

Callahan now waited on deck, turning the bat-jar *zemi* over and over in his hands. He was beginning to wonder if he was being ripped off. Beginning to obsess over it, actually. He had given up the first *zemi*—the armband—for 50K. But for all he knew, it was worth twice that. Now he was about to make the same trade with the gourd. It didn't look like much, but what if there was something valuable inside? *Those kids warned me not to open it. But it's not like they're watching out for my welfare . . .*

So to Cash's horror, Callahan opened the jar.

Nothing flew out. Callahan pulled a small flashlight out of his pocket and shone it inside the gourd. He saw damp ashes and traces of seafoam. Cash breathed a sigh of relief. (Or would have, if he still had breath.) But Callahan growled in disappointment, coming to the not quite rational conclusion that the teens were messing with him.

Another boat was approaching. Callahan resealed the jar.

However, at that exact moment, my attention was drawn to the approach of heels on cobblestone. I looked up from my vision of the ocean to find Hurricane-Santa-Julia-Guanayoa-*Hura-hupia*-First-Witch drawing near. She wore one of her more visually pleasant guises—though that didn't help her scent.

Of course, Maq wasn't smelling too fresh at the moment either. He was Dumpster-diving once again behind the Plaza del Oro Mall. It's shallow of me, I know, but I couldn't help wishing his behavior was slightly more dignified in front of the enemy.

Julia stopped before the bin, waited and then cleared her throat.

"Stop barking at me, Opie," Maq said from deep within the Dumpster—though I'm fairly certain he knew it wasn't me.

"It's not the dog," she said angrily.

He popped his head out. "No. Apparently not. 'The dog' has a better disposition."

She looked down at me. I pointedly yawned, opening my mouth as wide as possible, showing my teeth.

"What can I do for you, *Hura-hupia*?" Maq asked.

She winced at the appellation, then took a deep breath and said, "*You* summoned *me*."

"Did I? Why, yes, I suppose I did."

They looked at each other. I looked back and forth from her to him to her again, as if observing the world's dullest tennis match.

"Well?" she asked, finally.

"Can't remember. Sorry."

For a second, she looked so angry, I thought she'd smite him with a lightning bolt right there and then. The storm passed, though, and she said, "This is your way of gloating."

"Yes! I mean, no! I mean, I remember now! You owe Charlie Dauphin a quarter. Oh, and there's something I wanted to show you!" He ducked back down into the Dumpster and jack-in-the-boxed back up pulling on a torn and stained powder blue T-shirt. Since he couldn't be bothered to remove his straw hat or the fishing hooks on it, the process took some time. When the shirt finally came down—quite tight even on his semiemaciated frame—we could see the yellow oval decal depicting the stylized shape of a black bat.

His voice was low, gravelly and comically grim. "I'm Manbat!"

I barked in correction.

"Right. No, wait. Let me try again."

She didn't wait. She turned away, muttering, "I can't believe I'm losing to this guy."

By the time Maq had climbed out of the Dumpster, she was gone. He looked at me and said, "This *is* my symbol, you know. I'm the original."

We could argue over archetypes for hours, but he was distracted by half a fried fish sandwich—stuck by its mango-chutney dressing to the seat of his shorts. Like a puppy chasing his tail, he began turning and turning in an attempt to grab it.

I thought maybe I had better things to do and trotted off.

Half a block later, I passed the Flame & Surf Steakhouse, where Constable Jean-Marc Thibideaux was having dinner on the patio beside the big fire pit with Tess Mvua of Vector Control, Dr. Josef Strauss of the Coroner's Office, Deputy Constable Mariah Viento of the Ghost Patrol, and Ensign Chris LeVell of the United States Navy. Jean-Marc had originally invited Ms. Mvua because, well, because he was *attracted* to the smart and shapely 5'2" woman with the onyx skin and the short, short Afro. But at the last minute, he had . . . blinked . . . and invited Mariah to join them. When Mariah asked if she could bring her fiancé, Chris, Jean-Marc had at first been pleased at the prospect of a double date, before deciding it smacked too much of *being* a double date. So he had blinked again and invited Strauss.

Given this specific crowd, it was hardly surprising when the subject turned to the myriad strange events of the last couple weeks.

Chris LeVell listened with amused interest as Strauss and Mvua debated the lifestyles of mosquitoes and bats, and as Mariah and her boss discussed the likelihood of three preteen children surviving among drug smugglers for forty-eight hours. Chris listened carefully as the others discussed the bizarre witness reports that seemed to walk hand in hand with each case. For a moment, the ensign was tempted to top their tales with one of his own: the impossible appearance of a ruined B-17 bomber on one of the navy's landing strips on Tío Samuel. Military forensics and intelligence experts had descended onto the island in force, searching for explanations and finding few. But LeVell stopped himself from spilling. He knew better than to air the U.S. Navy's dirty laundry in public.

Distracted as he was by Tess Mvua's charms, Constable Thibideaux nevertheless recognized LeVell's abrupt attack of reticence. He noticed the pregnant pause and intake of breath before the ensign was about to speak—strangled off at the last second by LeVell's better judgment. Instantly, Thibideaux knew something strange had occurred over at Tío Sam's. Just as something strange had occurred over at Sycorax and here on San Próspero. And at the risk of me making the good constable seem a cliché, I sensed Jean-Marc Thibideaux determining then and there to get to the bottom of it all, starting with the three teenagers he knew were somehow involved: Rain Cacique, Charlie Dauphin and Miranda Guerrero.

Those three were on my mind too. But I was also keeping track of Callahan, Cash and Setebos.

The exchange of *zemi* for money had gone much the same this time as last. Callahan was still nearly blinded by a searchlight shone directly in his eyes, and even Cash could only see Callahan's employer in silhouette.

The Pale Tourist was furious when he learned just how big the score was. *Fifty K?!! He was only paying me two!! And now he doesn't even have to pay that!!* It made him more determined than ever to find a way to get even and help Rain.

He thought maybe he was about to get that chance as the topic of the clipped conversation turned to the search for the next *zemi*.

Callahan called over to the other boat, "Any hints where to start, chief?"

Setebos didn't feel the need to shout. His crisp English accent cut the distance between vessels nicely. "Search the cemetery on San Próspero. I'll e-mail you all the details I have."

"Right."

The interview ended. Silas Setebos departed into the night, and Callahan—with his ghostly stowaway—set a course for Próspero Bay.

I was there already, ending more or less where we started, with a small driftwood fire constructed perilously close to the rising tide.

Rain, Charlie and Miranda sat barefoot on the sand, using bent wire hangers and a package of marshmallows to add a little melted sweetness to the evening. Unable to partake, 'Bastian was perched on a rock nearby, enjoying the relative stillness of the night. Rain had a little bit of fluff in the corner of her mouth. Charlie pointed it out. Rain attempted to remove it but somehow managed to miss it—twice.

Charlie finally reached out himself and wiped the whiteness off her lip with his thumb. Miranda watched, shaking her head slightly, as he stared at that thumb for far too long, stranded among his confused, adolescent, pubescent yearnings. So I decided to help by slipping in beside him and licking the marshmallow off. He hardly seemed grateful, scowling at me jealously before exhaling loudly.

"Thanks, Opie," he said, but I could tell he didn't mean it. He tried making up for the sarcasm by rubbing my neck with sticky fingers. As he had chosen the one place on my person I couldn't reach with my tongue, I pulled away and plopped down closer to Miranda, who fed me a marshmallow and rubbed my belly nicely with her sandy toes.

A wave rolled in just shy of the tiny fire pit. And with it, Alonso's camera slid right up against the bottoms of Rain's bare feet. Stunned, she gawked at it for a few seconds. I barked sharply to snap her out of it before the surf reclaimed the camera. (What would they do without me?) Rain snatched it up.

The Dark Man and the three teens gaped. Miranda said, "Is that . . . *the* . . ." She didn't even bother finishing.

Rain stood abruptly and shouted, "Thanks, Auntie!" She waited for the unseen dolphin/Sister to respond, but no response came.

So she sat back down in the sand and turned over the camera in her hands, much the same way Callahan had been examining the gourd. Illuminated by the flames, the camera didn't seem any the worse for wear, and when she checked, all the photos and footage of Aycayia and her transformation were still stored in its memory.

Charlie looked over her shoulder as she scrolled through the pictures and played the video footage of Her transformation. "What are you going to do?" he asked.

Rain said quietly, "Give it back to my dad."

"Not with the camera! With the pictures! The footage."

Rain deleted every picture, one by one. Then the footage. "Aycayia deserves better than to be on display."

'Bastian and Miranda nodded. I wagged my tail approvingly.

Charlie persisted. "But I thought you wanted proof of all the weirdness . . . ?"

"I don't need proof," Rain said as the drums and flute of the *areyto* played in her head. "The weirdness is enough."

ACKNOWLEDGMENTS

MONDAY, NOVEMBER 11, 2013

Thanks to Michael Homler and the other helpful people at St. Martin's Press, including Bob Berkel, Elizabeth Catalano, Paul Catalano, Edwin Chapman, India Cooper, Stephanie Davis, Jennifer Enderlin, Joe Goldschein, Sarah Goldstein, Anna Gorovoy, Meryl Gross, Bridget Hartzler, Paul Hochman, Lauren Jablonski, Sarah Jae-Jones, Aleksandra Mencel, Lisa Marie Pompilio, Jessica Preeg, James Sinclair, and Geraldine Van Dusen.

I'd also like to offer a blanket re-thank-you to everyone who was acknowledged in the first *Rain of the Ghosts* book—the foundation upon which *Spirits of Ash and Foam* was built—in particular, the original DreamWorks conference room gang: Bruce Cranston, Darin Dusanek, Lydia Marano, John Skeel, and Jon Weisman. Thanks also to Kuni Tomita for her artistic inspiration. And thanks to the good friends and objective strangers who blurbed such nice things about *Rain*: Shannon Delany, Nicole

Dubuc, Jonathan Frakes, Stan Lee, Jonathan Maberry, and Danica McKellar.

Thanks to my pals at the Gotham Group: Elise Brown, Eddie Gamarra, Ellen Goldsmith-Vein, Julie Kane-Ritsch, Peter McHugh, Quinn Morgan, Julie Nelson, Matt Schichtman, and Joey Villarreal.

Appreciation to my *Star Wars Rebels* family for their scheduling patience during the writing of this book: Carrie Beck, Steve Blum, Tracy Cannobbio, Liz Cummings, Megan Engle, James Erskine, Dave Filoni, Henry Gilroy, Taylor Gray, Kiri Hart, Pablo Hidalgo, Kevin Hopps, Simon Kinberg, Vanessa Marshall, Charles Murray, Lindsay Perlman, Freddy Prinze Jr., Rayne Roberts, Tiya Sircar, Kira Thompson, Diana Williams, and especially my hero Athena Portillo.

For technical assistance on things like my Twitter account (@Greg_Weisman), ASK GREG (http://www.askgregweisman.com) and the *Rain of the Ghosts* Wiki (http://rainoftheghosts.wikia.com/wiki/Rain_of_the_Ghosts_Wiki), I'd like to thank Erin Weisman, Benny Weisman, Eric Tribou, Todd Jensen, Kevin Chafe, and Thailog.

For help with the animal research: Tuppence Macintyre. For the Spanish translation of the second message of the Cache: Frances "Demona Taina" Vázquez. For taking the picture of me on the book cover: Marcia Perel. For the map of the Ghost Keys: Rhys Davies. For putting up with 693 multicolored index cards "decorating" our office while I outlined the novel: Wally Weisman and Anita Nitta.

I also need to thank a few people (some deceased) who have no idea who I am or just how much assistance they rendered. For information on bioluminescence, I want to thank *Smithsonian Magazine*, specifically the March 2013 issue and an article by Abigail Tucker on the work of Dr. Edith Widder. A Taíno *areyto*, inspiration for much of the music in Rain's head, was composed by El Concilio Taino and can be heard at http://www.prfdance .org/taino.areyto.htm. Aycayia emerges from *Tradiciones y leyendas de Cienfuegos* by Adrián del Valle. Even more important, I must acknowledge my tremendous debt to the *Memory of Fire* trilogy, its author, Eduardo Galeano, his translator, Cedric Belfrage, and one of his sources, Benjamin Péret. Galeano's five short paragraphs on "Mosquitos" provided the lion's share of inspiration for *Spirits,* and his trilogy consistently brings me closer to Rain's world.

As there are bound to be people I've forgotten, my thanks *and* apologies go out to all of you.

Finally, I offer my special thanks to my wonderful semiextended family: Jordan, Zelda, Danielle, Brad, Julia, Jacob, Brindell, Jon, Dana, Lilah, Casey, Dashiell, Robyn, and Gwin. Ultra-double-thanks to my fantastically supportive parents, Wally and Sheila Weisman, my awe-inspiring children, Erin and Benny Weisman, and, of course, my amazing wife, Beth Weisman. I love you all!

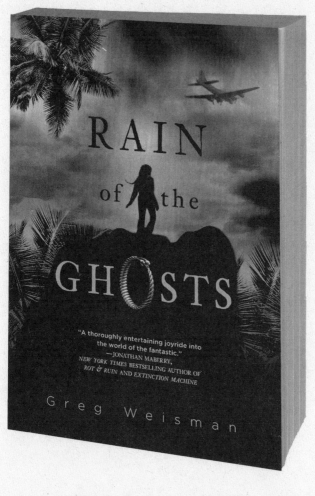